Books also by Mike Abbott

Straight Flush

Thirty

Preservation Man

To Muriel

Tordale

MIKE ABBOTT

ISBN 978-1-916838-04-8

Printed in Great Britain by
Biddles Books Limited, King's Lynn, Norfolk

Introduction

Jake Tordale had finally settled down into retirement at his idyllic home Wisteria Cottage in the County of Dorset. However he still had a few things to finalise over the coming three months, there was the Christmas festivities to share with his family in Devon, installation of his new Alarm System in the New Year, plus a few other bits and pieces before he retired completely.

It would be Christmas soon so he decided to take the families presents early, however during the loading of his faithful Lexus saloon he realised that the temperature outside had dropped considerably, the local weather forecast had predicted snow showers throughout the day, but as he had already arranged his visit to Devon, the journey would be mainly on the M5 motorway so he would be taking it easy in both directions.

Christmas Day was in three days time and he was glad he had pre-booked a seat at the busy Swan Inn for lunch, the Landlord Bert had said they were now totally booked with locals therefore it should make the occasion quite homely.

In April he was flying to Washington to meet up with Charlene for a week's holiday, but an unexpected earlier visit to the USA made another situation turn into what could easily have had an unhappy conclusion.

Chapter 1

With the clouds building up over Wisteria Cottage heralding possible impending snow showers, Jake made his way down the lane, passing The Swan, before quickly driving along the B road that led out onto the M5 motorway South West bound for Devon. The journey took nigh on two hours, and as he approached the town of his birth, he began to meander through the narrow streets of the village, before he became suddenly overcome with nostalgia, as thoughts of his youth enveloped him. A car's horn sounded behind him, bringing him back to the present ,as he realised he had stopped in the middle of the road whilst deep in thought. A few minutes later he pulled up outside his eldest daughter Clare's house and was greeted at the door by their boisterous Golden Retriever Becky who bounded towards him and nuzzled into his leg whilst waiting for the usual scratch to her head and rubbing of her back. Clare stood at the doorstep with arms folded against the cold wind, waiting for a greeting from her father followed by his usual hug.

'Looks like snow's on the way luv, I won't be stopping long, I've got presents for you and the children, I wondered if Sharon and Lottie were around today, if not I'll leave there's with you if that's OK?'

'Come on in out of the cold Dad, we'll sit down and have a cuppa first then I'll try Sharon' Clare replied, turning and heading back into the kitchen.

Becky followed Jake, waiting for him to sit down on his chair to give her another scratch.

His daughter sat down a little later cradling a cup of tea and proceeded with her usual questioning of her busy father's life. 'How are you Dad, and what are you doing for your Christmas meal this year?'

'I'm booked for Christmas dinner at The Swan, it looks like it's going to be a noisy affair, Bert the Landlord informs me he's fully booked with locals, so it will be like one of our old Christmas's, too much food and drink, but full of lots of laughter'.

She smiled, then said 'For once the whole family have booked into the Motel for our festivities, no dishes to worry about this year, and then back to ours for the opening of presents. Right, I'll try and give Sharon a ring and see what her and Lottie are up to, but I expect they are either seeing to the horses, or out somewhere with the dogs'.

Clare dialled Sharon's mobile, and surprisingly it was picked up right away.

'Hello you' Clare remarked, 'Where are you, Dad's here with Christmas presents for us all but he won't be stopping long due to the impending weather?'

'I'm at home with Lottie, we'll call around to see you in half an hour if that's OK with Dad?'

'Excellent, see you soon' Clare replied.

Clare turned to her Dad and said 'Mike's had to go into work today, so I'm afraid you'll miss him this time'.

'Not to worry luv, could I have a top up of tea please' whilst we wait for Sharon and Lottie.

She took his cup, then switched the kettle on for his refill, returning with his cup a few minutes later. he thanked his daughter then asked how her little family were. 'Everything alright luv, are Laura and Jake managing OK?'

'Yes, it's only been a few week's since we saw last you, things don't happen here as quickly as they do in your life, you know' she replied with a grin.

Twenty minutes later Sharon pulled up outside, her and Lottie were dressed as usual in riding attire, and following loud greetings to her sister and auntie they walked into the kitchen. Clare's children had arrived the meantime, Jake kissed them all before confirming that he wouldn't be stopping long due to the approach of possible wintery weather.

He walked out to the car and returned with presents for the whole family, separating Sharon and Lottie's from Clare's family.

With Becky at his feet he outlined what he had on his programme for the next few months. After the summary was completed they stared aghast at their father and grand father before identifying all the items he had just explained to them.

'Dad I thought you had finished your gallivanting around the world and had at last decided to settle down, obviously retirement has been removed from your DNA, I feel quite tired even talking about your little adventures. Did you also intimate that you had to go over to

Singapore to sign paperwork for the sale of a property you own over there?'Clare asked.

'Yes I did, I might even fly on to Australia whilst that way to visit Mrs Choo as I'll be more than halfway there'.

'When will that be, after America I assume?' Sharon asked.

'No, I expect to fit it in after the Alarm system has been installed in January'.

'Goodness me Dad, your passport must be full of stamps over the past few years of travelling?' she said with amazement.

'I haven't looked recently but I expect you could be right', he replied with a grin.

A little while later having distributed the presents he said his goodbye's to everyone and headed back to Dorset.

On the way he rang Maureen Donaldson to check that she was home and asked if it would be alright for him to call in for a chat.

She confirmed it would be and said she was looking forward to seeing him again.

As he approached Taunton the clouds overhead appeared to be getting darker heralding imminent snow showers, so he decided it would only be a brief visit with Maureen for a catch up.

As he pulled into the kerb he could see her looking out of the Lounge window obviously anticipating his arrival. When he turned off the engine she was lost from view and knowing her she had rushed to the kitchen to put the kettle on.

Before he could lift the knocker on the Victorian front door, it opened, and with a broad smile Maureen greeted him with 'Good to see you again Jake, did you have a nice visit with your children', whilst ushering him into the kitchen and closing the door.

'It's good to see you again Maureen, yes indeed it was nice to see them again, I just called to deliver Christmas presents for them as I will be spending the festivities at the Cottage with the main day being spent at the Village pub for lunch'

She smiled at him before saying 'I'll be hosting Christmas this year and thankfully all the family have agreed to come for Christmas Day, then I shall visit my son's family for Boxing Day' Maureen explained.

'Please forgive me for asking, and I don't wish to pry, but do you intend staying here or will you be downsizing at a later date. I actually feel comfortable alone in my three bedroom Cottage, but there are times when I think that the property needs someone else in it as I potter about. Forgive me for wittering on, I do apologise, sometimes my mouth speaks before my brain is in gear' looking at Maureen's face he realised that he could have overstepped the mark with his intrusive remarks.

Maureen laughed quite loudly as she carried across the teapot, cups and milk. 'I have actually thought about it recently Jake, but as Graham and I spent quite a period of time here together, I think this is my home for always, why do you ask?'

'I don't wish to be insensitive but there is a lot of housework to carry out for one person, and as you get older it could become a bit of a burden for you. May I suggest you look into hiring a cleaner for say once a week to help you out with the mundane chores?'

'I understand your concern Jake, perhaps when the time comes I will arrange for someone, but at present it gives me lots to do, and it take my mind off the loss of my husband'.

'I fully understand Maureen, I have only just settled into my forever home in Dorset, and I still miss my wife, who was a knowledgable and very keen gardener, she would tell me what to dig up and what not to in the garden, together with the daily chores in running a house, but I now have plenty of time and have made myself a weekly chart of things to do, albeit not the way a woman manages a house'.

There then followed a pregnant silence for a while as they both took in the significance of the views they had both expressed.

Having finished his second cup of tea, Jake checked his watch and said to Maureen it was time for him to trundle on home, whilst thanking her for his cup's of tea.

'Keep in touch Jake' she said, 'it's always nice to talk to you' Maureen exclaimed.

'I certainly will' he replied kissing her on the cheek, 'I hope I wasn't too pushy about you downsizing, I sometimes speak before I think'.

'Don't worry Jake, I appreciate your concern, take care and we'll speak soon'.

Jake returned to the car, waved to Maureen and headed back to Dorset.

Pulling up at Wisteria Cottage, he was surprised to see the accumulation of snow that covered his front garden since he had left earlier that morning. He thought to himself it looks as if his visit to

The Swan for Christmas lunch would have to be on "shank's pony" and even then with great care.

He turned off the engine and locked the car, then on opening the front door he was confronted by an accumulation of envelopes that had been delivered that morning, which he assumed were Christmas cards. He picked them up, dropped them onto the dining room table to be opened once he had put the kettle on for a cup of tea. The answerphone was flashing announcing a new message, again he would see to that after his cuppa.

The kettle whistled loudly announcing it had boiled so he poured his tea and sat down to open the mail whilst sipping his drink.

There were cards from Charlene in the States, Olivia from Sweden, even Mrs Choo from Australia, which surprised him. There were cards from The Swan, his Solicitor and the Butchers shop in the village, and lastly a card from Daniel Frobisher in Kent wishing him the compliments of the season. Tucked amongst the flyers there was an official looking one, on opening it he found it was from Henry Bates at MI6, it contained a Company Christmas card and within it a cheque for £5,000, and a note on plain paper saying it was his salary for recent exploits, and for him to enjoy the Seasons festivities. He put the cards in the Lounge and sauntered over to the landline and pressed the play button to listen to his missed calls.

The first was from the Alarm Company wishing him a Merry Christmas, and confirming that his installation was booked to commence on the 10th January at 8.30am.

The second was from Henry Bates checking if everything was OK and that he would be leaving for his holidays that evening at 5.30pm and if he was available, to ring him before he left his office. Checking the time he realised he had a twenty minute window, so he rang the office number before checking any other messages. Henry picked the phone up at the second ring with "Henry Bates'.

'Hello sir, it's Jake just returning your call, thanks for your card its much appreciated'.

'That's OK Jake, you certainly earned it, I wanted to catch you before I left this evening, something has cropped up in the States that needs the Security Services attention, and I wondered when you were visiting the lovely Charlene?'

'I fly out the first week in April sir, why?'

Chapter 1

'I won't say anything over the phone, perhaps you could pop up to London the first week in January and I'll run through the details with you then, now forget all about it and have a lovely Christmas break'.

'Thank you sir I will, I'll call up to the office around 11am on the 2nd January if that's OK with you?' before putting the phone down he pondered over the message and thought it meant an early visit to the States for him in the New Year.'Bye sir, have a good one'

Having put the phone down, his mind all of a sudden turned to work mode as he wondered what new adventures lurked in the USA.

He continued with the answerphone messages and the next was from Bert, as tomorrow was Christmas Eve he decided to ring The Swan and see what he wanted. Bert picked up the phone and he could hear the hubbub of the clientele in the background as he shouted 'The Swan'.

'Hello Bert its Jake, what can I do for you?'

'I'm glad you rang Jake, I've sorted the details out for the rugby, and all the lads are coming here this evening to check through the costings and pay their dues, how are you fixed for about 7pm?'

'I'll be there mate, looking forward to a couple of pints'.

'See you later Jake' replied Bert, then the phone went dead.

There was one other message left to answer, and when he played it he felt a warmth in his heart, it was from Olivia, asking him to give her a call.

Checking the time, he decided to ring her mobile on the off chance she wouldn't be driving home, however the call went unanswered.

He fired up his laptop and sent a quick message to Olivia, explaining he had just returned home, had tried her mobile to no avail but would call her later that evening.

Deciding to make a sandwich he checked the fridge's contents, and plumped for a blue cheese and pickle concoction, accompanied by a cup of black coffee.

He had just taken the first bite when his mobile rang, checking the caller he realised it was Olivia, so quickly emptying his mouth of food he pressed the green button and replied 'Jake Tordale', knowing full well who was on the other end of the phone.

'Stop teasing me you naughty man, did you receive my Christmas card and present?'

'Yes I did, thank you so much it was a wonderful surprise'.

'You are most welcome, what are you up to over the Christmas period?'

'I've just returned from visiting my family in Devon, having delivered their presents, then after I finish my tea I am going down to The Swan for a few drinks before returning home. Christmas Day I am having my meal at The Swan, where I'm guaranteed a great time as the pub is fully booked, what are you doing?'

'I have decided this year I'll be returning home to my family, which will be the first time in five years, my brother and sister will also be there, making the occasion quite enjoyable for my elderly parents'.

'Thank you for ringing Olivia, I hope you have a nice time, I'll ring you on New Year's Eve, if that's OK?'

'I'll look forward to it Jake, miss you', and with that she was gone.

Sitting back in his favourite chair he carried on eating his sandwich and drinking his coffee, whilst contemplating his walk to the Pub at 7pm having an enjoyable evening with the lads who he will join to discuss their trip to France for the anticipated Six Nations Rugby, final and deciding game. A smile spread across his face as he contemplated the busy weekend they would be having, as together with watching the game, they would be indulging in plenty of local food and wine as befits the occasion.

At just after 6.30pm he donned his winter attire and walking boots, put his trusty torch in his pocket, locked the front door and made his way down the lane to the Pub.

The snow had stopped, but the temperature was extremely cold, he decided the car would be staying put over the Christmas period, therefore Christmas Day would be another walk for him, which would help move the predicted excesses of fare and alcohol.

He strolled carefully along the lane taking care not to turn his ankle over on hidden stones, arriving at the Pub at a quarter to seven, needless to say his other companions were already well imbibed. He just made it to the Bar before he was presented with a pint of Best on the house, from Bert the Landlord. 'I'll leave the counter for half an hour and chat to you and the lads before they have had too much to drink, and they won't take in what I have to say to everyone' he said with a smile.

'OK Bert, I'll find a space at the table' Jake replied.

Ten minutes later amidst the babble of conversations within the Bar, Bert tapped the table with an empty beer glass and asked for a bit of quiet.

'Right lads, as we discussed at the last meeting I have arranged flights, hotel accommodation and tickets for the match in France, and the total for each of us is £430.00. This also includes a minibus to Bristol Airport and back. I trust you have all brought your Debit cards, so if you are happy I'll get my reader and do the honours'.

Tony raised his hand and asked 'Does that just leave food and drink to sort out ourselves?'.

'Yes, that's all Tony' Bert replied.

'I for one am happy with the figure Bert, thank you for organising everything for us' Jake answered for all of them.

Looking around the table, they all nodded in agreement, and produced their cards, apart from Tony who got his wallet out and produced cash.

Tony smiled as they all looked at him, 'It's easier for me, the wife does the accounts and would be aghast at me spending this amount of money on myself' he informed the remaining members, who sat there with beaming smiles.

Bert then produced a few sheets of paper showing a breakdown of his figures which divided amongst them came to £430.00 each.

He then stood up to retrieve the card reader and a few minutes later returned, together with a tray brimming with full pint glasses for everyone.

Once they had paid their dues, general conversation took place with individual accounts of their movements over the Festive period.

After another pint, Jake asked if all present would like a snorter with him, only a short delay before Bert was back to the Bar to collect numerous shots for the gathered friends.

A little after ten, they decided to make their way back to their family homes and the meeting dispersed with a shaking of hands all round. Jake was last to leave and asked Bert if the figure covered all the expenses he would have to pay out. Bert smiled and said he was quite happy that everyone had parted with the agreed figure.

Shaking hands, they finished with, see you at lunch time tomorrow, with beaming smiles, enhanced with the alcohol consumed over the past few hours.

The air outside the Bar was quite bracing as Jake made his way home, glad to have the illumination from his powerful torch to guide him along the lane. The silence was deafening as he inserted the key in the front door, and for a brief moment he felt quite vulnerable until he had put on the lights and locked up for the night.

Turning the kettle on he thought he would have a cup of drinking chocolate to cheer himself up and watch the TV for half an hour, checking on the latest News headlines.

Nothing startling on the News but the weather forecast wasn't too good, as it looked as if heavy snow would be falling over the South West of England, late Christmas Day and for all of Boxing Day.

Picking up his empty mug, he washed it and put it away, then made his way upstairs to bed. His mobile rang just before eleven, looking at the caller he saw that it was his daughter Clare. 'OK Dad, we just wanted to wish you a very Merry Christmas'.

'Thank's love, I've just got back from the Pub, we had a meeting regarding our trip to France in February to watch the rugby, then I'm back there for lunch on Christmas Day. Hope you, Mike and the family have a lovely time also, thank's for ringing, night, night'.

'Night Dad, luv you'.

With that he got into bed to read more of Umpire Dickie Bird's book.

Chapter 2

The dawn chorus woke him, but apart from the bird songs there was just silence. Pulling back the curtains he was greeted with a completely white landscape, a sight he had not seen for many a Christmas Eve. He got dressed and rushed downstairs to pick up his camera and record this extremely unusual weather event.

Donning his boots, he opened the kitchen door and took panoramic photos of the back garden, before taking more shots around the front area. The trees were heavily laden with snow that had accumulated on the branches, the multicoloured leaves with their natural greens and browns together with a build-up of snow resting on top, made the dawn even more eerie.

Walking back inside he removed his boots, shook them off to remove the melting snow, then into the kitchen to make himself some breakfast.

Turning on the radio to the local station, he was pleased to hear Christmas Carols being played, so he turned the volume up high to make the Cottage envelope the Festive mood. Knowing Sharon would be up early, he rang her mobile attempting to catch her before she made her way up to the horses. The call was picked up after three rings and he wished her a very Merry Christmas. 'You're up early Dad, couldn't you sleep?'

'We have had quite a lot of snow here, so I got dressed at dawn and have been taking a number of photos before it disappears again. I hope you and Lottie have a lovely Christmas, I spoke to Clare last evening and everything appears fine with them, so I'll speak to you again later, bye for now luv'.

'Bye Dad, luv you'.

With it being a few hours before his walk to the Pub for lunch, he thought he would clean the house through starting with the bedrooms and bathroom. Then working his way down the stairs polish the furniture and give the carpets a good clean.

The whole operation took him up to eleven o'clock, so he put his cleaning utensils away, and poured himself a coffee with a good measure of brandy before sitting down to listen to the radio.

A few minutes later the phone rang, picking it up he found his daughter Clare on the other end wishing him a Merry Christmas and thanking him for the families presents. 'I hope you have a lovely lunch tomorrow Dad, see you in the New Year'.

'Thank's luv, I must admit I am looking forward to my lunch especially with no cleaning up afterwards'. They both laughed at his remarks before ending their conversation.

Twenty minutes later he donned his boots and wet weather gear, locked the front door and made his way down the lane towards The Swan for a few drinks.

The build up of snow had banked up against the hedges, and with the sun peering out weakly it gave off stunning colours for the short period of time the rays penetrated the clouds. Looking in the distance towards Devon, there were a big build up of dark clouds heralding possibly more heavy snow.

Thoughts of the weather suddenly moved to the back of his mind as he opened the door to the Pub to be greeted by a cacophony of noise from the accumulation of happy customers sat at tables laughing and joking with each other, their countryside faces ruddy due to the heat from the roaring log fire. Jake approached the Bar and ordered a pint from Bert who shook his hand and wished him the compliments of the season. He ushered him over to a table where Tony Bailey and his wife Joyce were sat, he shook hands with both of them and sat down, conversations started immediately regarding the weather and Jake inquired if they had been able to carry out all the farming chores they needed to do. 'Yes thanks Jake' answered Tony, 'I must admit, this is a first for us, I think we deserve a break, or should I say Joyce does, we've been really looking forward to tomorrow for a few weeks, and it's great to have your company to share it with'.

Blushing Jake replied 'I couldn't wish for anyone better to share Christmas lunch with, would you like to share a bottle of wine or two with me tomorrow?' looking at Joyce for an answer.

'That would be lovely Jake, thank you'.

'Red or white?' he asked.

They both spoke at the same time, Joyce asked for white and Tony red, so that answered the awkward question, he walked to the Bar and ordered a bottle of each for tomorrow, asking for the best Bert had on the shelves. As they sat back relaxed in their chairs sipping their drinks, Tony started the conversation again with 'I take it your on your own for Christmas mate?'

'Yes I am, but I expect I'll be spending time here with Bert over the festivities'.

'Joyce and I would like to offer you lunch on Boxing Day if you fancy it, tomorrow's meal will be nice but you can't beat a farmers spread, what do you say'.

'I don't wish to intrude on your busy lives Tony, but if it's OK with Joyce it's fine with me'.

'I tell you what, so you will enjoy it more, I'll pick you up in the Land Rover and drop you back afterwards, as it appears we are in for more snow. So that's settled, I'll pick you up around eleven' Tony said with enthusiasm.

'You are both very kind, and I really appreciate it, thank you'.

Over the next hour or so they refilled their glasses twice before the Bailey's took their leave. Jake made his way back to the cottage feeling slightly light headed but quite happy as he was looking forward to tomorrow's lunch, followed by a farmers homegrown meal on Boxing Day. The rest of the day was spent watching TV, and reading, interspersed with checking over the photos he had taken over the past two years.

Chapter 3

Christmas Day had arrived, but there was only silence outside, no dawn chorus, nor the sound of wind whistling through the trees, nothing at all. He pulled back the curtains and was taken aback at the amount of snow that had fallen overnight. He thought to himself that many of the villagers would have to revert to 'shank's pony' as well as him, as not many vehicles would be moving today especially for the diners at The Swan.

A shower and a shave was required before dressing, then as his thought's turned to access to the Pub, even on foot things would be difficult as no traffic would have ventured along the lane over the past few days, and snow on top of snow would make the going extremely difficult and quite time consuming for him. However time to venture outside and see what amount of snow he would have to clear away from the front and back doors to prevent any ingress of water. Access to the shed was hard work, as that was where he stored his shovel and broom, however only a few minutes later he was armed with the required tools. It took the best part of an hour to shift the snow, and when he walked back into the kitchen he was ready for a spot of breakfast, toast and marmalade was the recipe of the day, and after pouring a half glass of orange juice and a coffee he settled at the kitchen table to consume his fare. The landline rang at 8am no doubt someone ringing to wish him a Merry Christmas and to his surprise he realised the call was from Sweden. 'Good morning to you' he started, 'A very Merry Christmas to you, are you with your family'.

'A very Merry Christmas to you too, in answer to your question, yes I am' Olivia replied.

'I expect you have had a large quantity of snow making Christmas quite magical for you all?' he queried.

'Yes we have, but we are all very excited as it has been more than five years since the whole family has met at my Parents house, and they are so happy to see us all. I have told the family about you and if you just wait a moment, I have to say who is on the telephone'.

Olivia spoke rapidly in her assumed Swedish, before whoever was close by shouted "God Jul' in unison. 'Could you hear that?' Olivia asked.

Jake replied 'Loud and clear, if that means Merry Christmas, please send them all my regards for Christmas and for them to have a Happy New Year. Thank's very much for ringing, and we'll catch up again in the New Year, bye for now'.

'Bye Jake, miss you'.

He felt quite emotional as he replaced the receiver, thinking how Olivia had all her family around her for the Christmas Festivities. But he thought to himself he had made his bed, so he must get on with it. First would be his lunch at the Pub to look forward to and the company of the Bailey's, then tomorrow he would be feasting with them at Pentire Farm.

He switched on the radio for the latest local weather forecast and settled into his chair for the expected depressing news, however he was somewhat surprised when the forecast became quite positive with possible rain showers on the 27th leading to a thaw. His mood changed quite considerably with that thought, at least he wouldn't be holed up in the cottage for too long and only three weeks later he would be having the Alarm people starting their installation work, that's assuming he wouldn't be still in the States.

The hours passed slowly, he spent the time listening to the Christmas Service on the radio and reading an interesting book by Dickie Bird on his umpiring career.

With an hour to go before lunch he dressed in his warm trousers and sweater, over which he wore his faithful Barbour jacket and a cap on his head to complete his outfit. Even hardy as he was, he donned warm gloves and wellington boots for the journey to the Pub.

The half mile trek was a mammoth task as the snow had accumulated up against both hedges forming a dish like walkway, even at the centre of it, it was more than half a metre in depth. As he made headway in the cold morning air perspiration started to form on his brow, and he felt his whole body warming as if he was walking in deep water. He realised he had plenty of time, so therefore slowed down making his treads more methodical as he approached the end of the lane, tiredness spread over him. What a wonderful sight The Swan was to him, he was looking forward to removing his outer garments to prepare himself for the warmth of the Dining Room where he was sure there would be a roaring log fire blazing away to keep the many customers comfortable.

Pushing open the door he felt like an explorer arriving back from an expedition, as he was greeted by the diners already in their seats. Glancing across he could see his friends Tony and Joyce, so he made his way over to the table, noticing that the wine was already in position, he checked his watch and was amazed to see that the time was a quarter to twelve, making his foot journey almost half an hour, anyway he was here now so he took off his hat and coat and sat down to a warm welcome from his companions.

'Food is being served dead on noon, so you're well on time Jake'.

'Thanks Tony, it was certainly a slog, the snow has drifted against the hedges on both sides of the lane making it extremely hard work getting here, however Merry Christmas to you both' he said raising his glass.

'Thanks' said Tony and Joyce in response, 'Shall I pour the wine?' Tony questioned.

'Fine with me' replied Jake, 'I'm certainly ready for the first glass, and possibly a few more' he followed with laughter.

No sooner had their glasses been filled than the plates of turkey arrived, together with a huge platter of roast potatoes and seasonal vegetables and sauces. Joyce of course was 'Mum' and placed the accompaniments on each of the plates for them to began their feast. No conversation took place over the next hour, only the odd request for a glass to be filled. A waitress came by part way through their meal and asked if any more veg was required, Tony asked for more 'roasties' which were duly delivered.

They had ordered Christmas pudding for dessert, Tony and Joyce had clotted cream with theirs, but Jake had asked for custard which was his favourite.

This was followed by mince pies and cream and coffee. Jake asked if they fancied a 'short' to have with it, Joyce asked for a Tia Maria, Tony a whisky and Jake a brandy.

When they had finished they all sat back feeling extremely full, Jake was glad he had a hard walk back home afterwards to move his excess around a bit.

Chapter 3

Walking up to the Bar Tony and Jake paid their individual bills, and Jake passed over a £20 note as a tip for the staff.

Jake bade his farewell to everyone, Tony giving him a reminder that he would be collecting Jake at 11am the next day.

Wending his way along the lane he was glad of the coolness of the air, which was in total contrast to the warmth of the Dining Room and the heat from the log fire in the Pub.

Reminiscing as he slowly walked along, he realised that this would be a first for him away from family, but what will be will be. He had decided to move to Dorset after the cottage was gifted to him by his late brother, and for his retirement, his Devonshire family was only ninety minutes away from Wisteria Cottage, making it quite accessible when the weather was OK.

The return journey took a good thirty minutes but as he opened the front door he was welcomed by the landline ringing so he rushed to it without removing his boots. He picked up the receiver with a 'Hello' in between puffs, before listening to a chorus of Merry Christmas from his family who were spending the day together. He chatted to everyone for about fifteen minutes before putting down the receiver.

Feeling very tired he sat down in his armchair and drifted off to sleep. When he roused it was pitch dark and checking his watch realised it was 11pm, so he trundled off to bed.

Chapter 4

The high pitched ringing from his landline brought him out of his comfortable dreaming and back to reality and lifting the receiver he just managed 'Hello'.

'Good morning Jake, its Tony, ready for another feast. I've just finished milking so I thought I'd give you a bell to confirm, I'll pick you up at eleven.'

'Thanks Tony that's fine with me, I'm afraid the alcohol got the better of me and I'm still under the covers, anyway thank's for the early morning call'.

'Early morning, I've been up since five' Tony exclaimed.

'OK mate see you soon' Jake replied feeling slightly annoyed by his friends retort and put down the receiver.

Checking the bedside clock he noticed that he had slept in as it was now five minutes past nine. Pulling back the bedclothes he went to the bathroom and carried out his ablutions, before dressing and wandering downstairs for a light breakfast.

Sitting back in his armchair nestling his second cup of tea, he decided to look through his wine rack and pick out a bottle of red and white wine to take with him to the Farm.

Getting up he opened the back door and to his amazement was confronted by green grass poking through the melting snow, the temperature was still he thought around freezing but if the thaw continued the recent weather forecast could possibly be correct.

Turning back into the warmth of the kitchen, he washed and wiped his dishes, then selected the two bottles of wine he would be taking later.

Ten minutes went by before his mobile buzzed and to his surprise he noticed the call was from London, 'Jake Tordale' he answered.

'Good morning Jake it's Henry, did you have a nice Christmas Day at The Swan?'

'Yes the Pub was packed and the food and company were most enjoyable, how about you?'

'The wife and I also pushed the boat out and feasted the day with some close friends of ours. Why I rang was to keep you up to date on the condition of Janet's health' there was a couple of seconds delay before he spoke again. 'I'm sorry to say that she passed away at 5am this morning, the Hospital tried everything, but her injuries were too extensive and her body just gave up. The Police as you know have arrested two men but they will be out on bail until coming up for trial in the New Year, on a date yet to be determined'.

The silence was deafening as both of them were lost for words until Jake spoke in a slow and concise manner. 'What the hell had Janet done to deserve that sort of beating Henry'.

'Unfortunately with the Justice System in this Country at present the perpetrators, will have a long period of time at large if their Briefs delay the actual trial. Even then if they are sentenced they will face a ridiculously short period of time incarcerated that most likely will be even more reduced by good behaviour in prison, It truly sucks!!', Henry exclaimed with utter fury.

'Thank's for letting me know Henry, at least now Janet is at peace, because even if she did recover her life would have been extremely difficult and debilitating for her, but I am truly upset at this eventual outcome' Jake replied with extreme sadness. 'See you in the New Year sir, I hope it will be more peaceful for everyone.'

'The same to you old man, I think it will still be a busy and stressful time for you when our meeting is completed, but don't think about it now, I'll tell you all about it later, bye for now' and with that the line was disconnected.

His concentration was shattered as the sound of a car horn heralded his lift to Pentire Farm with the arrival of his friend Tony Bailey and his faithful Land Rover.

He rushed to the door, waved quickly returning inside to don his coat, hat and scarf and pick up his bag containing the wine for their lunch.

Locking up he jumped into the passenger seat and shook hands with Tony, who beamed and asked him if he was ready for a farmer's lunch.

'I have looked forward to it since we parted yesterday, I hope I am not putting you both to too much trouble, barging in on your precious time?'

'Think nothing of it Jake, all the farming work was done by ten, and the 'Boss' has been slaving over the stove since dawn. We really appreciate you coming as we have no immediate family to see over the Festive Period, and it will break up our very work regimented daily lives'.

'It looks like a thaw is on the way, does it disrupt the farm at all for you?'

'Not really, the only problem we get is when it freezes, we have to collect all the animals and house them in the sheds, as its difficult to get to them and the troughs freeze as well. Anyway enough farm talk, what will you be doing for the remainder of the Christmas period, visiting The Swan do doubt?'

'Strangely enough, prior to the break I topped up from the Butchers and supermarket, and will no doubt stay in until the New Year when I will call down there for a few pints. Then the first week of January I have to go up to London. I'm glad the rugby trip is all sorted, dear old Bert is a good organiser, I'm sure it will be a great weekend for us all'.

With no further talk they pulled into the farm. 'Here we are welcome to the Pentire exclusive restaurant for Boxing Day' he said with a chuckle, opening the front door for Jake.

Joyce was laying the table as they entered the Kitchen/Dining Room, so Jake placed the wine bottles on the table, and kissed her on both cheeks.

'The smells from your kitchen are intoxicating Joyce, I thought we would be having cold meats and pickles today, not the gargantuan hot feast that I spy?'

'As we had lunch at The Swan yesterday there was nothing to have cold, but we have an alternative to the traditional turkey, we have beef and gammon with roast potatoes and vegetables, all from the farm' she replied with a smile. Tony looked at Jake and asked him what he would like to drink, or would he prefer to wait for the wine as they ate. 'I'm in your hands Tony, if you fancy a beer first, I'de quite happily join you, but I don't wish to appear rude'.

'So beer it is then' he said with a wide smile, 'Believe it or not I bought a small keg of real ale that has yet to be opened, so I'll get that sorted for us'.

'Can I help with anything Joyce?' Jake enquired.

'No, sit yourself down Jake and enjoy your beer, lunch will be ready in about half an hour'.

Sitting alongside Jake,Tony poured a pint glass of real ale for each of them and sat back ready to hear any dialogue Jake was prepared to divulge. Sipping from the glass Jake let out an enthusiastic sigh as the alcohol slid down his throat, before a smile spread across both of the men's faces showing their satisfaction.

'Many years ago Tony I used to enjoy a pipe of tobacco with my beer, but thinking back it used to take the taste of the beer away and in retrospect I am glad I gave up the thing.'

Tony replied 'I have never smoked in my life, I've nothing against smokers but I think it must deaden their taste buds from the enjoyable food that is available. Now we have a bit of time to ourselves, how about you running through your working life, and enlighten a poor farmer's interest' Tony asked with a grin.

'Not a lot to say really Tony, after college I trained as a Building Surveyor and after passing my various qualifications I was lucky enough to fill a position with a local Construction Company where I spent the majority of my working life, until the tragic death of my wife, I then took early retirement'.

'What have you been involved with over the past couple of years since you moved to Dorset. You appear to have been visiting a lot of Countries and not necessarily for holidays. As a friend I don't wish to pry but I find your secretive life most interesting' Tony's forehead creased in concentration, thinking he had gone too far with his inquisition.

A pregnant silence followed before Jake gave a guarded rhetoric of his past exploits, starting with telling Tony that what he was about to outline was to go no further as the details were covered under the Official Secret's Act.

'My resumption into working started a couple of years ago when I went for a holiday in Kefalonia, Greece. I rented a bungalow up on the hillside away from the holiday clatter, to enable me to expand my hobby of photography. I had booked the property for two weeks, and on a day trip to an adjoining Island I witnessed a shooting which changed my quiet holiday into a nightmare. This was due to the fact that I had taken a few shots of the surrounding area where the shooting took place, and to cut a long story short the perpetrators caught up with me and removed the SD card from my camera. This led to a confrontation with them, an intervention with a lady CIA agent eventually leading to me returning home. Thinking that was the end of it I was then contacted by MI6 and recruited to seek out the gang, who in fact were headed by the best man at my wedding.

The details thereafter are likened to a comic book with travels to Singapore and Australia, which culminated in my return to Devon where an explosion in the local Paper Mill almost killed me, but it unfortunately took the lives of the head of MI6 and the CIA agent, but unfortunately not the person responsible for the murders. I spent a period of time in a Plymouth hospital recovering, then returned to the Far East where the man involved met his painful demise'.

Joyce then saved Jake from further explanation as she called them to say that the meal was ready. Tony was sat in his chair with his mouth open wide, staring at him as if he had just listened to a horror movie.

Jake got up from his chair, asked Tony if he was OK, then with no reply he walked to the table and sat down as Joyce started plating up.

Tony never spoke a word as he opened the wine bottle, but occasionally glanced at Jake in disbelief at what he had just been witness too.

Joyce thought that her husband wasn't himself and asked him if he was alright. He just stared at her with no reply, just a nod of his head. He took his place at the table and started carving the meat, with the odd shake of his head.

'This feast looks mouthwatering Joyce, I assume all the fare is from the farm? Jake enquired.

'Yes it is, we are very lucky in that regard, making us self sufficient. Although it is a seven days a week life we wouldn't have it any other way, would we Tony?'

Tony was finishing pouring the wine, but there was no reply forthcoming to Joyce's question, just a couple of nods of his head.

'Are you OK Tony, come and cut up more meat and stop messing around' Joyce said in a stern tone.

Tony walked around the table, picked up the carving knife and fork and proceeded to cut slices off the cooked beef and gammon carefully placing them onto the plates in front of him. Joyce stared at him in disbelief before asking Jake what they had been talking about in the Lounge.

Jake's reply was short and to the point, 'Just this and that' whilst smiling at his hostess.

Completing his chore Tony made his way back to his chair and sat down awaiting his plate which Joyce was filling with potatoes and vegetables together with Yorkshire puddings. Jake looked on, waiting for Joyce to finish pilling up the plates then sit down to commence their meal.

A few minutes later Jake could wait no longer, and had to express his gratitude to both of them for the invitation they had made to him for this Boxing Day feast. 'It's no problem at all Jake' Joyce answered, 'We are glad of your company, with our busy working life, our only visitor's tend to be the Vet' she said with a smile.

'OK, I'm diving into this sumptuous meal' Jake answered.

Over the next half an hour, only small talk took place, with Tony's contribution being just grunts and nods of his head.

Both bottles of wine disappeared during the meal and as Joyce cleared the table she confirmed that Christmas pudding was for sweet and did Jake prefer cream or custard.

'I'm a traditionalist Joyce thank you, clotted cream if I may'.

A huge plateful was placed in front of him, which made his digestive system make a bit of a growl, however he tucked into the dish with some gusto.

As the three of them completed their dessert, Joyce asked if they wanted tea or coffee which she would bring into the Lounge. Jake said 'Coffee for me Joyce, and can I give you a hand with the dishes'.

'It's OK Jake we have the wonderful up to date facility called a dishwasher, and I don't mean Tony', she said laughing.

Both men stood up and walked into the Lounge, on their way Tony asked Jake if he fancied a drink before the tea and coffee arrived. 'I'd love a brandy to complete that fabulous meal mate if you don't mind'.

'Not at all Jake, I won't join you if you don't mind, the wine at the dinner table was enough for me, as I have to drop you home later, and then milk the cows when I return'.

This was said with no hint of humour, with Tony still deep in thought regarding Jake's previous revelations.

After pouring Jake's brandy, Tony sat in his favourite armchair, whilst looking directly at Jake with the obvious intentions of asking for further information regarding his mate's exploits.

Jake sensed Tony's hesitation and felt he had to start the conversation, as his friend was at a loss over his previous details regarding his employment in MI6 and its implications.

Before he had chance to start Joyce walked in with their tea and coffee and sat down with them, asking Jake if he had any further plans over the Christmas Period.

'I'm lucky really Joyce, I only have myself to see too. I have an appointment in London in the New Year, and a local Company are installing an Alarm System to the Cottage on the second week of January which is scheduled for ten days, after that I have nothing planned. Oh, I just remembered something else I have to do, and that's make a visit to Kent, where I have to disperse my recently deceased relatives ashes out into the North Sea'.

'You are going to be busy Jake, so much for retirement, eh?' Joyce answered.

At last Tony looked as if he was about to join in their conversation when he looked at his wife and said 'would you like to look around the outside before you have to head home mate, I'd like to show you the guts of the place that we have to farm?'

'Yes I would Tony, if it's not rude to leave Joyce here on her own' he replied.

Looking at her husband who nodded at her, 'It's OK Jake, have a bit of man time with Farmer Tony, he needs a bit of male company now and then' answering whilst grinning at her guest.

With that Tony got up, walked to the kitchen door and put on his boots. Jake followed behind retrieving his overcoat from the coat hooks alongside the back door.

'Are you alright Tony, you have been very quiet throughout the meal and I think Joyce is a little worried about your demeanour?'

'I'm just in shock from the account of your recent activities and wonder what else you are prepared to divulge regarding your recent times?' Tony said quizzically.

'I shouldn't have told you anything at all, but as you are a good friend to me I thought you would take my revelations in your stride, and not go so quiet at the dinner table causing alarm to you're good lady with your non communication'.

'I'm sorry Jake, I'm just a rural farmer where my only excitement is the birth of a lamb or calf, your recital was like an Agatha Christie 'who done it' extract, and I'm afraid muddled my head for a while. Do you have anything else to say, or do you feel that you have told me too much already?'

'I think we'll leave it at that Tony, I don't wish to freak you out, and I'm sure you will be in for an interrogation once I have left your home'

You could be right mate, I'll leave any more questions for another day' with that Tony formed the first smile he had shown for a while. After Jake's tour of the shed's they returned to the house just as Joyce had finished clearing the table. She smiled, looked at Jake and asked ' do you fancy being a farmer?'

'Not in a million years, you both do a wonderful job, but you have to be completely dedicated for all the hours you put into your business that are needed to carry out the multitude of tasks required to run a successful farm like your's'.

'Thank you Jake, its a joint effort, and we both appreciate your comments, not having a family we have quite a solitary existence but we get on well and should be grateful for small mercies' Joyce replied.

Tony scratched his head before putting his arm around his wife and kissing her on the forehead. 'It's a seven day, three hundred and sixty five days a year job but thoroughly rewarding at times, you have to love the work or it would eat you up. Day's like today with you as company makes it bearable for the both of us, thank's for coming Jake'.

'I thoroughly enjoy your company as I am in the Cottage on my own for most of the time, but as the saying goes 'if you make your bed you have to lay in it', I think we have to be thankful for what we have, life is too short to be miserable. Now I think I'd better leave you to your numerous chores and return home, if you would be so kind to drop me at the end of the lane Tony I'll walk the rest of the way. Thank you Joyce for that wonderful feast, and we will meet up in The Swan later where I'll foot the bill for our next get together'.

Driving back Jake could feel that Tony was in turmoil, itching to ask for more insight into his recent exploits, but unless he asked he would not mention it again. Thanking Tony for the ride he wandered back up the lane to Wisteria Cottage.

Feeling grateful for the walk, he felt less bloated as he entered the Hallway, noticing that the answerphone was blinking, showing a missed call and a possible message. He quickly went upstairs and changed into his lounging clothes, then put the kettle on for a cup of tea, before pressing the button on the phone to hear what messages that had been recorded. The first was from his eldest Clare, hoping he had a nice meal with his friends. The second message was from Olivia who just said that she was returning home the next day and would he return her call. The third was a short one from Henry Bates for him to return his call as soon as possible.

Checking the time of the calls, he decided to ring Henry first on his mobile. The call was picked up after only a couple of rings with 'Thanks for ringing Jake, I didn't want to disturb you, and hoped it could wait until we met next week, however certain things have taken on another twist'.

'OK Henry, what can I do for you?' Jake asked with some trepidation.

'Well I'll just give you the basics, the investigation into Janet's case has taken a bit of a twist, the drug dealer that the Met took into custody was interviewed but let go through lack of firm evidence, but he has now absconded to the USA. With the Police having no jurisdiction there they have given it back to us. I sent George off on Christmas Eve to attempt to locate him and to keep me informed, but unfortunately his mobile went off late on Christmas Day. His last location was San Diego, so I was wondering if you were up to taking on the baton and attempt to first, locate George, then this drug dealer?'

'When will you be back in the office, before I say yes I will need the full facts from you, and as much details as you have of the man George was attempting to locate'.

'I can be in the office tomorrow, if you are up to coming up to London?' he tentatively asked.

'I'll travel up first thing, and meet you in the underground car park at 10.30am, OK?'

'Thank's for that Jake, I'll see you in the morning' with that the line went dead.

With his head spinning he dialled his daughter Clare's number and with a few short sentences explained what a good time he had with the Bailey's and hoped everyone's Christmas was enjoyed. He then rang Olivia's number which went to voice mail, he left a message to say that he had to go to the States for a while but would call her occasionally when he was over there. He finally rang the Alarm Company and put his installation off until February unsure how long his impending visit would take him.

Chapter 4

Climbing the stairs he packed a suitcase with essential's and toiletries, together with his passport and cash ready for his possible departure to the USA the next day.

Chapter 5

Much to his surprise he woke up to sunshine streaming in through his bedroom window which lifted his spirits for the task ahead. Quickly carrying out his ablutions, he repacked his toiletries, dressed, made the bed and headed downstairs.

After a quick breakfast he checked the fridge removed all the perishables, and threw away the last of his milk as he was unsure when he would be returning to the Cottage.

Unlocking the front door, he was pleased to see that the snow had melted, making his escape from home easier than he first envisaged.

Wiping off the remnants of sleet from the Lexus, he lifted the bonnet and checked the oil and water, before putting his suitcase and carry on bag in the boot.

A last scan around the ground floor before he collected his mobile and laptop, placing them in the car and making his way off to the Capital.

The roads were reasonably quiet as the holiday was still in full swing, and families were still enjoying each others company, however as usual the closer he got to London the more busy it became, but not to the extent of a normal working day, he therefore pulled into the underground car park of MI6 at 10.20am. As he turned off the engine and exited the car, he was greeted by Henry Bates who had an extremely concerned expression on his face.

'Thank's for coming at short notice, let's go up to the office and I'll fill you in on the whole situation, and give you as much information as I can so far'.

The journey in the lift was taken in complete silence, with both men deep in thought. Entering his office Henry gestured for Jake to take a seat opposite him, and again thanked him for coming up to London at such short notice.

'It's obviously not as straightforward a visit I assume as you intimated on the telephone. I suppose I'll be off to the States, so I've packed a couple of bags together with my passport'.

Henry pulled a manilla file from a drawer and pushed it over to Jake, the file was marked 'Janet Hill'. 'This is all the information I have at present, it was forwarded to me by the Metropolitan Police as the case for them is going no further. But due to George going off the radar I fear that something untoward has happened to him, possibly with contact from the drug dealer'.

Jake picked up the file and swiftly scanned through the limited details that were there. The offender was called Roland Withers, it gave his last address as Walthamstow, his age, family details and a list of arrests in his short career, none of which lead to Court action. There was a detailed copy of the interview that took place, together with an alibi that had been provided by an 'Employer' who happened to be his second cousin who owned a Tyre Fitting company.

'No wonder the Police had nothing to go on with this reprobate, the alibi looks dubious, but obviously they followed it up and found the Tyre Fitting business was a bona fide Company'.

Henry looked up into Jake's eyes with concern etched on his face, appearing at a loss on what to say further until he gathered his thought's and started his speech.

'The time delay between Withers leaving Blighty and George following on his trail was three days. The Met scrolled through flight manifests at Heathrow and he travelled under his own name to Phoenix, Arizona on British Airways, but they found that he hired a car and then drove to San Diego, which is the last location we have for George until his phone died. I would like you to take the same trail, Heathrow to Phoenix, hire a car to San Diego and play it by ear after that. I realise it is a sketchy situation but you know what I know, I feel that you'll have more success at ground zero. I've booked a First Class flight for you, leaving at 4.30pm today, assuming you were prepared to leave at short notice'. He passed over a sealed envelope to Jake 'there's $4,000 American dollars in the envelope for expenses, anything else please keep receipts, which I'll sort out at a later date'.

Checking that the time was approaching mid-day he smiled at Henry and said 'I had better make my way over to the Airport and book into an Hotel where I can leave the car, by the time I have done that I will need to get to the Terminal, so I'd better be on my way'.

Henry stood and shook Jake's hand before saying 'I wish you were 25 years younger, you would have had a lot to give to Her Majesty's

Secret Service, but I'm grateful for the time you have given already, thank you for doing this Jake'.

'I'd like to say no problem Henry, but I feel I'm heading into the unknown with the little information we have in this file, I think it'll be luck that get's us over the line this time, I hope to see you soon' he finished with a sly smile.

Looking bemused Henry quickly caught up, slapped him on the back and said 'at least your humour is still alive old man'.

'We must remain positive otherwise life isn't worth living, is it?'

'Quite right Jake, if things turn out OK, a visit to a London restaurant will be waiting for you on your return to the UK, best of luck my friend, get back safely'.

'I'll do my utmost on that score, and return with George hopefully as well, in one piece if I have my way. I'm not sure about the other character'. With that he turned and left the room without another word.

He took the lift to the underground car park, got in his car and made his way to the Airport Hotel he had used previously on his visit to Australia. He parked in the underground car park alongside the Hotel, explained his situation to the Receptionist and handed over the keys to the Lexus for his return, as and when that would be he couldn't say. He paid a deposit for the use of the parking area, picked up his luggage then waited outside for the shuttle bus to pick him up.

He quickly made his way through Customs where his case was deposited, then he walked into the First Class Lounge. As he was a couple of hours early, he ordered a meal and a glass of wine to while away the time. His brain was racing as to a plan he could come up with to trace the path that George and Withers would have taken.

But first get to Arizona and then hire a car for his onward journey to San Diego and see what he could glean in that City, then he looked through the file whilst he waited for his food to arrive. His meal was delivered ten minutes later which he calmly ate, not paying much attention to it as he was still deep in thought anticipating the scenarios ahead of him. The waitress asked if he wanted a refill of his wine glass, but he declined and asked for a cup of black coffee. Completing his meal he picked up a magazine and glanced through it before sitting back to relax for the almost eleven hour flight he was about to undertake. Three quarters of an hour later his flight was called so he made his way to the

Departure Area, their were quite a few people queueing already but as he was in First Class it didn't affect him at all, and five minutes later he was greeted by the stewardess who directed him to his seat. Picking up The Times he turned and followed her to his seat. 'As soon as we take off sir I'll return and take your order for food and drink, I hope you enjoy your flight with us today to Arizona'. With that she turned and walked away.

Twenty minutes later the giant plane wizzed down the runway and soared up into the cloudy sky heading for America, taking Jake to unknown territory.

Chapter 6

The journey to the States was punctuated by visits from the stewardess offering refreshments and drinks, whilst he watched two films that were on offer. Four hours into the flight Jake dropped off to sleep to charge his batteries for an hour or so ready for his ongoing journey once the huge aircraft landed and taxied to its allotted spot .

Eventually with the long flight over he and the rest of the passengers disembarked with to go through the normal Controlled Area's before retrieving his luggage from the carousel, then making his way out to locate an available cab. The driver put his two cases in the truck before asking him which destination he required. Jake, deep in thought asked the man if he could recommend the most reliable car hire company for someone who had just arrived from the UK.

'Avis is the most popular in Arizona sir, I know the Manager Pete and could take you there if you like and introduce you to him'.

'That would be great, I appreciate that, sorry what's your name?' he enquired.

'Chad sir, could I have your's?'

'I go by Jake, shall we make our way there now?'.

Chad looked in the mirror and smiled whilst saying 'I'm on it' then drove off.

Twenty minutes later Jake could see a huge illuminated sign that read AVIS in three metre high letters. The parking area was full of all types of cars that looked to him from a distance in good condition. Chad pulled up to the entrance and asked Jake to follow him to a massive glass enclosed building occupied by numerous staff rushing around tending to customers looking to hire vehicles. Following in Chad's wake, they made their way to a bank of rooms until they approached a large office with MANAGER stencilled on the exterior. Chad knocked and entered the room with Jake following. A large African/American man stood up as they walked in and enveloped the driver with his massive arms in a bear hug before standing back and addressing Jake.

'Pete Chamber's sir, nice to meet you, not many people come to my office but Chad and I go back to High School football day's and once you're involved with the game, that's it for life. Now what can I do for you today, I assume you need a car?'

Jake shook his hand and explained that he was trying to locate another Brit who arrived in Phoenix on Christmas Eve and is hoping that there could be details of his booking a car for an onward journey to San Diego.

Chad looked at Jake and said 'I have to get back to the Airport, it's nice to meet you Jake, I'll get your cases from the car and bring them in'.

'What's the damage I owe you, $20 dollars OK?' he asked the driver.

'Sure, you can pay when I come back in with your luggage'.

'OK, what sort of vehicle do you need today, I'll see what we have, when I have a word with Accounts about your friend?' Pete Chambers asked.

'If you have a Toyota Camry available that would be my preferred vehicle', Jake replied.

'Give me a few minutes and I'll see what I can do for you' said the huge man as he walked out of the office.

With that Jake was left alone pondering over what the chances were that George had hired a car from this outlet.

The Manager eventually returned with a beaming smile on his face, and couldn't wait to sit back down in his chair to dispense the good news that he was holding in his hand, it was an itemised printout that he had retrieved from the Company archives.

'I hope you won't be disappointed with the details I have here and trust your patience will be worth the wait' he said almost on the edge of excitement with the details that his client obviously needed.

Jake adjusted his seating position, almost on the edge of the chair whilst placing both hands on the desk in front of him, he was almost salivating in anticipation for more information from this slow and frustrating man.

'I see you are urgently awaiting the details I have here and I'll not keep you waiting any longer. They are as follows, a Mr George Adams hired a basic car from us for two days, for his ongoing destination of San Diego where he would deliver the car to our Depot. He paid the invoice in cash and left our Depot there at 1600 hours three days ago, I rang the office in San Diego and they confirm that they have taken back the car with no damage, plus it was full of gas as requested. Mr Adams apparently asked a few unusual questions, the Manager said he was attempting to locate a cousin of his that had arrived a week previously and wondered if he had any idea where a UK citizen would head to once he arrived in the City'.

This information opened Jake's thought's as to George's next moves, the obvious one would be for him to now take his hired Toyota Camry and head to San Diego as soon as possible to hopefully locate the whereabouts of George and the man he had been chasing. He then stood, shook hands with the Manager and thanked him for his information and walked to the front of the building to give the Toyota the once over. Once satisfied he signed the paperwork and paid the invoice. The vehicle was full to the brim with fuel so there would be no reason to stop until he reached the outskirts of the City of San Diego. Placing his luggage in the boot, he got in the car and set the sat nav directions for San Diego, with the priority location of the AVIS Branch there. Settling back in the luxurious seating he eased his way out of Phoenix City and onto the Highway for his long journey to San Diego.

The readings estimated a drive time of between six and a half and seven hours for the distance of over 400 miles, he would have to stop partway for ablutions and a snack but he realised his trip would take the best part of the day, allowing him to locate accommodation before darkness fell.

A pit stop at Yuma for a burger and a coffee broke up the drive, plus it allowed him to stretch his aching muscles before completing the second section of the trip.

The AVIS unit was smaller than the one at Phoenix but still well laid out with similar cars that he had encountered there. He pulled into a parking area and entered the Sales Office. Introducing himself to the Manager he explained that he had just driven from Phoenix and assumed he remembered the call from Peter Chambers the Manager at Phoenix regarding his attempt to locate his friend George Adams. Following a short question and answer session, the Manager explained that he had directed George to a Hotel close by, which was roughly a mile away. He asked Jake his intentions regarding the car, which was paid for until 10am the next morning. The Hotel has a parking area at the rear, and he gave instructions to the quickest drive there, he also rang the desk to inform them of Jake's imminent arrival.

Thanking the Manager for his help he returned to the car, parked in the rear car park then booked into The Lafayette, asking if he could have a word with the person in charge. He was ushered into a plush office where a man stood and introduced himself whilst giving Jake a firm handshake. 'Welcome to the USA and the Lafayette Hotel Mr Tordale, how may I be of assistance?'

'A colleague of mine came this way from the UK a couple of days ago and stayed at your establishment, I am attempting to catch up with him but for some unknown reason I am getting no reply from his mobile, I wonder if you have any information that would help me locate him. His name is George Adams and I'm sure he would have given that name whilst possibly asking about another person he was trying to locate'.

'Quite a story sir I must admit, are you by any chance with the Authorities in the UK, as Mr Adams asked me virtually the same questions, but about another man?'

'I'm sorry to sound so vague, but as I am here in America and not in the UK I have no way of explaining why I need to locate the other man, only to say he is a rather dangerous individual, and needs locating as soon as possible and extraditing back to Britain. If you have any helpful information regarding George Adams I would be extremely grateful, otherwise I will have to make contact with the local Police Headquarters or the CIA to assist me'.

'Give me a minute sir, and I will see what details I can obtain for you' the man appeared flustered as he looked through a filing cabinet, trying locate what information he had available to help Jake further.

'Ah here we are, this is a copy of my conversation with Mr Adams, as you can see it is quite detailed, as I thought it important to keep relevant details in case in the future something happened to him and the Authorities would need my input', he placed the paperwork on the table in front of Jake.

A few minutes later having perused the information, Jake looked up and thanked him for the details.

'I trust this is some help to you Mr Tordale?' the Manager inquired.

'Yes, thank you, do you know when Mr Adams booked out and left the Hotel, did he leave a forwarding destination?'

'I found Mr Adams an interesting person, we had a few chats during the time he stayed here, myself being a person's person, I did in fact ask him where he was off to next, but his reply took me back a little. He said he would be taking a flight to LA and then on to Washington before returning to the UK in the New Year. I thought his journey appeared rushed but he was obviously anxious to catch up with the other man'.

Tordale stood and shook the man's hand thanking him profusely for the information he had provided, he heading out of the Hotel and back to his car, to check further details at the Airport and then book a flight for the next morning to LA.

Parking in the short stay car park adjacent to the Terminal building, he then made his way towards the Information Desk to obtain the details he required. The short stocky African/American gave him a stern look before checking through flight details for LA taken recently. After ten minutes or so he located a booking for George Adams who took a flight yesterday at noon, but he had also enquired about another Englishman who's flight departed on Christmas Eve to LA.

'Thank you for your help, I also wish to book a flight to LA, would you kindly point me in the right direction to obtain a ticket?'

After receiving the information, he made his way to the ticket counter and booked a flight for first thing the next morning.

Driving slowly back to the Hotel, he parked in a bay at the rear of The Lafayette and made his way up to his room feeling completely drained. Before he dropped off to sleep he rang AVIS and told them to collect the car from the Airport after 10am tomorrow.

It was almost 9pm when he awoke, and the rumble of his stomach told him that his body required some nutrition. He made his way down to the front desk and asked the Clerk for recommendations for decent food establishments nearby.

The young lady smiled and asked him what preference of food he was partial too.

Smiling, he replied 'At this present time anything would do'.

'If you walk out of the Hotel and turn right there are at least half a dozen Restaurants within a few hundred metres I'm sure at least one of them would meet your requirements'.

'Thank you that is most helpful, I'll let you know where I end up'.

Each of the establishments looked in good order but he ended up in one that supplied Mexican food.

Chapter 6

As he walked in there was quite a babble of conversation going on as the customers were tucking into their plates of food, he thought also that it was at least half full which was a recommendation good enough for an exhausted and starving Brit Abroad. He was shown to a table for two and handed a menu, the waiter asked what drink he would like and Jake asked for a cold beer.

The extensive menu was quite inviting, so just as the waiter returned he had made up his mind to have San Diego Burito with a Taco salad, together with another beer.

An hour later feeling a lot better he paid the bill and returned to the Hotel and back to his room, he tried George's number one more time however there was still no reply.

Chapter 7

When he awoke the next morning for a short while he felt disorientated, mainly because of jet lag, but also the long drive he had made just after a long flight, and of course his advancing years. Checking his watch it was 9am local time so he quickly showered and dressed, then made his way to Reception. The lady he spoke to last evening was at the counter, he explained where he had eaten and that he had thoroughly enjoyed the cuisine.

The Hotel provided breakfast so he made his way to the Dining Room, where half a dozen tables were already occupied. The buffet was laid out at the far end of the room and as he sat down a waitress asked what drink he required, he replied black coffee, then made his way to the buffet.

Still feeling reasonably full from last night's indulgence he collected some fruit and asked for pancakes from the hot counter.

His companions all appeared to be business people as they were dressed in formal wear, engrossed in each others conversations, appearing unaware of Jake's presence.

After his breakfast was consumed he collected his luggage from his room and handed the key back at the Reception Desk. Just as he turned to leave the Manager appeared from his office, and wished Jake good look in locating his friend. He thanked him for his help, indicating he was off to the Airport for an onward flight to LA.

Before leaving he decided to ring Henry Bates to give him an update, he dialled the number without a thought of what the time was in the UK, however Henry picked up on the fifth ring.

'Hello Jake, how are you, and have you located George?'

'I am in San Diego at present, but just on my way to the Airport for an onward flight to LA, which is where George was bound according to the Manager of the Hotel that both he and I stayed at,The Lafayette. There is no further information as to why he has gone to LA, I therefore assume he has found that our suspect has also headed that way.'

'If you get further info that involves the American underworld, please take great care before heading into those murky waters. May I suggest that you have a word with the Police Force and possibly the CIA or FBI prior to any confrontation' Henry pleaded.

'I understand Henry, but at present I'm flying blind with little or no information, which I hope to obtain in Los Angeles. If I find anything of interest I'll ring you again tomorrow, I also tried George's mobile number, once after I landed, and again last night when I arrived in San Diego, but the line is dead'.

Take care Jake, I look forward to your call tomorrow'. Henry replied with finality and he rang off.

Shaking his head, he felt out of his depth with this whole situation, but was determined to give it his best shot into finding his friend George. He made his way to the car park, placed his belongings in the boot and drove to the Airport. There was an AVIS office there, so he handed the keys to the person in charge and made his way into the concourse to await his flight to LA.

Sitting in the Departure Area contemplating the 25 minute wait for his flight he decided to get a coffee from the vendor and a copy of the local paper to pass the time. Returning to his seat he was flanked by two very large men dressed in dark suits, nodding to them as he took his seat he noticed that they didn't return his greeting they just stared straight ahead. Sipping his coffee he leafed through the newspaper until he got to page 14 where a headline caught his attention, it read 'Unidentified person found in alley with life threatening injuries. Robbery appears to be the cause as there was no wallet, money or identity found on the person. He was taken to Scripps Mercy Hospital, LA where he remains.His world ground to a halt for a moment before he realised he was in America and this report was possibly replicated daily in such a large metropolis, plus the odds of it being George must be thousands to one. Before he could read any more of the paper the flight was called, he decided to wait until the men either side of him moved to join the queue but unfortunately neither of them budged. Rather than get paranoid with the situation, he folded the paper and stood to deposit his empty container into a trash bin located nearby.

He joined the line of travellers at the gate and onto the waiting aircraft to take his seat. The plane was filling rapidly but there appeared to be no sign of the two burly men as the doors were closed and the engines accelerated propelling them towards the runway.

The stewards walked the aisle checking that all passengers had engaged their seatbelts, before returning to their seats in preparation for takeoff.

Ten minutes later they were levelling off at their cruising height onwards to Los Angeles, Jake looked around at his companions in the adjoining seats to find that he was sat next to a heavily pregnant lady and a businessman deep into whatever work he was involved with on his laptop. The lady smiled at him but no response from the businessman, across the aisle sat the two burly men he was with at Departures, but they made no attempt at eye contact. Opening the newspaper again he read the stories therein from front to back, before folding it and settling down for the short journey ahead.

As the plane landed and taxied to its gate a number of passengers stood up to retrieve the hand luggage they had put in the overhead compartments, ready for the scramble to exit the plane. Seasoned traveller Jake let the businessman pass him and he sat down until almost everyone had trudged down the narrow walkway. He did not turn to see if the two men opposite had left their seats until he stood to join the last of the people, feeling more relaxed the two men were not in sight, however he expected to see them in the luggage collection area.

Luckily as he waited at the carousel there was no sign of them, so he concentrated on looking out for his case which he quickly spotted on the belt on the other side, but decided to stay where he was as it would exit alongside him in a matter of a minute or so.

With all his belongings collected he walked towards the Information Desk and enquired the location of the nearest hotels to the Airport. The helpful young lady gave him an information pack which included all the hotels in LA, but she marked three that she recommended that were also the closest to the Terminal. Thanking her he took a seat alongside the Information Desk and perused the documents before walking over to the taxi rank.

The driver took his cases and put them in the boot, before asking where he was bound.

'The Marriott please driver'.

'British are you sir?' he replied.

'Yes I am, have you by any chance taken a fare for another Brit in the past few days?' he asked quizzically.

'Funny you should ask, I dropped a burly Brit off at the Marriott only a few days ago, and he asked me a similar question about another man. He gave me a rough description but I couldn't remember anyone like that'.

'I'll ask at the Marriott when I get there if they possibly have any more information, thank you anyway you have been a great help. I'll only be staying the one night, and if possible I would like to arrange a pick-up tomorrow to return me to the Airport'.

'No sweat' replied the driver handing Jake a card with his direct number on.

A quarter of an hour later they pulled up at the front entrance to the Hotel with Jake tipping the man quite generously on top of the fare.

'I'll await your call tomorrow sir' the driver said as he got back in the car and drove off.

Jake walked into the foyer and approached the Reception Desk asking for a room for the one night.

The smartly dressed man checked the board and handed over a key for Room 278 and a request for $150 dollars which included breakfast.

Jake couldn't wait any longer and asked the young man if he had any information on a friend of his who had stayed at the Hotel a day or so ago in the name of George Adams.

'Bare with me for a minute and I'll check the details for you. A'h here we are, George Adams from London, England booked in for just the one night as he was catching the Washington flight the next day'.

'Did he ask about another British person he was looking for do you know?'

'There is a side note attached to his receipt that said he did in fact ask about another man but no additional information has been written with it'.

'Can you say who put that note on the computer system, if so is it possible to speak to them. It is an extremely delicate subject that involves the British Secret Service, who I know have no Authority in the States, but the person we are after is a dangerous criminal and your help would be greatly appreciated'.

Blushing considerably the man said to Jake 'Your friend spoke to the Manager as its his login details, he will be back at work at 2pm and

I will tell him you wish to speak with him, I'll give you a call in your room as soon as I have spoken to him Mr Tordale'.

Jake thanked the man and handed over cash to pay for his stay.

Taking the lift to his room he deposited the cases in the corner of the room and lay on the bed to try George Adams number for the last time.

To his amazement he heard for the first time a ringing on the receiver and he waited in anticipation for the call to be picked up. After 15 rings there was a click before a male voice issued a one word reply of 'Hello'.

Jake still shocked was gobsmacked that the phone was answered unfortunately the voice was not George's and as the seconds ticked by he was in a turmoil as to a reply.

Eventually he boldly said 'Hello to you, could I speak to George'.

'I no George, you have wrong number' it was answered in a highly accentuated Mexican tone.

'I'm sorry could I just check the number with you' quickly giving the number to George's mobile. 'Right number, but no George' the man repeated.

'It's been good to talk to you, I'm sorry I didn't get your name sir' Jake asked.

'My name is Miguel'.

'Thank you Miguel, where are you at the moment, only I am in Los Angeles and I have come over from Europe to meet my brother George and I thought this was the mobile phone number he had a couple of weeks ago'.

'I am in Hospital in Washington in Men's Ward, man across from me come from Europe and I answered mobile for him, as he no well. I get Nurse for you, hold line'.

A long silence before a female voice picked up the device and said 'Staff Nurse McDonald how may I help you?'

'Good afternoon Staff Nurse, my name is Jake Tordale, I'm ringing from Los Angeles, and I'm trying to locate a colleague of mine from England called George Adams. I understand he left LA a few days ago and was heading for Washington. I am booked on a flight there tomorrow and hopefully the man the other patient mentioned is in fact George, Is it possible you could confirm if that is so'.

'You must know Rules and Regulations in Hospitals are the same the World over regarding patient confidentiality, but I will confirm that is indeed the persons name we have logged. However your friend is in an extremely sorry state, having been beaten quite badly, and the Police are waiting to interview him once he regains consciousness'.

'Which Hospital are you from please, as I should be in Washington mid afternoon tomorrow and would like to call and see him, and then visit the local police to get an update on what happened to him'.

'I am at the Medstar Washington Hospital Center, where your friend is also, ask at the Reception Desk and they will give you directions to the Ward'.

'Staff Nurse you cannot know what a relief it is to find out that George is in capable hands, if you are on duty tomorrow it will give me great pleasure to thank you in person, for spending the time to speak to me, thank you and goodbye for now'.

'Goodbye Mr Tordale, perhaps I will see you tomorrow'.

Falling back on the bed Jake almost cried in relief at the conversation he had just been involved with, so he immediately dialled the UK number for Henry Bates.

'Hi Jake any news?' was the short retort.

Jake outlined what had happened during the last 24 hours culminating with the distressing news about their colleague.

'Where are you going now?' Henry quizzed.

'I'll be flying to Washington in the morning, and heading directly to the Hospital. Unfortunately I can't imagine I will get any information from George as he should be still out of it. But I'll make a few inquiries on how he arrived at the Hospital and possibly speak to the Police regarding what happened, as soon as I have anything I'll ring you, speak to you tomorrow'.

'Thank's for everything Jake, take care of yourself' was the final words spoken by Henry as the line went dead.

Thirty seconds passed and he had just laid back on the bed for a rest when the Hotel phone rang. Jake picked up the receiver and said 'Jake Tordale'. The reply was from the Manager, 'Hello Mr Tordale my name is Stevan Charles. I understand you wish to ask me about a previous guest at the Hotel, Mr George Adams'.

'Yes I do, can I call down to Reception and speak with you if you could spare a few minutes of your precious time?'

'Certainly sir, just ask at Reception and the young lady will direct you to my office'.

'Thank you Mr Charles, I'll make my way down right away'.

Ten minutes later he was sat opposite the Manager and commenced his questioning.

'Firstly did Mr Adams give you any details of himself, or why he wished to contact the other man in question?'

'He did inform me that he worked for the British Secret Service and he was attempting to locate an absconded criminal, who should not have left the UK as he was a suspect in a homicide, with drug offences also under scrutiny'.

'Secondly had the other person stayed at the Hotel before Mr Adams' visit'.

'Unfortunately no, we checked through our records and there was no-one by the name that Mr Adams gave me'.

'Just on a whim, did the Hotel receive another man with a British accent under another name in the past week or so?'

'Ah I see your reasoning, let me look again'.

He booted up his computer and scrolled through recent guests over the last 3 weeks before retorting 'Bingo, I have a British male who stayed at the Hotel for one night by the name of Ronald Kray who paid in cash and stayed in Room 101'.

As he turned, he was taken aback at Jake's beaming smile, then asked 'What is so funny Mr Tordale?'

'It's just that Ronald Kray was one of twins, he was a highly dangerous criminal in London in the 60's and 70's. It appears quite apt that this individual took his name to put us off the scent. However George didn't fall for it and followed this individual to Washington where I will be heading tomorrow. Thank you for all your help on this matter and I'll trouble you no more'.

'Glad to be of some help to you Mr Tordale, and I hope you find this felon as soon as possible and get him back to the UK to pay for his crimes'.

Jake shook hands with the Manager and returned to his room for a doze.

Chapter 8

The Washington flight left at 10am local time, so Jake had an early breakfast, then phoned his driver for a return ride to the Airport.

His driver was extremely quiet throughout the journey, but just before pulling up at the entrance he said 'I wish you good luck on your visit to Washington'.

'Thank you for your wishes, if I return to LA again I will certainly contact you should I require any transportation'.

Jake collected a trolley and placed his luggage in it, before shaking the driver's hand and paying for his trip.

'Good luck sir' was the driver's passing remark.

The shuttle left on time and with 5 hours flight time Jake scrolled through what he had encountered since landing in the USA. But he still had the worrying scenario he was headed for, how bad were George's injuries, when had his injuries been inflicted and most of all by whom.

As the plane was only half full he was lucky enough to only have one companion who was sat by the window, whilst he took the aisle seat. The lady in his row was a professional person of fifty or so, and spent the flight attacking her laptop, most likely sending emails to her work colleagues or clients.

The flight was uneventful and after collecting his belongings from the carousel he obtained a yellow cab, giving instructions to be taken to the Washington Hilton which was the closest Hotel to the Medstar Washington Hospital.

Booking in at Reception he told the pleasant man he would be staying for a minimum of three days, which he paid for in cash.

After unpacking, he made a call to the UK and informed Henry he had landed in Washington and was settling into his room before making a visit to the Hospital to find out George's situation.

He had a wash and a quick change of clothes before heading back to Reception where he asked for a cab to take him to the Medstar Hospital.

The Receptionist dialled a number, obviously for their favoured Company and ten minutes later the cab pulled up at the front of the Hotel.

Jake gave the destination to the driver and twelve minutes later he stood at the entrance to the Hospital where his friend lay in a bed, gravely ill.

He walked up to the Main Desk and explained who he was here to visit, then mentioned a contact, Staff Nurse McDonald.

The lady dialled a number before giving Jake the floor and Ward location for him, whilst directing him to the lifts.

As the doors opened at the required floor, Jake felt a knot in his stomach wondering how badly injured George might be, but he strode across the corridor and approached the Information Desk. Explaining who he had come to see the lady buzzed a number that he could hear going off in an adjoining Ward, a few moments later a lady appeared and as she walked to the desk, he could see her name badge, it was Staff Nurse McDonald. She spoke a few words to the Receptionist before turning to Jake and introducing herself.

'It's a pleasure to meet you in person Mr Tordale, you made good time from Los Angeles, there is no change at present with your friend, but I must warn you that when we go in to see him there is a Police presence'.

'Thank you Staff Nurse, It'll save me going to the local Police Station to get an update on how the injuries were inflicted and hopefully by whom'.

'Follow me' she said whilst looking at Jake with sadness.

Opening the door to the ward he was surprised to see that George had been moved to a Private Room as he was the only patient in the room, apart from a uniformed officer together with he assumed a detective sat on opposite sides of the bed.

At first glance George looked a sorry sight with tubes attached to him together with a breathing tube via a tracheotomy, both arms in plaster and bandages over his face.

Before stepping any closer to the bed Jake had to take a few deep breaths as he was feeling extremely lightheaded at the sight that confronted him.

Chapter 8

Staff Nurse McDonald held his arm and introduced him to the Police Officers. The uniformed officer stood and offered Jake his seat which he took before he keeled over.

The detective scoured Jake's featured before asking him his name and relationship to Mr Adams. 'Mr Adams is a colleague of mine from London, we have worked for the same Security Department for a few years, why do you ask?'

'Do you have any form of identity Mr Tordale?'

'Yes I have' with Jake producing his MI6 credentials.

'I see' said the detective, deep in thought.

'Can you tell me what happened to George, and where he was found?' Jake asked.

'We had an anonymous call, saying that a person had been attacked at the rear of a night club and it looked as if he had been seriously beaten and to send someone straight away.

You must understand we receive a number of these calls daily, with a large percentage being bogus ones attempting to get our officers away from some other break-in or homicide that is taking, or has taken place. However we had officers and an ambulance at the scene within 10 minutes. Mr Adams was still in possession of his wallet and credentials, plus credit cards, so we therefore assumed that robbery was not the motive for the attack on him'.

'Were there any witnesses for you to interview as to why this had happened?'

'Yes indeed, we had two witnesses that gave us an account of an argument within the club between Mr Adams and two other men, one of which was also British. The first witness confirmed that he saw all three men exit the club about half an hour before the call was made to the station informing us of the affray. The other witness is the person who made the call to us after Mr Adams had already been attacked, but there was no-one else on the scene'.

We have a description of both men that were arguing with your friend and the team are arranging for a photofit picture to be made for you to peruse and possibly recognise one of the possible assailants. Officer McGregor is here to prevent any unauthorised persons from visiting this ward until further notice'.

Jake turned to the Staff Nurse and asked what George's medical situation is and what the possible outcome would be on his health.

'I'm unable to give you a full report but your colleague's Doctor will be doing his rounds in 30 minutes, and I'm sure he will give you his up to date diagnosis'.

'Thank you Staff Nurse, should I wait outside until called?'

'I would suggest that, there is a family room just down the corridor, I will show you and arrange some refreshments for you'.

'Thank you'. Turning to the detective he asked if he could cadge a lift with him to the station later to possibly look at the pictures.

'Certainly Mr Tordale, I will be staying until the medical report is given by the Doctor'.

Jake sat on a comfortable chair in the allocated room with a cup of black coffee brought to him by a young nurse, he was deep in thought regarding the future of George and the length of time he would be detained in this establishment.

He had just finished his drink when the Staff Nurse popped her head around the door to say that the Doctor would be in the patient's room in the next minute or two so would he follow her back.

The Doctor introduced himself as Sean Fortescue and shook Jake's hand, before returning to the clipboard at the bottom of the bed to check the patients stats.

With a few um's and ah's the Doctor looked at the detective first, before addressing Jake with his up to date assessment of George's condition.

'Firstly as you can see, your colleague is in a very poor state of health. His main injuries are what you can see are a broken tibia of the right leg, two bones broken in both arms, a serious wound to the scalp which needed 15 stitches, followed by heavy bruising around the midriff consistent with a kicking attack. We were concerned initially that this would have caused internal bleeding, however following extensive X rays and due to his superb condition he was obviously in a position to repel some of the attack and the bruising on his torso was external only. We have placed him in an induced coma temporarily to allow his body to prepare itself for the severe pain he will feel after the beating and subsequent intrusion by the surgeon's but I can confirm there are no life threatening injuries'.

'Thank you Doctor I appreciate your directness and excellent work, do you have any idea how long his recuperation will be, before he'll be fit for repatriation back to the UK, as I will have to arrange it with my Superior's?'

'My verdict at the moment can only be given with a rough guide. The damage to his leg and arms will require time in plaster, the other injuries to his body and head give me a lot of concern and I reserve judgement on those until further observations over the coming week. Mr Adams is a middle aged man in superb physical condition and I judge from that his recovery will be a lot swifter than the average human being, however I cannot tell what his mental condition will be until he is brought out of his induced coma. That is all I can tell you at this time Mr Tordale', Dr Fortescue concluded.

'Thank you for your direct report sir, I will be staying in Washington for at least a week to hopefully see a change in George's condition and take it from there' Jake replied shaking his hand firmly.The doctor returned the clipboard to the foot of the bed and left the room, with the Staff Nurse in tow.

The detective stood and said to Jake, 'If you follow me Mr Tordale, I'll take you back to my office and we can run through the details I collated from the Scenes of Crime Officers, together with information on the assumed attackers. When I have completed my report I'll arrange transport back to your Hotel'.

They walked out of the room without any further ado while the Uniformed Officer remained seated at the window.

Chapter 9

The drive to the Police Station only took 10 minutes, then after signing in at the desk he followed the Officer through a door where his name was etched on the glass DETECTIVE INSPECTOR RYAN DREW.

'Take a seat Mr Tordale, firstly I must apologise for not introducing myself to you, but I assume after looking at the door you realise I'm Ryan Drew, may I offer you coffee?'

'Thank you I could do with a caffeine injection, to enable me to take in what I have seen over the last half an hour'.

After pouring drinks for them from an aged glass percolator he sat at his desk and opened a manilla folder, then ran through the details within it, together with the statements of the two witnesses.

'I can't understand why George would have been given such a beating, I assumed he would only be looking for information on the whereabouts of the British man we are attempting to locate, and then return him to the UK to stand trial'.

'From the limited details I have been able to put together, it appears that your friend asked the wrong questions to a local high ranking drug baron unfortunately with dire consequences. It's not easy to apprehend these people as they all have corrupt lawyers at their beck and call, so even if we get them to the Station they just call their brief and then are released within a few hours' the detective replied frustratingly. However I have two mugshots to show you that have been put together by a Police Artist?'

'What I don't understand is that the only question he would have likely asked is if anyone knew the whereabouts of a fellow Brit named Roland Withers, however I would like to see these mugshots?' Drew passed over a sheet of paper with faces on but Jake was unable to recognise either man shown.

'That name means nothing to me', Drew replied 'But if drugs are involved I can arrange for his possible contact to be brought in for questioning. If I drop you back to the Hotel I'll ring you once this arrest has been made, allowing you to return and listen in to the questioning later'.

Jake stood and thanked the detective for this information and followed him to his car.

After being dropped at the Hotel he made his way directly to his room, he sat immobile for half an hour with his head churning with all the information the detective had divulged, then picked up the phone and rang Henry to give him the latest up to date details.

'Hello Henry can you spare a minute, if so I'll run through George's situation, then what we have regarding the attack, I gleaned from Detective Inspector Ryan Drew who has been most helpful?'

'Go ahead Jake, I await in anticipation'.

Ten minutes later after Jake had completed his rhetoric, there was complete silence from Henry, before he asked Jake what his intentions were for the next few days.

'I'll visit the Hospital whenever I am allowed, and as soon as the offenders are brought to the Police Station Detective Inspector Drew will contact me and I will sit in on the interviews, hopefully gleaning more information on the whereabouts of Roland Withers'.

A slight hesitation before Henry continued with 'As soon as George is out of the woods, I will arrange transport to have him returned to the UK for further treatment and recuperation. If the Police are able to locate Withers, you are not to intervene, do I make myself clear Jake. Leave it to them and we will arrange for his extradition this end with no interference from you, OK'

'Fully understood sir' said Jake with underlying anger.

'I get your fury, but there is nothing you can do for Janet now, so let the Authorities meet out their Justice for her'.

'Yes sir' Jake replied finally, then disconnected the call.

Calming down after a few minutes he decided to give Charlene a call and tell her he was in Washington. The call was picked up almost immediately, and as soon as Jake said where he was situated at present she screamed with delight.

'Would you like to meet up for a coffee and a chat today?' he asked.

'That would be lovely Jake, shall I come to you?'

'It would be easier, as I have no transport at present, my visit here was at very short notice, but I'll explain everything once we meet up'.

A slight hesitation before Charlene continued, 'I'll be at the Hotel in half an hour, I'll see you in Reception, bye for now'.

Jake thought he had best change his clothes after having a shower and make himself presentable for his lovely visitor.

Twenty minutes later he was sat in one of the plush armchairs in Reception casually reading a paper when the delectable Charlene made her entrance rushing over to him and clutching him to her body in a loving embrace.

'So good to see you Jake, it seems forever since we were in Santorini, how have you been and why are you in the States?'

'Slow down Charlene, I have lots to tell you but not here. I am not familiar with Washington, so I'll be led by you where we can go to eat and talk without being overheard' Jake answered trying to calm her down.

'My car's outside, so if you're ready follow me, I'll provide you with a guided tour of my City' she replied in an obvious state of delight.

Her car was a large station wagon that made British cars look like toys, he had just buckled up as she pulled out onto the road with expertise, and amalgamated into the City traffic like a true professional.

Jake looked out the window as they drove along and the landscape was surrounded by skyscrapers that enveloped the City as if they were ancient stalagmites, almost blotting out the light, however Jake was staring at the amount of traffic on the roads together with the hustle and bustle on the pavements as hundreds of pedestrians rushed along with mobile phones gripped in their hands still somehow avoiding each other as they rushed to their intended destinations.

'Are you OK?' Charlene questioned as he hadn't spoken since they had got in the car.

'Sorry, yes I am, I can't believe the rush and noise of Washington, it appears even worse than London' he replied.

'You should see it in rush hour, first thing in the morning and last thing in the afternoon, its like a swarm of ants on the sidewalk, but the roads are jammed with workers who decide to take their vehicles, and together with the multitude of cabs makes for slow going, but everyone knows it will be the same next day, next week, ad infinitum, so we just have to live with it'.

'How much further are we going Charlene?'

'We are almost there, I just have to pull into that multi-storey over there' she answered pointing to the next turning. Travelling down in the lift Jake smiled at her, which was the first time his face had done that since he had landed in the US.

'What?' she asked.

'It's so good to see you Charlene' he answered smiling from ear to ear.

'Don't get all sentimental with me Jake Tordale, I'm waiting to hear why you're in the States earlier than expected?'

'Lets wait until we are sat at a table and I'll tell you all I have so far'.

They stopped at Level One with Jake following in Charlene's wake as they headed to a Cafe only 20 metres from the lift. Sitting at a table for two she ordered coffee for them then sat back awaiting Jake's report on his visit to Washington.

Drinking his coffee slowly, he looked into Charlene's intense grey eyes before he started his explanation.

'Life is full of ups and downs and I had no intention of visiting America until I was coming to see you in April. However the house of a lady who previously worked for the Secret Service, was broken into in late November and she was badly assaulted. She sustained severe injuries and following a couple of operations, unfortunately passed away without regaining consciousness. The perpetrator was arrested, but placed on bail, prior to a Court appearance in the New Year. Unfortunately he absconded and was traced to the States. My colleague George Adams, whom you met, followed him but unfortunately asked the wrong questions at a nightclub here in Washington and received a terrible beating and is at present residing at the Medstar Hospital.

The whereabouts of the fugitive is being looked into by the local Police. I have just spoken to Henry Bates and once the doctors pass him fit to travel George will be airlifted back to the UK. I intend to stay until there is further information to hand and to then arrange for the extradition of the fugitive Roland Withers, however long that will take. That is all the details I have up to date'.

'Goodness gracious Jake your life is as busy as it has been over the past 12 months' Charlene replied, with wide eyes at his description of recent events.

Having only just noticed how lovely Charlene looked after being entrenched into his narrative, he smiled and quickly apologised at how 'off the wall' his attitude had been since they had met up. He stood, walked around the table and gave her a deep and passionate kiss which was reciprocated, until they both came up for air.

Charlene blushed before saying 'I've certainly missed that'.

'Sorry to be so forceful and in public as well, but I needed that' he replied.

She smiled at him before continuing with 'What plans do you have for the rest of the day, only I have to return to the office?'

'Sorry Charlene, I forgot you have to work, if it's not too much trouble could you drop me back to the hotel and I'll catch up with you later on in the week'.

'That's fine with me' she replied.

Half an hour later he was back in his Hotel room, then just as he sat on the chair by his bed his mobile rang.

Picking up the phone he was surprised to se that it was Detective Inspector Ryan Drew. 'Hello detective what can I do for you?'

'Just an update for you Mr Tordale, we have brought in both men for questioning, and I wondered if you would like to sit in on the interview?'

'Thank you, I'll call a cab and be with you as soon as possible'.

Cancelling the call, he rushed down to Reception and asked them to arrange a cab for him.

Ten minutes passed before a yellow cab pulled up outside, then thanking the receptionist he walked out the doors, got into the vehicle, and explained his destination to the driver.

Chapter 10

Walking into the Police Station, he signed in and was directed to the Detective's office. Knocking on the door, he entered, then walked over to the desk and shook hands with Ryan Drew.

'Thank's for coming in so quickly Mr Tordale, both men are in a holding room, I'm giving them a little time to stew and work on their stories. It should be interesting to see if they come up with the same details. I think the first man will be the weakest link, not knowing his surroundings and the way US Police carry out their interviews. Do you fancy a cup of java before the fun begins?'

'A good idea sir, I think it could take a while'

'Call me Ryan when we are on our own and I'll call you Jake if that's OK?'

'OK' is all Jake could come up with.

'Right let's have a cuppa' as he poured out two cups of black coffee.

Sitting back in his chair he stared at Jake for a while before asking him about his time in MI6, then the following minutes were taken up by Jake's abridged details of what had happened over the past few years, leaving the detective taken aback by his story, and he could only shake his head in astonishment at the information he had just been privy too.

Quickly changing the subject he stated 'Let's get to it, I intend talking to my drug dealer first, and then I'll have a go at your man, you can go in the Observation Room which has a one way mirrored wall and a loudspeaker, allowing you to check reactions to the questions and the replies they give'.

'I'm ready when you are Ryan' Jake said whilst standing up.

'Follow me Jake and I'll show you to the room, there will be another officer with you taking what necessary notes he feels are appropriate.

Jake followed in the Detective's wake, as they approached the third door along the corridor he opened it and was introduced to the Officer sat in one of the two seats.

Five minutes later a man was sat in the chair facing the mirrored wall with a brief alongside him, before Ryan entered the room and sat with the other Detective who would operate the recording device.

Questions were asked by the detective over a period of ten minutes with only one answer given by the arrested man which was to give his name and address, all remaining questions were answered with an abrupt NO COMMENT, as directed by his Brief. Ryan excused himself for a minute, then re-entered the room with Jake and the policeman who had taken a few notes.

'As you can see Mr Tordale, these bastards know the system, having been in custody numerous times, so it's like getting blood out of a stone'.

'May I suggest that you tell a white lie and say that the person attacked is in a serious condition with a 5% expected survival rate, which was advised by the surgeon who operated on him to see if he places the blame on my man. Also the arrest for affray and grievous bodily harm is one thing, but it could be changed to murder if the patient dies'.

'Excellent idea, I'll try that with my second approach' then he walked out of the room and returned to his seat in the Interview Room.

'Sorry about that' he said to the two men opposite him, 'where was I, oh yes, I forgot to say that my reason for this interview is based solely on affray and GBH, but of course due to the patient's condition and the surgeon's diagnosis. he has only been given a guide of 5% survival rate, which takes the case to a new level and brings in the possibility of a murder charge. Addressing the lawyer he said, 'Before you suggest no comment again to your Client, I wish to emphasise that I also have three witnesses to the attack and their statements, so think very carefully before you say anything further'.

The lawyer's face took on a deep red complexion as he turned to his Client and whispered a few instructions to him, before facing the front again awaiting the detectives further questions.

'My Client is willing to answer your questions, if you would start the interview again', the lawyer confirmed as he turned to his Client, who just acknowledged with a snarl, then nodded in agreement.

In the other room the policemen and Jake looked at each other with grins on their faces, but nothing was said as they waited for the interview to start again.

Chapter 10

Twenty minutes later with questions and answers completed Ryan left the room once more, with the other two men following in his wake. A little while later Jake and Sean met up, and following a quick update walked back to his office. They sat down and had another coffee, then talked about the British man who was in custody.

'As you eluded when cornered these long term criminals pass the buck to anyone other than themselves, so it looks as if your man is in for a very rough ride with his interview. I'll let him stew for another half an hour, then grill him on his take on the attack. You're most welcome to listen in again if you so wish, if not I'll get someone to drop you off wherever you wish to go!'

'I'll stay if you don't mind, as if he is arrested I will have to arrange with my office for his extradition back to the UK, hopefully on the same aircraft that will repatriate George for rest and recuperation, also myself'.

'That's fine Jake, can I get you a sandwich or something, as I'll start the interview just after 1am'.

'I'm fine thank you Ryan, I had a nice breakfast that will see me through until later today'.

Clutching his mug of coffee the detective sat back in his chair totally relaxed, before asking Jake a little bit more of himself.

'Believe it or not I retired a couple of years ago and settled down in a little Cottage in SW England. Having lost my wife in a tragic car accident, I felt lost for a while and visited a few of the Countries we enjoyed together to relive the good times we had together and indulge in my hobby of photography. Unfortunately when I visited Kefalonia in the Greek Islands I witnessed a murder, and my life changed completely over the next few years.

I have two children and three grandchildren who live a couple of hours from me, who I have seen frequently and hopefully this will be my final episode with the UK Secret Service. Do you have family?'

'Yes, unfortunately being a full time detective, it's not the glamorous job that is shown in the movies, therefore my time with them is sporadic. My wife and I have been married 20 years and we have a boy and a girl who I love dearly'.

With that his mood appeared to change completely, as his head dropped to his chest.

'You OK Ryan?'

'I'm sorry, last week my wife was diagnosed with breast cancer and she will be having an operation within the next two weeks, then quite invasive treatment afterwards. Thankfully my parents live locally and they will be able to sort out the children's school activities'.

'That's rough Ryan, but at least you have your parents to help out'.

'They are a great help, but I feel guilty not being there for my family. Anyway back to business. I'll get your man up and start the interview, if you make your way back to the room I'll start in about 15 minutes'.

Jake walked slowly back to the gallery with a heavy heart, thinking about what he had just heard from the detective, whilst reminiscing on his married life when work had intervened with his children's early years. However time has passed and unfortunately there is no going back to change those early years but when his time in the States was over he would return to Devon and spend more time with the family.

Chapter 11

A nervous looking Roland Withers entered the Interview room, as he settled into his chair he certainly looked out of his comfort zone. His clothes were disheveled, he hadn't shaved for a few days and his ginger hair also hadn't seen a barber for weeks. Sat next to him was a State lawyer, who looked no older than twenty five, he was dressed in a light grey suit, blue shirt and multi-coloured tie, beside him was a black briefcase which Jake thought was just for show as he made no attempt to open it.

Ryan switched on the recording machine and nodded to his Assistant who was there to take any necessary notes that would be in addition to the recorded conversations.

He then sat back and gave both the men opposite him a blank stare that Withers could not match and his eyes dropped down looking at his hands that were in his lap.

'My name is Detective Inspector Ryan Drew, and I am interviewing Mr Roland Withers who is accompanied by the Court lawyer Mr Julian Goldberg' the detective stated into the recording device. 'Would you confirm that my statement is correct?' both men nodded their agreement.

'Right Mr Withers, I will ask you firstly, were you in the back yard of said night club with another person following an altercation or disagreement with a third party?'

'Yes' Withers replied.

'Then did both you and another person give the third person a severe beating causing serious harm, which lead to that person being transferred to hospital for a series of operations'.

Withers looked at the lawyer and nodded.

'Please answer the question Mr Withers, yes or no?'

'Yes' he replied with head bowed.

'Please tell me exactly what caused this altercation and why you were involved'.

There followed a long pause before Withers explained 'The man approached me in the club and started asking questions about why I had come to the USA and for what purpose, I refused to answer any, and he became quite aggressive towards me.

The man who was with me got involved in the verbals, then we continued the situation outside, then someone threw a punch and I can't remember what happened afterwards'.

Ryan said nothing for a while until he opened up with another important question 'Did you throw the first punch, your colleague or the other person. Think very carefully before you answer Mr Withers'.

Withers turned to the lawyer who was non-committal, before returning his gaze to the policeman and then said 'It was me, I felt threatened, but that was the only blow I gave the man'.

'So you are saying that the main injuries were inflicted by your friend?'

'Yes I am, but he is no friend of mine, just someone who's name I was given in LA'.

Again Ryan waited a blink or two, satisfied with the reply Withers had given him, that with luck his testimony would bring down one of the most influential drug dealers in Washington.

'Until we can determine the full extent of the injuries to Mr Adams and how long he will be incapacitated, it is not known what incarceration time can be expected if found guilty, but I expect you will be returned to the UK to carry out whatever sentence is passed, do you understand'.

'Yes Sir' Withers replied with a sigh.

'I will have you taken back to the cell until I have the rap sheet typed out for you to sign, and then bring you up later to confirm your statement, do you understand the consequences'.

'Yes Sir', he answered with a look of relief.

It took a whole lot of self control to stop the detective from smiling as he picked up his papers and left the Interview Room.

Jake met Ryan in the corridor and as they approached each other they both had beaming smiles, before the detective said a few words that meant a book full 'Check mate I think,

'Very rarely do you end up with two bad eggs in a basket, but I think that is what we have today Jake' Ryan exclaimed with a look of total satisfaction.

'Excellent work my friend, there is just the final work to do, and that's to get a conviction, but at least my man can be extradited back to London for his sentence after the formalities. Let's just hope that George is as strong as I think he is and can pull through from his injuries'.

'I'll get a car to drop you back to the Hotel Jake, so you can relax and give your Boss some good news for a change'.

'Thank's for everything Ryan, I'm just glad that things have turned out positive in the end'.

'I would also like to thank you for your invaluable input to date, I'm sure there is more that will come out from this case over the coming days'.

Chapter 12

Back at his Hotel room he took a beer from the Mini-bar and made himself comfortable in the chair by the window before dialling the number for Henry Bates. It rang for about 30 seconds before Henry's familiar voice answered with a cheery "Hi Jake how are things'.

The following 10 minute conversation was carried out totally by Jake with no interruptions as he outlined what had taken place at the Police Station.

After Jake took a well earned breather Henry replied with 'Excellent result Jake, let's hope the same will be said for George over the coming days'.

'What is the procedure for bringing Withers back to the UK sir?' he asked.

'I'll arrange for a specialist Officer to fly out when the paperwork has been completed to meet the US Police at the Airport to hand over Withers, and they will fly back the following day. In regards to George I would like you to stay in Washington for another week to ascertain his condition regarding his repatriation, assuming that is OK with you?'

'I have one or two things I wish to do whilst in the City as well as visiting George and keeping in touch with Inspector Drew regarding the on-going case, so another week will be no trouble at all'.

'Perhaps you could give young Charlene a call and meet up with her?' Henry said cheekily.

'I've seen her already, but will no doubt meet her again during the next week' he replied.

'Ok Jake, you appear to have everything in hand there, keep in touch as often as you can and look after yourself'.

'Thank you sir, bye for now'.

As he disconnected the call to London his mobile sounded with a message, he saw it was from Charlene wondering what he was doing that evening. He quickly dialled her number which she picked up right away.

'You have been busy on the phone Jake!'

'Sorry, I've been speaking to London to give them an update on the situation here, what can I do for you?'

'I was wondering if you would like to meet up for dinner?'

'That sounds a wonderful idea, what do you have in mind?'

'There is a lovely Greek Restaurant close to where I live that I would like to try, I know your preference for Greek cuisine and thought we could enjoy it together, shall I pick you up in, say an hour?'

'Excellent I'll be waiting in the foyer, see you soon'.

Buoyed by the call, he jumped into the shower for a blast of cold water before having a shave. Checking his wardrobe he chose a warm green turtle neck jumper and dark slacks, and due to the cold conditions put on a three-quarter length overcoat and gloves.

He made his way down to the Foyer to await Charlene and sat in one of the comfortable chairs facing the glazed entrance doors.

He had no time for contemplation as minutes later Charlene arrived looking gorgeous, dressed in a light blue pant suit under a grey overcoat with matching gloves.

Jake stood as she approached the doors, and as they met gave her a light kiss on both cheeks and said 'Your timing is impeccable as I have only just sat down in the armchair'.

'I am always on time Jake, it's part of my makeup I'm afraid to confess'.

'I must admit I changed when I married my late wife, she was a stickler for time and usually arrived at any appointment excessively early, but that was her way, bless her' Jake reminisced.

'OK, let's go' Charlene replied before Jake became embroiled in his past, then walked out to the car.

As they settled into their seats she said 'I hope you'r hungry, I have been told that the meals are extremely generous in this Greek establishment and as I am famished myself there will be no small plates of food put in front of me this evening'.

Jake gave her a broad smile before managing a genuine chuckle at her remarks.

The trip into central Washington took them twenty minutes and after parking the car at the rear of the premises, they entered the restaurant by the front entrance to be greeted by a waiter.

Charlene gave her name and the smartly dressed man ushered them to their table.

They ordered drinks and tapas as starters before sitting back and discussing what had happened to them both since they last met.

An hour later with their starters complete Jake ordered a bottle of wine to go with their main course of Lamb Kleftiko. As the plate was put in front of Jake he could only look at Charlene with popping eyes and wide open mouth before saying 'I see what you meant when you asked if I was hungry'.

They ate and drank in silence before they both sat back fully sated by the gorgeous food they had devoured. Jake asked if she could manage a sweet but a shake of her head confirmed his already realisation that she had had enough lovely food for one evening.

Jake gestured to the waiter for the bill which he paid with a generous tip.

The waiter returned a few minutes later with a complimentary drink for them both.

Charlene asked Jake if he would like to come back to her apartment for a coffee before she dropped him back to his Hotel, or did he want to do something else.

'You could drop me back to the Hotel if you like and we could have coffee in the Lounge or in my room and have another chat about things to get us fully up to date' Jake said with a glint in his eye.

'Perhaps that would be best, as I think my friend will be home all evening, not that she isn't great company, but three's a crowd I think'.

'I totally agree, the Hotel it is then' he replied with a cheesy grin.

Back in the Hotel Bar Jake ordered a cafetiere of coffee before they settled down in the plush armchairs to continue their conversation.

Charlene asked Jake how long he anticipated staying in the States, as perhaps they could bring his holiday forward from the intended April weeklong visit.

'It depends on George Adams's recuperation and when he'll be fit to travel back to London. I have spoken to Henry and advised him I'll be staying on until arrangements can be made to extradite his English attacker, and then escort George back to the UK, so my stay therefore will be as long as it takes'.

'I assume it will be at least a couple of weeks, so perhaps I'll take a week's leave and I could spend the time showing you around Washington and highlights of the District'.

'That sounds like a good plan my dear, I will of course be visiting George every couple of days to ascertain his condition, together with visiting the Police Station as and when required during that period'.

'Good, that's a plan then Jake, I'll express my intentions for a week's leave tomorrow morning and plan our week from Wednesday', she exclaimed with excitement.

Jake smiled before saying 'Excellent, knowing your efficiency I assume you will come up with a daily itinerary for us with classy eating establishments every evening'.

In reply Charlene stated 'I would have been organised if this was now April as planned, but I expect I can formulate something before Wednesday that will meet with your approval'.

'Looking forward to a busy week ahead already. During the time I'll need to visit the Hospital and Police Station to keep up to date firstly with George's condition, secondly the completion of the extradition details for Roland Withers'.

'We can work those visits in as and when necessary Jake, my time off is flexible to suit whatever conditions prevail'.

The time was approaching 9pm and Charlene smiled at Jake before saying she would have to return home as she had an early start the next day to enable her to clear her workload before leaving in the evening for a week away from the office.

'I fully understand, I can wait another day to have you all to myself for the following weeks adventures'.

They both stood and walked out the door with Jake following in her wake and out to her car, they embraced with a lingering kiss before waving goodbye.

Back in his room he decided to ring his daughter Clare before settling down for the night.

Checking the time in the UK he dialled her number which Mike her husband answered with a "Hello, how may I help you'.

'Hi Mike it's Jake, is Clare there a minute i'm just calling from Washington DC, and just wanted a quick catchup, I won't keep her long'.

'Off on your travels again Jake?'

'Something like that Mike, speak to you when I return to the UK'.

'OK Jake, here she is'.

'Hello love, just a quick catch-up, I'm in Washington at the moment, I'll be here for at least another week, I've got a few bits and pieces to clear up but should be home again later in the month. Everything OK in Devon with you all?'

'We're fine Dad, what on earth are you doing over there?'

'Just had a complicated issue to attend to, but everything is OK now and should be completed as I said in a week or two. When I get back I'll pop down and see you again before I go to Singapore and Australia, prior to the installation of my Alarm System'.

'Thank's for ringing Dad, take care of yourself and I'll tell the rest of the family you're whereabouts etc'.

'Thank's my luv, take care and I'll see you soon' he replied before ringing off.

He thought to himself he would give Henry a ring in the morning and check the timings for George's repatriation and Withers return to the UK.

Chapter 13

He roused early and realised he had the day to himself, so following his breakfast he contacted the Police Station and spoke to Ryan Drew for an update and a guide into the possible date Withers could be extradited. Ryan couldn't give him any good news at present as all the paperwork he would have to prepare for the Court hearing wasn't to hand at present, but on a positive note he expected everything to be ready in 3 days time.

Feeling quite buoyant by that conversation he decided to walk to the Hospital and see what George's condition was and to check if he had been brought out of his induced coma. The weather was quite cold so he put on his overcoat, cap and gloves and walked to the Hospital in an optimistic mood, approaching the Reception desk half an hour later he hadn't realised how far the walk was as he had taken a cab on his last visit. However his mood was still buoyant as he approached the desk and explained who he had come to see. The Receptionist as usual rang through to the ward and spoke to someone before confirming it was OK to visit his friend. Taking the lift, a minute later he was outside George's room and greeted by Staff Nurse McDonald with a beaming smile. 'Good morning Mr Tordale, how are you today. I have some good news for you, Mr Adams is out of the induced coma and in fine spirits, I'm sure your arrival will lift his mood further', she then turned and opened the door to the Private Ward with Jake in her wake.

As he walked over to the bed Jake felt quite moved as he looked at his friend covered in bandages and bruises, however he was smiling as he viewed his fellow Brit.

A weak 'Hi mate, what are you doing here?' George asked.

Jake managed a quick chuckle before answering 'Checking on my 'house sitter', as he seems to have got himself into a bit of a pickle, don't you think'.

'They caught me off-guard but wait until I'm up and about again' George said optimistically.

'I don't know what you know at present, but the good news is that your attackers are in custody and trying to say that the other inflicted you're injuries, so they are both going to be charged with 'ABH',causing danger to life, and affray'.

A quizzical look on George's face was followed by 'How did you know where to find me Jake?'

Looking George straight in the eye he said 'I took the same route as you and followed the trail by interrogating the Hotel staff and AVIS representative's where you visited and the journey led me to this Hospital, mainly thank's to Staff Nurse McDonald. I have kept Henry up to date on the situation so far, and a plane will be sent whenever you are fit to fly, and all the papers have been completed for the extradition of Roland Withers'.

'I can't believe how I fell for the 'let's talk about this outside' comment, but it happened, perhaps I'm getting a bit long in the tooth for these confrontations'.

'It's a good job you'r in such good condition mate, as the Surgeon said to me when I arrived that a mere mortal person would not have survived the attack that you were subjected to' Jake replied with feeling.

'You could be right Jake, but I feel a right prat falling for that scam, I thought I had done the hard work in finding Wither's, but fell for the involvement with the drug baron which had nothing to do with him, but of course he took over and accelerated the situation by giving me a thorough beating and leaving me for dead'.

'Have you spoken to the Doctor and found out the time scale for leaving the Hospital?'Jake asked.

'He did his rounds before lunch and was pleased with my stats after coming out of the coma, but anticipates it will be at least another seven days before he can release me, why do you ask?'

'Well as I said previously, Henry has to arrange for transport to take us all back to London, and arrange for an armed Police escort to fly over to take Withers back home. I'll also be on that plane, so it will kill three birds with one stone if we all go together, pardon the pun.'

George smiled, then closed his eyes, obviously after all this talk it had tired him out.

'Now I've seen you awake I'll leave you to have a doze' Jake whispered to his friend and nodded to the policeman as he walked out of the room.

Chapter 13

As he approached the lift he bumped into Staff Nurse McDonald who smiled at him and said with sincerity 'Good to see your friend awake I expect?'

'It certainly is but the dear old chap is feeling a little tired, so I'll call back and see him this evening. He's a strong willed man and I think he'll be ready to return to the UK in a few weeks'.

'I think your judgement of medical matters is a bit hopeful, but looking at his stats and body condition, I think we will find it difficult to contain him much longer than the few weeks you hope for'.

'Keep up the good work here and I might bump into you again this evening'.

'Bye for now' she remarked as the lift doors closed.

As he descended to the ground floor he decided to ring Ryan Drew at the Police Station to see if he needed him at all, and to ask how the paperwork was going.

Unfortunately the detective was out on another call, but the person who answered his phone said he would arrange for Ryan to ring him back on his return to the Station.

He had the rest of the day to himself, so decided to go back to his room and make a few phone calls. First to Olivia in Sweden, followed by Mrs Choo in Australia, Clare and Sharon in Devon, and finally Henry Bates.

With the last of the calls completed he realised how much time had passed and it was now past midday, so he decided to check out the eateries in the Hotel's vicinity. Within 100 yards he came across a steakhouse, so he thought he would give it a try. Walking in the front entrance he was taken aback by the number of diner's already tucking into their lunch, which he thought was a good sign as to the place's popularity, he was shown to a table by a waiter and handed a menu, and asked what he would like to drink.

He ordered a beer from the waiter and would give his food order when he returned with his drink. Checking the menu, 'steak' was on each of the individual items, you just had to decide on the size of the steak and what accompaniment to have with it.

He quickly plumped for a 12oz sirloin steak (medium rare) with prawns, fries and a side salad, together with a bottle of house red to go with it.

Over the following hour of bliss he devoured all that was put in front of him together with the beer and wine, then relaxed with a large black coffee to complete the meal. He paid the bill then made his way back to the Hotel for a couple of hours rest in his room.

He woke up just after 5pm and thought he would wander down to the Lounge and have a coffee before making his way to the Hospital to visit George. as the next week would be taken up by Charlene's whistle stop tour of Washington.

As he opened the door to the Private Room he was taken aback when he discovered George out of bed, and with some effort limping with small strides. The Officer who was sat by the window was grinning from ear to ear at the grit and determination that the patient was showing.

George turned to face Jake and smiled, 'Not bad for starters Jake' he said with some effort showing on his face'.

'I wouldn't expect anything less from you George, has this been OK'd by the Doctor or do you have your own clearance'.

'You know me Jake, I'm not one to let the grass grow under my feet' George answered whilst making his way back to the sanctuary of his bed.

'At this rate my anticipation of a couple of weeks to Henry could be a go-er for you returning to the UK, what do you think?'

'If the physio works over the next week I think Henry should arrange for my return the week after, if of course I have the OK from the Doc'.

'Great George, it all hinges on the paperwork for Withers to go through and we will all be winging our way back home'.

With that the Doctor entered the room with Staff Nurse McDonald at his heels. 'How are things Mr Adams, I understand you have been up and about over the last hour, how do you feel?'

'A bit shaky Doc I must admit, but a few days of exercise and physio and I think I will be ready to go home'.

'Excellent, If you would step outside for a few minutes gentlemen I'll give Mr Adams a check over to update my notes'.

Jake and the officer left the room as requested, with the policeman stationing himself at the door, Jake walked down the corridor to locate a seat.

Chapter 13

The Doctor spent 10 minutes examining George before he and Staff Nurse McDonald exited the room, leaving the officer and George to return. On passing the Doctor explained to Jake that his patient was making remarkable progress and he should be fit for his return to the UK in 10 days, this of course being a provisional arrangement.

Jake spent another hour in the room discussing the current situation and asking if there was anyone George needed contacting back home, which he replied negatively.

They finally shook hands and Jake took his leave.

Chapter 14

His mobile phone rang at 7.30am, with a chirpy 'Good morning sir, your adventure day has arrived' Charlene chipped with mild amusement.

'Good morning young lady what is the itinerary for today, and do I have time for breakfast?'

'I suggest you have a big breakfast, as today we will be quite busy, I have arranged transport to take us to The White House, The Lincoln Memorial, National Air and Space Museum and finally Jefferson Memorial and Tidal Basin. This will take us the best part of the day, and then it will be time for a nice meal to complete our first adventure'.

'Excellent, what time will you be collecting me?'

'Be in the foyer at 9.45am sharp and prepare yourself for an enjoyable day in my company'.

'I'll be ready, see you soon'. he said before racing out of bed.

Down for an enjoyable big breakfast and coffee as he was told, he was ready and sat in the foyer at 9.30am, ready to be collected just in anticipation of Charlene arriving early, and he wasn't disappointed as she bounced in 10 minutes early.

'Ready for your Tour Jake?'

'I was born ready' he replied.

As they stepped out into the cold weather he was taken aback by the limousine that Charlene had organised for the day.

'Nice motor' Jake remarked.

'Nothing but the best for my UK visitor, I'm glad you decided to wrap up warm as although we will be cozy in the limo, visiting the sites we'll be exposed to this cutting wind that has greeted us this morning'.

As they fixed their seat belts the limo glided away from the kerb on its way to their first site, the impressive White House. Jake took numerous photos as they walked around the areas that the public were allowed, and although early in the morning there were already hundreds of sightseers gazing at this most impressive of buildings.

Chapter 14

The rest of the morning and early afternoon were taken up by the other three sites before the final attraction's of the day Jefferson Memorial and Tidal Basin. They stopped for a quick snack before visiting this impressive site, but the wait was worth it. The sun although weak this time of the year cast shadows over the area making Jake's photos even more startling.

With this final location completed the tour was over for the day, Charlene asked the driver to take them back to her apartment's address, and as they pulled up outside the huge block Jake grinned and asked which floor she resided on.

'We are on the 12th floor, but don't worry there's a lift' she replied grinning.

She thanked the driver and offered a tip for his patience, saying they would see him again tomorrow for more exploration's of the wonderful City.

Jake followed Charlene into the building, where they boarded the lift for the 12th floor apartment she shared with a friend.

As she opened the door Jake was taken aback by the size of the apartment, it consisted of two bedrooms both ensuite, a huge kitchen/diner and a lounge the size of the ground floor of Wisteria Cottage.

'Your face is a picture Jake, as the saying goes 'everything is big in America', however the cost also matches the size, but with two of us sharing it works out quite reasonable'.

They walked into the Lounge where Charlene offered Jake a drink, 'Coffee, tea or a drink drink?'

'I don't suppose you have any Ouzo, my dear' he asked with a grin.

'Strangely enough as soon as I returned to the States I ordered four bottles for your proposed visit in April, but I suppose we can have a drop earlier now that your'e here. Do you want anything in it, or just another Ouzo?'

'Are we eating out again, or are you ordering in?' he asked.

'Why?' she enquired.

'It all depends on how much I drink if I would be fit company to go out on the town'.

'You're here on holiday, what would you like to do?'

'I feel quite tired after our intense sightseeing, so I will either have to have a nap before we go out or stay in and have a few drinks and wait for the food delivery'.

'Let's see how the drinking goes first shall we, my friend will be home from work around six, therefore our state of inebriation can be judged by her reaction as to our eating arrangements after her suggestions'.

'After our first drink, perhaps we could have a bit of fun before your friend gets home' he asked with a wry grin.

'A good idea perhaps it's best to take our drink, and the bottle into my bedroom, as I have a lot of pent up energy to release, you being the target'.

Jake followed her into the kitchen, then carried the bottle and ice, whilst Charlene carried the two glasses into her splendid boudoir'

No sooner had Charlene put the two glasses on the bedside tables she started shedding her clothes, Jake put the bottle and ice down and mirrored her movements.

He was immediately in a state of arousal as soon as he looked at her outstanding figure, they then fell onto the bed in a long and sensual kiss. Charlene took charge and in a matter of minutes they both fell back completely exhausted.

They reached for their drinks and downed them in one go, before laying back in each others arms.

'I think we'll stay in Jake, I would like round two before Heather get's home'.

'Fine by me, but I'll need at least half an hour before round two'.

A bellowing laugh from Charlene followed by 'You're on', made Jake laugh as well.

Fully exhausted after round two, they decided a shower was required before Heather returned home so at least they would be sat nursing their drinks on the settee when she walked in the door.

To their surprise Heather was late home today, Charlene surmised that she had called into the shops on the way to collect a few items, just in case Charlene had brought Jake home with her.

A key was inserted in the door 20 minutes after they had settled down and Heather breezed into the Lounge with a cherry 'Hello' to Charlene, 'So this is the mysterious Mr Tordale I have heard so much about, It's a pleasure to meet you Jake, you certainly live up to the description I had been given by Charlene'.

Jake stood and shook her hand, 'It's nice to meet you Heather' he replied, then sitting back down on the settee.

Chapter 14

Charlene followed Heather into the kitchen for a quick chat before returning a few minutes later. 'I explained that we will be ordering a take-out and she is most welcome to join us, I assume that's OK with you?'

'No problem at all, what does anyone fancy, I'll pay for the food, and I won't take no for an answer, OK'. he said with some authority.

'Fine by me, Heather will have a shower and a change of clothes before she feels human, so I'll ask her what she fancies for eats and we'll put the order in'.

Charlene ordered Chinese which was the unanimous decision, with a mixture of starters, mains, rice and noodles.

Three quarters of an hour later there was a knock on the door with their delivery just as the table had been set out by Charlene.

Two bottles of wine were placed in the centre of the table and the mixture of containers were spread out and within easy reach of the three of them.

An hour and a half later with both bottles empty and most of the food containers clean they retired to the Lounge to relax with their coffee.

The remainder of the evening was spent outlining each of their lives so far, and at 9.30pm Jake said he would catch a cab back to the Hotel. With pleasantries completed he took the lift down to the ground floor as a cab pulled up to the pavement to take him to his destination.

Making his way back up to his room after a straightforward journey, he felt sleep coming on after a long and arduous day, had a quick shower and settled down for the night, as tomorrow would be another busy day.

Note to himself as he settled down was to make a visit to the Hospital to see how George was progressing, and to ring Henry Bates with an up date.

Chapter 15

Day Two of the itinerary had arrived as Jake woke at 7am to an overcast morning, it even looked as if a snowstorm was imminent so he quickly carried out his ablutions before making his way down for breakfast. He had just started buttering his toast as his mobile rang. He picked it up knowing full well it would be Charlene, however he was mistaken as it was in fact Ryan Drew.

'Hi Ryan, you're up with the lark, what can I do for you?'

'I thought I would ring early and give you some good news, both parties will be in Court today, and by close of day should be charged with the offence of GBH and common assault, if convicted they could be down for at least ten years. Your man Wither's will be free to return to the UK on conviction, to serve his time there. My drug dealer if convicted could have additional charges brought against him. So if all goes well with Mr Adams's recovery going well you could be back in London as soon as two weeks'.

'Good news Ryan, how hopeful are you of that result?'

'90% if all goes well with the Judge and the Lawyer's don't find something to jeopardise the case'.

'Thank's for letting me know Ryan, also on the plus side is that George Adams is up and about and the doctor reckons he will be fit to travel in a couple of weeks'.

'So good news all round, what are you going to be doing with yourself in the meantime?'

'It so happens that a young lady I met on holiday last year lives in the City, and we have made arrangements to spend this week sightseeing together. I was initially coming over in April to see her, but as I'm here now albeit on official business I thought I would 'kill two birds with one stone' as the saying goes'.

'Right Jake I have to go but give me a ring before you go back home and we'll have a drink or two together'.

'Fine bye me Ryan, I'll give you a bell next week and we can set up a day and time to suit your busy schedule'.

'Great Jake, look forward to your call'.

Closing his mobile he thought to himself it was a nice gesture of Ryan to say about going out for a drink or two, and he was looking forward to it already.

Finishing his toast he asked the waiter for pancakes and bacon which when brought to him went down a treat.

Breakfast over he made his way back up to his room and as he opened the door his mobile rang and looking at the number he realised it was Charlene.

'Good morning are you ready for another fun packed day Jake' she said without any introduction.I've booked the 'chariot' for 8.30am so I should be with you around 9am, see you in the Foyer, OK?'

'Wonderful, what's the itinerary today, if I may be so bold?'

'I was going to surprise you when we meet, however I'll quickly tell you. First to the International Spy Museum, then the Washington Monument and finally we are going to see a show at the National Theatre'.

'That sounds great I'll see you in a while, bye for now'.

9am on the dot she breezed into the building and asked him if he was ready for day two's adventures.

'As I said yesterday I was born ready Charlene' he replied with a grin.

The International Spy Museum was of great interest to Jake, and the two of them spent two hours pouring over all the exhibits deep in thought at all the intrigue that had taken place over the years, and of course was still carrying on to the present day.

The next visit was to the Washington Monument, a most impressive sight, with Jake taking many photos as they walked around its perimeter. There was a slight flurry of snow as they had completed their time there, and they both were glad that the final visit would be an indoor location and warm.

Charlene decided to dispense with their driver and vehicle once they were at the Theatre, telling him they would make their own way back after the show.

The programme they were booked to see was Pretty Woman : The Musical, Charlene was really looking forward to it and hoped that Jake would feel the same. She had pre-booked their seats, so went straight to the Restaurant to order food and drinks. The show started in an hour and a half's time so they sat relaxed and enjoyed the fare that Charlene had ordered. They had more alcohol after their plates were removed, then sat back for a chat about the remainder of the weeks programme.

Entering the auditorium they were shown to their seats, with Jake unsure if this show was to his taste, but he would go with the flow.

As the show came to an end after two hours, he was full of praise for the performance they had just witnessed and thanked Charlene for booking the impressive show.

In the lobby she called for a cab, then on the way she suggested that if it was OK she would stay with him for the night but return to her apartment early in the morning to await the transport for tomorrow's visits.

Grinning from ear to ear, Jake said he thought it a very good idea, but wondered about a change of clothes and toiletries etc for her.

She half read his mind and said 'I'll get the cab to stop outside my apartment for me to collect an overnight bag that I've already packed' sh answered grinning from ear to ear.

'You are a very organised young lady, you'll make somebody a good wife' Jake said with a smirk.

'Why are you offering?' she replied.

'I'm far too old for you my dear, anyway we live thousands of miles apart' he retorted.

Eventually the cab pulled up to the Hotel, where they went straight up to Jake's room. Charlene unloaded her overnight bag as Jake raided the mini-bar and had drinks on the coffee table ready for them as she breezed into the room.

They spent a couple of hours discussing their lives and the situation with George, before Jake told her that he would be returning home within the next two weeks.

With Charlene taking this information in he suggested they walk down to the restaurant he had visited previously for a slap-up meal.

Charlene thought this was a great idea and popped into the bedroom to change and make herself presentable for supper. Within half an hour they were sat at a table enjoying a cold beer and tucking into their mixed starters. This was followed by crispy duck and pancakes with the main course of sweet and sour king prawns, and chow mein. The meal was washed down with a bottle of house wine.

Chapter 15

Back in the room they had coffee and brandy before retiring for a 'nightcap'.

Chapter 16

Charlene was up and dressed by 6.30am, and down in the lobby as her cab pulled up outside 20 minutes later.

Jake decided to lay in until 7.30am, and wander down for breakfast at eight making himself ready for when Charlene returned.

It was the same driver as yesterday Jake noted as the limousine pulled up outside just before 9am and Charlene strode into the lobby to collect him. She looked bright as a button, and asked if he was ready for another excursion.

'What do you have in store for me today?'

'We have a shorter day today, first the National Gallery of Art, then the Museum of National History and finally The Capital. This will leave us plenty of time to do a bit of SALES shopping' she finished with a grin.

'Tomorrow we only have one place to go and that is on a boat trip along the Potomac, it is an all inclusive trip so we can have a leisurely day after three busy ones, what do you think?'

'You have thought of everything my dear' he remarked impressed with her organising skills.

Jake always loved Art and History at school, so took in the first two locations with great interest, spending far too long in each of them, before their final destination The Capital.

Today's visits were completed by 2pm as the cab dropped them outside Charlene's apartment, before going up they picked up some snacks from a Deli nearby to have with a coffee before visiting the shops later.

Charlene asked Jake what presents he wished to purchase before returning to the UK as she would work out their route for each shop.

He wrote a few quick notes of the items he would like for his family, himself and a few friends, then they were off pounding the streets visiting a multitude of shops within reasonable walking distance of the apartment.

Chapter 16

Two hours later they were laden down with the various items they had purchased and were glad to return to the sanctuary of the apartment.

She put on the percolator for a coffee while Jake opened up the many bags containing the purchased articles to double check if he had something for everyone. Satisfied that he had just as Charlene came in with the drinks, he sat back in the plush sofa and said 'That's what you call Sales shopping in earnest, I'm bushed'.

She laughed at this remark before taking a sip of her coffee. 'What's on the agenda now?'

'I think I need to return to the Hotel, make a few phone calls, then go to the Hospital and see how George is fairing, if that's OK with you my dear?'

A scowl spread across her face for a brief moment before she said 'OK'.

The cab arrived 10 minutes later and took him and his shopping back to the Hotel. Up to his room he rang Charlene first to apologise for leaving her so soon but she fully understood.

Next was a quick update with Henry Bates, then he rang both daughter's explaining he would be coming home in a couple of weeks, and would make arrangements to visit Devon to see everyone.

Putting his overcoat back on he decided to walk to the Hospital to stretch his legs after today's excursions. He reminisced as he walked along at how much he had enjoyed the performance at the National Theatre yesterday, as it was something he wouldn't have visited in the UK but he intended putting that right when he got home.

Making his way up in the lift he hoped to find his colleague up and about and in good spirits, however as he walked down the corridor he was surprised to be intercepted by the Nurse who was at her station behind the desk, asking for his name and who he was visiting. Jake had not seen this lady on his previous visits, so quickly introduced himself and that he was a friend of George Adams. She quickly scanned her paperwork before smiling at him and saying for him to carry on in, apologising for her rudeness.

'Please don't apologise, I prefer intervention as I could have been anyone, thank you for your concern' he smiled at her as he walked to George's door.

He knocked and walked in to see to his amazement, George playing cards with the Policeman, obviously in fine fettle. George got up as Jake approached and shook hands.

'What have you been up to mate?' George asked.

'Luckily Charlene has taken time off work, and we have been visiting landmarks around the City over the past few days. Today was a shorter day so I thought I would pop in and see how you are progressing. I've had a conversation with Inspector Drew and it appears we should be in a position to return to the UK within the next 10 days or so'.

'Great, I have spoken to the Doctor and he feels I will be in reasonable order to travel by the end of next week, so you can make arrangements with Henry regarding transport, plus a Security Guard to look after Withers'.

'I have just updated Henry on the current situation, but will ring him again next week to make the final arrangements. Can I get you anything whilst I'm here, or is the food better than the NHS hospital's back home?'

'The food is good and plentiful, the only thing I would like is a book of some kind to break the monotony, Jose here loves a game of cards but time passes slowly for the both of us, I also fear that he will be leaving in the next few days as any threat to me appears to have disappeared now that our friend is in custody'.

'I'll pop down to the shop and get a couple of books for you, do you have any preference on topic?'

'Crime Fiction for me if that's OK?'

'I'll go down now and see what I can find for you, I hope you'r not playing for money Jose?' Jake said as he walked out the room, the man grinned as he left.

Twenty minutes later he returned with two books and a magazine for George, and placed them on the bedside cabinet, shook his hand and left.

Feeling quite peckish he collected a takeaway as he made his way back to the Hotel and ate it in his room. Wandering down to the Bar later he sat in the corner nursing an ice cold lager and munching on a few nuts, when to his surprise Ryan Drew walked into the room.

'Hi Ryan, what brings you here, no problems I hope?'

'Nothing to worry about Jake, as I hadn't heard from you lately I thought I would call into your Hotel and take in that drink we spoke about'

'Fine with me, I've nothing pressing this evening in fact I have only just started my drink, I don't like drinking alone so I welcome you're company, what can I get you?'

'Lager's fine with me' he replied.

Jake got the bartender's attention and ordered Ryan's drink.

'Are you off duty at present, if so I won't ask any questions regarding the ongoing case, leaving us time to discuss our lives'.

'I'll get work out the way as we enjoy our first drink, which I always think is the best. The paperwork will be completed on Monday for the extradition of Withers, the other person will take a little longer to put away. So as far as I am concerned you can make arrangements with the powers that be to organise the flight for the return to the UK of Withers, George Adams and of course your good self, at your convenience'.

'That's good news Ryan, I have tentatively made a start on the arrangements with my Boss for the end of next week, which I will confirm with him early tomorrow morning. George is in fine fettle, unfortunately though he's feeling a tad bored so I took him in a couple of books to tide him over'.

'I guess he'll be glad to get back to normal after his attack, I hope the breaks to his arm and leg mend as soon as possible, and the New Year will be more comfortable in his home surroundings'.

'Unfortunately I don't know anything about his private life, but I assume Henry will place him in plush surroundings on his return'.

'Good, that's that out the way, do you want to stay here or shall we 'hit the town' for a meal and drinks?'

'There's a great restaurant down the road, and I don't mind a few drinks Ryan, but doing the town is a bit too much for me if you don't mind'.

'Fine by me, I'm feeling a bit peckish after a busy day at work, so shall we drink up and head out for some grub?'

'Ready when you are Ryan' Jake agreed, downing his drink before going to the bar to sign for the drinks.

The weather outside was extremely cold but dry, so they made their way down to the Mexican Restaurant on foot, and as they walked in the waiter that served him previously recognised him and shook his hand before showing them to a table.

Scanning the menu Ryan asked if there was anything Jake didn't like.

'No, I like all Mexican food, why do you ask?'

Ryan smiled before explaining that a friend of his always prepares hot Mexican food whenever he visited him for a meal, and his palate had become accustomed to spicy food.

'I'll leave the ordering to you, but I insist on paying for our meals, I won't take no for an answer?'

The waiter returned and took their drink and food orders, before departing with a huge grin on his face.

A few minutes later he returned with their beers, and a dish of chillies as a starter.

Relaxing back in their chairs Ryan started outlining his life at home with his parents before taking the exams he required to become a Police Officer. He had been in the Force for 15 years working his way up from a beat officer pounding the streets of Washington, to a Detective and his eventual promotion to Detective Inspector.

Just as Ryan finished his story their main course arrived, and when the waiter had completed the chore of placing all the different dishes on the table, there was only just enough room for their plates to be placed in front of them. Jake ordered more beers to accompany the gargantuan feast in front of them, before saying he knew Ryan was feeling hungry, but they would struggle to finish all that had been placed in front of them.

'There's no rush Jake, take your time and wash it down with a few more beers'.

The food was spicy with more chillies that indoctrinated each and every plate they delved into, but surprisingly an hour and a half later the majority of the dishes were empty, of course washed down with more beers.

With his mouth and senses glowing Jake started his story of his early days, the demise of his late wife and the three encounters he had been through during the last few years.

Ryan's mouth adopted the same pose that his friend Tony Bailey had on Boxing Day when he had explained his life only a few weeks ago at his farm, a look of bewilderment and disbelieve at how one man could encounter so much and travel so far to eventually bring each crisis to a satisfactory conclusion.

'I know it all sounds a bit far fetched to you Ryan, I hardly believe it myself, but I can confirm the details I have just relayed to you actually all took place'.

'I think I had better finish the meal with something stronger, how about you 'Superman', do you fancy some Tequila?'

'I think that would be most acceptable, shall we make them large ones?' replied Jake beckoning over the waiter with his order.

A nod in acceptance from Ryan was all Jake needed to confirm their drinks order, with coffee chasers.

They left the Restaurant just after nine and Jake insisted that Ryan took a cab home and collect his car in the morning.

Ryan laughed loudly as they walked back to the Hotel, before saying 'I thought it would be a good evening with you Jake so I got a cab here, so I'll ring for another to take me home'.

Jake returned Ryan's laughter as he hadn't thought of the possibility that he had taken a cab originally, but he supposed that the Detective Inspector would have thought ahead for his evening out.

They shook hands half an hour later as the vehicle pulled into the kerb, and Jake waved his friend goodbye thanking him for his company this evening.

Up in his room he poured himself a black coffee, before musing over the enjoyable evening he had just had with Detective Inspector Ryan Drew (off duty), hoping that it had given the officer a bit of normality away from his daytime duties.

Chapter 17

The mobile rang at 8am bringing Jake back to reality with a pounding headache, 'Jake Tordale' he answered.

'Good morning Jake, today we are taking a trip up The Potomac on an all inclusive boat ride, I trust you are looking forward to it?' asked Charlene.

'Of course, what time will you be collecting me?'

'The trip doesn't start until ten, so you can take your time today, I'll collect you around 9.15am. Are you feeling OK, you sound a mite drowsy?'

'I had a surprise visit from Detective Inspector Ryan Drew last evening. He was off duty so we had a few drinks, then a few more together with a lovely Mexican meal so I'm slightly fragile at the moment'.

'Have a good breakfast and plenty of black coffee and you should be revived by the time we board the boat, see you later'.

"Bye' was all he could manage.

A hot and cold shower, before downing a litre bottle of water from the mini-bar, livened him a bit before he went down for breakfast.

Toast and black coffee settled his stomach, but he still possessed a pounding headache, cursing Ryan under his breath.

He asked the young Receptionist if there were any Aspirin's or their equivalent on the premises, as he had a pounding headache.

She fished in her handbag and handed him two tablets together with a glass of water. He thanked her profusely and made his way up to his room, deciding to get a bunch of flowers for the young lady to thank her for her kindness.

He decided as they were on a river trip today it would be prudent to dress for the occasion, so in addition to his overcoat and gloves he wore a scarf and woollen hat.

The car arrived on time and the lovely Charlene walked into the foyer looking like an actress from a Christmas movie. 'Ready for your final adventure of the week?' she asked.

'The headache is just beginning to subside, thanks to a couple of tablets the Receptionist kindly supplied me with'.

'Good, then if you'r ready we'll make a move'.

Jake slowly followed in her wake and was really glad of the heating in the car, as the temperature outside was almost arctic.

As they settled back into the plush seats Charlene explained what they would be doing today. 'Our cruise starts at 11am so I thought we would utilise our transport to visit other highlights of Washington before we our ready to board, if that's OK with you?'

'I'm in your hands, or should I say the driver's' laughing as he peered out the window.

Charlene said to the driver 'Carry on as we discussed', the driver nodded in compliance.

The next hour or so was spent driving past the properties that Charlene described in infinite detail, allowing Jake to understand why she had chosen this route.

As time approached 11am the cab pulled up alongside the jetty where the boat was moored waiting for all its passenger's to board. Their driver opened the doors for them and said he would be waiting here when they returned.

As they walked up the gangplank they were greeted by a smart individual dressed in a dark suit and bow tie. 'Welcome aboard for today's trip along the Potomac may I please have your names'. Charlene gave him the details, and he ticked them off the i pad he was carrying, before directing them into the bowels of the vessel where they were met by a waiter dressed in similar clothing as the first man.

'A table for two?' he asked.

'Yes please' Charlene answered.

There were already quite a number of passengers seated but the position they were offered was far superior as the table only seated two people whereas the majority were for four or more.

At exactly 11am the cruise commenced with the Captain introducing himself and outlining the various landmarks that they would be passing. The cruise would be taking around 3 hours, with drinks being offered immediately and the meal being produced an hour into the journey. Jake suggested they have a bottle of white wine to drink first and a bottle of red with the meal. Charlene agreed, the waiter took their order after 5 minutes into their journey.

Jake didn't need the details given over the loudspeaker by a member of the crew, as Charlene kept him ahead of the game as she knew what was coming up and carried out a running commentary, which slowed as they worked their way through the wine.

The views they were able to see from this angle were of interest to Jake, so he took a lot of photos to show his children and grandchildren when he returned home.

They were interrupted by waiters delivering there food after an hour into their journey, and this was accompanied by their bottle of red wine. The food was enjoyable and quite filling, but they were still entertained by the continuous commentary as they ambled along the Potomac.

Their meals complete they sat back drinking their coffee and enjoying the ambience, together with the hustle and bustle of the passengers and staff. Pulling alongside the quay exactly 3 hours after they had departed they carefully negotiated the walkway and spied their driver waiting for them. As they settled back in the plush seats of the limousine they were asked where they would like to go next. Charlene looked at Jake wanting him to decide on their destination. However he was non committal, so Charlene gave her home address.

The smooth journey took 20 minutes and as they alighted from the vehicle, Charlene asked Jake if he had done all the shopping he required. Jake nodded so they then took the lift up to her apartment.

As they sat down Jake thanked her for her time and energy organising all the trips over the past few days, clarifying that he had enjoyed every minute. 'I have a lot of memories to take back home with me, I trust you've enjoyed the time with me as well?'

'I certainly have, but I think it would have been better in April with the warmer weather, however timings are completely out of our hands, and I wouldn't have seen you this early unless poor George hadn't been assaulted'.

'I think things are meant to be, so at least we have been able to have time together' Jake replied with a sense of guilt.

'I don't know about you but those two bottles of wine have gone straight to my head, I think I need a lie down, how about you?' she asked with a sheepish grin.

He looked at her briefly, nodded and they headed for her bedroom.

Two hours later they both woke up, smirked and got up ready for another cup of coffee.

Tomorrow would be the weekend so they decided to have the both days apart, Charlene to prepare herself for returning to work, and Jake to organise his return to the UK with Henry Bates, and to check with George Adams as to his hospital release. He also wanted to visit Ryan Drew to thank him for his recent visit and to clarify the extradition date for Roland Withers.

They parted company at the front door as the cab arrived to take him back to Hotel, but promised to meet up one evening the following weekday prior to his return to the UK.

During the journey back he felt quite sad at leaving Charlene so abruptly, however all good things must come to an end. He also thought he would arrange for a bouquet of flowers to be delivered to her apartment after he had left the USA, with a thank you note.

Back in his room he made a few phone calls before feeling an urge for a nice curry to lighten his mood. Wandering down to Reception he asked the person there if they could recommend a Curry House in the vicinity.

He delved under the desk and handed Jake a business card for a good Restaurant about a 100 yards from the Mexican place he had previously visited. He thanked the man profusely and asked if he needed to make a reservation. However the man grinned and said 'If you get there in an hour's time Mr Tordale I'll have rung through and booked a table for you, I would also recommend the mixed starter and Chicken Madras. I have eaten there on numerous occasions and have never been disappointed with the service, or the delicious and plentiful cuisine'.

'Thank you for your advice, I'll be walking there within the hour'.

The Hotel Clerk was correct with his recommendation, as after one and a half hours he left the establishment feeling completely satisfied with his delightful meal.

Chapter 18

A call from Henry woke him at 6am, and with a slight panic in his voice he asked his Superior if there was a problem as it was only 6am in the States.

'Sorry old man' replied Henry 'It's 11 o'clock here. I just want to give you the heads up regarding your flight back home. There's a plane booked for next Friday, it will land at Washington mid to late morning. On board will be a plain clothes policeman to accompany Withers, plus arrangements have been made for some of the seats to be removed from the rear of the plane to facilitate a bed, if required for George. Once landed the plane will immediately refuel and return to the UK as soon as air traffic control provides a gap for it'.

'Sounds good sir, I visited George last evening and he's up and about. Unfortunately he will be in plaster for another 6 weeks at least, but his doctor will sign him off on Tuesday. So as far as he's concerned he will be ready to fly. I also spent an evening out with Detective Inspector Drew yesterday and he confirmed that the paperwork for Withers will be formalised by Monday so unless anything detrimental happens all parties will be ready after Tuesday of next week'.

'Well done Jake. I'll try and bring forward my arrangements and will contact you as soon as I can with the fixed date and time'.

'Thank you sir, did you and your family enjoy the Christmas festivities?'

'For the little time that I could, I did indeed, but on your return we'll catch up together and have a natter and a blow out at our favourite eating house'.

'Looking forward to it already, and to your confirmation details, bye for now'.

'Goodbye Jake, and thank's again for all your hard work on this, your latest tricky situation'.

He then dressed and went down for breakfast, as it was Saturday there were only a few guests in the Dining Room so he could sit apart from them and enjoy his privacy.

Chapter 18

Drinking his second cup of coffee he ruminated over what would occupy his time today, he had got used to being organised by Charlene for the past week, and thinking about it he was at a loss on what to do. Before he could think anymore on the subject his mobile vibrated with a message. Opening up the appliance he was taken aback by the text from Sweden, from the delectable Olivia it read 'A Happy New Year to you Jake, I hope you are OK, I tried your home phone but it went to answerphone so I assume you are tied up, please answer this message and let me know that you're alright. Olivia'.

A smile crossed his rugged face as his thought's reverted back to Santorini where he had spent a wonderful few days with the delectable Olivia, he quickly typed a reply giving the briefest of details, but to confirm he would be back in the UK by the end of next week and that he would ring her when he was back home in Wisteria Cottage.

A confirmation came back from her with two heart emoji's.

Checking the time difference in the UK, he then typed messages to his daughter's, again confirming he would be returning to the UK by the end of next week and would ring them soon after he left the Airport.

Returning to his room he checked through the presents he had purchased and realised he would require an additional suitcase to carry them all for his return journey so he would visit a shop nearly to purchase one.

Whilst out he thought he would find a gift for Ryan Drew who had been so helpful to him whilst he had been in Washington, but what he would get he hadn't a clue as to what would suit the Detective Inspector.

There were numerous shops in the vicinity so his plan was to window shop before committing himself, as he felt sure that something would catch his eye.

The full spectrum of retailers was within walking distance of the Hotel and for once he was looking forward to browsing each one. After ten or so windows viewed, he was drawn to an upmarket jewellers who had numerous silver ornaments in the window. He opened the front door and was immediately greeted by an elderly man dressed in a pinstriped suit, white shirt and striped bow tie. He wore half rimmed glasses that were perched on top of his bald head.

'Good morning sir, I saw you perusing my window display, did anything take your fancy, if so please let me know and I will retrieve it from the window for your perusal'.

'You have a silver ornament of a prancing horse I am interested in, could I look at it please?'

'Ah, I assume that is an English accent you have there, sir?'

'It is indeed, I am after a thank you present for a Policeman who has been very helpful to me whilst I have been in the United States'

'Very well, I'll go and get the horse and a few other items for you to look at, please take a seat, may I offer you any refreshment, tea, coffee?'

'No thank you, I have only recently had breakfast'.

The old man scuttled off to get what he hoped would be his first sale of the day.

Putting the various items on a felt lined display board on the glass counter, the old man stood back and scanned Jake's face with eager anticipation, he had watched this scene play out over a number of years and knew a sale of some kind was imminent.

No words were exchanged as Jake perused the items, lifting each one up to check the workmanship before deciding on not one but two items. He handed both to the old man and as his shirt cuff was pulled back the jewellers eyes popped wide open as he viewed Jake's watch. 'Please forgive my impertinence sir, but do I spy a Patek Philippe watch on your wrist?'

'You do indeed sir, why do you ask?'

'I have never been fortunate enough to have seen one up close in all my years. They are the most sought after high end watch in existence. I do not wish to appear impertinent, but could I possibly inspect it up close, you would make an old man very happy indeed'.

Jake undid the strap and carefully handed the watch over to the excited jeweller.

'How long have you had this masterpiece sir?'

'Only a few years, I was lucky enough to have purchased it whilst overseas at an extremely discounted rate and feel privileged to own such a beautiful work of art'.

The old man returned the watch and thanked Jake for the opportunity he had given him, then returned to the two items that Jake had put to one side.

'Let's see what the ticket prices are for these two, the horse is $200 dollars, and the dog is $150 dollars. I will sell both of them to you for $300, and wrap them up individually for you, is that OK'.

They shook hands and Jake handed over his credit card.

The old man took both items into another room and returned with a small glass of alcohol, 'Please have a drink with me, this is a Jack Daniels I trust that would be alright for you whilst I wrap your purchases'.

'Thank you very much, I appreciate your generosity'.

He returned a few minutes later with the two wrapped items just as Jake had finished his drink.

They shook hands before he left the shop, turned and waved before returning to his Hotel. He placed one of the parcels in his suitcase, together with his other purchases that were spread out on the bed.

Once finished he dialled the number for Ryan Drew, who picked up after half a dozen rings with 'Detective Inspector Ryan Drew'.

'Good morning Ryan, it's Jake Tordale. I know you are a busy man but could we have a catch up soon, as I will be returning to the UK the middle of next week and would like to see you before I leave. As you know I do not have a vehicle, and I wondered if you could meet me at the Hotel after one of your busy days. I won't keep you long I have something to give you which might be of interest!'

'I'm not working today, as there is nothing pressing so am taking the family out for a bit of retail shopping, but I could catch up with you later this afternoon, say 4pm in the Hotel Bar?'

Jake smiled then confirmed the appointment with 'Look forward to seeing you Ryan, bye for now, and don't spend too much'.

Ryan laughed and replied 'I won't, as Christmas has cost a fortune this year, see you this afternoon'.

After the call he decided a visit to the Hospital was required to see George, check on his recovery and give him the good news about their return to the UK.

Again as the weather was cold and dry as he walked to the facility then followed the usual protocol regarding his access to George's private ward. Thankfully he met Staff Nurse McDonald as he exited the lift, and spent a minute or two thanking her for her attention to his friend's recovery.

'We will be leaving for home on Wednesday assuming everything is organised at my end, please carry on with the good work you do here and I wish we had met in different circumstances' shaking her hand vigorously.

The Staff Nurse blushed before replying 'Seeing your friend recover to the point he is now from when he arrived is reward indeed. Unfortunately a lot of patients that are admitted with similar injuries do not survive no matter what attention we give them'.

'The body is a remarkable organ in itself and can take horrendous damage to it to survive and still recover, however medical staff such as yourself give the additional help needed with operations, drugs etc to allow the repair work to carry out it's job, I applaud you'.

With that he opened the door to the private ward to be greeted by George Adams with a beaming smile.

'Morning Jake, what brings you here this morning, I thought you would be out on the town with the delightful Charlene !'

'We have done the town for the last few days, and she has to organise herself a bit over the weekend for her return to work on Monday'.

George smiled and said 'So you're at a loose end today so you thought you would come and see me to check if I hadn't scarpered and gone AWOL, Eh?'

Jake gave a chuckle before replying with 'I've just done some last minute shopping and admittedly had a small window with nothing to do, but thought I would tell you that we will be off back in Blighty mid-week with any luck'.

'Great' answered George 'I enjoy the company here but can't wait to get home'.

'You realise that your assailant will also be on the plane, but he'll be attached to a plain clothed police officer from the UK and in handcuffs'.

'That's reassuring I must admit, if I had my way I would open a door and shove him out over the Atlantic to save the Government's money housing him in one of Her Majesty's Prisons'.

'I know where you're coming from George but we'll have to let it go through the Court System again, and I am sure Mr Wither's won't be seeing the light of day until he is very old, Is there anything I can get you whilst I'm here?'

'No I'm fine Jake, still working my way through the book you got for me thank's'.

Chapter 18

'Count down starts now mate for our return home, I have to meet up with the Detective Inspector this afternoon then I'm up to date with things, I'll call in to see you every day up until our departure and decide how we will be getting you to the Airport'. Shaking hand they said their farewells.

Chapter 19

The Hotel Dining Room was empty as he returned from the Hospital, so he sat in his usual seat and perused the menu. He was feeling quite hungry and when the waiter approached him he plumped for a steak and side salad with skinny chips, accompanied with a cold beer. Although it was late for lunch a number of guests wandered in as he consumed his meal, and ordered food but he didn't get involved with anyone.

He finished his meal with a black coffee, then went up to his room for a nap until his appointment with Ryan Drew at 4pm.

He woke with a start at 3.45pm as the alarm he had set on his mobile sounded, he had a quick wash and hurried down to the Bar just as Ryan walked in.

They shook hands and took seats in the corner of the room, Jake ordered drinks for them before handing over a parcel to Ryan.

'What have we got here Jake, you know it's not allowed to give presents to a serving police officer, it would appear as if you are giving me a bribe' before laughing as he noticed the shocked look on Jake's face.

'It's just a little something I wanted to give you as a memento for all the hard work you have done for my colleague George Adam's together with your friendship towards me. I hope it's something you will like and display in your home to remind you of a case successfully completed'.

Ryan carefully opened the paper and blushed as he took the silver statue of The Prancing Horse and placed it on the table in front of him. 'There is no need to spend your money on me Jake. This I think would be very expensive, but I am quite honoured to accept on behalf of the Police Force in Washington and throughout the United States. But of course I will place it in a prominent position in my home, thank you very much indeed'.

'You are most welcome, now tell me how you got on with your shopping?'

Chapter 19

Over the next two hours they opened up again on their life's paths, accompanied with a few more beers. Ryan was a keen NFL spectator, had played for his College side before joining the Police, he then got married. He has two sisters, and both of his parents are alive also living in the City.

Jake explained about his time in MI6 and his recent adventures, Ryan dipped in with a comment saying he was a bit like James Bond from the film series that had been aired in the USA.

Jake disagreed, saying that most of the time he was chasing shadows and all the people he met were either 'baddies' or people he had got close to who were then killed. He explained that there were also good times where he had met a few delightful females on route, a couple of which he was still in touch with, Charlene here in Washington, as she had kept him company during the last week and had shown him the sights of this wonderful City.

Ryan checked his watch and apologised to Jake for leaving but he had to return home as his wife would have his evening meal ready by seven.

They stood and shook hands formally, before Ryan thanked Jake profusely for his present and left.

Jake walked up to the Bar and ordered a sandwich to go with a brandy and coffee as he realised until he caught the plane home he would spend the rest of the time alone.

He was halfway through his sandwich when the mobile rang, he answered with the usual 'Jake Tordale' and was elated when he heard the sensual tones of Charlene's voice asking how he was.

'OK my dear, I was just thinking that I would be spending the rest of my visit alone, as it look's as if we will all be returning to the UK on Wednesday, anyway what can I do for you?'

'I am missing you already and was going to suggest that we met up tomorrow before I have to return to work on Monday and you have to go back to the UK?'

'I have nothing organised for tomorrow and would love to meet up with you, what do you have in mind, as we have done all the sights?'

'Well, I thought to begin with we could have a slap up meal in a Restaurant and then go for a nice walk followed by a visit to your Hotel room to finish the day, how does that sound to you?'

'Splendid my dear, shall I come to you or will you pick me up. The meal will be on me of course, whichever establishment we visit I will leave you to organise'.

'Excellent, I'll pick you up at noon and organise our eats for 1pm, don't have too much for breakfast I guarantee you will need that walk after we have eaten'.

'See you tomorrow Charlene, and thanks again for ringing'.

Finishing his sandwich he sat back nurturing his brandy whilst giving thanks to the lovely Charlene for contacting him and organising him for the following day.

Chapter 20

Waking from a long dreamless sleep he had a nice hot shower before shaving and preparing himself for another day with Charlene.

Deciding on a light breakfast he ordered a cup of black coffee to go with his bacon and eggs. Strangely he thought, looking around the Dining Room it was half full with what looked like late holidaymakers having a break before returning to work, and the buzz of conversation took him out of his misery at being sat alone.

Later he went back up to his room and adjusted his suitcases to even out the clothes and presents that he had purchased recently.

Leaving enough clothes in the wardrobe he would require over the next few days he felt satisfied, then placed the suitcases beside the wardrobe.

It was another two hours before Charlene would arrive so he decided to go for a stroll to breath in the cold fresh air, and possibly hunt out a small present he could hand over during their meal. He approached the jeweller's he had visited previously and scanned the window display, where his eyes were drawn to a figure of a woman reclining on a sofa. Before he could move the old proprietor drew back the curtain behind the display and beckoned him into the shop.

'Good to see you again sir, has anything taken your eye?' the old man enquired.

'Strangely enough yes indeed, the lady reclining on a sofa' Jake answered.

'Well, I have had that particular piece for a number of years and thought it would never leave the window, let me get it for you'.

He reached over carefully and placed the piece on the counter for Jake to check over. He lifted it up and checked it thoroughly before asking the obvious question 'There is no price ticket attached to this article, how much would you like for it?'

'I assume you realise that it is solid silver, it was made over 80 years ago by a silversmith in Germany. He was an uncle of mine, who lived in the Jewish Quarter of Berlin but was unfortunately one of the many who didn't survive the Second World War'. A tear spread down the cheek of the old man, which he wiped away with a blue handkerchief.

A pregnant silence ensued before Jake spoke 'I think it best if you hold onto this article as it is full of fond memories of your uncle and family'.

'No, no sir, the years have flown by and I have a number of items that remind me of my family and friends, so if you like it I would be pleased to sell it to you for $300'.

'That's fine, could you wrap it for me please'.

'Certainly sir, I'll bring you a little drink whilst I carry on with the wrapping', he disappeared behind a curtain before returning with a small glass of Jack Daniels.

Ten minutes passed bye before the old man returned again, the parcel he had wrapped was rectangular in shape so Jake assumed he had placed the figure in a box before wrapping it. He got out his wallet and removed four $100 bills and placed them on the counter, before thanking the jeweller for his help, then quickly walked out the shop before the old man could see that he had left too much money.

He decided a catch up with Charlene was required so he dialled her number but it went straight to answerphone, he left a message asking her to ring when she could and that it wasn't however too urgent.

He walked into the Hotel and took a seat in the lobby whilst nodding to the young lady on Reception. After a few minutes the Receptionist asked if he wanted a coffee or anything whilst he was waiting, but he thanked her with a 'No' and a smile.

A long ten minutes went by before a cab pulled up outside and the lovely Charlene alighted and strode into the Hotel. She was dressed in a long black coat, scarf and gloves with a bobble hat on her head looking as if she was intent on taking a walk somewhere in the cold.

'Good morning Jake' she said with formality as he stood and planted a kiss on either cheek. He noticed that the cab had pulled away from the kerb, so was unsure what she had in store for them. She sat down beside him and asked 'Is that a present for me you have there?'

'Well I actually was going to give it to you later but I realised the time had flown by so I suppose I had better give it to you now', handing over the parcel.

A big smile fell over her face as she said 'How exciting'.

Slowly unwrapping the carefully wrapped present she gasped as the sculpture of a young lady reclining on a sofa was exposed.

'How absolutely fabulous, I have never seen anything like it before, you shouldn't have done this for me'.

'I saw it in the window of a jeweller I had frequented before and thought it would be a nice reminder for you of my visit'.

'It's absolutely beautiful Jake, thank you' she leaned over and gave him a lingering kiss, before pulling away realising the Receptionist was only a few yards away.

They then discussed where they would eat and plumped for a diner of her choice within walking distance of the Hotel. They popped up to his room to freshen up, and also for her to leave her latest present from Jake there, before they made their way to the Restaurant.

Looking through the menu Jake was surprised to see that each item was a calorie overload, but hey when in another Country eat like the locals as he would be returning soon to basic English food.

Charlene laughed at him as he appeared confused at what to order, she therefore suggested number four on the menu. It was a huge steak with fries, onion rings, slaw and a side of green salad. When it arrived the steak covered almost half of the plate. leaving just enough room for the fries, onion rings and slaw, the green salad was in a separate container alongside, thankfully it was accompanied by a pitcher of ice cold water to wash it down.

Tucking into his meal he was delighted with the steak and after half an hour he put down his knife and fork on his empty plate. He looked at Charlene and smiled, as her plate was also empty, before casually asking her if she fancied a dessert and was somewhat surprised when she said yes.

Back to the menu Jake looked for something light, before deciding on strawberries and ice cream, but Charlene asked for blueberry pie and cream. Deep in thought Jake wondered how she put all this food into such a trim figure.

They completed their meal with coffee then sat back completely full before the bill arrived which Jake duly paid.

'I think the walk back to the Hotel will help move all this food around for me, I don't know about you my dear?'

'That was certainly most enjoyable, you must think us Americans eat like this all the time, I can assure you that this was a gastronomic treat for me, which I thoroughly enjoyed, thank you very much, what are your plans for the rest of your stay?'

'I have to tie up a few loose ends, namely George at the Hospital, a final meeting with the Police to clarify Roland Withers removal from the USA, finally to confirm with Henry Bates when the plane will be arriving to take us all back to the UK. It is provisionally booked for Friday but I feel it could be brought forward to Wednesday, as long as all the arrangements here fall into place'.

'Perhaps after today, we could meet up once more one evening before you leave to say your goodbyes'.

'That's fine with me, shall we put Monday evening down as a date for us, and I'll arrange for a cab to collect me and meet you at your apartment'.

The evening had turned considerably colder as they made their return walk to the Hotel, therefore glad when they entered the heated lobby, before walking into the Bar.

Jake looked at his companion and asked her what she would you like to drink, 'I'm having a warming brandy'.

'Same for me please' she replied with a smile.

This was followed by a coffee, before Charlene asked if she could go up to his room to powder her nose. Jake grinned at her, knowing full well what she meant.

Two hours later he waved goodbye to her as the cab pulled away from the kerb, transporting his companion back into the heart of Washington.

Chapter 21

Before he knew it Monday evening had arrived and the cab dropped him right outside Charlene's apartment building. He took the lift up to the second floor and rang the doorbell. She answered almost immediately and welcomed him into the room, offering him a drink of whatever he fancied. He decided on a small beer which would allow him to enjoy the evening more, and make room for another gargantuan meal if the restaurant and food was anything like the meal they had enjoyed previously.

She brought his drink to him and sat on a chair opposite with a gin and tonic in her hand.

Charlene smiled at him and said 'After our previous meal I thought I would leave it up to you as to which cuisine you fancied for our last meal together. It will depend of course on the location of the restaurant as how far we have to travel, either walk, cab, or train. Tell me what you fancy and I'll check on the location of an eatery?'

'Such a decision to make, but I could really eat food from a nice Italian establishment, pasta dishes, pizza's and the like with the lingering taste of herbs etc, takes a bit of beating'.

'Good decision Jake, there is a wonderful Italian place within walking distance, I have eaten there a number of times, and know the food will be excellent. I'll ring and book a table for say 7 o'clock'.

'Excellent, we can sit and have a chat for a while, what time is your flat mate home from work?'

'Not until late, she is meeting someone straight from work for a few drinks and shouldn't be home until ten at the earliest, why do you ask?'

Jake blushes before saying' Perhaps we could work up an appetite before we go out, seeing as we are alone?'

With that Charlene quickly drank the remnants of alcohol in her glass, stood up and dashed into the bedroom removing clothes as she went. Jake quickly followed in her wake also removing his outer clothes. Just to be on the safe side he shut the bedroom door before removing the remainder of his clothing and joining her on the bed.

They woke at the sound of an alarm clock, both looked at each other before they burst out laughing,

Charlene had set the alarm to go off at half past six allowing them time to freshen up before leaving for the Restaurant.

The short walk allowed them to arrive at just on seven pm, a waiter directed them to their table before handing over menus to them and asked what drinks they would like. Jake asked for a bottle of house white wine before perusing the menu.

A quick chat between them before they decided on their order. A nod to the waiter and he returned making a note of their requirements, before opening the bottle of wine and pouring the contents in their glasses.

Making small talk prior to their food arriving, Jake mentioned his thoughts on the time they had spent together whilst he had been in the US. He also mentioned that he would not be returning again in April as this visit unfortunately had to take the place of the previously organised one. Charlene sighed before touching his hand and saying 'I fully understand, I've enjoyed your company over the past week, and knowing you there are other adventures for you to be involved in, I hope we can meet again sometime, but we'll keep in touch anyway by email or mobile'.

Their food arrived shortly after a pregnant silence in conversation, which was a thankful distraction from the latest dialogue where Jake confirmed he would not be returning to the US in April. The food was ate in silence with just the interruption of their glasses being topped up. A coffee completed their meal before Jake paid the bill and they walked hand in hand back to her apartment.

Before ordering a cab, Jake looked at Charlene and said 'I hope I haven't upset you my dear, but I have my family to see more regularly, now, and I am also off to Singapore and Australia during the later part of January. Then I must settle down to my retirement and carry out work on the Cottage and gardens before everything deteriorates'.

'I fully understand Jake, this week has been really lovely and a bonus that was unexpected, I have a lot to do at work, but we'll keep in touch with each other'.

They had another drink before he ordered a cab to take him back to his Hotel.

Chapter 21

As he sat on the bed in his room he pondered over the time he had spent with Charlene over the past week, realising how much they had done together and the various experiences he had been shown by her, which otherwise he wouldn't have encountered during his stay.

Tomorrow he had to speak to Detective Inspector Ryan Drew to clarify that all the paperwork was complete for the extradition of Roland Withers, then visit his friend George Adams in Hospital and check if his discharge papers had been finalised by the medical staff. Finally ring his Boss Henry Bates to confirm the itinerary for the flight arrivals date, and time. Once it had all been confirmed he could arrange his check out from the Hotel and pay the invoice for his stay, what a busy life.

Chapter 22

Waking at 7am on an overcast Tuesday morning he thought for a moment he was in his cottage in Dorset, however that thought only stayed with him for a short while, as he realised he had a lot of organising to do today.

First priority was breakfast, he quickly dressed then took the lift down to the lobby, he exchanged pleasantries with the Receptionist, before walking into the Dining Room where his nostrils were enveloped with the aroma of cooked food.

He decided to have cereal and a cooked breakfast today with fruit juice and black coffee, as he was unsure if lunch would be an option for him.

Scanning the room he was surprised that he was joined by only two other occupied tables, one had a couple looking romantically at each other as their conversation was low plus they were holding hands whilst looking into each others eyes, the other table had one occupant, an elderly man in his fifties or sixties smarty dressed in a suit and tie with a pale blue shirt, alongside the table was a large leather briefcase. Jake assumed he was either meeting someone at the Hotel, or was perhaps off to a meeting in the City. He mused with his thoughts before returning to today's business. After finishing his meal he ordered another coffee before dialling Ryan Drew's mobile number, it was picked up after a few rings with 'Detective Ryan Drew'.

'Hello Ryan its Jake Tordale, just ringing for a catch up and to find out if all the paperwork is to hand for the removal back to the UK of said Roland Withers?'

'Hi Jake, yes I have all the paperwork at my office, myself and another two Officers will escort the prisoner to the airport, and hand him over to the UK Agent. Have you had clarification on Arrival time of the plane from the UK?'

'Yes it touches down at midday tomorrow, on my side George Adams has had his Discharge papers from the Medical Staff at the

Hospital and I will accompany him to the Airport and meet you there around 11.30am'.

'Fine Jake, I'll see you tomorrow' he then rang off.

His next call was to Henry Bates office, the number unfortunately went to voicemail so he left a message for a return call.

Returning to his room he packed all his remaining items leaving himself a change of clothing for tomorrow, his passport, wallet and toiletries.

Travelling back down in the lift, he approached the Receptionist and informed her that he would be checking out tomorrow morning and asked her to prepare his invoice which he would pay that evening. The young lady smiled and asked if he had enjoyed his stay at the Hotel and was he able to see all the sites he had wanted whilst being in the States. He replied that the Hotel was first rate, and he had indeed visited all the various 'Touristy' sites, and more during his stay.

Although only 10pm he walked to the Hospital to visit George to see if there was anything he wanted before they boarded the plane to return home, clothes, toiletries, etc and did he require someone to pack for him.

He spoke to the usual Staff before walking into the Ward, to be greeted by a smiling fully dressed George Adams.

'It's only January George, a bit early for shorts mate' Jake asked whilst grinning from ear to ear at his pal.

'It's the only way I could get something over the plaster my friend' he replied somewhat tersely.

'OK mate just trying to keep you upbeat, are ready for an update?' George nodded in reply.

'Right, the plane lands at noon tomorrow, the prisoner will be escorted to the airport by Detective Inspector Ryan Drew and two of his burly Police Officers, I'll collect you by cab, around 10.30 and we'll meet in the confines of the lobby and be transferred to the plane by the back door. Before I go any further do you need anything before we leave, clothes, toiletries etc. If so I could pick it up today and drop it off later this evening for you'.

'That's thoughtful of you Jake, I'd like to give the Staff a gift of some kind to thank them for looking after me, also perhaps something for my Police Guardian. Could I leave it up to your discretion as to what you think would be appropriate. With regards to to my personal requirements I think I'm OK on that front, but I would like to take back home a bottle of Jim Bean for medicinal purposes only, you understand' he finishes smiling broadly.

'I think I can manage that for you. I'll leave you to rest now, don't get up to anything between now and tomorrow morning, I'm waiting to get back to Blighty ASAP'

'I don't think there's any fear of that Jake, thank's for everything'.

'No problem George, see you this evening'.

Walking back to the Hotel he thought he would ring Charlene first, then Clare and Sharon before placing a call to Olivia explains he would be back home in the UK on Thursday.

The temperature was bracing this morning, so he bypassed the Hotel and walked along the adjoining road to visit the various shops to collect George's requirements.

Unsure what to buy for the Hospital Staff, he walked into a supermarket to obtain a bottle of Jim Bean for George, then whilst perusing the aisles he came upon a shelf full of chocolates. Possibly the wrong present for the Staff but its the thought that counts. The question was how many boxes to buy, there was the surgeon, two doctors, Staff Nurse McDonald and the Receptionists. After a brief moment a decision was made so he put six boxes in his shopping basket to join the whisky. This left him the Police Officer's gift, not such an easy choice, but as he turned the corner to the next aisle he had a light bulb moment so quickly went to the checkout to pay for his purchases.

Heading back up the road to the Hotel he opened the jeweller's door and was warmly greeted by the old man with 'Can't stay away young man, how may I help you?'

'On my last visit I noticed in the window a silver cigarette case for sale, could I look at it please'.

'Certainly take a seat I won't me a moment' he pulled back the curtain that shielded the contents of the window display and retrieved the case.

'You'r not a smoker are you sir?' he enquired.

Smiling Jake replied 'No, it's just a gift for someone who helped a colleague of mine who's at the Hospital, and is now able to return with me to the UK'.

The old man placed the case in front of Jake, who gave it the once over before saying 'I know the majority of the population are now non-smokers, but I know this fellow is a smoker although I have not witnessed it. So if you would kindly tell me what you would like for this article I'll gladly pay you'.

'Believe it or not this case used to belong to myself, it was given to me by my late wife over 25 years ago, but I gave up the smokes when she passed away 15 years ago. Only recently I found it and thought I would sell it as it is of no use to me now and I know she would approve. To you as a returning Client I cannot accept more than $25, which I will give to Charity, would you like me to wrap it for you?'

Jake took out his wallet and placed $50 on the counter before saying 'I am happy to give the additional money to your Charity, and would appreciate it if you would kindly wrap it. I am returning to the UK tomorrow and wish to say that visiting your establishment has been the highlight of my visit here. If I was staying longer I'm sure I would be here regularly not only to purchase things but to enjoy your company'. The old man thanked him before they shook hands, then he came from behind the counter and enveloped Jake in a bear hug. No further words were exchanged as Jake walked out the door.

Chapter 23

Walking back to his room he felt quite pleased with himself for the purchases he had made on behalf of his friend George Adams. he hoped he would feel the same when he brought them to his room.

The bits and pieces were quite bulky so he put them all in a shopping bag, he thought as it was January at least the chocolates wouldn't melt on his walk to the Hospital.

Up in the lift he mulled over what he had bought, and if they were good enough for his friend, so as he entered the private room he was glad to see that the Police Officer and George were in conversation over a game of cards.

Taking a seat alongside the bed Jake said 'Don't mind me, carry on with your game, I'll sit here and listen to you chat before you finish your game'.

Both of them laughed, before the Officer finally put the cards back in a box and placed it on the bedside table.

'Looks like you've been busy Jake, do you have anything for someone close to me?'

'Indeed I have, I had it wrapped if you don't mind, as I think it appropriate for the Officer to open it once he finishes his shift'.

Jake took the package out and handed it to George who gave it to the Officer and said 'A little token, to thank you for entertaining me whilst I've been hospitalised'.

'Just doing my job George, there was no need sir, but thank you I appreciate the thought'.

'I'll leave the other items in the carrier for you to distribute later George'.

'Many thanks Jake, I'll square up with you on the way home'.

'OK mate, I have a few things left to sort out so I'll see you in the morning, oh just one thing I assume you have your passport?'

'Yes, passport and wallet already packed in my case, see you tomorrow and thanks again'.

Chapter 23

As he arrived back at the Hotel the Receptionist handed him the invoice for his stay which included tomorrow's breakfast, rather than leave it until the morning he paid it there and then, thanking the young lady for her help during his stay.

Back up in his room he rang Henry Bates to confirm that George was OK to leave, and he had everything he required for the trip home. He then booked a cab to collect him in the morning to take him to the airport via the Hospital to collect George.

He sent a message to his daughter's Clare and Sharon to confirm the time he would be leaving the States, and that he would ring them as soon as he touched down in London.

He finally rang Olivia's mobile number, the various clicks as the International call was connected, took a few seconds before the delightful voice of Olivia picked up with 'Hello you delectable man, where are you'.

'Still in Washington but I'm travelling home tomorrow morning and will ring you once I have returned to Wisteria Cottage for a catch up. How are you, did you enjoy your Christmas with the family?'

'I didn't think I would enjoy it as much as I did, but everyone was so glad to see me and we spent three days just talking about the past and what we had all done since the last time we had met up'.

'I'm glad you were able to meet up again, you mustn't leave it so long the next time, life is very short and we must savour every moment'.

'I agree Jake, perhaps after you are settled we can meet up again?'

'When I am home I have a few things to carry out, I'm off to Singapore on business, then on to Australia to visit an important person who I will explain when we meet up. I assume that I will be officially retired by mid March so we will base our meet around then possibly with a week's holiday together?'

'Sounds a good idea, take care Jake and see you soon'.

Although he had paid the Hotel bill, he decided to eat in the Restaurant for the last time as he had been impressed with the cuisine on offer when he had eaten there before. He would pay the waiter for the meal when he had finished.

He had a shower and shave and a change of clothes before taking the lift down to Reception. He spoke to the young lady and told her that he would pay the waiter for his meal once he had finished, which she replied was no problem at all.

As he strolled into the Dining Room the young waiter he had dealt with during his stay ushered him to his table and handed him a menu.

'May I get you a drink Mr Tordale while you decide on your meal?'

'Yes please, I'll have a small beer and a look at the Wine list, I fancy a nice red wine with my meal tonight, as I'm off back to the UK in the morning'.

He quickly returned with the beer together with the wine list and handed them to Jake.

He scanned the impressive menu, which included American, Mexican, French and Oriental dishes leaving him spoilt for choice. But as he was in the States for his last meal he decided on American.

He settled on the Angus Beef steak with all the trimmings accompanied with No8 on the wine list a bottle of Merlot.

Just as he finished his beer the waiter delivered his meal and wine, Jake sat back in awe at the plate in front of him, drooling at the succulent beef cooked to perfection. The waiter smiled as he poured the wine as he saw the delight in Jake's eyes at the food in front of him. 'Enjoy your meal Mr Tordale'.

When he realised that he would get no reply from Jake he walked away with a smile on his face, thinking that his Client would enjoy the food and drink on his final day at the Hotel..

Not a scrap of food was left on the plate as Jake sat back wallowing in satisfaction at the delicious meal he had just consumed. He poured another glass of his lovely Merlot as the waiter arrived to clear his plate.

'Could I tempt you with a dessert sir, I could recommend the cheesecake!'

'Sounds good to me, I think I had better let the first layer settle down before you deliver it, could you give me 10 minutes'.

'Certainly sir, I would like you to enjoy your last meal with us in comfort'.

Grinning to himself as the waiter walked away, Jake couldn't remember the last time he had enjoyed such a lovely meal.

The wine bottle empty he waved to the waiter to deliver his sweet, of course like everything in America it was a huge slice almost covering the width of the plate, but as the first piece met his taste buds he agreed with the waiter that it was an excellent accompaniment to the main course, and to his surprise he cleared the plate.

He asked the waiter for the bill, explaining that he had paid the Hotel bill previously and would be paying for his meal separately. Paying with a card he added a $50 dollar tip for the waiter thanking him for his service during the stay.

Back in his room he sorted out his cases before laying out the clothes he would be wearing the next day before settling down to read a book he had purchased previously.

Chapter 24

At last the day to return home had arrived, a final packing of the remainder of his belongings and he was ready for his cab journey to the airport, via the Hospital to collect George. Making his way into the Dining Room the waiter approached and asked if he required a cooked meal. Jake replied that he would like pancakes, bacon and hash browns together with a pot of black coffee.

He sat alone for his last meal and thoroughly enjoyed the food washed down with an excellent coffee. As there was a short time before the cab arrived he decided to take a last visit to the Jeweller's to say his farewell and to thank the old man for his time and explanation of the items he had purchased.

Back up to his room he collected all his belongings and left them in a recess alongside the Reception Area then collected his receipt, finally making his way along the road to his destination. On opening the door the old man recognised him and with a broad smile said 'I didn't expect to have the pleasure of your company one more time Mr Tordale, aren't you returning to the UK today?'

'Yes I am, but I wanted to say a fond farewell to you, and to thank you for your help in providing me with my purchases, and also giving me an insight into your life here'.

'It was my pleasure, I am always glad to relieve my customers of money in exchange for my goods. Wait, I have a little something I would like you to take back to England, but would appreciate that you wait until you return to your home before opening it. Could I offer you a little refreshment before you leave?'

'No thank you, I have only just eaten quite a substantial breakfast at my Hotel'.

Jake could hear the old man rustling with paper in the back room and after a quarter of an hour he returned with a pocket sized parcel beautifully wrapped and handed it over to him.

'This item is of little value if sold, but it is of sentimental value to me, so I wish to give it to you as I value your calling here choosing my establishment to purchase your presents.

But more than that I treasure your time and thoughtfulness in spending time with an old Jewish jeweller, when in fact if you had walked further along the road you would have had a choice of at least half a dozen upmarket premises'.

'I understand, but you must realise I am an old school type of person myself, who notices class and beauty, therefore once I entered this place I sensed an aura about it and the stock that you hold, then of course we had a conversation and that was it for me. If I lived here in Washington I can assure you I would have been in to see you at least once a month. It has been a pleasure to meet you sir, should I return to Washington in the future you will be my first stop once I get off the aeroplane'.

The old man bent his head and a tear slowly slid down his cheek as he made his way from around the counter to embrace Jake. As he held him he said something in Yiddish before releasing him and standing back.

Just before Jake picked up the parcel, he wiped his eyes and blew his nose, before the old man noticed, then shook his hand and said farewell.

'God speed Mr Tordale, may you have a long and healthy life my friend'.

As he strolled back to the Hotel he felt quite melancholy after his latest conversation with the old Jeweller and the hard life he had endured, but back to reality his cab should be arriving around 10am to take him to the Hospital so he made his legs work a little faster and he arrived in the foyer with fifteen minutes to spare.

He shook hands with the Receptionist as the cab driver collected his luggage and placed it in the trunk. He then asked Jake for his destination, somewhat perplexed that he had to go to the Airport via the Hospital, however he thought that at least the fare would be higher for him than first anticipated.

Pulling into a parking bay alongside the entrance to the Hospital, Jake asked the driver to wait until he collected his friend from the Ward, explaining that he was in plaster and would need to ride shotgun to allow his leg ample room. The driver scratched his head then settled in the seat to await their return.

George was already dressed and sat in a wheelchair, with his belongings on his lap, a smile spread across his face as both men faced each other. 'Ready mate!' exclaimed Jake. 'Although everyone has been so good to me here I will be glad to get into the fresh air and aboard a plane to get back to Blighty'.

Jake stood behind the wheelchair and quickly pushed George towards the lift, as they passed the Nurses Station they all wished George good luck, and he thanked everyone there for all that they had done for him.

Was that a slight tear in the corner of George's eye thought Jake, soft bugger.

On the ground floor at last the driver saw them arrive and quickly got out of the car to help them with George's belongings, assisting him into the front seat and returning the wheelchair to the foyer.

Ten minutes later they were all settled in and on their way to the Airport. The ride was uneventful and the cab pulled into a pull-in by the entrance. the driver rushed out and collected a wheelchair from inside the terminal, George got in just as Jake returned with a trolley to take their belongings. After paying the driver with a reasonable tip, they entered the large building to be met by Inspector Ryan Drew together with a burly policeman attached to Roland Withers by handcuffs.

They exchanged greetings before Ryan led them through the terminal to a Priority Area which was separate from the General Public to enable them to access their aircraft without interference from onlookers.

Checking passports and luggage quickly they were approached by a plain clothes officer from England who took control of his prisoner and asked Jake to accompany him to the plane that had taxied to a hanger close by. After shaking hands with Ryan, Jake thanked him for his diligence and hoped that his ongoing investigation would have a fruitful ending. They exited the area through a wide door which helped with George's wheelchair, then arrangements had been made for George to be lifted onto the plane by a mechanical hoist.

Three quarters of an hour later the plane taxied onto the runway and soared into the clean blue winter sky on its way to Heathrow.

The men were fed and watered throughout the flight and as they were the only four passengers they were also entertained by inflight films, making the time in the air appear to zip by. The journey was uneventful and they landed on time being welcomed by a cold and overcast London. The aircraft taxied to a hanger where it was met by a Police Van that took the Officer and Withers away. Jake and George eventually reached terra firma and were at last on home territory but to their surprise were greeted by Henry Bates who shook both their hands vigorously.

George was whisked off to hospital to have his wounds checked over, whilst Jake and Henry made their way back to the Hotel to collect his car.

Reunited with his trusty vehicle after collecting his keys, he followed Henry back to the underground car park, then up in the lift to his office.

As they sat in the comfortable leather seats Henry remarked 'I expect you could do with a long hot shower and a good night's sleep back in Dorset after your recent escapades'.

'I could indeed Henry but I thought I would quickly give you a rundown of the events that took place in the States first'.

'No need for that now old man, just give me any receipts you have to hand together with any funds left over and I'll let you be on your way'.

A stern look spread across Jake's face as Henry said these words, but then he supposed it was all Government money.

Removing his wallet he handed over numerous receipts and the balance of US dollars he was left with for Henry, who put them all in a side drawer.

When he removed his hand it contained an envelope which he passed over to Jake. 'Disturbance money for you Jake, thank you for all you did for George and to get him back home'.

Jake put the envelope in his pocket, stood and shook his Boss's hand, then said 'I think I had better wend my way back to Dorset as I have a lot to do in the next month or so'.

'I hope it's relaxing things' Henry reiterated.

'First I have an Alarm System being installed next week, then I'm off to Singapore and Australia, then as I return to England I am off to France to see the final game of the Six Nations Rugby Tournament with half a dozen locals, to hopefully see England win the Grand Slam'.

'You tire me out just listening to your various exploits Jake, perhaps the day before you fly to Singapore you could call and we can go out for a meal, or if that isn't convenient when you return, its entirely up to you, but I think its time we indulged in the gastronomical delights of Marcus Waring's establishment sooner rather than later'.

'That sounds an excellent idea Henry, now I must be off before the jet lag sets in', he turned and left the room taking the lift down to the car park.

As he settled into the drivers seat his mind wandered back to the details he had just divulged to Henry, and even to him it sounded a busy few weeks.

The London traffic, for a better word ambled by, before he passed the vast expanse of Heathrow Airport, the further he drove away from the Capital the less dense the traffic became. The journey took him under two hours and he felt relieved as he drove down the lane and reached his wonderful home, Wisteria Cottage.

As he turned the key and brought in his luggage he nearly fell over the accumulation of post that was strewn across the coir yarn mat in front of him. The answerphone was flashing as normal whenever he was away for a while, but all thoughts of opening the mail and answering the phone thoughts were put to the back of his mind, before he had unpacked, loaded the washing machine, changed clothes and sat down for a cup of Fennel tea. An hour later he sat at the Dining Room table and placed the mail in front of him together with the envelope that Henry had given him. First things first, he opened Henry's envelope, and to his surprise it contained cash, a lot of it. Counting up there was a total of £4,000 in various denominations and a note that just said TAX FREE, and a smiley face. The remaining post included belated Christmas cards, the usual junk mail, a note from the Alarm Installers saying they would be commencing work in two days time. A letter from Maureen which he put to one side, finally a large envelope from his Singapore Solicitor that included details of the premises they were selling for him, the agreed selling fee, plus the proposed final settlement figure. He had to sign and return the documents within five days which was too short a time so he decided to ring the number and speak to them in person explaining the time problem, also that he intended visiting their offices in the next few days.

Chapter 24

Half an hour later Jake had confirmation that his visit would be acceptable due to the time problem with postage.

Now feeling quite tired he decided to have a nap upstairs before having something to eat and then listen to the messages on the answer machine.

Chapter 25

Checking the clock alongside the bed he realised his nap had been five hours long as it was now 10pm, although it was late he felt quite ravenous. In the kitchen he opened a tin of Mushroom Soup, then put a couple of slices of bread in his toaster for a late snack. Completing his refreshments he pressed the button on the answerphone to find out what messages he had received, one from the Alarm Company regarding starting work date, another from Bert regarding the Rugby in France, one from Olivia, one from the Solicitor regarding his Aunts ashes, finally a call from Mrs Choo in Australia.

The only people he needed to answer were the Solicitor and Mrs Choo, also a visit to the Pub would answer Bert's inquiry, but he would leave the others until the morning.

With the time approaching midnight he decided to settle down for the night and wandered back upstairs to bed.

After an exhausting two weeks he wasn't surprised when he eventually awoke the next morning that it was past 10am, but he felt a lot fresher than when he had gone to sleep. Drawing back the curtains he was greeted by brilliant sun rays shining through the malaise of trees on the hedge across the lane to his property, although it was only January the rays produced a reasonable amount of heat which had invaded his bedroom.

A shower was the priority before he needed to make the urgent phone calls which he intended to carry out before preparing his breakfast.

The first call was to Clare his eldest daughter to check on the family and to explain the details of his recent visit to the States, together with his imminent trip to Singapore and Australia. She informed him that Sharon and Lottie were OK but were up tending to the horses.

Next call was to Mrs Choo, unfortunately it went unanswered so he left a message saying he would be in Australia in a week or so and would call and see her, but he decided to ring the Solicitor in Kent after breakfast.

Half an hour later after he had cleared away his dishes he settled into his favourite armchair and rang the number in the Kent Solicitor's office, the usual professional answer came over the line from the efficient lady secretary, then after giving his name he was put through to Daniel Frobisher who thanked him for returning his call.

After explaining that he had had an unexpected visit to the United States Jake asked how he could help.

A short silence before Frobisher explained 'I still have your relations ashes which require moving to their final resting place and I was wondering when you would be available to disperse them?'

'I do apologise Mr Frobisher for not contacting you sooner as unfortunately I have just returned from the USA after two weeks there, tomorrow I am flying to Singapore then on to Australia on business. However when I return to London, I'll visit you to collect the ashes and make arrangements with someone who is available to take me out into the North Sea to carry out my duty'.

'Please forgive me Mr Tordale, there is no hurry I just wished to inform you that they are still with me for collection, that's all' he replied quite sheepishly.

'No you are correct, I'll certainly do as I said when I return. Perhaps you would be able to accompany me on the trip and I'll treat you to lunch when we get back to shore' Jake said with a chuckle.

'Unfortunately I suffer from a very sensitive stomach and could not accompany you on the boat, but would be happy to stay on land while you carry out the deed and we could have something to eat when you return'.

'Excellent, I'll be in touch'.

He wondered if the Alarm Company were available, but made the call anyway. It was picked up right away when Jake explained that he would be away for a couple of weeks and was leaving the Country tomorrow the person gave a loud sigh.

'However' Jake said, 'If someone could call today to collect a key you could carry out the work and put the key in the letterbox once you have completed your works'.

'Thank you Mr Tordale, I'll arrange for someone to call this afternoon to collect it, have a nice journey'.

He checked the contents of his fridge, then realised he hadn't replenished it for a couple of weeks, so would make do with what he had there for the rest of the day, and breakfast tomorrow morning.

He then rang Heathrow to book his flight to Singapore and an onward journey to Australia the following day. Due to the distance he booked Business Class, then rang the on-site Hotel he had only just left to check his car in with an overnight stay on his return in a week or so's time.

The flight out was in the afternoon, leaving him plenty of time to get to London, park his car and check in for the flight.

Feeling quite relaxed after making all his arrangements he just had to wait for a representative from the Alarm Company to collect the front door key, then finally call and see Bert at The Swan to find out what he wanted and of course have a last pint before he was off again.

He turned to the letter from Maureen and opened it to peruse its contents, it consisted of two pages and after scanning them he was pleased to read that she had had an enjoyable Christmas with her family and she was looking forward to the New Year as she had arranged to start a couple of Courses at the local College that would occupy two days a week for a year. Jake thought, note to self, reply before leaving the UK, however send the letter from Australia to give Maureen something else to think about.

He then took out a meal from the freezer to cook in the microwave, checking the label it said 'meal for 2' Spaghetti Bolognaise, that would do he thought.

Two hours later there was a knock on the front door, and as he opened it he was face to face with a swarthy man of 'fiftyish', dressed in a dark pinstriped suit, white shirt and red tie. 'Mr Tordale, my name's Brian Fellow's we spoke a couple of hours ago. I'm the MD of The Alarm Company I've called to collect the front door key, and just wish to confirm with your good self that you are happy to leave your premises unattended whilst the work is carried out'.

Jake shook his hand and ushered him inside. 'I am indeed quite happy with that arrangement, I have already put your company off once, and when I return hopefully the work will have been completed. I'll check it over when I get back, and if satisfied, which I'm sure I will be, I'll send off a Bank transfer for the outstanding balance'.

'Thank you' the man replied. 'I would still make sure that anything of value is safely locked away for both our sakes, my men have worked with me for years and I trust them implicitly however it's best to be on the safe side'.

'Thank you Brian, the only items in the house of value are sentimental only to me and will be secured. Of course any damage to the property whilst carrying out the works I would expect to be repaired at no cost to myself. I apologise for saying that, but before I retired I was a Building Surveyor working for numerous Companies and the number of times the Builders were accused of damage was considerable, a few times quite costly to them'.

'I fully understand sir, but the works involved are mainly external, but there will be someone overlooking the Contract each day and any problems found are reported directly to me'.

'Thank you for your reassurance, now let me get you that key'.

After Brian Fellow's left he checked the MG in the garage and the padlock on the door which he had exchanged for a digital one for extra security recently, and everything was as it should be. He started the dream car up to turn the engine over as it had been left for over a month, then whilst sat there he looked forward to the spring when he could give the old girl a good run out.

Donning his warm clothing he headed for The Swan for a chat with Bert and a pint or two before returning home and packing again for his latest trip.

As he walked in Bert gave him a beaming smile and said 'The wanderer returns, long time no see Jake, how the devil are you my friend'.

'I'll be a lot better once I've sampled a pint of Real Ale Bert' he answered with a grin.

'Sit yourself down and I'll bring it over, then you can fill me in on where you've been lately'.

As he settled down Jake felt a little uncomfortable at the thought of telling a Pub Landlord what he had encountered over the last few weeks, but in the end decided to embellish what happened with a little extravagance on the sights he had visited whilst in the States.

Bert walked over with a tray of drinks and sat opposite Jake with an enquiring face on him as he handed Jake his beer.

'Well I'll keep it short Bert, just after Christmas I had a call to say a friend of mine had travelled to the States but after two days had gone off the grid, his mobile went unanswered for a number of days, so I travelled over there to try and find him. Whilst there I contacted a lady I met in Santorini and spent a week sightseeing with her in Washington. My friend eventually appeared out of the blue and we both returned to England day before yesterday. I intended visiting the young lady in April but due to my off the cuff visit, I will now cancel that arrangement. I am off to Singapore tomorrow for a couple of days and then on to Australia to check on an old lady who recently became widowed, I think I mentioned it to you before when I visited her for her husband's funeral'.

'Globe trotting Tordale they should call you, you must have covered some air miles in the past few years, but it's best to do it when you can. Will you still be available for the rugby in France?'

'Of course Bert' he replied, 'I wouldn't miss that for the world. Anyway did you have a profitable Christmas, and of course have you recovered fully from such a busy time?'

'One of the best festive breaks ever mate, it made up for the lean spell I experienced over the last six months, and yes I am back ready for a busy month then a weekend in France with all my pals'.

Jake finished his drink and asked for a refill together with a snorter for Bert.

A smile spread across Bert's face as he walked back to the Bar to get the drinks.

On his return Jake asked if all the other lads had a good Christmas and were ready for the trip away.

'Most are in each night ,and the topic is Rugby and the weather, but all are in fine spirits even the hard working farmer who I see a couple of times a week'.

'I take it the message you left for me was to check up on my welfare, if so, you know where I've been and what I've been up to, was there anything else Bert?'

'No mate, just nosy me wanting to know your whereabouts'.

A couple entered and Bert returned to the counter to tend to them. Five minutes later Jake had emptied his glass and bade farewell to Bert with a wave.

As he entered the Cottage he smiled at his friend's nosiness, but that's what and where rumours spread. Although Bert he concluded was not the normal gossip, but was genuinely interested in Jake's welfare as a friend.

Next on the list was to check through the house and decide what of value he wished to place out of sight of the workman that would be at the Cottage working tomorrow.

He decided the safest place would be the boot of the MG, after collected a dozen small articles, he put them in a sackcloth and placed them in the car. After replacing the cover over his prized vehicle he shut the doors and twisted the dial on the digital lock, noting where the numbers had finished, he would double check on his return.

Walking in doors it was now bag packing time, using his new case he filled it quickly with what he needed clothing wise leaving it open to put in his toiletries in the morning.

He then realised he hadn't opened the present from the Jeweller Stefan Cohen, so sifting through all the packages he had spread on the bed he located the little package and carefully opened it. There was a note, he spotted first and opened it carefully, it said 'Dear Jake Tordale, I find it extremely difficult to put into words the joy it was meeting and talking to you during your stay in Washington, I hope to see you soon. Thank you, Stefan.

In the little packet he found a small solid silver photo frame, and within it there was another note 'To Jake Tordale from Stefan Cohen, God Bless'.

Chapter 26

To his surprise, when he woke up he realised that he had caught up on the jet lag as it was only a little after seven. There was one item he hadn't attended to and that was contacting Maureen in Taunton, but he decided to give her a ring instead of a letter when he got to London. Down for his cereal and coffee, he double checked what he needed to complete before leaving, money, passport and paperwork the Singapore Solicitor had sent him before locking the safe, then take the car to the Hotel car park, ring Maureen and collect tickets from Terminal. He checked the oil, water and tyres on the Lexus again, thankfully his fuel had already been topped up, so there was no need for any stops before he pulled into the car park.

A final check through, lock the front door and off again he drove, down the lane, past the Pub and out onto the motorway. A straight-forward drive with no delays brought him into the hustle and bustle of the largest Airport in Europe an hour and a half later. Leaving the car in the Hotel's car park he approached the front desk and explained his destinations to the young lady and his car number and name. She recognised Jake and asked if he would be staying overnight on his return. Thinking quickly he thought it would be advisable, so booked a one night stay for 10 days time (to be confirmed). Handing over his keys, he waited patiently for the shuttle bus to take him to the Terminal building.

Twenty minutes later he had collected his tickets, gone through Departures and Passport Control, and made himself comfortable in the Lounge. His flight was due to takeoff in an hour, so he perused the Duty Free Shop and picked up a few items for the Solicitor and Mrs Choo. He decided to leave any food and drink for now as he would be looked after on the long flight ahead of him to Singapore. He gave Maureen a call thanking her for her letter, saying he was going to reply but as he had just returned from the States and was actually at Heathrow on his way to Singapore and then on to Australia he would give her a call instead.

'Thank's for calling Jake its most kind of you, can I just reiterate how busy a life you lead, to my quite mundane one. I had a lovely Christmas thank you with my family, it was most enjoyable and every one was in fine fettle, perhaps you could pop in when you return home for a nice chat'.

I'll give you a bell once things settle down, then call down to Taunton and take you out for something to eat if you fancy an hour or so out'.

'That sound lovely Jake, have a safe journey and speak soon, bye'.

'Bye Maureen, take care'

Jake placed a call to Singapore and spoke to the Receptionist at the Solicitor's, explaining who he was, and as he was about to board a plane from England and that he would be in the office the next day. The lady confirmed the call and advised him she would pass on his message. As he completed the call the time to board was announced over the tannoy, he picked up his bag and duty free items and joined the queue for the aircraft.

He was directed to Business Class and was surprised to see how little this part of the plane was occupied, however he wasn't one to complain.

Settling back into the comfortable reclining seat he scanned through The Times he had collected as he walked into Business Class, before waiting for the usual Safety briefing and the start of the huge Rolls Royce engines that would lift this colossal plane into the air over England's Capital and onto the Asian country of Singapore.

Twenty five minutes later, the plane accelerated down the runway, up over London, then banking over and heading for Europe and onwards on its half day journey.

As they soared to their cruising height the Hostess asked Jake if there was anything he required from the menu in front of him. Quickly checking what was on offer he asked for a Club sandwich and a bottle of red wine, which would be sufficient until they left Europe behind. Deep into the flight Jake had a nap and was really surprised to find that they were a quarter of the way to their destination.

Oriental food was delivered at stages throughout the flight accompanied by coffee, as Jake spent the time watching movies on the screen in front of him and completing the extremely difficult Times crossword.

Almost thirteen hours later the Captain gave out over the tannoy that they would be descending for the next fifteen minutes before landing at Singapore Changi airport, he hoped everyone had enjoyed the flight and would look forward to seeing them all in the future. As they landed and taxied to the plane's parking slot, the usual hustle and bustle commenced as the tired passengers started collected their bits and pieces from the overhead lockers ready to disembark.

His Stewardess approached him and asked him to wait awhile before leaving his seat, however after another 10 minutes he walked into the Terminal, through Passport Control and on to collect his baggage from the carousel.

Walking outside he hailed a taxi to take him to the onsite Hotel that he had booked previously. He booked in, went up to the room and went to bed. It was early morning in Singapore, just after 6am so he asked for a call around 10am to his room.

Four hours later he was awakened by the call, dressed and went down for a late oriental breakfast. Whilst sat at the table he rang the Solicitor's Office explaining where he was and could he confirm his appointment. Having been put through the Solicitor said he would arrange for someone to collect him as soon as he was ready, then once the paperwork was completed take him to wherever he wanted to go next.

Jake thanked the man explaining he would be ready whenever someone could call and he would meet them in the Hotel Reception Foyer.

Twenty minutes later a young lady walked in with a card saying JAKE TORDALE, he stood and explained who he was and she directed him to her car.

No words were said on the journey into the city, but her driving was exemplary, and as she pulled into the kerb outside the Solicitor's offices, he thanked her and walked into the impressive building.

Taking the lift to the 2nd floor he was greeted in true oriental style as he walked towards the Secretary, who then asked him to follow her into a large office with the Solicitor sat at an enormous desk that was covered with files containing numerous amounts of paperwork. The Solicitor stood and bowed to Jake before extending his hand and asking Jake to take a seat. 'I have the paperwork you require here already signed by myself, I have left it undated, as I was unsure when I would arrive here'.

'It is no problem at all Mr Tordale, I'm thankful that you have taken this long journey to bring this to me and thank you for it. How long are you staying, if I might ask?'

'I will be catching another flight tomorrow to take me to Australia, why do you ask?'

'As you have put yourself to so much trouble, I thought it would be polite of me to take you to a famous Restaurant in the City before you leave us again'.

'That is most kind of you, I would be honoured to accept your invitation'.

He turned to Jake before replying with 'Let us complete the boring paperwork, then we can get away from the Office for a while'.

Jake stood and handed over the papers that had been sent to him. The man perused the documents with an occasional 'mm' and 'ah' before asking Jake to put the dates where he had pencilled in crosses.

The formalities completed the bespectacled man asked 'How would you like the funds transferred and where' with a twinkle in his eye.

Jake gave him the details, then asked if there was anything else he needed from him.

Shaking his head 'No everything fine. I just have to do a little more work then we go to have food.

Perhaps you wait in Reception I be no more than hour, lady will give drinks'.

Jake stood and shook the man's hand before leaving the Office and sitting himself in the plush seats opposite the Secretary.

True to his word, exactly an hour later the door opened and the Solicitor walked out of his office, he quickly said something to his secretary who immediately lifted the phone and barked orders to someone, then nodded to Jake.

They walked out of the office and down in the lift, exiting the front door where a limousine awaited them. Both got in the plush back seat, and the vehicle pulled quietly away from the kerb heading into the City.

As the car slowed and quietly pulled to a halt Jake looked out the window but failed to see a restaurant. Turning he was surprised to see the smile on the other man's face who then said 'You no see Restaurant, have to look up'.

Jake couldn't see to the top of the building as it must have been at least thirty floors above the pavement level. The other man gestured for Jake to get out of the car, and he followed him into the building. Taking the lift no words were spoken until they exited out onto the twenty eighth floor, they walked directly into the Restaurant where a waiter was stood, he bowed to the Solicitor, and directed them to a table alongside a bank of windows.

No menu's appeared to be available as the waiter brought along iced water to the table together with a carafe of wine, apparently ordered beforehand.

Gentle conversation took place as they sipped their wine with Jake divulging the details of his journey to Australia and his visit to Mrs Choo.

As he finished his explanation the waiter returned with the mixed dishes for the first course of their meal. It consisted of dim sum and sliced crispy duck accompanied by prawn crackers in delicate varying shapes and sizes.

Eventually their dishes were cleared away before the main course was placed in front of them. A platter contained huge king prawns in a sauce that Jake couldn't identify, prawn dumplings, a large fish that had been carefully deboned and placed on a bed of rice.

Separate plates containing different sized noodles, plain rice, egg fried rice, together with four different sauces.

The waiter placed the king prawns, dumplings and sections of fish on each of their plates then left the remaining dishes for each of them to add to their plates.

Smiles spread across both of the diners faces as the elder of the two gesticulated for Jake to help himself to the food.

An hour later they had finished the wine and their main course with the table cleaned and prepared for the dessert course.

The waiter delivered a concoction that reminded Jake of his previous visits to Marcus Waring's London establishment only on an oriental scale. It was huge, the article in front of them resemble a cake surrounded with meringue but covered in soft fruits and enclosed in a honey spun dome. The waiter leaned forward and set the apparition alight, but only for a few seconds just as the meringue took on a burnt look.

He smiled and walked away leaving utensils for them to delve into it and put on their plates. They each took a reasonable slice before tucking into their food in front of them. Jake had to break the silence to thank the solicitor for bringing him here to indulge in this magnificent meal. His companion smiled and replied 'The pleasure is all mine my English friend, its small compensation for the work you have put my way, I am glad you enjoyed the experience. I will call the driver to take me back to the office, then transport you back to your Hotel'.

'Before we leave I have a small token of my gratitude for the work you have carried out on my behalf' reaching into his pocket he handed the man a cigarette lighter and a cigar cutter knowing full well that although he had not witnessed him smoking, being an ex smoker he could smell the tell tale signs on the man's clothing.

His companion thanked him for his generous gift and signalled for the waiter to bring two glasses of alcohol for them.

Delivered in shot glasses, Jake sniffed the contents, looked at the other man and said 'Whiskey'. He nodded and said, 'Not just any whiskey, try it'.

Jake took a sip and realised that it was a single malt of excellent quality and downed the remainder.

'What a finish to a meal, thank you so much for entertaining me' Jake exclaimed.

'My pleasure also, I visit here quite often, entertaining my Client's but none better than you Mr Tordale'.

They stood and left the table, into the lift and down to the waiting car, they called by the Office to drop off the Solicitor before the driver returned Jake to his Hotel.

The connection to Australia flew at 10am the next day, so he had a decent stay-over at the Hotel and caught up on some much needed sleep.

Chapter 27

Waking in yet another Hotel in another Country he took a while to get his bearings as to where he was and the time difference. However after checking the clock beside him local time was 8am. Quick shower and change of clothes before he made his way down for a quick breakfast before heading back to the Terminal.

His journey through the various barriers took a little longer this time, as the local authorities were more interested in why he only stayed the one day before heading on to Brisbane, Australia. Was he carrying anything illegal, had he been asked to carry anything illegal, what was the purpose of his visit to to Singapore, etc, etc. then after his honest explanations he was let through to the Departure area.

Feeling slightly frustrated by the way he had been treated, he finally thought to himself, if I'de have been in their shoes I would have been suspicious as well, so he dismissed it as just another experience to encounter whilst travelling abroad.

Sat in the huge Departure lounge he felt conspicuous as being one of only a few Caucasians in the Area, however he only had to wait awhile and he would be boarding and on his way to see Mrs Choo. He was also flying Business Class again on this leg so once on board he would be isolated from the other travellers.

The journey would take almost 8 hours, however as usual he was well looked after with food and drink, whilst being entertained by another couple of films.

As they descended into Australian air space the vast expanse of this huge nation could be taken in with most of the surface covered by barren countryside, then as they approached Brisbane the outline of one of the Modern Wonders of the Natural World came into view, the Great Barrier Reef, It never ceased to amaze him as to this wonderful outline to the coast of Queensland.

The usual briefing by the Captain was given out, as they descended on their approach before landing, to buckle up their seatbelts and to leave them on until the plane came to a halt. A hubbub of voices permeated his space as the passengers prepared themselves for their arrival, or homecoming to Brisbane, Australia.

The usual Airport formalities are heightened in Australia and it was an hour before Jake was out of the Terminal and walking towards the stream of taxis lined up for fares.

Jake got in the first one and the driver placed his luggage in the boot before asking for his destination. After giving Mrs Choo's address he dialled her number and after a couple of rings in was picked up. 'Good day Mrs Choo its Jake Tordale how are you, I've just landed and will be with you in half an hour if that's OK'.

'Jake its so lovely to hear your voice, I've been busy cooking this morning, so I can give a lovely traveller a nice welcome, see you in a while'.

'Bye Mrs Choo, see you soon'.

As the taxi pulled up to the front of the house, the dear lady came out the front door to greet him, the driver took his luggage from the boot and up the steps to the front door, before collecting his fare, and then driving off.

After a quick embrace she followed Jake into the house with his luggage. 'You must be tired Jake, perhaps a cup of coffee will help, the percolator is on, I remember its black coffee you take'.

'Yes, thank you for remembering, how are you, you look quite sprightly and even younger than when I last saw you'.

'You were always a flattering young man, but yes I do feel a lot better, especially after what my dear husband had put aside for me, I have no worries money wise now'.

As she sat down in her favourite chair she started her inquisition of him. 'Let's hear what you have been up to since we last met, and I want to know everything' she finished with a chuckle.

Jake sipped his coffee, then commenced his tale of where he had been, what he did for Christmas, his visit to Singapore, then after twenty minutes sat back to finish his drink.

'You amaze me Jake, how one man can do so much in so little time, your brain must travel at a 100 miles an hour. Anyway I am so glad you have travelled all this way to come and visit dear old Auntie Choo, how long will you be here this time?'

'I'm afraid it will only be a quick visit, I have to return inside a week, I am having an Alarm System installed in my home as we speak, and the work is due for completion the day before I return. Then a couple of days after I have to visit Kent to spread my Auntie's ashes out to sea, which is something I have had to put off due to my previous travels.

Then a group of friends and I are off to France to see a rugby match, before I visit Devon to see my family'.

'I'll have to enjoy your short stay as best I can then' she replied with a hint of sadness.

'I had to come and see you, therefore as my initial visit to Singapore was more than halfway to Australia, I felt I needed to see my adopted Auntie to see how she is coping'.

'Not many people would be as thoughtful as you my dear boy, but yes I have settled into a nice routine since I last saw you. I have joined three separate groups with all people of my age, we have a craft group once a week, a painting section that meets twice a month and a group of men and women who are on their own for a chat and a meal once a month. I am busier than when I was a housewife'. As she finished a sad expression fell over her eyes, her brain obviously thinking back to her late husband.

'I am glad you have other things to occupy yourself, besides cooking lovely meals, which I am pleased to say I can smell from your kitchen' Jake replied trying to lighten the mood.

'Are you hungry Jake, please forgive me, the meal I have prepared will be ready in half an hour, I had better get back there and check up on things. Put your cases in your bedroom and I'll be back in a few minutes'.

'Thank you very much, the jet lag takes some getting used to but I'll be more refreshed tomorrow and if you are free we can take a ride into town for a bit of retail therapy and give you some time away from the kitchen'.

'You are so thoughtful Jake, I expect you will be visiting the Police Officer whilst you are here. The day after tomorrow I have my craft meeting so you will have a day to yourself'.

'I expect she will be busy but I will give her a call and possibly meet up for coffee and a catch up' Jake confirmed.

Half an hour later they were sat at the kitchen table tucking into her famous and delicious food accompanied by a decent bottle of wine. The meal was ate in silence, then after she cleared away the dishes, she produced a bowl of mixed fruit from the fridge and spooned out a large portion into two dishes.

After emptying his dish he said 'That was delicious, its a pity I live so far away, I could eat your food all the time Auntie Choo'.

'I'm glad you enjoyed it, and love your special name for me Jake, if I had a son I would hope he would be like you.'

Jake couldn't speak anymore and stood up to do the dishes with her.

A little while later they retired to the lounge, where Jake sat in his favourite chair, Auntie Choo walked over to the bookshelf and retrieved the hardback book he was reading on his previous visit and handed it to him. 'I thought you could get back and delve into the ancient warriors, 'The Samurai', you were reading about on your last visit'.

'Thank you Auntie, it's getting late so I think I'll retire if you don't mind, I'll take the book with me and read for a while. Thank you for your hospitality, see you in the morning'.

'Goodnight Jake, I hope you sleep well'.

Chapter 28

Jake woke with a start to darkness, wondering where he was for a few seconds, before he looked at his watch and noting it was only 5am local time. He turned on the sidelight and started reading the history book he had been given by Auntie Choo.

After half an hour's reading he felt tired again, put the book down, turned off ed the light and settled down for a couple more hours of fitful sleep. His mind kept going back to time's when the delectable Orchid slept in this same bed, then sadness filled his mind as to what could have been. Eventually sleep overcame him again, until he became aware of a slight tapping at the bedroom door. Auntie Choo opened the door and quietly said 'I've brought you a morning cup of tea, I hope I didn't disturb you'.

'No, I woke early at 5am and eventually dropped off again, what time is it Auntie?'

'Eleven o'clock I'm afraid, I thought it best to wake you for breakfast, sorry If you wanted to sleep on'.

'No I'm glad you woke me, I want to take you into the City, however it will be later than I first anticipated unfortunately. But after I drink my tea I'll have a shower and shave and be at your service'.

A big smile spread across her face as Jake uttered these words, so she turned and left the room scurrying off to prepare his breakfast.

Half an hour later the embarrassed Jake sat at the kitchen table to have the fried breakfast Auntie had prepared.

Just after one o'clock they got in her faithful car and made their way into the shopping mall they had visited previously and parked in the multi-storey car park.

Jake asked Auntie if there was any shopping she needed, she said there were a few items she required so they would visit the Supermarket first and bring the shopping back to the car. The few bits and pieces eventually filled four shopping bags so Jake insisted on paying the bill, as most of the items purchased looked as if they were bought for his consumption. As they left the car they took the escalator down a couple of levels and were on a floor with a multitude of retail outlets. Browsing each shop Jake asked if there was anything she needed in any of these outlets. After a slight hesitation on her part, Jake felt that there was something that Auntie wanted but was embarrassed to mention, however he asked anyway 'Please tell me Auntie, there is something you have seen that you would like?'.'Well as we passed that Hobbies shop in the corner I spied a starter pack for novice artists, I didn't stop as I thought it rude as the visit here was mainly for you to look at all the shops'.

'I decided to come here for you Auntie' so he turned and walked back to the Hobby shop and looked in the window as Auntie stood alongside him. 'Let's go in and look at the various items you need for your Workshop'.

As they walked in they were approached by a pleasant young lady who asked if she could help them in any way.

Jake smiled at her before stating 'My Auntie has just started an Art Workshop and is interested in the starter kit that she has seen in in the window'.

The assistant smiled and said 'The starter kit is for watercolours, is that what you require madam?'

'May I look at them please before I give my answer' Auntie replied, obviously unsure how to that question.

She retrieved it from the window and placed it on the counter for the customer to inspect.

Jake asked Auntie 'Do you work in watercolour or oils at present?'

She looked at him with slight confusion before saying 'Watercolours, but next year I think we are advancing to oils'.

'May I suggest you have the watercolours now and see how you get on this year before you need to purchase the oil paints as this is a completely different medium'.

'I agree with you Jake' turning to the assistant she asked 'Does the pack come with brushes or is that a separate purchase?'

'The brushes are a separate purchase and the range is vast, if you could tell me what stage you are at in the Course I can suggest the items you will need'.

The lady was very sympathetic in her sales pitch and only added six brushes to the paints together with two canvases.

Before Auntie objected, Jake paid for the collection, taking no for an answer to her remonstrations

The assistant smiled at both of them as she handed over the purchase and said 'Happy painting madam, if there is anything you need in the future I would be pleased to help you with the items'.

Both Jake and Mrs Choo thanked the young lady for her help as they turned and left the shop, with Mrs Choo chastising Jake for spending his money.

As they deposited their purchases back in the car, Jake explained that he was happy to buy her gift as a way of paying his way for his stay.

She kissed him on the cheek and thanked him again for the tools for her new found hobby. Next Jake suggested something to eat, he left it up to her regarding the location.

'I visit a coffee shop only a street away if you would like we could walk there?'

'Fine by me, lead on Auntie' he said waving her forward.

'I really like you saying Auntie, it makes me happy that you think yourself one of my family, which I think you are' she said with a tear in her eye.

The sun was extremely warm as they walked along the street and he felt that she was glad when they entered the air conditioned coffee shop. They took a seat by the window and were quickly attended to by a young waitress.

Jake asked for their drinks and a mixture of cakes and sandwiches, which were delivered and to his amazement were apparently similar to the cakes he used to eat when he accompanied his mother to a local cafe, in his youth. There were chocolate eclairs, meringue's filled with fresh cream, apple turnovers, iced buns and fairy cakes.

On the lower level there were delicately fashioned sandwiches containing, ham and mustard, egg and salmon, and cheese and pickle leaving Jake's mouth aghast at the selection.

Mrs Choo was almost salivating at the food in front of her and made a start on the lower level with a couple of sandwiches. Jake followed and had one of each of the petite mixture. Pouring their second cup of tea they then tucked into the sweet treats and to his great delight he saw a sparkle of life spread across Auntie's face, as they tackled the sweet extravaganza. Jake excused himself to go to the toilet and paid the bill on the way before Auntie could object.

Thanking the waitress he returned to his seat as his companion took the last bite of chocolate eclair. 'This is a wonderful cafe Auntie, the food brought back memories of my youth when my Mum treated me to tea in a nearby town, where we enjoyed similar food to this, the only difference being that the waitresses were dressed in black with white aprons and a white cloth crown on their heads, it was a long time ago but after what we have consumed it felt like only yesterday'.

Mrs Choo wiped her mouth before saying, 'Did I see you pay the bill Jake?'

'It's my treat for you Auntie, please forgive me if I have upset you, but you will be treating me during my stay with wonderful meals, so think nothing of my treat in return'.

Walking back to the car she took his arm and squeezed it, 'It's so lovely to see you again Jake, you make an old woman very happy'.

'It's such a shame you live so far away Auntie, I would love you to meet my girls, their children and family perhaps we can arrange something next year, after I retire'.

'I would love that Jake, it is such a long way though, the furtherest I have travelled before is to Singapore, I'm not sure if my old body is up to the journey, however time will tell'.

Driving back in the car they chatted about Australia and the remainder of her extended family who still lived in Singapore and about the recent contact she had with them.

Jake said he had almost had enough of travelling the world due to work and was looking forward to settling down to his upcoming retirement. With that the car pulled up outside the house, Jake collected their purchases and followed her into the kitchen.

'Go in Jake, sit down and read your book I'll potter around out here for a while. Don't forget to ring the Police Officer!'

He scrolled through his Contacts before he found her number and dialled, it was picked up with 'Jake Tordale, for what do I deserve this call?' she answered.

'I'm back in Brisbane at Mrs Choo's for a fleeting visit and wondered if you fancied a catchup as I had to leave early the last time, I'm here for a few days so if you are free any of them we could have a drink or a meal out?'

'That would be nice, I'm busy all day today but strangely enough I have a day off tomorrow, what time would you like to meet up?'

'Anytime after ten would be fine, shall I meet you somewhere or would you like to collect me from Mrs Choo's' he answered hesitantly.

'I'll pick you up at ten, see you tomorrow'.

A slight tingle went down his spine as he ended the call, and rather than dwell on it he returned to his book.

Later as Auntie came into the room, Jake told her about his plans for the next day and that he would be leaving at ten in the morning for a day out with Inspector Chi.

She smiled and patted his arm, in a way confirming her agreement of his meeting with the Police Officer.

Chapter 29

With his brain now accustomed to Australian time he woke at 7am feeling quite hungry, then after a shower and shave he dressed and walked into the kitchen.

'Did you sleep better Jake?' Mrs Choo asked as he walked in.

'A lot better thank you, hardly any dreams and now I feel completely refreshed and hungry' he replied.

'What do you fancy, an English Breakfast or cereal and toast?'

'Not to put you to too much trouble, I really fancy an English Breakfast, will you be having it as well?'

'It sounds good to me also, I have just boiled the kettle so help yourself to tea or coffee whilst I cook our breakfast's'.

With the speed of a chef the dear old lady went about her business and twenty minutes later they were tucking into their spread of eggs, bacon, tomatoes, mushrooms and fried bread. They each had another cup of tea, before both smacked their lips as they put down their knifes and forks on top of the empty plates.

Jake asked 'What time is your Meeting today Auntie?'

'We meet anytime after ten, so after you leave I'll lock up and make my way there, I'll finish around two, so will be home soon after if your meeting has finished. But there is no hurry for you to get back'.

'I expect the Officer has a little sightseeing for me to enjoy, then we will have some lunch before I return, so I anticipate being back here around four, but I'll ring you to let you know'.

'I hope you have an enjoyable day, now it's time for you to give me a hand with the dishes' she said with a wry smile.

When they had finished tidying up Jake sat in his chair and returned to the story of the Samurai which he had found quite intriguing, and somewhat ferocious in the lives of those dedicated men and what they became after all their training.

There was a knock on the front door which brought him back to the present, checking his watch he realised it was just gone ten, and the visitor was Chi coming to collect him.

Auntie opened the door and shouted to Jake that his friend was here for him.

He put his book down and walked out to the Hall to be met by Chi in 'civvies' and looking very attractive. 'Good morning thank's for picking me up' he said, then turned and bade farewell to Auntie with a 'See you later Auntie, have a good meeting'.

There was no reply as he assumed she was busying herself preparing to make her way to her appointment with friends.

As they settled in the car seats she asked him what he fancied doing today.

'I'm in your hands, I visited a few of the touristy places on my last visit here, so anything unusual will do followed by lunch at any restaurant you fancy'.

'OK, I know just the place as we've got all day, we'll take a river cruise and visit a Koala Sanctuary, the trip includes lunch and lasts just under 6 hours, you up for that Jake?'.

'Sounds good to me, lead on I'm in your hands young lady'.

'It will also kill two birds with one stone, as I've not had the chance to enjoy it myself, so it will be an experience for me as well'.

After parking the car they walked to the quayside where the boat was tied up, after speaking to the man who was stood alongside the walk-on gangplank they boarded the vessel and were approached by an officer who took their admission money. They were then shown to viewing seats, sitting alongside each other, Jake asked Chi how she had been since he last visited Brisbane. A guarded reply followed, as her explanation consisted mainly of Police work and nothing about her private life.

He thought it best not to pry, so continued to tell her what he had been up to since their last meeting.

A look of astonishment spread over her face as he continued with his narrative until his final tale of his American Adventure.

'My God Jake as a private citizen your life is more involved than that of a Police Officer, my life feels quite mundane in comparison to yours'.

'I only have a few outstanding things to carry out until I will finally settle down to my retirement, most likely in May of this year. I still say most likely, as things seem to follow me through no fault of my own, but I really intend to stop now as my body is beginning to feel the strain of it all'.

'Well today, sit back and enjoy the ride with this relaxing cruise and a nice spot of lunch on the river before we visit The Koala Sanctuary'.

As they cruised down the river, menu's were handed to them, allowing them to choose their requirements for lunch, they decided on different meals, with white and red wine accompaniments. The food was extremely nice and washed down with the wine as they gazed at the views on either side of the river.

Two hours later the boat docked and the passengers were shown to the Sanctuary where they spent an hour, they both held a koala and took each others pictures. Jake was amazed at how docile these creatures were, and thanked Chi for this wonderful experience. Heading back to the boat all their fellow passengers were chatting away, saying how delighted they were at the experience they had all encountered.

Back on board Jake asked his companion if she fancied a drink, they both plumped for coffee which the waiter brought to their table. The cruise back gave Jake a view of the opposite bank and Chi pointed out the various buildings as they slowly drifted along.

Pulling into the quay an hour later Jake let out a sigh and thanked Chi for a wonderful few hours.

She looked him in the eye and asked if there was anything else he wanted to do, after checking the time he thought he ought to return to Mrs Choo's, but decided to ring her first to see how she had got on. The call was picked up after a few rings, with 'The Choo residence'.

'Hello Auntie, it's only Jake, did you have a nice meeting?'

'Yes thank you dear, have you had a good time?' she asked.

Jake thought for a while before answering her question, then said 'I've just got off a cruise boat and will be back with you in a few hours time, see you about six, OK?'

'That's OK my dear you enjoy yourself in the little time you will be in the Country, I'll see you at teatime, bye for now' and with that she put the phone down.

She seemed a bit put out, he thought, before turning to Chi and asking her what she had in mind for the next few hours. A smile spread across her face before she answered with ,'Well if you have a few hours spare perhaps we could go back to mine and we could talk a few things over before I drop you back'. She finished with a glint in her eye.

'Fine bye me' he confirmed, then they walked back to the car and drove into the City. Her flat was on the fourth floor of a multi-storey block in a nice District, and when she opened her front door he was taken aback by the lush decor and furnishings he spied as he entered the property. 'Nice pad my dear, do you live alone?'

'Yes, there is no one else here apart from you, come on in I'll put some coffee on unless you fancied something stronger'.

'No thanks, coffee's fine'.

They sat opposite each other and each told their stories over the next two hours. She was taken aback a few times when Jake mentioned the number of women he had encountered over the last few years, but was certainly impressed by the variety of life he had been witness too.

Her tale consisted of work, work, work, with Gym training three times a week and the occasional meal out with friends from work. There was no-one in her life at present and the way things were going there would be no-one in the future, then as she finished, her demeanour changed to sadness, thinking what a mundane life she had.

Jake looked at her and thought she should be in the prime of her life and enjoying it to the full, surely there had to be a special person out there somewhere for her.

'I sound rather boring Jake, in fact my life has been rather boring for years, and I appear to be in rather a deep rut and my legs aren't long enough to get me out, any suggestions?'

Jake smiled at her before saying, 'Someone will come along and sweep you off your feet before you know it, you are extremely intelligent, are great company, you must turn the eye of many a person your age, so take a chance and drop your guard. Things will change one day and all these doubts you harbour will evaporate and you'll wonder what all the fuss was about'. As he finished his lecture he looked her in the eye and realised that the lightbulb moment was there behind her eyes as if she had just thought of something. She got up from the chair, walked over to him and planted a kiss fully on his lips. 'Thank you Jake, you have just given me the talk I required from someone. As you will be heading back to the UK soon I would like to be quite candid with you'. She took a deep breath before continuing 'Over the last two years I have struggled with my sexuality, that's why I haven't been out with anyone, male or female. So I just put everything into my work, which appeared successful as my promotion to Inspector shows the dedication I have to my police work. But over the last few months my thoughts have wavered, and I feel I have more of an affinity with my own sex, mainly with intellect and conversation and not sexually, I hope you can see my confusion'.

'You are very brave to talk to me in this way, but for your own peace of mind I think it would do you good to talk to a Specialist on these matters before you put anything into practice, there is nothing wrong with thinking what you do but if you put it into reality you might have a shock, or be treated badly by saying or doing the wrong thing. Do you understand what I mean'.

'I completely understand Jake, I thank you for your candidness and understanding. I will follow your suggestion and see what pans out'.

'Please give me a ring in a few months time to let me know how you are'. he asked like a doting uncle.

'I will indeed, now I had better return you to your Auntie Choo before you get into trouble' she said with a smile.

The drive back in the car was taken in silence but as they pulled up outside the house she turned and thanked him again. He kissed her on both cheeks and finally on the lips and said 'In another life I would have answered your doubts'.

'I know what you mean, thank you for a lovely day and I'll speak to you soon'.

As he closed the passenger door the car pulled aways swiftly down the road and as she reached the junction the horn sounded once for a final goodbye.

He walked into the Hall to be greeted by the intoxicating smell of Chinese food. 'I'm in the kitchen Jake, come and tell me what you have been up to today?'

He sat at the table and went through his time on the boat, the Koala Sanctuary, and his conversation with Chi back at her flat.

Auntie carried on with the cooking, but after a lull she sat down beside him and said, 'The dear girl appears troubled but I must agree with your suggestion, and I hope she takes heed of your wise words'.

Jake turned and kissed her on the forehead.

'I hope you'r hungry, I've made a feast for us, mainly to thank you for my presents yesterday'. She put a number of dishes on the table together with a large bowl of steaming rice and noodles, telling Jake to tuck in, he did so with no hesitation.

The evening was spent reading and they both retired to bed at 10pm.

Chapter 30

Jake's last day in Australia had arrived and he intended to treat Auntie to a day out in Brisbane, to do whatever she wanted. He got up early and dressed in a new outfit, packing the remaining items in his suitcase.

Walking into the kitchen Auntie was busy setting the table for their breakfast, welcoming him with a bright 'Good morning Jake, how are you today'.

'Bright and breezy Auntie thank you, I have booked my return flight to the UK for tomorrow, and today I wish to spend the day pampering you, to do whatever you fancy, apart from breakfast there will be no cooking for you as we will eat lunch and dinner out'.

Taken aback for a moment she looked sternly at Jake before replying with 'What do you have in mind Jake?'

'As I said today is your day, what would you like to do, visit any of the attractions in Brisbane that you haven't seen yet, some more retail shopping, trip down the river, whatever you would like to do today I'lll make happen'.

'Let's have some breakfast first and I'll give it some thought' she said turning and putting more bits and pieces on the table and turning on the percolator.

'What can I tempt you with for breakfast?'

'Toast and coffee is fine with me Auntie thank you'.

A little while later after they had finished their restricted menu, Jake sat back waiting for Mrs Choo to tell him where she would like to go today.

'Perhaps another visit to the shopping mall and a saunter around them, I expect you would also like to pick up a few things to take back to the UK, then we could have some lunch in the area. See how I feel after that as to what we do in the afternoon, if that's OK with you Jake?'

'I am your servant today Auntie, take as long or short a time that you feel happy with, please don't feel you have to do anything to make me happy. If you have had enough after lunch we can just return home, then pop down the road for our evening meal'.

'Fine Jake, perhaps you could drive again today, I can then conserve my energy for today's little adventure'.

'Certainly Auntie, let's clear up and we'll leave whenever you are ready, there is no hurry'.

Parking in the lower level of the multi-story car park they took the lift up to the second storey and took the walkway to the shopping mall.

They window shopped for a while before Jake said he wished to look in the small shop that he had been in on his last visit. The old lady smiled as he entered and said 'Ah nice, kind Englishman come back to buy more treasure from my humble establishment'.

'Good morning to you young lady, I was impressed during my last visit, but I see you have restocked with a number of fine items'.

'Flattery will get you everywhere, what have you seen that has taken your fancy?'she asked with interest, and hoping for a good sale.

'Nothing in particular, but I would like to browse for a while' Jake replied not wishing to let her force his hand into an early purchase. Looking through the window he noticed Mrs Choo casting her eyes over the various items on display, so he thought he would ask her to join him in the shop. As they came back inside the two ladies exchanged pleasantries in what Jake surmised was Cantonese, with the shopkeeper spreading her hands in a gesture of 'look at all I have'.

Jake asked Auntie if there was anything in the window that took her eye, an angry look passed over her face as she said there was nothing she required, but suggested a few items that he could take back for his family.

After another fifteen minutes he had parted with the equivalent of almost three hundred pounds, but the items he had purchased he was really happy with.

Next was a shop that Auntie wished to visit, a perfumery which also sold scented candles. Jake held a shopping basket as she walked along the aisles with items being placed in the basket as they worked their way along. Then as they reached the counter he added a new razor to their goods and paid for the items, after being admonished by Auntie.

'Where to next Auntie?' he asked her, feeling that they ought to return to the car so he could unburden himself from their recent purchases.

'There is just one more shop I would like to visit and it's on street level, so we can put the two bags in the car.

Returning to ground level Jake followed in her wake, before they stopped outside a Jeweller's, she walked in and approached a Chinese man behind the counter. They exchanged pleasantries in Cantonese, before the man produced three trays of gold rings. Auntie turned and asked Jake what was his birth month, he replied August. The assistant asked Jake for his hand and placed a 'sizer' on his pinky finger, then put one of the trays in front of the two shoppers. Auntie looked Jake in the eye and said 'I wish to purchase this ring for you to thank you for everything you have done for my family and to keep us in your thoughts whenever you look at this ring'.

A tear fell onto his face as he kissed her on the cheek, and gave her a hug, unable to speak he tried the ring that was offered to him, it was a perfect fit.

'OK Jake?' she asked.

'I'm sorry Auntie, I'm overwhelmed as you can see, you are such a special person to me'.

She removed her purse and handed over her Debit card for payment. The assistant put the ring in a case and carefully wrapped it for her.

Lost for words as they left the shop he thanked her for the generous gift and said he would treasure it forever.

They turned left as they left the shop, it was obvious that Auntie knew exactly where she fancied having lunch today, after crossing the road they had to walk another hundred yards or so before she opened the door to a Chinese Restaurant and walked in.

They were greeted by a smartly suited elderly man whom Jake assumed was the Manager or Owner, then after a few words were spoken between them they followed the man to a table close to the kitchen. As they sat down, the man moved away and she explained why they were visiting this establishment today.

'Mr Li, the owner is a member of my Art Class, that was why he welcomed me so kindly, you will certainly enjoy today's meal as we'll be having the Special, which is what the owners eat and not available to the Public'.

There were a number of filled table even at this early hour, mostly with Oriental customers that were either on holiday or as he thought local residence. He felt quite honoured being placed so close to the kitchen, it was obviously due with his friendship to Auntie.

The man returned with menu's for them and asked what they would like to drink. Jake asked for a beer, Auntie plumping for a pitcher of iced water. Looking at the menu Jake was surprised to see that it was not in English but just the unmistakable Chinese signage.

He quickly looked at his companion, who was smiling at him and said 'What do you fancy Jake' and then laughed, knowing full well he had no idea what anything meant.

Jake returned her smile before answering 'I'll have the same as you'.

'The menu's are just for show and a laugh on my part, I already ordered when we walked in, we are having the Banquet, which is a specialty here'.

Over the next hour and a half Jake was subjected to the most delicious and unusual food that his taste buds had ever encountered, and he could only repeatedly say how wonderful the food was to his companion at regular intervals.

When the meal was finished Mr Li came over with the broadest grin, asked Auntie something in Chinese before turning to Jake and said 'You enjoy?'

Jake smiled and said 'More than enjoy, I have never tasted such delicious food, thank you, could I have the bill please'.

'No bill Mrs Choo is friend and you are her 'son' from England, this my treat to you'.

Feeling absolutely gobsmacked he turned towards Auntie and said 'I need to give him something to thank him for the meal, do they have a charity box or something ?'.

She turned to Jake before saying 'Please don't mention money to him as he would be quite offended, this is certainly an unusual gesture for him'.

I have known him for a while now and this is certainly against the grain for him. When we leave just be demonstrative with your handshake, he will be happy with that'.

As they stood to leave the man followed them out and Jake turned and offered his hand which was taken and he shook it vigorously, he said something in Chinese that made Auntie smile, as they turned and walked away.

'What were you smiling at?' Jake asked.

'He said how unusual it was for non Chinese man to shake his hand with such force, but it made it worthwhile and he was glad that I brought you to his establishment'.

They pulled out of the car park and headed home, bringing in their purchases once there, Auntie suggested a cup of coffee as Jake took his purchases to the bedroom.

Taking out his passport and putting it in his jacket together with his return ticket he packed the remaining items in his suitcase, and went back to the Lounge to read his book, Auntie came in with the coffee and asked what time his flight was tomorrow.

'I have to be at the airport by 11am so I'de better book a taxi for the morning. Unless you would like to go out again this evening Auntie, I would like to spend the rest of the time home here with you and finish this book'.

'I have had enough for today thank you Jake, I'll just do a light tea and we can have another English Breakfast in the morning, what do you think?'

'I'm relieved actually, it's been a hectic few days here and after I get back home I will have jet lag to contend with again. However I will have an evening out with a friend in London, before going to Kent to disperse the ashes of a relation of mine out into the North Sea'.

'That's sorted then Jake' Auntie replied with a certain thankfulness in her demeanour.

After a sandwich and cake they settled down with books before retiring early at just after 10am.

Chapter 31

Jake took his suitcases down and placed them in the hallway ready for his departure, in anticipation of the taxi 's arrival, he walked into the kitchen where Auntie was busying herself with their last breakfast together.

'Good morning' he said with a smile on his face, as he carefully placed a kiss on her cheek, careful not to take her attention away from the stove.

Without turning her head she said 'I hope your hungry as there is a large meal coming up for you today'.

He smiled and sat at the table that had already been laid out, and was lost for words. A cup of coffee was placed on a coaster, then a large plate of food was put in front of him. On it was two fried eggs, three rashers of bacon, fried potatoes, mushrooms, together with fried bread and tomatoes on top.

Salivating at the lovely start to the day, no sooner had Auntie took her place at the table before he started tucking into his plate of loveliness.

The time quickly went by as they chatted about what they had done since Jake's arrival, after which they tidied up their breakfast dishes before going into the Lounge to read. Jake was still only three quarter of the way through the book which Auntie had noticed, and said for him to take it back with him so he could read more on his long trip home. Jake thanked her for the gesture and confirmed he would telephone her as soon as he had finished in London and arrived back home in Dorset.

There was a knock on the door signalling the arrival of his taxi, but before opening the door he hugged her and told her to enjoy herself with her new hobbies and he would be keeping in touch with her regularly. They were both in tears as the front door opened, the driver took his cases and put them in the boot, then got back in the car to wait for his passenger. Jake could hardly speak as he bade a final farewell to Auntie Choo who stood on the entrance porch and waved vigorously as the vehicle drove off.

'Emotional farewell sir?' the driver speculated.

'It was indeed, I'm off back to England and that dear lady is a very special person in my heart. She is not a relation of mine but I have grown very fond of her over the last few years'. 'I can understand that sir, it's a good job they invented 'Whats App' it's a cheap way to talk to people far away, and also to see them, almost as if they were close by'.

'You are exactly right, I have a long day ahead, giving me lots to ponder over before I arrive back in the UK'.

The remainder of the journey was taken in silence as the understanding driver realised his fare was in rather a sombre mood and wanted time to think.

Pulling up outside the Terminal the driver jumped out collected a trolley before placing the cases on it ready for Jake, then stood before him to collect his fare. 'Have a nice flight sir' he remarked before getting back into his vehicle and lining up in the taxi rank ready for his next fare.

Checking in at the Singapore Airlines counter Jake collected new labels for his return flight and attached them to his cases. Then through passport control and into the Lounge for First Class and Business passenger's.

He had an hour and a half's wait before boarding would take place, so he took advantage of the facilities and sat back in a plush seat and read the local paper.

To his surprise an announcement was called over the tannoy asking 'Mr Tordale to please exit the VIP Lounge, and meet a visitor in the corridor outside. Astonished at this call he followed the announcement by opening the door, and walking out into the Corridor to be met by Inspector Chi in full uniform, smiling from ear to ear. 'I bet that was a surprise for you Jake, I rather liked the discreet call, imagining what your reaction would be, thinking to yourself that you wouldn't be flying today. I thought it would be nice to say a final cheerio to you at the Airport and thank you the time you allowed me during your short stay'.

He walked towards her and hugged her in a tight embrace. 'I hope you find what you are looking for my love, my time in Brisbane spent with two lovely ladies could not have made my visit here any better'.

As he pulled away she gave him a long lingering kiss on the lips before pulling away. 'I've a feeling that you might have made a momentous decision for me Jake and confirmed the way I will be moving forward, thank you'.

'It's my pleasure, I wish I could have stayed longer and spent more time in your company, however I have a lot to sort out back in the UK that cannot wait, so finally thanks for coming to see me off and before I start blubbering you had better get back to work Officer'.

She gave him a final kiss, turned and walked away without further ado.

He returned to the Lounge and immersed himself back into the newspaper rather than ponder over her final farewell.

He was three quarters of the way through the paper, when the flight was called. There was a bustle in the VIP Lounge as his fellow passengers started collecting their hand luggage and proceeding to the Departure Area.

Formality's were rapid as they handed over their tickets and for the third time he handed over his passport before boarding the plane through the covered walkway.

He was shown to his seat by the Singapore hostess who handed him another paper and magazine, he put them in his carry on bag alongside his book that Mrs Choo gave him about a Samurai warrior's life and settled in.

The aircraft lifted off half an hour later on its way to Singapore, during the flight he was treated to food and drink, spending most of the time watching a film and deep into his book. The journey flew by without any hiccups and they landed for refuelling on time.

The stopover took a couple of hours before they lifted off for the onward journey to London. Twenty five hours in the air is a long time, but Jake being the seasoned traveller he was could pace himself with a film, eating, drinking, reading and sleeping thus making the long flight acceptable. As they started their descent into the Capital the usual announcement was given out by the Captain, confirming that the flight was on time and explaining what the weather conditions were in the UK.

As the passengers funnelled through passport control and the baggage area Jake rang the Hotel, giving his name to confirm his booking of an overnight stay. Walking outside he boarded the shuttle bus that dropped him there and within twenty minutes he was settled in his room and tucked up into bed for much needed sleep on home soil.

Chapter 32

A surreal feeling crept over him as he slowly opened his eyes the next morning, as travelling through many time zones over the past few weeks, he didn't know if it was Christmas or New Year, however after a few minutes of contemplation and reminiscence he decided he was almost home.

He rose showered, shaved and dressed then went down for breakfast before calling Henry to confirm he was home and would soon be making his way to Kent to meet the Solicitor and finalise arrangements to disperse his relations ashes into the North Sea. On his return to London he would call into the office for a chat and take up his offer of a meal out.

It was 10am when he rang Daniel Frobisher the Solicitor and explained that he was on his way to Kent, and if it was convenient today to catch a boat out into the North Sea.

He hesitated for a while before confirming that he would make the arrangements for him if he could get to the office by 1pm.

Jake carried his belongings down into the foyer and paid his dues to the Receptionist, before collecting his car keys. He drove out of the car park and pulled up outside the front doors to load his cases, set the sat nav before pulling out of the Terminal and pointing the car in the direction of Kent.

The Kent countryside was looking lovely today as the sun shone over the green fields, it almost felt like spring apart from the chilly conditions outside. He was glad that somewhere in the bowels of his suitcase he was still carrying his overcoat, gloves and scarf which he would surely need for his boat trip out into the North Sea.

He drove into the parking space behind the Solicitor's office just before 1pm, before walking into the office he decided to locate his warm clothing and put them on before travelling down to the harbour.

As he opened the door, the Receptionist recognised him and stood to greet him with a 'Good morning Mr Tordale, it's so nice to see you again' before walking to the Solicitor's door, knocking and saying 'Mr Tordale is here for you Mr Frobisher'.

Frobisher stood up as Jake walked in and shook his hand vigorously before saying 'You look ready for the chilly Kent weather today sir'.

'It's quite balmy to what I encountered in Washington a little while ago, so Daniel what's the situation today, are we OK to carry out what's required of me?'

'Everything's under control, I have the ashes to hand and the boat is moored ready for you. Would you like to shoot off now and get it over with or do you fancy a spot of lunch first?'

'I think I would rather make a move now, then after I return if my stomach is up to it we could have something before we return here, if that's OK?'

'Fine bye me, would you like me to drive, or are you happy to take your's?'

'I'll drive, I've been sat in an aeroplane for a long period of time and I feel that driving is quite soothing and gradually bringing me back to normal life'.

'Right, then let's go' he said turning and retrieving the box containing the ashes of Jake's relative, whom unfortunately he had never met.

It was a 45 minute drive to the coast and as he parked alongside the harbour a swarthy man of about sixty walked over to the car, he was dressed in a well worn wooly hat, yellow wet weather gear and a grey woollen jumper.

'Morning Mr Frobisher, I take it that this is passenger and your Client, Mr Tordale, I'm Wilbur Friend, pleased to meet you sir' he said shaking Jake's hand.

'Good morning Mr Friend, it looks a bit choppy today, how far do you intend going out?'Jake asked.

'As far as you want sir, I would suggest at least a mile if that's alright with you'.

'Fine, I'm ready when you are' Jake replied with a little trepidation, handing his keys over to Frobisher. Jake followed in the sailor's wake as they strode towards a small fishing boat, blue and white in colour moored further along the harbour. Frobisher had quickly returned to the warmth of the Lexus and watched the boat as they quickly pulled away from the mooring and headed out into the choppy grey waters of the North Sea.

Jake was still strapping himself into his life jacket as Wilbur said 'See that buoy over there it's a guide that I use, it tell's me I'm a mile off shore, so when we are in line with it I'll just drift after cutting the engine, to allow you to say a few words and disperse the ashes'.

'Thank you Wilbur, I won't take long' Jake answered.

The following 10 minutes was spent in silence, with just the call of the seagulls and the throb of the boat's engines, the only sound breaking the silence.

Jake's memory returned to his grand father's life, as he pondered on what information he had never been privy to about the lovely old man, and now finally he was putting to rest the remains of what was most likely a lovely woman who had been in love with his relation.

Life is so precious he pondered, years passed so quickly and records of one's past relative's if not kept in words, get lost forever, and once that person has gone their details can never be retrieved.

He was shaken out of his reminiscence as the engine sound was cut and he realised that the boat had reached its destination.

He looked at Wilbur who nodded his head, as if telling him silently that it was time. Jake stood and collected the box from the wheelhouse, walked to the stern and emptied the contents into the water, saying a few words under his breath, before returning to his seat with his head bowed for a while.

The Captain started the engine and turned the boat towards shore, drifting into the harbour in silence. As they moored Jake shook the man's hand and palmed him a fifty pound note thanking him for his time and the use of his boat.

He returned the life jacket then slowly walked back to his car to be greeted by Daniel Frobisher who asked if everything went OK?.

His companion just nodded and got into the car and pulled away from the harbour making his way back to the Solicitor's Office in silence.

Pulling into the car park, he came out of his thoughts, before apologising to his passenger of his rudeness on the drive back. 'Do you still fancy something to eat Daniel?' he asked.

Chapter 32

'I think it best if you return to London Jake, before the rush hour traffic descends on the Capital, perhaps another time when you're in the area'.

'Thank you for organising today Daniel, unfortunately I'm a little more upset than I thought I would be about what I have just done, for a poor old lady that I never had the chance to meet, so yes, I think I'll make my way back, and thank you again' he said shaking the Solicitor's hand quite vigorously.

Jake pulled away as Frobisher disappeared back into his Office, and he was glad of the solitude as he prepared for the drive back.

Pulling into the underground car park he began to feel more himself, up in the lift his thoughts returned to his meeting with Henry Bates and finally the drive back to Wisteria Cottage.

Walking into the Reception Area he was greeted by a new lady who smiled as he approached her desk. 'Good afternoon Mr Tordale, I understand you have come to see Mr Bates, head on up he's waiting for you'.

Jake checked the nameplate in front of her and replied 'Thank you Eleanor, it's nice to meet you'.

She blushed before replying 'Nice to meet you also Mr Tordale'.

Jake knocked and walked into the office and to his surprise there sat opposite his Boss was non other than George Adams.

A huge smile spread across Jake's face as he spied his friend, who looked considerably better than when they exited the aircraft from Washington.

'Great to see you looking so well George, how are things?' he asked.

'Better than I could have thought, I have had superb care in the Hospital here, they have had to do a few tweaks to my old body but I am now recuperating well thank's to you'.

Henry broke in with 'I've invited George to join us tonight at Marcus's for a slap up meal to thank you both for bringing Wither's back to Blighty to serve his lengthy prison term'.

'Excellent sir, I haven't eaten since breakfast so I'm sure the delights of that restaurant will be enjoyed even more this evening, what time are we booked in?'

'An hour's time Jake, will you last out until then?' Henry asked whilst grinning at him.

'Certainly, but in the meantime I could kill for a coffee' he said with a beaming smile.

Henry rang through to the Receptionist who walked in five minutes later with a tray holding three cups, milk, sugar and a cafetière of coffee.

The next three quarters of an hour was spent talking about what happened in the USA with George and then Jake's visits to Singapore and Australia.

Henry brought the conversation to a close as it was time to get a taxi to take them to Marcus's restaurant for a slap up meal. George had never been to the establishment but said he would be on his best behaviour whilst indulging in the fine cuisine.

The taxi pulled up outside the impressive frontage at a minute to seven, and the doors were opened by a muscular fellow who was there to keep any 'riff raff' out.

As they approached the usual table that Henry preferred, Marcus himself came out of the kitchen and shook Henry and Jake's hands who had visited many times, before Henry introduced George to the World renowned Chef.

'What are you having tonight Henry drink wise?' Marcus asked.

'We have a celebration, so I think a bottle of bubbly would serve us just right, as a starter of course' Henry replied with a grin.

'I take it food wise, you would like a 'Special' of mine to welcome Mr Adam's for the first time?'

'Most acceptable Marcus, thank you'.

'If you two would prefer a beer or two during the meal, just ask the waiter and he will deliver it for you'.

An hour and a half later there were three beaming smiles on the diners faces as they completed their meals, whilst sitting back, relaxing with coffees and brandy's.

The Dining Room was filling up as the evening drew on, with more diners arriving, so the three of them stood as Marcus shook hands with them, trusting that they had all enjoyed the fare.

Marcus handed a small envelope to Henry who quickly put it in his pocket, the other two realising that it most likely contained the invoice, that would be paid at the end of the month.

Jake turned to his Boss and said 'Due to the alcohol I have had I'm going to book into the usual Hotel and head back home in the morning.

I can walk from here sir, and I'll leave the two of you to get a taxi back to the office'.

Shaking hands all round they parted company at the door, just as the taxi pulled up.

Walking into the foyer of the Hotel Jake had used previously, the Receptionist recognised him and said 'Just the one night Mr Tordale'. Smiling he said 'Yes please, and I'll stay for breakfast as well, thank you'.

Chapter 33

Before going up to his room he indulged in a quick drink at the Bar, just a small beer and a coffee afterwards. The same waiter was on duty as on his previous stay there, remarkably he remembered his name, with, 'Nice to see you again Mr Tordale, have you been on your travels again?'

The Bar was empty so he spent a little time indulging the man in the various Countries he had visited since Christmas, then when he finished the Bartender walked away to clean a few glasses, with a strange look on his face.

Just before ten o'clock he decided to go up to his room, so he paid for his drinks and took the lift to the third floor, on opening the door he realised he didn't possess any luggage which meant no change of clothing and not even a toothbrush. This wouldn't do at all, so he turned, exited the room and took the lift back down to the Reception Desk, asking the man behind the desk if there was anywhere he could purchase clothing and a toothbrush this time of the night.

A smile spread across the man's face realising Jake's situation before offering details of the shops that were open within walking distance.

Half an hour later he returned with his purchases, nodded to the Receptionist, then retiring to his room feeling quite sheepish as he took the lift again.

Rising early the next morning he had a long hot shower before changing into his new clothing, then placing his dirty clothes in the bag, together with the toothbrush, ready to take away after he had had his breakfast.

Jake plumped for a full English with toast on the side and an orange juice, together with a black coffee.

Collecting his shopping bag from his room, he walked into Reception, handed back the key and paid for his overnight stay, then made his way back to the underground car park to collect the Lexus. Although it was still rush hour he decided to make his way back to Dorset and two hours later he parked outside his Cottage.

Chapter 33

Scanning the front elevation of the building he spied the box containing the bell for the Alarm System, and to all intents and purposes could not see any visible damage to his property. Opening the front door he forgot that the alarm would be activated, so before it went off he walked to the unit on which the telephone stood and noted the number he required that was left by the Installers and shut the system down.

A number of envelopes were spread across the mat together with a few more neatly stacked on the table alongside the telephone, obviously put there when the men were in the house fitting the alarm, so he scooped them all up and dropped them on the table.

He took his belongings upstairs and put them in his bedroom, he then checked all the windows upstairs and down, and was extremely happy with the workmanship that showed no disruption to the windows or surrounding areas.

Before addressing the post, he arranged for a Bank Transfer to be made for the balance of his invoice, that had been left in an envelope, that also contained the Alarm details.

Gasping for a drink he put the kettle on for a cup of coffee, then sat at the table to open the remainder of the accumulated mail.

Once finished he walked upstairs to collect the dirty washing from his case and put them in the washing machine, following that he separated the various presents he had purchased in America and Australia for the family and put them to one side to wrap later.

Feeling a tad tired he sat in his favourite armchair and had a snooze for an hour before deciding to walk down to the pub for a couple of good old English pints and a natter with Bert the Landlord.

When he woke it was closer to two hours he had been asleep, obviously his body needed it he thought, so after a quick stretch he donned his outer clothes and was just shutting the front door as the landline rang. Turning he picked up the receiver with his usual 'Jake Tordale'.

'Hello Mr Tordale, it's Brian Fellow's here from the Alarm Company, I just called to thank you for your payment that I've just received. I trust you are pleased with the work that we carried out, and on time as agreed?'

'I certainly am Brian, thank you very much indeed and should anyone I know require any work in your line, I will certainly pass them your way'.

Thank you again' Fellow's replied and put the phone down.

Jake then, set the alarm, locked the front door and walked down to the Pub for a much needed drink.

It was just five thirty as he opened the door, but there were already half a dozen customers sat enjoying drinks, then as he approached the Bar Bert was pouring his pint, with a wide grin on his face, obviously waiting for Jake's details on his recent trip away.

'Good evening Jake, nice to see you, how did your trip away go, Singapore and Australia if I remember correctly, anything of interest to tell me?'

'Perhaps after my first pint has settled I might release some tasty morsels for you?'

'Excellent, I think Tony's popping in for a drink around six, I'll get the missus to serve here and sit down with the both of you for a natter when he arrives'.

'OK Bert, I'll take a pew in the corner'.

As usual the first pint slid down his throat with ease and as he walked up to get another in walked Tony Bailey. 'Pint Tony?' Jake asked.

Tony nodded in agreement with a 'Thank's mate'.

Bert smiled and said he would bring their beer's over to the table.

Tony was just about to say something to Jake when Bert arrived carrying a tray with three pints on, he sat down alongside them and handed over their glasses, retaining one for himself.

Tony stared at Bert for a second, before the Landlord explained that Jake was going to divulge the details of his trip abroad.

A grin spread over Tony's face as he realised that another sparkling tale was about to be described to the pair of them.

'Let's just enjoy our drinks for a few minutes and I'll then tell all' Jake said with a smile.

Before he could commence his tale Bert was called back to the Bar to change a barrel, so Jake looked at his friend and muttered quietly 'He's like an old woman lately, he's got to know where I've been and what I've been up to?'

'I understand his interest Jake, I'm no better, your life is 50 times more interesting than ours being stuck in the same old routine day in and day out, so I look forward to your most detailed report as much as Bert does'.

Ten minutes later Bert returned saying 'Sorry for that, where were we, Oh yes Jake I'm all ears'.

'Well as you know I went off to America at short notice to locate a friend of mine who had gone off the radar. I flew to Phoenix, Arizona first, hired a car to drive to San Diego, a short flight to LA where I found that he had flown to Washington. I tried his phone number before I left and it was answered by a patient in a hospital there, he said he was in a bad way, so I flew the next day to meet up with him. He had been set upon by two thugs who gave him quite a pasting and his stay in the hospital took a few weeks. During my wait I met up with a lady friend who I met in Santorini on holiday last year, and we had a week doing the touristy spots in Washington, then I returned with George to the UK a few weeks ago. After that I had a letter from a solicitor in Singapore asking me to sign a few papers relating to a property I was selling out there, but the letter had arrived whilst I was in the States and I arranged to deliver the details by hand. I decided whilst I was halfway there I would take an onward flight to Brisbane, Australia to spend a few days with an old lady who is very close to my heart. When I returned I had a small duty to perform, which was to disperse the ashes of an aunt of mine into the North Sea, which had been her wish. Since I had been away I have had an Alarm System put in at the Cottage. There I think that brings you both up to date' as he finished he took a long swig of his beer, whilst peering over the glass to see his friends faces looking aghast at him.

Bert spoke first 'Do you chaps fancy a chaser?' while shaking his head.

Jake said 'Brandy please Bert'.

Tony's face was a picture, and he could only nod in agreement.

As the landlord walked to the Bar a couple of other people walked in, both of them regulars that would be joining them on their trip to France for the rugby, and a few minutes later they were all sat together discussing their impending visit abroad.

After another pint Jake took his leave, shaking hands with everyone, making his way along the lane back to his Cottage. As the door opened the now welcome sound of the alarm buzz reminded him that he had to de-activate the device.

Making himself a coffee, he sat down to make a quick list of items he required to stock his fridge, freezer and food cupboard which he would replenish the next day, realising he wouldn't be galavanting off again until a trip to Devon to see the family and finally the journey to France for the rugby Grand Slam game.

Chapter 34

First thing the next morning he finished his shopping list before cleaning the windows of the Lexus from a sharp frost that hung over the area. Driving into the town he parked outside the Butchers, strode into the shop with his list of requirements. The assistant smiled at him and asked the usual question 'Have you got other shopping to carry out Jake, as it'll take me half an hour to prepare your order'.

Jake was ready for the question and replied 'I have to get groceries in the Supermarket next door and I'm popping into the Solicitors so I'll be at least an hour, OK?'

'Fine, see you later Jake'.

Walking into the large superstore he collected a trolley, then made his way up and down the aisles, stopping occasionally to talk to people he knew, before turning into the last area before the checkouts, and coming across Joyce Bailey who was deep in thought as to what wine to purchase.

'Good morning Joyce nice to see you in different surroundings, may I help you with your wine selection or are you OK'

'Well, I enjoyed the wine you brought to the meal on Boxing Day but Tony threw the bottle away and I can't remember the name of it, as I thought I'de get a couple of bottles in when you lot are all away watching the rugby in France'.

Jake smiled at her and pointed to the wine in question, Joyce put two bottles in her trolley, thanked Jake, and walked to the checkout.

Strange thought Jake, a bit short on Joyce's reaction, still he thought she most likely wanted to get back to the farm to carry out the numerous daily duties she had to perform.

Jake collected half a dozen bottles of red and white to keep in, then looked at his trolley which was half full and decided enough for today.

When he approached the checkout he noticed Joyce just exiting the shop, only ten feet away from the till area but she made no effort to turn and say goodbye, strange he thought.

After paying for his goods he took the trolley to the car and loaded the groceries into the boot of his car, before returning to the butcher's to see if his order was ready.

A smile spread across the man's face as Jake walked in before saying 'All ready Jake, is it cash or card?'

'Card, what's the damage?'

'£92.00 I'm afraid, I assume it's just for you, so I've put the bits and pieces in separate bags for freezing, I hope that's OK?'

'Yes it is, I intended to ask you to do it for me anyway but I forgot, thanks' he answered handing over his Debit card.

'Bye for now' he said finally walking out of the shop and back to the Lexus again.

He then walked across the road and entered the Solicitor's office, nodding to Joan before asking if Bryan was available for a chat.

Joan smiled then said 'No appointment I assume Jake?'

'I was just passing and wanted to ask him a question, I will only be a few minutes' he replied with a coy look.

Joan stood walked to Bryan Fairfax's door, knocked before opening the door and saying 'Jake Tordale's here. could you spare a minute or two?'

'Of course', he replied 'send him in'.

As Jake entered Fairfax stood and shook his hand, 'What do I owe this pleasure, dear boy'.

'I need to make out a new Will, Bryan, I have received a few investments that have come to fruition recently and I wish to prepare a new Will, there's nothing wrong with me health wise, I just need some sound advice on that quarter'.

'No problem Jake, have you finished navigating the world now and starting to settle down to retirement, or are there still a few adventure's left in you?'

'To be honest Bryan I think I have just about reached the end of the road on the adventure days, but you never know what's around the corner'.

'What about the day after tomorrow, about two o'clock, it should only take about an hour if that's alright with you'.

'Fine Bryan thank's very much' he stood, shook Bryan's hand, turned and walked out of the room, saying goodbye to Joan as he walked past her desk.

Walking back to the car, he realised how much he had to divulge to his Solicitor and thought he would prepare the details when he returned home, after putting away his purchases.

He was just getting into the car when he spotted Tony Bailey coming out of the Butcher's shop, a smile spread across his face as he noticed Jake, and shouted a greeting with 'Hold on a minute Jake'.

Jake closed the car door and walked around the vehicle as Tony approached with his arm outstretched ready for the shaking hands.

Jake was first to speak 'This has got to be a first seeing both you and Joyce in town at the same time , away from the farm, within an hour of each other'.

'I've just delivered some meat to the Butcher's and Joyce had some shopping to do in the Supermarket, so what have you been up to mate?'

'First, I've just bought some of your meat from the Butcher's, then I had to stock up on groceries, as I had virtually run out of everything whilst I've been away. Oh, I also popped in to see Bryan Fairfax about something, by the way, is everything OK with the two of you, only Joyce appeared quite pre-occupied in the supermarket and hardly spoke two words me?'

'Yes we're fine, it's been a bit hectic since the New Year and with me going away for a weekend to the rugby hasn't helped, but she's fine with it, it just mean's there will be a lot more work to sort out once I get back to catch up on with all the various chores'.

'If it makes things too difficult Tony I'm sure Bert wouldn't mind if you pulled out, its only a game of rugby after all, but its your call?'

'I know what you're saying Jake but I truly need some time away, although I enjoy the farm life sometimes it gets to me, so no, thanks for your thought's but I will be going to France' he said with finality.

'Ok Tony, I'll get off then, see you soon' Jake turned and walked back to the car and made his way along the lane to the Cottage.

Unloading all his purchases and putting them away took more than an hour, mainly due to his thoughts regarding his friend Tony's conversation and how intense farm work must be for him.

After pouring the hot water from the kettle into his cup, that had two spoons of instant coffee in, he sat at the Dining Room table and prepared a list of items he needed to amend for his Will. The Cottage would be sold on his demise and the proceeds would be split 50/50 with his two daughter's. The priceless MG in the garage would be sold at auction, the proceeds of which would be split between his three grandchildren. Now the tricky item, the money he had in the Bank. He would be guided by his Solicitor Bryan as to how this would be worded, and of course how best to show it on his amended Will.

The details completed he put the hand written document in the safe, whilst it was open he counted the money he had in cash, or various other currencies, and to his surprise found it totalled £10k.

With just a visit to Devon to see the family, a couple of hours with Maureen in Taunton on the way back, that just left the Rugby trip outstanding to complete his busy schedule.

There was of course the proposed meet up with Olivia for a holiday somewhere in Europe to organise, so he rang her mobile to find out when she would be available.

'What do you want now you lovely man, I'm too far away, but will see you soon I hope?'

'That's what I'm calling for Olivia, when would you be available for a couple of weeks away, only I thought I could organise a seven day holiday somewhere in Greece so that we can relax together and be pampered'.

'The earliest I will be able to get away will be the first week in May, where do you want to go in Greece, of course I'll leave it up to you?'

'What about a return visit to Santorini, if its OK with you I'll book the same Hotel I was in last year, I still have vouchers that the Manager gave me so why not use them in May?'

'What a good idea, shall I make arrangements to have the time off and meet you on the Island or shall I fly to London so we can go together?'

'Entirely up to you my dear, there will be plenty of time to make the final arrangements once I have booked the Hotel. Leave it with me and I'll get back to you OK?'

'Wonderful, you are so thoughtful, I'll have to repay you in some way I think best'.

'Just being with you will be all the payment I need, I'll be off now and send you an email once I have further news, bye'.

'Bye Jake, thank's for everything' and that was that as he ended up listening to the annoying end tone.

Then he walked over to the safe to retrieve the vouchers which gave the direct number for the Hotel and dialled the number. Although it was out of season he wondered if there was a skeleton staff still there keeping the property ready for out of season travellers.

The telephone was picked up after a couple of minutes with the confidant voice of the Manager that Jake had dealt with on his previous visit.

'Good Afternoon how may I help you'.

After a slight hesitation Jake replied 'Good afternoon to you my friend, my name is Jake Tordale I stayed with you last year and you were most kind to me'.

'Ah Mr Tordale how could I forget you my friend, what do I owe this pleasure?'

'I'm looking to return again the first week in May for two weeks and wonder if I could book my previous apartment for two weeks, but this time with myself and a lady companion'.

'No trouble at all sir, I will put your booking into the diary as we speak. Do you wish to pay directly to the Hotel or will it be through a package holiday?'

'I will pay directly to the Hotel, also if you remember when I left you gave me an envelope with vouchers in. I'll keep those until I arrive and it will pay for some meals or drinks'.

'That's quite alright sir, if you ring again with your flight times I'll arrange for you to be collected as before. Once I have the details I will give you the invoice figure and you can either pay by phone or when you arrive, I will leave that entirely up to you'.

'Thank you very much for your time and I'll be in touch with you later, goodbye for now'.

'Goodbye Mr Tordale, it's so nice to speak to you again'.

He thought to himself, that's one thing out of the way, next he checked flight times from Bristol for the first week in May for two, and then book two seats. Before doing anything else he sent off an email to Olivia confirming the date and details of flights from Bristol Airport, with a suggestion she arrived a day earlier and he could collect her from whichever Airport was best for her.

The computer pinged an instant reply from her with numerous emojis and an 'OK'

Right he thought that's a few things completed, now to make a list of other items to do.

First and foremost, a trip to Devon to see the families and take presents to them he had purchased from the various Countries he had visited since Christmas.

Secondly he would give a spring clean throughout the house tomorrow, the next day he had a meeting with Bryan regarding his Will.

Third on the agenda was a call to Mrs Choo, then a call to Inspector Chi, followed by an up to date call to Charlene in Washington.

Chapter 35

The following morning after breakfast he set out his agenda for the day, starting with phone calls to America, Australia and then to Devon.

Calls completed an hour and a half later, he set out an itinerary for his return holiday to Santorini with Olivia. He would need her full details to help him book their flights, once completed he would confirm the details with the Hotel Manager. As it was only February there was no immediate rush for these details, so he sent Olivia an email with confirmation that the Hotel was booked for the first week in May, and the details he required from her.

The rugby match in France would be taking place the following weekend so he needed to visit his children and grandchildren in Devon to give them their presents in the next few days. He decided to ring the girls and explain that he would be calling the day after tomorrow, arriving around noon. Should that be inconvenient and they would prefer to see him after their work had finished, he would call and see Maureen in Taunton on the way down to Devon rather than the reverse visit he had initially intended.

Clare answered the call on her mobile and confirmed she would prefer the second option of her father calling after five, as she thought it would be more convenient for her sister Sharon. However she would speak for everyone and arrange to meet at her house where they could all meet. Next, he rang Maureen explaining what his intentions were in 2 days time, thankfully she agreed saying she had nothing organised and would be pleased to go out to lunch with him.

He sat back and sighed, pleased with what he had just organised, noticing that the best part of the morning had passed by, he poured a coffee and sat back to check over the notes he had made for his visit to Bryan Fairfax tomorrow.

Later he hoovered the house throughout, stripped his bed, washed and dried the bedding before ironing them and remaking his bed.

Making himself a sandwich for lunch, he wasn't sure about the quiet life he had decided to take after the turmoil over the past couple of years, and thought he would ring Henry Bates to check up on his friend George Adam's health.

The phone was picked up almost immediately by Henry and a surprised voice answered 'I thought you had retired Mr Tordale, however it's nice to receive a call from you,'.

'Hi Henry, I thought I would just check up on George's condition, how is he fairing?'

'He's had a couple of operations, one on his leg and another on his arm, but apart from that he's on the mend. I hope to have him back to work next month, but is that all you rang for or do you have something else on your mind'.

'Well apart from going to France this weekend to see the final Six Nations match with the lads, a visit to Devon to see my family, and a holiday in May with Olivia I have nothing pressing and wondered if there was anything I could do for you at present?'

'I knew it, once you get a taste for the fast life it's difficult to leave it alone, especially in your case. Strangely in George's absence I have a little something I need doing but I would have to speak to you face to face, is it possible for you to come up to London early next week after your return from France. If so I will give you all the details then and if you are agreeable the jobs your's'.

'Sounds good to me sir, I'll drive up early on Monday and meet you in the office about ten' he replied.

'Excellent, see you on Monday old man'.

'Will do, bye for now'. With his mood lifted, he decided to give the Lexus the once over, check the tyres, oil, water etc, then give it a run into town and fill her up with fuel before his trek to Taunton, and then on to Devon.The rest of the day was spent pottering around in the garden and reading, before an early night beckoned and a good book to eventually send him off to sleep.

Chapter 36

Up early the next day he decided to take the MG out of the garage and take her out for a spin, then whilst he was out he would fill her up with fuel.

So after breakfast he went to the garage, removed the cover and checked the oil and water before driving out and down the lane, then making his way into the town past the Pub. The local garage was quiet this morning and the owner Reg made his way out as soon as he heard the unmistakable sound of the car pulling into the forecourt for fuel.

As Jake got out to speak to the Owner, Reg did a quick survey of the motor he had previously serviced and asked him if everything was alright. Jake quickly said 'she's in tip top order Reg, I just need to fill her up with fuel, thanks'.

'No problem, I'll get to it'.

They chatted as usual about everything local as the filling of the tank took place before Jake followed him into his old fashioned office and paid his dues.

Back in the car he drove back home, put the car back in its place , before putting the cover over it and locking the door.

He prepared himself a snack for lunch as two o'clock he had his appointment with the Solicitor to finalise and update his Will.

True to his word Bryan Fairfax completed the work on the Will in just under an hour, giving Jake a copy and retaining one in his safe should anything happen to his Client, they shook hands before Jake took his leave, saying goodbye to Joan on the way out.

On his way home he called into the Pub for a quick pint and a natter with Bert about things regarding the trip to France at the weekend, then drove home about five.

Tomorrow he would be calling to Taunton around midday to take Maureen out for lunch, before travelling down to Devon to visit his family and distribute their presents he had purchased whilst abroad.

The presents were still in one of the cases he had bought in America so rather than wrap them he thought it best to leave them there, and take them in the boot of the Lexus tomorrow.

He went up to the bedroom and took them out of the case and placed them on his bed, before putting individual labels on the presents for each recipient. Once done he put them back in the case and took it downstairs leaving it in the Hallway.

He then rang Maureen to double check that she was OK for lunch tomorrow, saying if so, he would be calling on her around noon.

She confirmed the arrangements saying she was really looking forward to his visit. He then rang Clare to clarify the previous arrangements, which she said was fine and that all the family would be there.

His computer pinged with an inbound email, so he opened it up and saw that he had a reply from Olivia with all the details he required to order the two seats to Santorini, so he put in a call to the Airport and paid for the flights, receiving a receipt and copy of tickets by return.

He then sent return email to Olivia asking her to arrange for a flight to arrive in England the day before to enable them to fly out the following day from Bristol.

He sat back satisfied on his day's work, before thinking of going down to the Swan for a slap up meal. A quick change of clothes and he made his way down the lane to his second home of late, to be greeted with Bert and Tony Bailey who were in animated conversation.

'Hello you two, everything alright?'

Bert smiled at him before saying 'We were just discussing the weekend and what we anticipated the result was going to be with the rugby, what do you think Jake?'

'It should be a very tight game as both teams are unbeaten up to this decider, so as long as it's a free flowing game it could go either way'.

Tony smiled before replying 'I am really looking forward to the whole affair, I can't remember the last time I left the farm, let alone fly abroad'.

Jake looked at him in astonishment before saying 'Although abroad its the shortest distance I have travelled for a few years by air'.

'Lucky bugger' Bert retorted, 'You'll have to tell us all about it over the weekend'.

'All depends how much liquid we consume' Jake answered.

Chapter 36

'Right get the beers in Bert, and could I have a look at the Special's for this evening, if their's a steak there I for one will be having one' Jake said in anticipation.

Bert looked at him before saying 'If there isn't I'll make sure you get one my friend, but don't tell everyone'.

Bert handed over the menu together with a separate piece of paper which read 'SIRLOIN, RUMP OR FILLET AVAILABLE for you, also Turf n' Surf if required, Signed Bert.

Jake smiled at the landlord before ordering the fillet medium rare with two large prawns.

'Can I get anything for you Tony, or are you just here for alcohol?'

'I'll just have a couple more beers before I return home for tea, thanks Bert, but I'll have a packet of pork scratching with the next round' Tony answered sheepishly .

The food as always was superb, there was not even a scrap left on Jake's plate as he wiped his mouth with his serviette.

They had talked together whilst Jake consumed his meal, mainly about the recent news in the town and local current affairs, before Tony took his leave after his third pint.

Jake ordered a brandy and anything Bert fancied, before paying his bill.

Walking back up the lane as the darkness started to envelope Dorset Jake mulled over the chat he had enjoyed with his two friends, whilst also thinking about his meeting with Maureen tomorrow lunchtime and then his visit to Devon to see his family.

As he turned the key in the lock and walked into the Hall his mobile rang, looking at the number he realised it was from Henry Bates.

'You're surely not working this time of the evening Henry are you?'

'No, I've just got home but just wanted a quick word with you about what we discussed earlier'.

'Oh yes, have there been further developments with that situation?' Jake asked.

'I have further details of the whereabouts that will help you, I would prefer not to divulge any more information over the phone but will tell you when we meet. A plane is available to take you from London City Airport around noon on Monday to your destination'.

'I'll get to the office at 9.30am which will give me plenty of time for us to go through the details, and get to the airport'.

'Excellent old man, look forward to seeing you, by the way enjoy the rugby'.

'Thanks very much Henry' Jake said finishing the call.

Chapter 37

A dull morning greeted Jake as he pulled back the bedroom curtains, but at least it was dry outside. He was tempted to take the MG down too Devon today but although the car had a good heater he would feel more comfortable inside the modern Lexus.

Having his cereal and pondering over what time he would leave for Taunton and Maureen, he was brought back to reality with a knock on the front door.

On opening it, he was confronted by Charlie his local postman, who greeted him with a smile and 'A parcel and numerous envelopes for you Jake'.

'Thank's Charlie' he replied 'A nice dry day for your job, everything OK with you?'

Charlie handed over the articles before saying 'The family have had lingering colds since Christmas, but apart from that everything is cushty thanks Jake' he turned and walked back to the Post Office van.

As he sat down in his chair in the kitchen he spread out the post on the table intrigued as to what was in the various envelopes and the parcel, but he thought he would finish his breakfast before seeing to them.

He poured himself a cup of tea before opening the post, starting with the parcel. Checking the postmark and stamps he noticed it had come from Australia, in fact Brisbane, so he carefully cut through the brown outer covering to be met with another covering inside that was sealed almost completely with sellotape. This item was about 300mm square and quite sturdy, so he commence the cutting of tape to expose within a white envelope and a painting.

A grin spread across his face as he realised it was obviously from Auntie Choo, most likely a painting from her recent Class. He opened the white envelope and read the note inside 'One of my attempts with the new paints you bought for me, I would appreciate your honest opinion dear boy. Auntie Choo.

A tear spread across Jake's cheek as he recognised that it was a portrait of her daughter, which was making him very emotional ,and extremely thoughtful of her to send it to him.

For someone who had only commenced painting in latter life he was very impressed with the way she had carefully reproduced a picture of her late and well loved daughter.

After wiping his face he placed the painting and letter to one side and commenced the opening of the letters.

One from Charlene in Washington, reminiscing over his recent visit to the States, and how much she had enjoyed his company.

A confirmation from the Solicitor in Singapore advising him that the funds had been despatched with a receipt and other details for him to keep in the safe.

A note from Bert with a receipt for his payment, plane ticket details, match day ticket, together with the itinerary for the weekend. Jake laughed at Bert's organisation skills assuming he had sent all these items to his fellow travellers as well.

A receipt and guarantee from the Alarm Company for the recent installation work, signed by the MD himself.

The remaining envelopes contained receipts for various purchases and a couple of flyers.

The rest of the early morning was spent cleaning and putting various items in the washing machine before retrieving his suitcase from the bedroom and placing it in the boot for his trip later.

As the time approached eleven he decided to make a move to Taunton to collect Maureen for lunch. He would let her decide on the venue as he was unsure where to suggest, then it would be most likely somewhere that Maureen had visited previously.

A nice leisurely drive to his first destination brought him to the kerb outside Maureen's house at ten to twelve, as usual as he walked up the path the door opened and she appeared ready for her lunch out. Jake greeted her warmly and asked where the next destination would be. She looked at him and smiled, before saying 'I've booked a table at The York Inn for 12.30pm so your timing is impeccable'

'Could you give me the address and I'll tap it in to my sat nav?'

'I knew you would ask me for that so I wrote it on a piece of paper' which she handed to him. As he opened the passenger door for

Maureen, he asked her how far the Pub was from her house, she replied less than twenty minutes.

He put in the address, and off they went. She asked a few questions as they drove along regarding what time he intended meeting his family in Devon, also how long it would take him to get there from Taunton, and before they realised it Jake pulled into the Pub car park. Jake opened the door to the hostelry for her and she strode to the Bar saying who she was and that she had a reservation. The man behind the Bar acknowledged her name and informed her she would be on table seven near the window, whilst asking what drinks they would like. Maureen asked for a white wine and Jake a tomato juice with the trimmings.

Looking through the menu Maureen said she would like soup of the day, followed by hand battered cod, chips and garden peas. Jake went for halloumi fries as a starter and gammon steak for main course.

As they sat down Maureen continued her enquiries of Jake, who replied as best he could about his recent trips. Their conversation was interrupted a few minutes later by the delivery of their starters. Jake asked if she fancied another drink with her main course, but she only asked for iced water, whilst Jake plumped for another tomato juice.

Their main course arrived just as a group noisily entered the Bar, and by the look of them they were walkers going by their haversacks that each one was carrying, but thankfully after ordering drinks and food they went outside to sit in the Beer Garden.

Only one other table was occupied in the Lounge and that was with an elderly couple, who looked like locals as there was little or no conversation being uttered as they consumed their food.

With plates empty Jake asked if she had room for a dessert, but she declined before asking if he would like to come back to her house for coffee or tea.

'That sounds very nice indeed Maureen, thank you. I'll just go and sort out the bill and we'll be off'.

The landlord asked if everything was satisfactory after taking the payment, which Jake said both of them were delighted with the meals.

The drive back was taken in silence after Maureen thanked him for taking her out. As they drove through Taunton, Jake asked if there was anywhere she needed to go whilst they were out. But she said no, there's nothing she needed, so they made their way back to the house.

She put the kettle on after showing Jake into the Lounge, then a little while later she came in with a tray full of cakes, biscuits and coffee.

She handed him a plate on which he put a piece of sponge and two biscuits to go with his cup of black coffee. They spent the next couple of hours talking about their lives since they had met previously then Jake offered to help with the dishes. She said that she had a suitable dishwasher and wouldn't think of asking him to help, and as the time had sped by he ought to make his way down the M5 to Devon, to see his family otherwise he would be late getting back home.

He thanked her for her company and trusted she had enjoyed her lunch saying they would have to do it again another time. With that he took his leave, then off in the Lexus to Devon.

He pulled up outside Clare's house at 5.30pm, no sooner had he turned off the engine than the front door opened and the whole family came out and made their way to him.

'Lovely to see you all together again, I think it best if you make your way back into the house, as the temperature has certainly dropped again. As they made their way back inside the house, he collected his case from the boot and followed them into the warmth.

As he stepped inside he was collared by Becky, the golden retriever, who nuzzled up to him, wagging her tail ferociously and wouldn't stop until she had received a scratch of her head and a pat on the side.

As he walked into the Lounge Clare asked 'Are you staying the night Dad?'

'No luv, I have a few presents that I bought on my recents trips abroad for you all, and as i'm off to watch the rugby in France with the boys from the pub at the weekend it seemed a good time to call and see you all, OK?'

'What else have you got on after that Dad?' Sharon his younger daughter asked.

Jake blushed before answering with 'Well, I have to go to London on the Monday after the rugby to discuss the possibility of going back to France to locate an individual that the Government is interested in. Also I've just booked a holiday for the first week in May to return to Santorini. Right, now make way for me and I'll open up the case so I can give you all your individual presents'.

There was an anticipated chatter as everyone spoke at the same time whilst making space on the sofa for him to sit, with Becky at his feet.

Twenty minutes later everyone had their gifts, with all of them thanking their Dad and Grandad at his thoughtfulness towards them all.

Then Jake said 'Is there any chance of a cuppa I'm parched after all that'.

He stood and followed Clare to the kitchen for a quiet chat, and as the kettle boiled he told her about his revised Will and that she was named as The Executor.

She stared at him before asking him if everything was OK with him.

'There's no problem health wise but its something I had to do as your old man's quite wealthy even after my gifts to you financially'.

Carrying a tray full of drinks back into the Lounge, Clare handed over cups to everyone before sitting down deep in thought at what her father had just told her.

Everyone chatted for the next hour before Jake stood and said he would make his way home now as it would be at least 9pm before he got there.

He kissed all his family before driving out onto the A38 and then joining the M5 heading for home, after a busy but productive day.

Chapter 38

Up reasonably early he dressed in what he called scruffs for a days fussing around.

A meeting had been called at the Swan that evening at 7pm to check if everyone received the paperwork from Bert together with the detailed arrangements for the next day. Although he had outlined the timing of the minibus's arrival at the Pub car park he wished to confirm that everyone was OK getting there on time and that they all had passports, match and flight tickets ready for the journey, only one or two of them could be absent minded when they are not in control. That was the evening sorted, now what to do for the rest of the day.

The weather was dry and there was a hint of sun attempting to appear through the thin cloud cover, so it bade a good time to tackle a bit of gardening. After a light breakfast he raked the back lawn to remove moss and dead grass before giving it a light mow, placing the accumulated cuttings into his compost heap. Although his small greenhouse was a basic one, he had purchased a couple of oil lamps recently to take the chill off any seeds and cuttings he would be potting on reasonably soon. Checking the container he kept his seeds in, he placed to one side lettuce, runner beans, broad beans together with various flower packs ready for potting up. In his shed he retrieved a bag of seed compost and filled numerous pots on his bench in the greenhouse and after a couple of hours he had filled over thirty plastic pots with seeds marking each one with a tab that said what they were and the day they had been planted.

Next he gave the borders the once over, removing dead leaves that had fallen off the trees surrounding the Cottage, together with dead heading various flowers and bushes, this took another hour but he felt better for the workout. Standing back by the kitchen door he surveyed the garden and felt quite pleased with himself.

It was just before noon when he removed his boots and walked into the kitchen, after washing his hands he walked to the front door to see if there was any mail, unfortunately it was mainly flyers from local business's touting for work, together with menu's for the local takeaway shops, plus one handwritten envelope. He pushed the flyers to one side and opened the white envelope to see who it was from, and to his surprise he noted that it was from George Adams.

It read 'Just a quick note mate, to thank you for all you did for me in Washington, I really appreciate your kindness and apologise for not paying you for the presents you bought for me, I enclose a cheque for £100 and please don't question me, saying you will send it back, please accept it as a token of my appreciation. Now health wise, I am uncertain at the moment if I will be returning to active service with the Firm, the injuries I sustained are healing quite well but I feel quite anxious at present and wonder if I could carry out the work I was involved with satisfactorily. I have spoken to H, he is quite understanding about it but said for me not to rush into any decision which I have agreed to do. I understand you will be off to France shortly, take care and perhaps you could call and see me when you return to Blighty. I have attached my address and home telephone number should you wish to contact me. Yours G.

The note took him completely by surprise, he put the letter in his pocket deciding to take it with him for his meeting with Henry next Monday.

Now, what to have for lunch, he felt like something different so he spent quite sometime preparing the ingredients for a Beef Madras and rice with a nan bread. With all the ingredients prepared he heated up his wok before carefully placing in the beef to brown off, then putting the meat to one side, he put the spices and onion in to cook before replacing the beef and turning the heat down to simmer for an hour.

Taking a nan bread from the freezer he put it in the microwave ready for the completion of the curry. Fifteen minutes before the curry was ready he prepared his pilau rice and with good timing on his part all the items were ready at the same time. Setting the table he sat down to one of his favourite meals. However they never taste quite the same as a traditional Indian Restaurant, but not bad at all, he thought to himself.

After clearing away his dishes he opened up his computer to check the weather forecast for tomorrow, for the Bristol flight and conditions in France for the rugby International, satisfied what was predicted, he then checked his emails, there was nothing of interest. Whilst it was opened he sent off notes to Mrs Choo and Inspector Chi in Australia, Charlene in Washington and Olivia in Sweden, explaining that he would be away in France over the weekend and wouldn't be available, but he would contact them all later.

Thinking past the weekend his meeting with Henry would surely be a precursor to him going off to France so he thought it best to lay out a few clothes and put them in a separate case as time would be short following his return from the rugby.

The timing of their return would be in the air, literally, until they pulled into the Swan's car park late on Sunday, but life is never straightforward is it, he thought.

The weather was a little better now as the clouds had thinned and the sun was heating up the air to almost an early Spring afternoon. Next on the agenda was a check over of the front garden, a light cut to the lawn seemed in order, a bit of weeding and dead heading followed, before tiredness set in and he returned all his tools and boots to the shed.

He spent the rest of the afternoon reading before having a mug of soup at six in preparation for his Pub visit.

He would only have a couple of drinks that evening he thought, then realised once everyone was in attendance the ale would be flowing, so he would see how things panned out.

Walking down the lane he could hear the hubbub of noise, and as he approached the bar he noticed he was the last to arrive.

Before he could speak Bert placed a pint in front of him and said 'You'r the last, but at least you're on time. I'll just pour one for myself and we'll get down to finalising tomorrow's itinerary'.

There were ten men going on the trip the next day and they were spread over two tables, Bert was positioned at the end of the tables but within earshot of everyone. He banged the table for a bit of silence before running through each item.

'I would like everyone in the car park at half past five, our flight leaves at 7.15am so there is no room for error. We arrive in Paris at 10.35am, we then make our way to the Hotel to be allocated rooms. I suggest we then have something to eat together before I arrange for a minibus to take us to the Stadium for the three o'clock kickoff. Everyone with me so far, and are there any questions. No, OK so far so good, did everyone get my letter with your plane and ground tickets'.

Everyone said they had. 'Good, so all you need as well will be your passport and spending money'.

There was a small amount of chatter before Bert stood and said 'Right anyone ready for a refill'. Everyone was ready, but Bert wouldn't take anyone's money, saying this round was on him, but he didn't expect to buy another drink throughout the whole weekend.

Everyone laughed loudly at this comment but all agreed with Bert's remark.

An hour later the group dispersed with the shaking of hands all round, and everyone said that they were looking forward to the weekend together.

Walking back along the lane by the beam of his torch Jake reminisced at the time a Jaguar car almost ran him over, and most recently with the access to his property almost impenetrable by the accumulation of snow that had built up.

Walking into the Cottage, then locking the front door behind him, he felt secure in the knowledge that he was safe from any intruders because of the installation of his new alarm system.

Before settling down he packed an overnight bag for his weekend away and set his alarm for 4.45am giving him ample time to walk to the Pub.

Chapter 39

It didn't seen five minutes had passed before his alarm sounded that it was time to get up and sort himself out. It was pitch black outside, obviously he thought it wasn't even five o'clock yet, however he quickly set his mind to the task in hand and carried out his ablutions before finally packing his overnight case.

Taking the bag downstairs he quickly got himself some breakfast and a warm cup of tea before it was time to head down the lane to meet his colleagues and their minibus to transport them to Bristol Airport. Jake decided to take the Lexus for the short journey, so he could park in the Pub's car park.

Within five minutes of his arrival all the supporters of the England Rugby team were sat in their transport with Bert still taking a head count, just in case he had missed someone. However to his delight they were all present, so with a muted cheer they were on their way. Just under an hour later the driver dropped them as close to the Terminal as he could, before wishing them a good time, and to confirm that he would be at the same place for their pickup on Sunday.

Into the entrance they all filed, making their way to the EasyJet station, producing their passports and tickets, before making their way to the passport control and baggage area. Everything was in order as they made the way to the Departure Lounge. Although the Bars were open everyone went for a bacon roll and coffee, to tied them over until they reached the Hotel in France.

Half an hour later they were walking out onto the tarmac, up the steps and onto the plane. Luckily they were seated together in a group, with Jake alongside Bert and Tony Bailey.

As they took off dawn was appearing in the distance, as the aircraft banked over heading towards Europe Jake felt his stomach muscles tensing as if he was on another long haul flight, but he quickly relaxed, safe in the knowledge they would only be in the air for an hour and a half. Of course with the all of them in a group the chatter got louder and louder the closer they came to Charles de Gaulle Airport, and Jake could feel the excitement within his fellow Rugby supporters.

They landed on time and taxied to their allotted station, disembarked, then through passport control before collecting their baggage from the carousel.

Bert then took charge and walked towards a minibus stationed away from the normal taxi's, spoke to the driver and signalled for them to get in. He gave the driver the Hotel they wished to be taken to in English, thankfully he was fluent, and asked if he could book the vehicle later to take them to the Rugby International.

The driver smiled and asked what time they wished to get to the Stadium, Bert thought for a moment before saying one forty five, allowing them time to seek out the bars and have a couple of beers before the start of the game.

Outside the Hotel the others got out and walked into the building, leaving Jake and Bert to get a card from the driver and confirm the time he would be outside.

The others were gathered alongside the Receptionist, waiting for Bert to confirm the party, and their names before each of them could be allocated their room keys. This only took a few minutes as the individual's displayed their passports, which the man behind the desk scanned and retained until they left. Bert was last to hand over his passport and asked if they could eat in the Dining Room before going to the Rugby later. The man smiled, before saying 'we expected you to have lunch with us so we are already prepared to see to your needs'. Bert smiled and shook the Receptionist's hands before saying 'I expect we will be down for food around noon, if you could book us three tables please'.

'No problem at all sir, I trust the rooms will be to your satisfaction'.

Their rooms were on the first floor so they all made their way to each of the rooms that had been allocated to them, all saying they would see Bert in the Bar in about fifteen minutes. Bert smiled thinking that some of them would be down earlier than that, but he needed the time to ring home to make sure all was in hand with the Pub, hoping it would run smoothly in his absence. After the phone was answered by his wife, saying there was no problems, just enjoy your time away, he relaxed completely ready for the day ahead, and whatever it would bring for them all.

Later, as he made his way down into the Bar he saw that everyone had their pints in front of them, and they certainly looked in good spirits so he walked up to the Bartender but before he could ask for a drink he was intercepted by Tony Bailey who said 'you're not paying for any drinks today mate, what will you have?'

Carrying his pint back to where the others were sat he asked 'Is everyone happy with their rooms and ready for a nice meal followed by a good game of rugby?'

There was silence for a moment before everyone shouted 'Ready, we were born ready'.

'Right lads, we'll just have the one then go through to the Dining Room and see what scram's on the menu for us, OK?' Bert said to everyone.

They quickly downed their drinks and followed their 'leader' into the plush Dining Area, where three tables were laid out for them to accommodate the diners in comfort.

Thankfully the menu was set out in multi language's one of which was English, which was OK for the men from Dorset.

The waiters gave them a little time to peruse the fare before they stood in front of their guests, taking down the orders given to them from all of the men.

The meals varied from basic English food to a few indulging in French cuisine, Jake being one of the latter. Once finished they all had a light dessert giving them a base for the alcohol the would be having at the Rugby Stadium.

They each paid for their meals before retiring to their separate rooms to freshen up, before meeting again in the Foyer to board the minibus that had been booked for a quarter to two. The trip to the Stade de France ground was slow due to the numerous vehicles and supporters lining the approach roads, however the bus dropped them close to the ground leaving them a walk of only fifty metres to the entrance.

Making sure that they were gathered together Bert made his way to the area where they would be seated, each displayed their tickets which were scanned, before they walked into the vast arena. The ground held a capacity of 81,000 people, and with what was at stake today, anticipation was that there would hardly be any room left for latecomers.

Chapter 39

On the way to their seats they stopped at a Bar and each purchased a plastic glass containing a pint of lager which would see them into the first half of the game. They all bought a souvenir programme before walking through the aisle and into their seats.

Scanning the stadium the men were flabbergasted at the number of people that were already seated, there was a huge gathering of English supporters but they were outnumbered by French men, women and children singing, waving flags and thoroughly enjoying the build up to this crunch game.

All the Dorset boys were looking through their programmes when a roar went up as both teams ran out from the dressing rooms and stood in a line to be introduced to the crowd, also to everyone that would be watching on TV, and those listening to the radio.

There then followed the playing of the National Anthems of both teams, with individual singers for France and England leading the way.

As the time approached 3pm the giant men stripped off their tracksuits and took their positions ready for the referee's whistle to herald the start of this momentous final game of the Six Nations Tournament.

Scanning the sky, it was a little overcast but Paris had been dry for the last few days which meant the ball would be thrown around amongst the backs making it an open game.

The excitement rose to a crescendo as the referee's whistle blew and the game was on its way with the ball being kicked high into the French half, it was taken by a second row forward but unfortunately it was spilled, and after less than a minute the big men would be forming the first scrum of the game.

Both teams had shown great strength in their previous games they were involved in, which gave each the upper hand in the distribution to their forwards. So this was a massive start to see who would be the stronger eight, but most importantly not to concede a penalty.

Although the crowd were in fine voice the crunch of bodies as they engaged in the first scrum could still be heard, then the whistle blew for a penalty against the home side for pre-engaging, one up for the English.

The number ten took the penalty kick sending it into the French twenty two, which led to a good attacking throw in for England.

An accurate throw to the middle of the line out allowed one of the big men to collect it and as he came down his fellow forwards gathered around him and they headed for the try line gathering momentum as they inched forward. The referee's arm went out as the French forwards brought the maul down then his arm raised vertically for another penalty, however the scrum half collected the ball and passed it to the half back who kicked diagonally for the flying winger to collect and touch down for the first try of the game. The referee signalled for the clock to stop, as he wanted to see the infringement on the big screen. This could be a critical start to the game and leave France with fourteen men for ten minutes if it is found to be a bookable offence. The time seemed to stand still for the next minute or two, before the referee ran towards the French Captain and asked for the hooker to come over to them both.

The replay was shown in slow motion on the large screen and it appeared that the hooker pulled his opposite number to the floor with a callous neck roll and he was show a yellow card which meant ten minutes in the bin. There then followed a reshuffle of the French side before the try was allowed and the subsequent kick was taken successfully. Seven nil to England.

The following ten minutes play was frenetic, with penalty after penalty awarded against France as they endeavoured to halt England's strong play. However as the ten minutes was up and the hooker returned England had scored another converted try and the number ten had put over an additional three penalties. After twenty minutes the scoreboard read twenty three nil to the away side.

The rest of the first half saw two penalties each, as the sides were playing a careful game not giving away further silly penalties as the whistle blew for halftime.

The Dorset boys quickly vacated their seats to dash to the toilets and collect refills of lager for the second half. Much chatter amongst them as to the quality of the England play away from home, but still there was the niggling feeling that the French wouldn't take the second half lying down and would be throwing the ball about in their usual Gallic style.

A slight wind had started to blow as France kicked off for the second half and there was doubt as to who should collect the ball, and it bounced once before screwing into touch on the England twenty two.

Chapter 39

Throw in to France under the new rules, neatly taken and passed back to the scrum half who launched a huge up and under, but unfortunately the wind blew the ball back and sideways directly into touch, thus only gaining a few yards for a throw in to England.

Again taken cleanly the forwards strode powerfully onwards with the French pack in disarray, the backs had to come into the melee to prevent too much momentum by the visitors, but this left the open field full of gaps, England's crafty scrum half saw the opening and passed quickly out to the inside half who punted the ball over the depleted French line to be gathered by the left wing who strode over under the posts for another try that was converted. Making the score thirty six to six to the away side, almost out of sight now and looking like the Championship for England.

The remainder of the game was frantic as France didn't lie down, but threw panicked ball around from all parts of the ground, however England were clinical and when the whistle blew for the end of the match the final score was forty eight points to nineteen. The end of a fantastic game of rugby for the purist, not so for the French supporters but a wonderful advert for positive rugby.. The boys stayed for the presentation and to cheer the players, as they walked to all parts of the ground displaying the Trophy for their ardent fans. As they walked down the steps the seats were almost empty, then leaving the Stadium Bert was glad to see their minibus stationed there, with a disgruntled driver stood alongside it having a smoke.

Rugby supporters are completely different individuals from other sports, as win or lose there is never any animosity, usually an hour or so after the final whistle they are quite happy to share a pint or two with the opposition, as would most likely happen later on as the 'Pub boys' take to the town.

Safely on board the minibus the driver asked if they had enjoyed the game, which they all confirmed by thanking him for being there to collect them. He smiled with a knowing nod, and asked if they wished to be taken back to the Hotel or directly 'on the town'.

The unanimous decision was to return to the Hotel for a lie down, before having a clean up and then to hit the town during the evening.

'If you like I could collect you and show you the best areas of Paris before taking you to a nice restaurant?' the driver said.

'Bert looked at all his mates and answered for them with 'That would be great, could you pick us up at 7pm from the Hotel?'

'I'll be waiting outside for you gentlemen' the driver replied.

As they got out Bert said to them 'Not too much drinking before we leave the Hotel chaps, have a nap if you can, before getting ready to go out and enjoy Paris. Before we part may I suggest that someone holds a drinks kitty rather than each and every one of us order our individual beverages. Jake would you do the honours and perhaps Tony could help with collecting them with you. May I suggest 30 euros each, and see how far that will get us, it should be enough as long as we don't go silly. We have to get on the plane tomorrow in a reasonable condition otherwise we might not get back to England until later'.

They all agreed and went straight to their rooms arranging to congregate in the Bar at half past six to hand over their kitty money.

A few hours later they were all in the Bar, where Jake went around to collect their kitty money before the driver arrived to take them into the City.

Bert asked for a bit of hush before saying 'I think it best if we all stay together, does anyone have any preference of what we do this evening. I suggest something to eat first to line our stomach's before the alcohol takes over, are we in agreement?'

They all nodded their acceptance before Bert carried on 'I know a middle of the road restaurant that dishes up good food and is not too expensive, I suggest we head there first then after that we can wander around having a beverage here and there whatever takes out fancy before heading back to the Hotel around 11pm'.

Jake looked at Bert before answering for everyone 'Sound good to me and I think everyone else as no-one else has said anything. Thanks Bert'.

Back in the minibus the atmosphere was full of excitement as some of Jake's friends hadn't left England for years and were acting like young teenagers, following the euphoria of the rugby they had just witnessed.

Before they drove off Bert said to the driver 'Could you drop us off at II Elait Un Square Restaurant please, and if possible could we ring you around eleven to collect us again to take us back to the Hotel?'

'No problem sir, I might take a while to collect you as there are many English out tonight enjoying Paris, but I will be there as soon as I can'.

'Thank you very much, let's go you have some very hungry passengers, waiting to sample the lovely food of France' he finished with a toothy grin.

The food at the restaurant was exceptional and everyone thoroughly enjoyed the cuisine, which was washed down with a few beers.

Leaving the establishment Bert scanned the area before asking them which way shall we go left or right. The majority turned right so off they went, they checked the numerous Bar's to see what room was available and if there were any rowdy Englishmen in them already well imbibed.

Over the next few hours they visited four Bar's and with the kitty going downhill fast Bert decided to try the driver's number to check when he would be available .

The time was fast approaching eleven, and he preferred to be back in the Hotel drinking rather than on the streets as his companions were getting to the high stage of inebriation. The driver picked up the phone but answered in French, Bert said 'Hi its Bert with his other English companions, are you busy at the moment, if not could you possibly collect us and take us back to the Hotel'.

'I have a group on board at the moment, who I am taking to a strip joint, but could be with you in half an hour, where are you?'

Bert panicked for a minute before saying the name of the Bar they were in, and they would be waiting outside in thirty minutes for him.

Two more beers were consumed before the minibus pulled up outside and the revellers boarded. Bert asked for a bit of quiet, before saying to them 'We'll just have a nightcap in the Bar and then retire for the night as we have to be at the airport by 11am, so after a good breakfast and plenty of black coffee we'll be on our way'.

As they exited the vehicle Bert arranged for a collection in the morning at 10.30am the next day, to take them to the Terminal, for their onward flight too Bristol.

Gathered in the Bar a few of them were worse for wear and as Jake took the various orders Bert walked with him suggesting discretely to a couple of the revellers to go steady on the intake of alcohol.

As everyone sat down with their drinks Jake divided up the remaining euros from the original kitty money and handed it over to each of them.

Everyone was in fine spirits and they all thanked Bert for his organisation skills, saying how they had all enjoyed the short time they had had being away together.

They wandered off to their rooms shortly after midnight all feeling content before saying goodnight as each of them dispersed on the first floor landing.

Chapter 40

Jake was up bright an early and had a lukewarm shower before dressing in a change of clothing, before making his way down to the Dining Room, where Bert was sat with Tony and a couple of others downing black coffee's, they decided they would wait until they were all gathered together before commencing breakfast which would help for the staff, and they could eat in unison. Their remaining friends appeared over the next fifteen minutes and once gathered they ordered their requirements.

The food was delicious and quickly took away the woolly event of too much alcohol and late night syndrome, that they had all suffered after last night's revelry, however before long the throng became quite animated talking about the previous day's game and the enjoyable evening hat they had all had.

Bert then walked out to the Reception to settle up the invoice and for the stay and obtain a receipt before they all went back to their rooms to pack up their cases and hand back their keys to the Manager.

Exactly on 10.30am the minibus pulled up outside to take them to the Airport, then within a few minutes they were off on the final road journey in France. The group quickly retrieved their belongings from the boot, shook hands with the driver, each of them handing over a tip together with the payment made to the drivers for their various trips.

Through passport control and luggage check-in then through to Departures the gang sat down for a few minutes before taking in turns to visit the Duty Free Shop for souvenirs and alcohol with the remainder of their euros.

Their flight was called later for their return journey to the UK, with the flight direct to Bristol Airport, and they landed on time an hour and a half later to be greeted with a clear blue sky. Half an hour after landing they walked out into the brilliant sunshine to be greeted by another minibus that would take then back to The Swan's car park, for them to collect their vehicles for the short trip back to their homes.

Jake was amazed to see a few of the men still glad to get back to the bar for a decent pint, but Jake shook Bert's hand thanking him for organising their excellent weekend away, saying he would be going home as he had to be up early the next morning for a meeting before taking a flight back to France on business.

Bert shook his head with dismay saying 'I don't know how you do it mate, but I look forward to the tale when you return, stay safe'.

'As always Bert' he answered shaking hands with the landlord.

Fifteen minutes later he had parked the Lexus, retrieved his case, put the dirty washing in the machine and prepared the ingredients for his evening meal, before sitting down and drinking a nice cup of coffee.

As he finished his coffee his eyes felt extremely heavy so he put down the cup and settled into the chair for a nap. Surprisingly when he woke some two hours later the phone was ringing so he quickly got out of the chair to answer it.

'Jake Tordale' he said to the receiver.

'Hi Jake its Henry. I just wanted to make sure you got back from the rugby in one piece, what a great result, I assume you hit the town in the evening for a nice meal and a few bevies?'

'We certainly did, I arrived back home just after two, and have just had a welcome nap, are we still OK for 10.30am tomorrow?'

'That's actually why I rang, can you possibly get here earlier, say 9.30am, only the flight is leaving two hours after that, and once we've had a quick chat you will have to get to the Terminal, check in and board in a very short window of time'.

'I'll get there a little earlier say 9am, I'd rather do that than be late for the flight'.

'OK Jake 9am it is, see you tomorrow, Oh just one other thing, you can leave your car in the car park as I intend to drive you to the Airport myself'.

'That's fine with me, I'm only going to pack an overnight bag as I only hope to be there for a couple of days, if longer I'll buy some extra clothing whilst there'.

With the call completed he was now wide awake thinking that Henry Bates had something else up his sleeve that would be forthcoming when they met, or perhaps he would leave it until they were driving to the Terminal.

Chapter 40

Walking up to his bedroom he gathered up some clothes he would be taking, plus other bits and pieces and placed them in his overnight bag, his toiletries he would put in tomorrow. He opened the safe tucked in alongside his library, the face of the safe was discreetly hidden by a false frontage of books. He removed a reasonable amount of euros together with his passport and put them on his bedroom cabinet ready for tomorrow. Satisfied he was now organised for the early drive, he started the cooking of his evening meal, which would be Beef Stroganoff with fried rice. The rich meal was washed down with a bottle of red wine and completed with a couple of cups of Earl Grey tea.

Feeling more alive after his previous nap and the substantial meal, he decided to watch some TV before retiring around eleven o'clock.

Chapter 41

His alarm went off at 6am, although he was already awake, so he quickly got himself ready, rushed downstairs to have some cereal and toast before putting his case into the car placing his money and passport into his inside pocket, locking the door after setting the alarm, then off to London.

He knocked and walked into Henry Bates' office at a minute to nine and was met with a beaming smile from his Boss.

'Always a stickler for time you are, if I need to rely on anyone its Jake Tordale. I take it there were no problems getting here this early?' Bates asked.

'No Henry, I allowed plenty of time, trying to get here before the bulk of the traffic slows to a stop on the outskirts of the Capital'.

'Right, take a seat Jake, let me run through the up to date intel I have for you. This is a completely different scenario than you will have encountered before. The plane will take you to Caen Carpequet Airport, I have booked you into a small boarding house close by in a town called Mondeville. This file gives you the description of the person I need you to make contact with, but before that you need to approach the local Police and speak to my contact there, the details are all in the file. The man you seek is known to the contact and he will give you his whereabouts. If you quickly scan through the file, make notes if you wish, it will help you fully understand what you are dealing with. Then you can ask me any questions that you like regarding your task'.

Jake picked up the brown folder and slowly read through all the information contained within. To be doubly sure what he had just read through, he went through it again whilst shaking his head at the files contents.

'If you feel that this is beyond what you wish to engage in I fully understand, but as you know it appears that George will now have to remove himself from the frontline and take a more sedentary role in the future, and all other agents are engaged in operations in various areas around the globe'.

Chapter 41

Jake stared into Henry's eyes before replying with 'So what you're saying Henry is that I contact this felon, arrest him and bring him back to the UK for crimes that are elaborated on in this file. Do we know if he is alone, part of another gang in France, or just hiding from the Authorities in a quaint village in the Country?'.

'Unfortunately I cannot answer any of those questions, because honestly I don't know, however if you get my contact involved with possible surveillance you should glean the information you require at ground zero. So, what's your decision as the clock's ticking?'

'Obviously I'm going back to France, but I must admit this is a little outside my realm of work, but until I get there I cannot ascertain the severity of the problem, so I will fly there today and ring you once I have talked to your Contact'.

'Excellent Jake, I knew I didn't have to pressure you at all, before you kindly took up the baton. Let's make our way down to the car. Oh, by the way here's an envelope for you, it contains 1000 euros to tide you over, I expect you have a pocketful as well. So any other out of pocket expenses you have please retain the receipts for me, as usual'.

Without further ado they took the lift down to the underground car park, Jake collected his bag from his car, then Henry drove out into the traffic heading for London City Airport.

There was no small talk on the way there, as both men were deep in thought about the operation Jake was about to undertake, so nothing more was said about the task ahead.

Parking outside the Terminal entrance Henry shook Jake's hand and said 'Take care Jake, my contact will cover you, discuss everything with him and I'm sure it will terminate in a good result for all of us'.

Getting his case from the car, he shut the boot just as Henry pulled away with just a single toot from the horn heralding his final farewell.

Checking his bag in and through passport control he was amazed how quiet the Departure Lounge was at this time of the morning. However he wasn't worried about any company on the flight as it was only an hour and a half before they would be landing in France, he had a lot to think about whilst in the air, so he scrutinised the notes he had hastily made in Henry's office. The man he was after was named as Silas Blackledge, his actual name, or not, God only knows. He had absconded from the UK whilst on remand, he was tagged but the device had shut down a week ago, obviously having been removed from his leg and deactivated. He had been arrested 6 months ago for serious drug dealing, being part of the County Lines fraternity, it would appear that he was at a very high level in the hierarchy, being heavily involved with the distribution of people and drugs throughout the Home Counties. He was obviously hoping to melt into this nondescript area around Caen and away from the eyes of the Authorities, until his disappearance lost interest in them. Little did he know that he had been rumbled and he was now being hunted by MI6.

As he left the aircraft and headed into the impressive Terminal building he took out his passport and produced it to the efficient security staff, then collected his overnight bag from the carousel, before heading outside to the Hertz car rental. The young lady behind the desk asked if he had booked a vehicle in advance which he confirmed he had and once shown his driving licence and passport she handed over the car keys to a Citroen that was just being valeted. He explained that he would be staying in the local region, and could she direct him to the Police Station as he had to see a friend there.

With directions inputted into the sat nav he carefully drove out onto the right hand side of the road heading to the Police Station, it was only a drive of fifteen minutes or so and he pulled into a car park opposite the old building. Walking up to the desk he asked in French if Inspector Jean-Paul Dupont was available. The policeman scrutinised Jake for a few seconds before asking for his name. Jake handed over his passport which was checked over thoroughly before he handed it back and asked Jake to take a seat. He picked up the phone and rattled away in French to someone, then a tall grey haired man appeared, dressed in an Inspector's uniform, from the back of the Office and walked over to Jake 'Mr Tordale its a pleasure to meet you sir, please come this way'.

Jake followed him along a dark corridor before entering the Inspector's Office, the tall man said for him to take a seat, opposite where he sat at his desk.

'Your Henri Bates as told me all the details about your fugitive and as you no doubt understand you are booked into the same Hotel as him. We have observed this character over the past few days and he appears to be a man who is trying to be, what is it you English say 'nondescript' or as we French would say 'incognito'. He usually appears after breakfast around ten, walks into the town and calls into a coffee shop where he stays for an hour and then carries out a bit of 'window shopping' before returning to the Hotel.

Jake appeared bemused before replying 'Does he meet anyone at the coffee shop, do you know?'

'Obviously other customers come and go whilst he is in the cafe, but my men have only observed from the street and they were unable to see if he made any contact with anyone inside'.

'Is it the same ritual each day, or do the times vary?' Jake asked.

'Always the same time over the past five days, I can confirm' the Inspector said with firmness. 'From now on I will cancel the surveillance and let you take over, but should anything happen that you require assistance, my officers will be close by. May I suggest that you do nothing for the first day and go in a different direction to Blackledge, also leave the Hotel earlier than he does, so he doesn't think you are tailing him'.

Jake pondered on this for a few seconds before saying 'Good idea Inspector, I'll most likely settle into my room, and should the opportunity unfold to engage in conversation with the man, I will make small talk regarding why I am in France and try to find out a bit about him and what brings him to France'.

'OK Mr Tordale, I think that is all we can talk about at the moment, if you wish to contact me at all about anything ring me on my mobile, it's over there' he said handing over a card.

'Thank you Inspector for your assistance on this sensitive matter, and with a bit of luck I will remove this reprobate from your Country and back to the UK to be put away for a long time'. He stood shook the man's hand, before asking the location of the Hotel, then left the Station and returned to his rental car. He sat there for a while unsure what his next move was, before deciding to go to the Hotel and book in and drop off his overnight bag in his allotted room. When he explained who he was to the pleasant young lady at the Reception Desk she asked for his passport before handing over the key to his room number 8 and wished him a pleasant stay. She also handed over a few pieces of paper regarding the requirements of the Hotel and times for breakfast, and if required evening meals. The room was smallish but acceptable he thought, having been spoilt with the facilities he had encountered over the past few years.

He had a quick shower before dressing and walking downstairs and into the compact bar. There was no-one there, just a bored looking barman of about sixty, who was making himself appear busy drying a glass.

Jake walked up to him and before he spoke the barman seemed to come to life with the thought of having a customer. 'Would you like a drink sir?' he asked with almost no interest in his customer.

'Beer please' Jake answered with a smile. The man poured it and brought it to a small table in the corner of the room where Jake had positioned himself.

In the opposite corner sat his quarry, Jake just nodded to the man before checking a message he had just received. It was from Henry Bates, asking if he had arrived at the Hotel. Jake's fingers quickly tapped in a reply 'Sat opposite our man now, also I've just had a good meeting with your contact and we are all up to speed as to how we are going to proceed, I will send more information tonight with a possible photo of our man'.

'OK Jake, I'll leave you to carry on, speak later'.

As he disconnected the call he checked to see if Blackledge was paying any attention to him but he appeared immersed in a paper, although his profile was in view. So Jake quickly took a photo of him, before taking a sip of his drink.

Blackledge was dressed in a patterned sweater over a white shirt, together with denim jeans, on the seat opposite him was draped a Barbour jacket. His face appeared swarthy and he sported a three day stubble of beard, and he could really do with a haircut.

Jake thought to himself that was a quick character assassination of someone he didn't know.

The man turned over the last page of the paper before standing, putting on his jacket and walking out of the room with no acknowledgement to either the bartender or Jake.

Checking his watch he wondered where the man was going, this was against his routine perhaps he was heading into town to meet someone, so Jake downed his drink and quickly left the room hoping to keep the other man in his sight. However as he walked out the front door there was no sign of him, but a large black saloon was pulling away at speed so perhaps he was waiting for a lift.

Unsure what to do next, his stomach told him where to go, find food as it was way past lunchtime as his last meal was early morning at his Cottage.

Walking along the street he spied a restaurant offering local cuisine and walked in. He was shown to a table by a waiter who spoke fluent English and handed him a menu. He informed Jake that the dish of the day was a mixed seafood platter accompanied by hot bread, so Jake ordered it with a bottle of white wine. The meal was delicious and when the waiter cleared his plates he asked for a black coffee and the bill.

Feeling a lot better he walked further into the town to take in all that it offered and to his surprise, the car he had seen speeding off outside the Hotel was parked across the road from a Funeral Directors Office. How strange he thought, unless it was a cover to transport drugs in a coffin back to England. Then he thought to himself, steady on your mind is wondering into the fantasy world, however it would be a possibility if that was what he was up to. Further up the road there were seats for locals to sit and natter amongst themselves, so Jake took the opportunity to sit and watch the car for however long it took, as he was in no hurry.

He didn't have to wait long, as he thought his hunch could be correct, two men walked out the front door of the Parlour, followed by a man dressed in black who he assumed was the Funeral Director, and shook hands with both the men who turned and got back in the black car, before speeding off.

A lot has happened in the few hours since he arrived in France he thought, he had spoken to Henry's contact, booked into the Hotel, met his quarry in the Hotel Bar, and bumped into him in the centre of the town. Fuel for both Henry and the Inspector to mull over he thought, so he made his way to the Police Station to talk to the Inspector first, before ringing Henry when he returned to the Hotel.

Chapter 42

Walking up to the desk, the policeman he saw just a few hours ago looked at him with recognition. 'Do you wish to see the Inspector again Mr Tordale?'

'Yes please if he's in, Officer' Jake replied.

The policeman lifted the phone and gabbled away in French, before he smiled and gestured for Jake to come through and down the corridor to Inspector Jean-Paul Dupont's office. Jake tapped on the door then opened it following the welcome 'Come in'.

The Inspector stood and shook Jake's hand, then gestured for him to sit in the seat he had vacated only a few hours ago.

'I take it you have news for me Jake?'

'I do indeed, before I telephone Henry Bates I thought I would tell you what I witnessed less than an hour ago, just a short distance from here'.

'Proceed' Dupont almost ordered with urgent enthusiasm.

'I followed our man into town after he had been collected from the Hotel by a car and driver, and at a discreet distance observed them as they pulled up in front of a Funeral Director's offices in the High Street. I parked the car and walked towards a couple of seats in the square where I could observe them when they left the offices. They were there for at least half an hour, before they left, got back in the car and drove off. Perhaps my mind is rushing ahead of the situation, however I thought it would be a good way to export drugs from France to the UK, or vice versa, what do you think?'

'I have had dealings with the Owner of the Funeral Parlour for a number of years, and he has indeed been involve in dubious goings on in the past, however nothing to do with drugs. Perhaps your man and the driver are involved in shady dealings and have co-opted the other man into making a lot of money on the side, it's certainly worth looking into' Dupont concluded.

'Before my target left the Hotel we were sat in the Bar having a drink, then when he left we nodded to each other as he walked past me and left the room.

He would most likely recognise me if I became involved at the early stages, but I can keep him close to hand if he stays at the Hotel'.

'Of course we could be on a fools errand and their visit to the Funeral Home could be quite innocent but personally I think there is something more suspicious going on. Why, for instance did he flee Britain and come to a small town close to an Airport, unless he already had contacts here on the ground, such as the driver of the car, and of course the Funeral Director, what do you suggest we do next Inspector?'

'Please call be Jean-Paul, and if you don't mind I'll call you Jake' the Inspector retorted.

'I feel it is best to take it slowly, I'll keep two of my plain clothes officers on the case, one near your Hotel and another close to the Funeral Home, and together with your observations in the Hotel, we will hopefully have their movements covered. However it is not known where the other man resides so once I have his car number I will trace the owner'.

Jake thought for a while before answering with 'Luckily enough I took the number whilst I was waiting for them sat on the seat in the square' so he handed a copy of the number to the Inspector.

'Well done Jake, let's see what I can find on my old but extremely efficient machine. He tapped away for a few minutes before a beaming smile spread across his face.

'Bingo, I have his address and name, and guess what he is known to the Authorities for importing drugs from the Far East, although to date he has not been caught in the act. So it appears that your initial assumption is correct and we have stumbled on a drugs Import, Export scam'.

'What do you think he deals in, heroin, cocaine, or others?'

'If he imports from the Far East it could be anything, from the information we gleaned from our initial inquiries regarding this man, he is an offshoot of a larger group based in Paris, that seems to be spreading like wildfire from the Capital. So your help in this matter could break not just the people we see here but the far larger group around the Country'.

'Believe it or not Jean-Paul this is the last operation before retiring, so I'm not sure what I've let myself in for'.

Dupont chuckled before replying with 'You'd best go out in a blaze of glory then my friend, if we can crack this case between us I'm sure I for one could be looking for higher things and I'm sure you will be also rewarded in some way, on your side of the Channel'.

'Let's not jump before we can walk, these dealers are extremely clever and although we think they could be exporting drugs, until we catch them at it, we are really still in the dark'.

'I agree softly softly does it, which I think is one of your English sayings' replied Dupont.

Jake left the office and headed back to his car, before driving to the Hotel.

Collecting his key from Reception he asked if there were any messages for him, but there were none so he went up to his room to phone Henry and pass on his current news.

They chatted for a while, until Jake was told in no uncertain terms to watch himself, and leave the actual arrest of the criminals to the French Police'.

'OK mother' Jake answered with a chuckle, before ringing off.

After all the excitement Jake realised he hadn't eaten since his breakfast, so he trundled down the stairs and into the Dining Room to be met by a waiter who directed him to a table before handed him a menu. Scanning what was on offer he plumped for soup as a starter, Duck a'la Orange for a main course, with cheese and biscuits afterwards, to be accompanied by a bottle of red wine, and finally a filter coffee.

After an hour of gastronomic delight, he sat back sipping his coffee as his quarry, Blackledge entered the room and sat as far away as was possible from Jake before receiving a menu from the waiter, immediately placing his order. He then took out a paper and became engrossed in it until his starter arrived. Jake decided to leave the room and go for a walk to help his digestion. Although still winter the temperature was a lot warmer here in France than in the UK, and as he wandered along he could see the buds starting to form on the trees and bushes.

He was surprised to notice that after ten minutes or so's walking from the Hotel, he was deep in the Countryside, away from the hustle and bustle of town noises, and in tune with the bird life, they obviously felt secure as they were singing at the top of their voices.

He sat on a bench just outside a small wooden area and felt quite at home, there wasn't a soul in sight, then to his surprise a robin came and perched on the arm of the bench and sat looking at him.

Jake remembered his wife saying many years ago that a robin will come to a person it feels comfortable with, and will sing you a message from a departed one.

After a couple of minutes the bird started singing which left Jake feeling melancholy, as thought's of his dear departed wife, who he missed terribly, before tears started flowing down his cheeks as he thought of her.

The robin flew away after a few minutes, but only as far as an adjacent oak tree, where he sang merely until Jake stood to walk back to the Hotel.

His thoughts were deeply into his early married life back in Devon with his lovely wife and two young girls, as he trudged along the pathway, before he was brought back to the present by a Golden Retriever that nudged his leg. He looked up and saw two people approaching him whom he assumed were the dog's owners, but he was mesmerised by the dog who sat down and looked directly into his eyes. He bent down and gave the animal a rub to its head and was rewarded with another leg nuzzle as it stood up. The couple smiled as they approached him and he was surprised that they were British as they said 'Good evening, someone has taken a liking to you'.

'I used to have a 'Goldy' many years ago, and my daughter has one now, they are certainly very affectionate dogs and wonderful companion's. Do you live here in France or are you on holiday?' he asked.

'We live here in the village, in fact we have only settled here in the last six months, away from the turmoil back in England, what about you?' the man replied.

'I am only here for a few days catching up with a friend of mine, anyway must press on nice to talk to you'.

'Where are you staying, I just wondered if you would like to pop in and see us whilst you're here, I'm sure 'Alfie' would like to see you again'.

'That's extremely thoughtful of you, I'm staying at the Hotel at the end of the pathway, its nice to meet you, I'll try to visit you in the next couple of days, if you give me your mobile number I'll give you a bell to see if it's convenient'.

They exchanged numbers and then walked their separate ways.

Back in his room he contemplated how simple it was to meet people you have never come across before and quickly form a bond, he decided once he had sorted things out with the Police he would indeed visit the couple again before he had to return back to London.

Chapter 43

The fresh air must have done him a power of good, as after ten minutes he dropped off to a deep sleep before being woken by his mobile's loud ringing heralding a call. 'Jake Tordale' he said into the appliance.

There was a pregnant silence before the call was answered with 'Hello Jake, its Giles Brown we just met on the pathway. I'm sorry to call you so soon, but wondered if you had thought any more regarding meeting up for something to eat at our's'.

'Sorry Giles, I've just come off a couple of calls from the UK and dropped off to sleep for half an hour or so, I'm afraid I haven't had time to think about a meet up yet, I'll return your call tomorrow and we can arrange something then, if that's OK with you?'

'That's fine, sorry to put pressure on you, if its inconvenient please don't be afraid to say'.

'No its OK, I'll ring you back sometime tomorrow' with that he rang off thinking to himself, how odd it appeared for someone who met him on a pathway, then after a very brief conversation would want to invite you to their house for a meal. Perhaps, he thought he was becoming a little paranoid at the couple's generous offer, however he would take his time before deciding to go to their property as there were more pressing things going on in his life at the moment.

Dialling the number for Inspector Dupont he was surprised how quickly the call was answered with 'Hello Mr Tordale, how may I be of help'.

'I just wondered what position you are in at present with our on going problem?'

'Well I have despatched two officers on the case, one outside the Hotel where you are staying and the other across the road from the Funeral Directors Duboise and Laurent. They are in constant contact, directly with me, but to date I have nothing to report on either location. Have you seen your man recently?'

'He was in the Dining Room of the Hotel earlier, I left to go for a walk in the countryside, and when I returned he had either left the property or gone to his room. Do you have any thought's regarding approaching the Funeral Directors and searching the property?'

'What excuse could I have for that, anyway I would have to get a search warrant and then what grounds could I give for such a search in a delicate industry?'

'I fully understand, but my concern is that where drugs are concerned if they are in a storage situation they are not making any money for the suppliers or dealers, and if we are not careful they could make their move without us knowing, thus leaving us empty handed'.

'I understand your concern but it is a delicate situation we are in, we really need one of them to make a mistake to enable an arrest to be made. Perhaps you could make contact with your man and get into dialogue with him, regarding his reason for being in France and see what excuse he comes up with, then at least we will have a starting point, which could possibly push him into a mistake with his other contacts'.

'A good idea, I'll approach him first thing in the morning at breakfast and let you know what I find out, speak to you tomorrow'.

Jake then contemplated how he would start a conversation with the drug dealer, with nothing coming to him immediately he put it to the back of his mind and walked downstairs into the bar and ordered a glass of red wine. He turned to see where to sit and was taken aback by Blackledge staring at him over his glass of beer. Jake nodded and sat down at a table alongside him.

As he walked over he had already decided how to start his enquiry, he turned and said 'Nice Hotel don't you think?'.

Slight hesitation before Blackledge answered with 'Yes, are you staying long?'

'A week or so, I'm quite flexible though as I'm retired and have no urgent worries about going home, I'm trying to catch up with an old school friend of mine who settled in France some ten years ago and lives in this area, how about you, are you on holiday?'

Jake stared him straight in the face, but the other man looked away before taking a swig from his glass to give him time to adjust his thoughts. 'I also have a friend here who I have caught up with, and we have a few things planned over the next week or two'.

'Is he in the village or does he live locally?' Jake pushed for an answer.

'No he lives a few kilometres away, but he collects me most days'.

'That's nice, can I freshen up your glass, I'm sorry I forgot to introduce myself, I'm Jake Tordale and you are?' he asked offering his hand.

Blackledge shook his hand thanking him for his drink before replying 'Charles Storey, nice to meet you Jake'.

Jake walked to the bar, and ordered another red wine and a beer for his companion with a false name. As he walked back to the table Blackledge stood and excused himself saying he had to go and use the facilities, but would be back.

Thinking to himself he was most likely going to make a phone call to his buddy explaining that he was being interrogated by another Brit in the Hotel, but he could be wrong about that. The man was only gone a few minutes and as he sat down he said he felt better after relieving himself.Jake smiled at him, lifted his wine glass and said cheers.

The next half hour was spent talking pleasantries regarding families, the weather and the state of the UK at the moment, before Jake stood and said he was going for a walk to get some fresh air. 'Thank's for the chat, it was nice talking to you, see you at breakfast' Jake said as he left the room, walking out the front door, and back on the trail towards the woods. He sat on the seat he had occupied only recently and lifted his mobile to dial and speak to the Inspector, unfortunately the number went to voicemail so he left a short message saying he had something to report but would call again in the morning.

Chapter 44

Jake was sat at his breakfast table at 8am tucking into toast when Blackledge entered the Dining Room and sat at the table opposite him, saying good morning in an almost friendly manner. The waiter took his order, then he turned to Jake and asked what he was up to today. ‘I was able to contact my friend last evening and he is looking forward to meeting up later this morning, so I thought it best to get some food inside me early in preparation of my visit, how about you?’

‘My friend should be picking me up around nine, and we will be visiting some sights around Caen today, the weather looks reasonable so I expect we will be out all day’ and with that the waiter placed his breakfast in front of him.

Jake caught the waiter’s attention and asked for scrambled egg and bacon, with mushroom’s, together with another cup of coffee. As the waiter walked away Jake’s mobile rang making him a little flustered but as he looked at the caller he realised it was his daughter Clare so he answered it whilst sat at the table. The conversation was quite innocuous and he finished the call with ‘I hope to get down to Devon in 10 days time to see you all’, as he disconnected the call Clare was still saying something so he would ring her again once he got back to his room.

‘Nice to get a call from your family I would think, unfortunately I never married so have no one that would call me from England’ Blackledge said.

‘Sometimes its a blessing, however there are times when you need to be left to your own devices rather than the interrogation you receive from your siblings, such as where are you, what are you up to, when will you be home, but I wouldn’t be without them really’.

Blackledge gave a chuckle before replying with ‘Perhaps overall I’m better off with not having any baggage then’.

Jake smiled but obviously didn’t agree with this retort.

The meal arrived and the remaining time they were sat there was spent in silence thankfully.

Chapter 44

Checking his watch he excused himself from Blackledge and left the Dining Room to return to his room where he would make calls to the Inspector and Henry Bates with his update on the latest proceedings.

He called Henry first, explaining everything that had transpired and his doubt's on the other man's story, Henry told him to hang on in there and work with the French Police as he really had no jurisdiction over Blackledge and his associates, but he was sure that everything would work out OK, but he knew how organised and 'bloodhound' like his contact worked in situation's such as this. A few more minutes was spent on George's medical condition before they completed the call.

No sooner had the line cleared than it rang again, it was Inspector Dupont, Jake answered with 'Jake Tordale' as usual.

'Hi Jake, it's Jean-Paul Dupont just returning your call, what do you have for me?'

'I've just finished a conversation with Henry Bates in London explaining my up to date details, and I wished to give the same information to you. I had a couple of drinks with Blackledge last evening, after I introduced myself to him, however he said his name was Charles Storey and that he had no family at all in the UK. He said he came to France to meet a friend of his who was escorting him around the area to get a taste of the French countryside and cuisine. Obviously it was a load of rubbish but I think he felt satisfied with my response. Reading between the lines I think they are almost ready to proceed with their operation, what do you think will be the next move, a possible visit to the Funeral Director's?'

'I have my doubt's regarding that approach, but have given it a lot of thought regarding their transportation of the drugs and feel that a coffin would certainly be a clever way of concealing them. I wonder if they would go as far as to use an actual corpse to hide the drugs or would they just take a chance that the Authorities wouldn't ask for the coffin to be opened, either at Caen Airport or Central London'.

'Drug dealers are gamblers, but if the haul is considerable and they lose this consignment, prison would be the least of their worries. I think with the extreme pressure they are under they would have the funeral home involved in the scam, and there are ways they could conceal whatever they need transporting to the UK' Jake suggested to Dupont.

There was silence for a few moments before Jean-Paul replied with authority 'Could you call in at the Station in the next hour and we'll thrash out a plan between us, after speaking to my men on the ground and get an update on their reports'.

'No problem, I'll make my way there now' before he ended the call.

Parking his hire car in the Station car park he walked to the front desk, explained who he was to the Officer and was directed to Jean-Paul's office along the corridor.

Jean-Paul stood and the shook hands before, walking past Jake to close the office door, just as the phone rang. Jean-Paul took the call in his native language as Jake looked on, then a smile spread across the Officer's face as he relayed the conversation to his companion in English. 'Blackledge and his companion arrived outside the Funeral Home fifteen minutes ago, after getting out of their vehicle the boot was opened and each man took two bags into the front door. Most unusual to take bags into that premises unless it was clothes for the departed, but four bags, my guess is, that it's to drop off drugs that we think are to be concealed in a coffin'.

'I agree, what do you suggest the next move is for the Police?' Jake asked.

'It's a tricky one, we are only guessing at this time what is happening, and I would need a signed search warrant before I could proceed, however I think initially I will remove my officer from the Hotel and go two up outside the Funeral Home, leaving you to oversee Blackledge at the Hotel' said Dupont scratching his head.

'I personally think we need to catch the drugs being hidden in the coffin before it leaves the premises, otherwise you would have to either stop the hearse on the road to the airport, or get the Security Staff to check the coffin when it's being unloaded, which is rather a sordid approach, but I'm completely in your hands Jean-Paul'.

'OK, I'll phone my man at the Hotel and arrange for him to relocate to the square, then I will sort out a search warrant, before calmly walking in the front door, while my men seal off the rear where they keep the hearse and funeral car. It would be best to do this when Blackledge and his friend are not around, as I'm sure the funeral people, although involved, would be compliant with our investigation. If everything went to plan we could then hunt down the other two and arrest them, for you to take Blackledge back to England for trial. How does that sound to you Jake?'

'A very good plan indeed as long as the bird doesn't fly before we are ready sir'.

'If any movement took place before I have the search warrant we will storm the premises, and I trust my superiors would be kind at my approach assuming everything worked out successfully'.

He sat back in his chair before taking a big breath, looked and Jake and said 'Coffee?'

Jake smiled with, 'Please, that sounds a good plan'.

Whilst Jake drank his, Dupont rang the officer stationed in the square and outlined the operation to him, but on no account's was he to either approach either of the men or enter the property without his instructions. He then rang through to make arrangements for a search warrant asking the person he spoke to how long it would take. He appeared happy when he replaced the receiver and said to Jake that he would have the papers by the end of the day.

Jake stood, shook Dupont's hand and left the Station. Sitting in his car he pondered over the proposed operation, and although he thought the scheme to get the drugs to the UK preposterous, it was that stupid that if he hadn't come to France it would have worked, right under the Police's noses.

The most important thing now was to hit the Funeral Home within the next forty eight hours before the drugs were removed, but he must let Dupont do what is necessary in the Police's own schedule, and he would go along with whatever he was required to do. He drove back to the Hotel and parked at the rear of the premises, then went to his room, but not before the Receptionist called to him and said that he had a phone call from his 'brother' in London. Jake thought 'brother', then realised it could only be Henry Bates, and asked for the number lthat had been left, only to confirm it was from the Office.

Sitting in his comfortable bedside chair he dialled Henry's number, which was picked up immediately with 'Hi Jake, I've just had a call from Dupont, he outlined you're conversation with him and I suggested you get on with it without further delay, he proposes that they hit the Funeral Home tomorrow morning just as it opens to the Public at 9am local time. He said for you to keep an eye on Blackledge and inform him when he leaves the Hotel after breakfast, and to confirm that the other man has collected him. Give it a few minutes and then follow in the car and park up in the square, he will approach mob handed with armed officers and enter the building. When it has been secured he will send an officer to fetch you and you will be able to see the final stage played out'.

'Sound's good sir, I hope that my assumption is correct and that they propose to transport the drugs in a coffin, otherwise I will end up having egg on my face, but one way or another these trafficker's will be arrested together with the funeral directors for helping them. Once Blackledge is arrested will you send a specialist Police Officer from the UK to take him back to London, or do you expect me to bring him back?'

'No Jake, I wouldn't expect you to bring him back, however once the exchange is made you can return on the same flight and sit with the officer as back up, but Blackledge isn't a violent man so the return should be quite smooth'.

Completing the call to Henry, he then rang Clare to apologise for his completing his call with her so abruptly before he explained in minimal detail why. Clare had a chuckle, then said Dad you get more mysterious as you get older, take care and I look forward to your visit here soon'.

Checking the time, he realised that it was past midday, and with the rumble in his stomach thought it was time for something to eat.

He decided to go to the Dining Room to see what was on the menu and possibly have lunch there, as he entered the room he was surprised to see quite a few people sat at tables, and in the corner sat Blackledge with another man. Not having seen the driver before he assumed that was his companion, so he sat down some six tables away from them. The friendly waiter walked towards him with a menu and asked what he would like to drink, so he plumped for a carafe of red wine, whilst he perused the food on offer. After a few minutes he decided on the 'special' which was braised beef sautéed potatoes and vegetable's.

There was considerable noise being generated by the other diner's so he was unable to pick up any conversation from the two drug dealer's, but whilst waiting for his food he sent off a message to Dupont that both men were sat having lunch at the Hotel, and he would keep a close eye on them.

Chapter 44

The meal as expected was delicious, and as he finished off the acceptable red wine he noticed that his quarry were just completing their meal's and had asked for the bill.

Jake stood and made his way to Reception, picked up a paper and sat on one of the Lounge chairs by the front door, so he could see where they went. He didn't have to wait long, as he turned the first page of the paper they came out of the Dining Room and straight out of the front door. He watched as they turned right then after a few seconds he followed to see if they were going to the rear car park. However they walked past the entrance and along the road where the other man's car was parked, got in and drove off in the opposite direction to the town. Jake dialled Dupont's mobile and explained what he had witnessed, he wondered if they were going to the Airport to book a flight for Blackledge and make arrangements for the coffin's transportation. Dupont 'Hm'd' a little before saying 'I'll ring the Transport Police and explain but also get one of my Officer's up there immediately to confirm our thought's, thank's Jake for you're detective work, as soon as I know something I'll get back to you'.

Chapter 45

Now in limbo Jake decided to take a walk along the path he had been on before and as the weather was quite pleasant explore the wooded area that he had only just viewed the last time, before turning and returning to the Hotel. He got to the seat without anyone appearing on the path and sat for a while, the colours around him were quite vibrant so he took a few snaps with his mobile before standing up and heading into the woods where the trail meandered between the huge trees that dwarfed him, as he walked deeper and deeper into the woods. As the trail appeared well trodden he didn't feel anxious at all, but was glad when he saw the path lighten as he got to the end of the woods. To his amazement he was confronted by a huge lake, no more than twenty yards from the end of the path. There was another path that took walker's around the perimeter of the lake, and he assumed this would also be a great location for a paddle or swim during the warmer month's of the year for local people and holidaymakers alike.

Casting his eyes over the expanse of water, he noticed in the distance there was a person swimming near the far bank, it looked as if they were clad in a wet suit together with a rubber hat thus covering most of the body. The strokes were that of an accomplished swimmer and someone that swam regularly during all times of the year apparently. Then Jake noticed that there were seats at various locations around the lake so he plonked himself down and watched the person carry out their programme of varying strokes. After some ten minutes the swimmer changed direction and headed towards Jake's location before stopping and waving to him.

In French he asked Jake if he fancied a dip, but he replied he had no gear and also it was too cold for him. He let out a huge guffaw before turning away and returning to the other bank. Jake stood, turned right and walked around the path to approach the position where the man had left the water, but there was no-one in sight when he got there. He carried on the circumnavigation of the lake and then wandered back through the woods along the pathway before returning to the Hotel.

Chapter 45

As he entered the Hotel he changed his mind about going to his room and walked to the car park at the rear and got in his car. His destination was the Airport, where he would go to the Viewing Gallery and watch the aircrafts movements, acclimatising himself also with the loading of baggage etc and its whereabouts, also to see if the two men would be visiting today.

Parking in the short term car park he walked into the terminal and made his way to the raised area where he could observe both Ticket Booths and the outside area whilst looking like a 'plane spotter'.

He spent an hour watching various planes arriving and departing, and became quite transfixed at the organising it takes for this industry to run so smoothly, during that time he noted where the luggage etc, left and came into the terminal building, however there was no sign of the two men he hoped to see, so he thought he would get back in his car and pop into the town to do a little shopping. However as he walked down the steps to exit the building he was dumbfounded to see Blackledge and his companion walking towards the ticket stand. He stopped, turned and walked back up the stairs to prevent them seeing him and as he walked he dialled Dupont's number. The call was picked up immediately with 'Jake this is getting a regular call from you, how may I help?'

'Just an update for you really, I thought I would visit the airport today to check where the coffin would be stored and taken to the plane, also the off chance that our quarries would turn up here. I've been here for an hour observing the place and pretending to be a plane spotter, I was just leaving when the two of them have just walked in and are at the ticket counter., I think someone ought to get here post haste as I have no jurisdiction here to ask any pertinent questions. In the meantime I will stay and observe for you, shall I leave the line open?'

'I will come myself Jake, together with two of my burly officers in case of a confrontation, see you shortly, and yes I would appreciate it if you leave your phone on'

Now in a quandary, he looked around before boldly walking down the stairs and turning away from the position the two men were, they didn't notice him as they were deeply involved in conversation with what appeared to be the Airport Manager who was waving his hands about in a somewhat aggressive manner towards them.

Jake sat in a chair some way away from them but keeping them in view, he picked up a discarded paper and watched as the circus continued at the ticket counter.

Ten minutes passed by, but the man was unrelenting in his manner as if they had asked for something extraordinary that appeared unattainable which left Jake quite bemused, however he thought he would soon get an answer as Inspector Dupont strode in flanked by two burly policemen.

Jake stood to watch what would happen next as the three men walked towards the confrontation, and proceeded to gabble away in French. All those involved became quite animated in conversation before the two policemen restrained the drug dealers with some force and handcuffed them. They were then escorted out of the premises by the officers, which was a signal for Jake to walk towards Dupont unobserved by the criminals.

Jake shook Dupont's hand and said, 'could it really have been as easy at that?'

Dupont shrugged and said 'It's only part one my friend, we have to raid the Funeral Home now whilst they are in custody, and attempt to locate the drugs before we arrest the Owners of said premises, then after all that we have to prove that one belongs to the other and when and how was it to be despatched to England'.

A wide smile spread across Jake's face before he answered with 'That's the easy part you smooth talking policeman, they will delay as long as possible but I'm sure they will confess to a lesser charge, as they didn't have the drugs on them'.

'Um, I see your point you clever Englishman, however I'm glad we have reached stage one of this investigation, I'll just go and speak to the person they were attempting to purchase airline tickets from and find out when they or just your man intended to fly'.

'I'll come along with you if that's OK, I could be your witness, but unfortunately the conversation will be in French which I can only just hold a short conversation'.

Dupont scratched his head before replying with, 'good idea Jake, I'll say that you are an undercover detective and was the officer that first recognised the two men we were after'.

'Excellent, I'll follow you' Jake replied.

Chapter 45

Walking to the desk Dupont asked for the Airport Manager, who was in an office adjacent to them he walked out after a minute or two and approached them with a quizzical look on his face before asking how he could be of service.

Dupont explained the circumstances and what had just happened, explaining that he wished to interview the person they were talking to about the purchase of tickets by the arrested felons. Also could he take the young lady away from her station and talk to her in a quiet room.

The Manager talked to the young girl for a couple of minutes, before she stood put a sign up to say that this booth was unattended and walked into the Manager's office. The room was quite extensive and there were a number of chairs available. The Manager said he was due a coffee break and left them to it.

Dupont explained to the woman that there was nothing to be alarmed about and handed over his warrant card for her to look at, he also said that Jake was a fellow detective who would take any notes that were necessary.

A quarter of an hour later Dupont had all the information he required from her, which was the flight they had booked, together with a coffin that would accompany them under freight. They had paid their necessary dues and the tickets were in their possession.

She was then excused to go back to her work, and as the door closed the Manager returned to retrieve his office from the Police.

'Thank you for your assistance on this delicate matter, I cannot explain what these people's intention's were but I can assure you that they were not relative's of the person in the coffin, and there might not even be a body in the coffin anyway, but that is the only explanation I can give you at present as this is an ongoing investigation' and with that he shook the man's hand and left his office with Jake trailing behind him.

As they walked out into the fresh air and headed towards the car park Dupont patted Jake's arm and said 'thank you' with some relief, Jake just nodded at him.

As they approached their cars Dupont turned to Jake and said 'I'm now authorising a raid on the funeral home, so would you like me to follow you to your Hotel car park, then come into town with me to witness the raid?'

'Fine with me, I would like to see it to the end and check if my initial thought's were correct'.

'OK, let's go then' Dupont said with some urgency.

After collecting him from the car park, Jake was securely strapped into the Inspector's large Citroen estate as they raced into town and pulled up alongside other police cars in the Square.

Two officers in full combat gear were stationed either side of the front door allowing Inspector Dupont to enter first, he knew there were other officers stationed at the rear of the premises just in case they tried to escape that way when they were confronted.

As they entered the front parlour there were two oldish men dressed all in black sat at their desks, together with a lady whom they assumed was their secretary. As Inspector Dupont and Jake entered they looked up in absolute horror as to the intrusion on such a sacred establishment and blurted out their annoyance to boot.

However the Police Officer was armed with a signed search warrant which he waved in front of the Secretary, and then to the two Funeral Director's, who nodded in acknowledgement before protesting and asking what they were looking for.

'This warrant allows my officers to search this building and its surroundings for concealed drugs, may I suggest that your secretary leave's the office and goes home for the day. We will be here sometime carrying out a detailed search and unfortunately you two gentlemen will be accompanying my officer's to the Station for separate interviews once we have finished here, do you understand?'

They both nodded rather sheepishly, before attempting to say something. However Dupont raised his hand and said 'wait till we get to the Station before you say anything.' he beckoned the two officer's outside to come into the office and guard the two men whilst he investigated further.

He walked past the startled secretary who stood up and walked out of the office, then he continued into the Chapel of Rest which housed one coffin on stands in front of a small alter with a gold cross on. Dupont approached the coffin and looked at the inscription on the lid. Jake also looked at the inscription and with some amusement said 'I think this is the one Inspector, check the name of the 'deceased?'

It read 'ALBERT TATLOCK 1928-2003'

Dupont looked puzzled and asked Jake why he thought it was funny.

'Albert Tatlock was a character in a soap opera in the UK, not a real person, Obviously Blackledge thought it would pass the French Police as they wouldn't understand the significance of the name, so it's a good job you have a boring English guy here who could interpret the pun the dealer's attempted to get away with, may I suggest we get one of them in here to open the lid and let us see what lies within'

Dupont turned and walked out the door, before returning with one of the Director's.

'Would you please open the coffin for me, now' he said with some authority.

The man looked at him before walking to the corner of the room where there was a concealed door, Jake quickly followed him to make sure he wasn't trying to make a bolt for it, however he only went to fetch some tools from a cupboard.

It only took a few moments for him to release the fixings before he took off the lid and set it to one side. He stood back and said 'as you can see it is just a corpse that is due to be transported back to England on a flight tomorrow'.

Both Dupont and Jake looked inside the casket and to their astonishment inside was an old man dressed in a suit, with a white shirt and coloured tie, complete with socks and shoes. Out the corner of Jake's eye he noticed a slight smirk on the man's face before it quickly disappeared, there was obviously more to this than meet's the eye he thought. They are definitely being paid well for the concealment of the drugs and have worked hard on wherever they are hidden.

Dupont read Jake's mind and he looked directly at the man and said 'I want this body removed from the coffin, transported into your embalming room and opened up,

I will get your fellow Director to help you with the work but I want it done immediately, do you understand?'

'Yes Officer, but before we do this unchristian act may I say that we were forced to carry out this work, much to our distaste, with threats to our business and lives, and although we went along with it I understand you will treat us the same as them'.

'Let's see what pans out over the next few hours before decisions are to be made, now let's get to it'.

Chapter 46

Over the following hour and a half the two men stripped the clothes off the body and with dignity removed the crude stitches that adorned the corpse to expose the cavity within. It appeared that all the organs had been removed and the shell was solidly packed with plastic bags containing a white powder which they guessed was heroin.

Dupont turned to the men and asked who the deceased person was, they refused to comment or give any reply at all, only that they would give all details back at the station. He then took out his mobile and spoke rapidly into the device asking for two drugs squad officers, to attend and that the two policemen in the outside office to come and collect the funeral directors and take them back to the Station for interview under caution.

They locked up the premises and left officers at the front and rear of the property, who fitted police tape over all the external doors, then remain on guard until further notice.

Dupont and Jake then returned to the police station to commence the interviews of the four men now held under caution. The four had been kept in separate cells to prevent them collaborating their stories, or if to stay silent under interrogation.

Jake followed the Inspector to his office, sat down in his chair and let out a huge sigh, and showing the relief and pleasure at how easy the capture of these criminals had panned out, but most of all the capture of the huge amount of drugs.

There was a knock on the door as one of his subordinates came in and spoke rapidly in French to his Boss, then turned and left the room.

Jake looked confused as he couldn't grab a word of what the officer had just said to Dupont, but there was nothing wrong as he explained to Jake. 'The older of the two Funeral Director's would like a word with me urgently, he obviously want's to get his version off his chest as soon as possible.

I will be interviewing him in a room that has a two way mirror and has a sound connection to the room so if you follow me I will show you the room and you can listen to everything that will be said'.

'Excellent, this should make interesting listening, and a possible explanation as to how they got involved in the first place'.

'I agree, it should be a quick interview, as up until they got involved with these criminals the firm has been in existence since 1920 and has served the town and surrounding areas with great professionalism and dignity to all the people that have required their services'.

They walked along the corridor with Dupont showing Jake the door to his Observation Room, whilst he walked further along the corridor to the Interview Room.

Jake sat down in the chair and donned headphones to listen to the Interview although it would be made in the national language.

Looking through the large picture frame window the Funeral Director was already seated with what he assumed was an agreed local solicitor, and they were talking furiously, a few words of which he recognised 'Listen, keep quite, not guilty' were some that were amongst the many. They fell silent as Dupont and a fellow officer entered the room, Dupont shuffled some papers around until he looked up and obviously read him his rights under caution, before commencing the interview.

It was mostly a one way conversation with Dupont asking a lot of questions, then all of a sudden the man broke down and gabbled away with the solicitor trying desperately to prevent his Client from saying too much at this early stage, however he continued to gabble on which appeared to Jake like a confession.

Ten minutes passed before the man completed his oratory and placed his head on his hands that were resting on the table and burst into tears.

Dupont stood and left the room, a few moments later he entered Jake's room and said 'that tells us all, they were coerced into their involvement by Blackledge initially, before he threatened their families with harm if they didn't carry out their requirements, they even located the corpse, from where the man doesn't know. All they had to do was to provide a coffin, place the plastic bags inside the cadaver and dress him up. Then when they were ready to meet them at the airport and sign over the coffin to the freight office. I asked about payment for their work and they were informed that once in the UK the would send ten thousand euros to the office. I said to him if they left on the plane he could guarantee that no payment would be forthcoming as they were hardened criminals'.

Jake looked at Dupont's face before saying his bit 'They must be quite genuine and so afraid that their families were in danger unless the carried out the criminals demands, so although they were totally integrated with the operation, their involvement was minimal, and also under extreme pressure'.

'I agree Jake, I will now be speaking to the other Director, then later today I will have a go at the other two, why don't you get off now and have a break, as you were originally at the sharp end and the main person who carried out the ground work of the operation. Myself and the French people thank you for your involvement in the arrest of these drug dealers and their accomplices, together with getting a huge amount of drugs off the streets of France and of course the UK'.

He stood and shook Jake's hand before giving him a firm French embrace.

This form of affection was used throughout French life, however Jake felt slightly uncomfortable for a brief moment before he realised that Inspector Dupont was really thanking him for his help in solving what he had originally been unaware of as a huge haul of drugs, having been brought into the Country and then concealed for transporting on to the UK.

Jake turned and walked out of the Office before anything further was said. He realised that Dupont now had the hard task of completing this investigation, before hauling the accused up in front of a Court to obtain the necessary convictions.

As he left the Police Station he dialled Henry Bates' direct number to give him the good news. The call was picked up immediately, then over the following ten minutes Jake gave him all the details of the 'sting' at the airport and the raid on the Funeral Director's premises and everything that had been found within.

The only negative was that Blackledge could not be extradited until they were taken to Court and a conviction made, so Jake suggested that it wouldn't be any point him staying in France, and that any extradition would have to be carried out by a member of the Police Force when the prisoner was ready to be returned to the UK to serve his sentence.

Chapter 46

'I agree Jake, if you book out tomorrow morning and catch the early flight back, perhaps you could call and see me before you return back home'.

Chapter 47

After breakfast the next morning, he paid for his accommodation and any other costs at Reception before ringing the Car Hire Company explaining that he was returning home later and would leave the car at the Airport. The person gave him the total of his invoice which he paid for over the phone, asking for a receipt to be sent via what's app.

Driving to the Terminal he was deep in thought of the various incidents that had happened over that past few days, then realised that he hadn't informed the two people that had offered him a homely meal, that he was returning home this morning. He scrolled through his saved numbers and dialled the number for them, then realising that he didn't know their names as only mobile numbers were exchanged. However he decided he would just blag it with whoever picked up the call. It must have rung twenty times before it was answered with 'Helen Markrum, how may I help you?'

'Good morning its Jake, we met on the path to the woods'.

'Hello Jake, are you calling to arrange a visit to us?' she enquired.

'Unfortunately no, I have to return to the UK as a matter of some urgency, and I will not be returning to France in the near future, I'm just ringing to thank you for your generous offer and apologise for not ringing sooner, I only knew of the urgency of the situation an hour ago'.

'That's fine, I hope everything works out OK for you, and just remember if you do return to the area in the future, please give us a ring'.

'Thank you Helen your generosity bodes hope for the future, bye for now' then he disconnected the call.

Pulling up at the car park he walked over to the Car Hire office and handed over the keys, then the receptionist gave him his paper receipt and wished him a safe journey home.

Walking into the Terminal he handed over his return ticket then through to Passport Control and into Departure's for his wait for boarding. He felt relaxed but still a part of him would like to have been assured that Blackledge would have already been sentenced and ready for deportation before he left for home, however the justice system has to be in order before that could take place.

Also it was really not his problem any more, as the drugs had been seized and four people were in custody facing trial, he could therefore return home pleased that he had been a large cog in the operation that trapped the smugglers.

His flight was due to leave in an hour, so he spent some time looking around the Duty Free shop picking up a few items for himself and one for Henry Bates.

The Lounge area started filling up as two flights were leaving within minutes of each other, but thankfully his was first to leave, and the call went out for passengers for London to make their way to the Exit door. The plane was only half full as the steps were pulled away and the door was closed. The engines built up in intensity before the aircraft made its way to the end of the runway, a wait of a few minutes before the acceleration thrust, then down the tarmac before the pilot lifted the huge machine into the air for its short flight to the UK.

Landing at London City Airport on time the small amount of travellers left the plane in an orderly manner and twenty minutes later Jake was stood outside in the fresh London air.

Getting in the taxi he gave the address he required which was a street away from his actual destination, for obvious reasons. The short walk felt good to be on UK soil, but as he slipped down the ramp of the underground car park where his Lexus had been parked he felt glad to be back to reality. Placing his bag in the boot of the car, he took the lift up to Reception and asked for Henry Bates, explaining who he was to the young lady, who smiled and confirmed that she knew who he was and for him to make his way up in the lift, and she would forewarn her superior that he was on his way.

Jake was deep in thought as the doors of the lift opened onto the fifth floor having spent the short period of time in the enclosed box running though the details of his latest exploits in preparation for his debrief with Henry.

He knocked and walked straight into the luxurious office that housed the head man of MI6, who stood ready to shake hands with his Agent. 'Welcome back Jake, from what I can work out the arrest couldn't have gone any smoother. I have had a long conversation with

Dupont, and he was full of praise at the way you handled the whole affair, in fact he was up to offering you a post in France, but you would have to brush up on your French he said' Bates said whilst laughing loudly. 'Enough of that take a seat and run through the whole event, starting from your landing on French soil'.

Jake thought for a while and over the next quarter of an hour outlined everything that had happened, from landing at Caen to his leaving this morning.

Henry sat back in the chair, digesting the tale that had just come out of Jake's mouth before saying 'I wish I had a 'Youth Pill' I could give you, as all the time I have been in this position, no-one has come anywhere near you for sorting difficult things out with such professionalism as yourself, and I commend you most sincerely. Now priorities, what is your next move, I expect you are exhausted, do you want to head back to Dorset, or would you like to stay in London overnight and we could visit a certain Restaurant that isn't too far from here and have a celebratory meal together with a few drinks?'

'I am indeed tired, however there is nothing pressing at home at the moment and a stay in the Capital rather appeals to me especially a visit to Marcus Waring's delightful establishment and his delicious cuisine'.

'That's sorted then, do you want to go to your usual Hotel and book in, and have a wander around the City until say 6pm, and meet me by the underground car park for a taxi'.

'Fine with me, I'll take my leave, and catch up with you later sir' Jake said getting up from his seat.

'Just before you go, could I have your receipts and I'l sort out the cash when we meet' Henry explained.

Jake fumbled in his wallet and handed over all the receipts he had acquired which Henry sorted and put in an envelope.

Twenty minutes later he entered the Hotel and booked in, strangely he was given the same room that he had used previously, so it was if he had come home. He had a quick shower and a change of clothes, before he decided to do a bit of shopping for replacement clothing. He decided to hit his Debit card hard and splashed out on a designer suit, fitted white shirt finished with an elegant silk tie, new socks and a pair of brogue shoes. Looking in the mirror he thought he really looked the business and would appear part of the elite in the Restaurant later.

Chapter 47

As he paid the bill he cast his mind back to the days when he wasn't so well off and thought to himself that what his outfit had cost him today, was at least two months pay not so very long ago.

Pleased with himself he strode back to the Hotel and walked into the Bar. The room was only graced with two other people so he walked up to the counter and was surprised to see the usual man in position ready to take his order. 'Small beer is it Mr Tordale, or would you like something else today?'

'Nice to see you again Giles, and I'm impressed with your memory. I have just returned from France and feel it would be appropriate to drink some wine, so I'll have a chilled bottle of Chardoney please, and take one for yourself. I'll sit at my usual table if you would kindly bring it to me'.

Walking towards the table he nodded to the other guests before taking a seat in anticipation of his wine delivery.

He didn't have to wait long as the Bartender walked over carrying a silver tray that contained his wine with a glass and a selection of nuts in a bowl.

Giles poured a small amount of wine in his glass, which he sipped and nodded his approval whereupon the glass was filled up, then he turned and went back behind the Bar. Over the next hour he slowly drank the bottle whilst devouring the tasty nibbles and took his leave of the room after signing for his drink.

Retiring to his room he laid out his newly acquired clothes ready for this evening's event, then stripped off and settled down for a nap.

He awoke, checked his watch and noticed that he had slept for an hour and a half, the time now being 4.30pm. Quickly having another shower, and shave he dressed in his new attire, before heading down to Reception and ordering a taxi.

The taxi dropped him off fifty yards from the underground car park and as he walked the short distance to the entrance he was met my his Boss.

'My God Jake, you scrub up well, new outfit is it?'

'I thought it was time to purchase some decent attire for special occasions, but forgot what the prices are here, they must be three times that of rural Dorset. But as my mother used to say 'you get what you pay for'. And I must admit this outfit is extremely comfortable and well worth the money'.

'Right Jake, I hope you're ready, Marcus is looking forward to seeing you again, and here comes the taxi now'.

Jake turned and smiled before replying with 'I expect he says that to all his customer's'.

'I doubt it, when I booked he actually asked if you were coming with me'.

'That's nice, I must admit I feel quite honoured', they then got in the taxi and headed off to their venue.

Met at the door by the Manager, handshakes were made all round before they were ushered to their table, whereupon the man himself exited the kitchen and strode towards them, shaking hands he expressed his pleasure at welcoming them both.

Marcus waited before they sat down then explained that there was the usual menu available together with a 'special dish' not on the menu this evening, if they were interested in sampling it.

A glint in Henry's eye made Jake speak first, 'Sound's very interesting, are we allowed to ask what the main ingredients are or just take a chance that we will enjoy it?'

Marcus grinned and replied with 'I would prefer to deliver the goods first then ask for your opinion once you have sampled it, what do you say gentlemen?'

Jake looked at Henry who nodded his head in approval, then Jake replied with 'It looks as if you have two guinea pigs at your disposal'.

'Excellent' Marcus replied, 'I'll get on with it, just give your drinks and starter order to the waiter, and I hope you enjoy the experience this evening'.

And with that the renowned Chef disappeared back into the cauldron that is a Restaurant kitchen. Both men smiled before Henry frowned and said 'I hope it isn't too flamboyant, so I think we had better decide on a small starter and a bottle of bubbly to keep us going'.

Henry ordered some sort of fancy fish dish with salad, whilst Jake plumped for his favourite starter of prawns marinated in various sauces with a side of thin sliced oriental vegetables. There was a break before the main event arrived, however it was worth it. Marcus walked to the table carrying a gargantuan plate of food that he placed in front of them, he stood back and waited for a response from his diners. Henry stared in astonishment at the mix of ingredients on the platter but could only utter one word 'Unbelievable'.

Jake also stared in wonder, trying to decipher what they were being offered, there were shellfish, various meats, accompanied with an assortment of vegetables and salads. There was an array of sauces intermingled around the plate, before finally the waiter placed a side dish of potatoes cooked in various ways.

Marcus stood back as the two diners stared in awe at the incredible dish that was displayed in front of them before Henry opened his mouth to reply to the Chef and Owner with 'An incredible display of culinary art, I hope that it tastes as good at it looks, but I'm sure it does, any comments Jake'.

Jake sat there open mouthed before replying with 'It never ceases to amaze me how you replicate food as an art form and I applaud you for it' he answered, standing and shaking Marcus's hand.

'I'll leave you to Pierre who will cover your plates with whatever you fancy, enjoy' he bowed and returned to the kitchen.

Both men turned to each other and smiled as their plates were carefully filled with a selection of the platters contents, before Pierre the waiter also bowed and left them to their food.

An hour later both men sat back from their empty plates, chatting quietly about the sumptuous meal that they had just consumed, and as the waiter cleared their plates Marcus returned to the table presumably to ask for their comments.

They obliged with positive murmurs, before he asked if they had room for dessert. Henry smiled at him before saying 'He would like one of his fancy sorbet's', and Jake seconded his suggestion, also adding they would like to have a nice Port to go with it.

A smiling Marcus returned to the kitchen, explaining to Pierre what his Client's requested, he then followed in his employer's walk ready to deliver their dessert's after they had been prepared. He walked back with two glasses and a bottle of Port, whilst informing them that the drinks were on Marcus, so he poured the Port before saying he would be bringing their food shortly.

Half an hour later Henry made a call to the usual taxi Company to collect them as soon as possible for the short journey to Jake's Hotel and then onward to the underground car park. Henry thanked the waiter with a generous tip and asked him to forward the invoice to his office as usual. They stood and walked to the front door where Marcus stood waiting for them with a handshake to both, thanking them for coming to his humble establishment.

As they finished talking, the taxi pulled alongside and they made their way back to their destinations, with Henry shaking Jake's hand as he alighted the vehicle five minutes later. 'Have a nice trip back to Dorset Jake, and thank's for everything you have done recently'. Jake turned before replying with 'Thank you Henry for your generosity and help in the past two years, perhaps you and your good lady could come and visit me sometime, stay over for the weekend and I'll show you the sights as well as treating you to an all expenses 'free' break'.

'That sound intriguing Jake, I'll have a word with the dear lady and will be in touch soon'.

With that the door closed just as Henry wiped a tear from his cheek, which Jake thought was most likely caused by his sudden offer of time away from London.

Collecting his keys from Reception he suddenly felt quite tired, and decided to have an early night, allowing for an early start the next morning.

Chapter 48

After an enjoyable deep and relaxing sleep he woke at 6 am feeling totally refreshed, he got out of bed had a cold, followed by a hot shower, then shaved and changed into casual clothes. He packed, then walked down to the Dining Room for breakfast, although he had a sumptuous meal last evening, after cereal he plumped for a good old English Breakfast consisting of two fried eggs, bacon, mushrooms, black pudding and fried bread. Followed by two slices of toast accompanied by a pot of strong black filter coffee.

Half an hour later feeling as if he could go a couple of days without any more sustenance he paid for his room at Reception, went to collect his bag and sauntered down the road to retrieve his car from the underground car park.

As it was still early, the bulk of traffic was heading into town, therefore he made his way swiftly out of City of London and an hour and a half later he pulled up outside his home, Wisteria Cottage. As he opened the front door and deactivated the alarm, he sighed with relief as he inhaled the unmistakable smell of home. There was an accumulation of mail waiting for him on the mat, which he collected and placed on the Dining Room table. He collected his luggage from the boot of the Lexus and took it straight up to his bedroom. He then unpacked, took clothing down to the kitchen to run through the washing machine, then went back to the bedroom to hang up his external garments and put his toiletries in the bathroom.

First things first, he put the kettle on for a cup of tea before sitting down and addressing the pile of mail.

There were flyers from various Charities, advertising from Double Glazing Companies, details of Funeral Plans, so on and so on. Before he spied three hand written letters, one with a Swedish stamp attached, obviously from Olivia, another from France, and the last one from Australia. The last object was an A4 package with no indication of who it was from, but it had British stamps on the front.

Opening the envelopes in front of him, he started first with the Swedish one, and to his surprise it was from the Police from Stockholm. It was written officially from the Head of the Police Force there, requesting Jake's presence to attend a medal presentation ceremony that was coming up in a week's time.

Between the fold's of the letter was a first class plane ticket to Stockholm, how strange he thought I was given money etc for helping in the arrest of the thieves who had infiltrated the whole of Europe and beyond, in their drugs distribution together with all the other illegal trades, they where eventually cornered at Wisteria Cottage by a simple trap that was sprung by himself. The letter was signed by the Commissioner of the Police, therefore another visit to the Scandinavian country appeared his next outing. At the bottom of the letter the proposed date for his attendance was in two days time. This would need a little thought as he would have to return to London to catch his flight, as he had only just left there, still he was quite intrigued what it was all about, should he ring Olivia and find out or just turn up at the allotted time. The other item in the package was a formal programme of events, thankfully the one he had received was written in English, as he quickly scanned through the pages, two lines stood out to him. They read 'SPECIAL AGENT JAKE TORDALE ATTACHED TO MI6 - SPECIAL AWARD FOR SERVICES TO THE SWEDISH NATION AND THE WHOLE OF EUROPE.

He read it two or three times before his mind went back to his initial thoughts, that he had already been to Stockholm and received a monitory reward for the same act, however he thought another trip could clear up an outstanding meeting again with the delectable Olivia, assuming that she would be in attendance.

He made a quick call to Henry Bates to find out if he had been notified of his invitation to Sweden, however his number was diverted back to Reception. The young lady said, after the formal enquiry as to his name. 'He's out at the moment Mr Tordale shall I ask him to return your call when he is back in the office or do you wish to try his mobile?'

'If you could ask him to ring me back on this number when he can, it's not that urgent, thank you'.

Next one he opened was the French one, It was from Inspector Dupont, informing him that all four of the defendants had been up before the Court, and various sentences had been given out, Blackledge had been sentenced to four years in a UK prison, his accomplice who was a French citizen received a total of nine years, finally the two Funeral Director's were let off with a huge fine of ten thousand euros each together with a two year suspended sentence. He confirmed that he had already informed Henry Bates, who was making arrangements for Blackledge's extradition. Finally he thanked him for his awareness in the matter and how helpful he had been in the solving of the crime.

The final letter was from Australia, and it was on headed Police notepaper, quickly scanning through to the end of the letter he noticed it was signed by Inspector Chi.

It was not Police business but outlining her recent life since he had left Brisbane. She thanked him again for their formal conversation and understanding regarding her turmoil over her sexuality, but would like to confirm that she had reached a decision in that regard. Although she harboured thought's of Lesbianism she had recently stepped out with a bachelor schoolteacher who lived near her, and was now 100% sure that she was straight.

They were very serious about each other she confirmed, and would like to give him fair warning that if things progressed to the marital stage he would do her the honour of giving her away.

The letter was signed with two kisses.

He now turned to the brown A4 envelope with a certain amount of scepticism, so he carefully inserted the paper knife into the top of the package, then eased the lid so he could peer inside. All he could see was another smaller package so he turned it onto the table gently, and with care the article slid out. There was a note on the front that said TO JAKE TORDALE, THANK YOU, AND I HOPE THIS TOKEN WILL REMIND YOU OF ME.

He slid open the top of the envelope and pulled out a small note together with a box that contained a gold pocket watch. The note was from the old jeweller which said the following 'A token from me to show you how much I enjoyed and valued your visit to my small establishment during your stay in the USA. It's most unusual for any of my customers to engage in conversation, let alone make purchases without haggling over the price. But I felt that you were a kind and understanding human being and I would like to have got to know you better in the short time that we conversed. In case you are wondering how this envelope reached you, the Receptionist at your Hotel is a

Client of mine and I cheekily asked her if she had a forwarding address for your good self. She said that she could do better than that as she was visiting relations in the City of Birmingham in England soon, and would take it to the UK and post it on to you, obviously I gave the young lady the cost of the postage. Anyway I digress, since you left I had to visit the Hospital for tests and unfortunately I have been diagnosed with an incurable brain tumour, therefore I am at present selling my stock and closing the shop within the next few weeks. Please treasure this watch and I hope it will remind you of the time you spent with an old jeweller who became very fond of you. Yours Stefan Cohen (Your Friend).

Turning over the watch he was taken aback when he saw the inscription on the back FROM ONE FRIEND TO ANOTHER, and the sentimental man that he was, tears streamed down his face, and he had to reach for his handkerchief as memories of the old man overcame him.

He quickly scrolled through his mobile searching for the phone number of the Hotel where he had stayed, when he came across it, he pressed the green button.It took a while to connect before the Receptionist answered. He quickly explained who he was and asked if she could give him the number of Mr Stefan Cohen, the Jeweller, whilst also thanking her for posting his parcel. She laughed loudly thinking of the old man, before asking him to hold while she found the number he required.

She came back on the phone after a few seconds, confirming Stefan's recent diagnoses before giving him the contact number.

Jake replied with 'That is why I wish to speak to him, thank you so much for your help and I'll give him a call now, goodbye'.

Five minutes later the mobile was ringing the number he was given, it appeared to ring for a long time before it was answered by 'Stefan Cohen, how may I help you?'

'Mr Cohen it's lovely to speak to you, it's Jake Tordale from England. I'm just calling to thank you for my parcel which I have just opened, I was able to get your number from the lovely Receptionist at the Hotel that I was staying at. I'm so sorry that you have recently had such unhappy news, is there anything I can help you with, I would not hesitate to return to the States if you require any help with the shop?'

Chapter 48

'So nice to hear from you Jake and thank you for your kind words. I have made good headway in reducing the stock by selling it to other jeweller's in the City, but should you come back I'm sure I could offer you some good deals'.

Jake laughed into the mobile and he could also hear the old man chuckling. 'Always the salesman my friend'.

'I have spent fifty years in this shop, and its part of my DNA, so the patter comes naturally, It will be another two weeks at least before the shop is empty and ready for someone else to take it on or turn it into another type of retail outlet, there's no pressure, but if you could I would love to see you again before its too late'.

Jake pondered for a few seconds before he replied with 'I have to go to Sweden for a few days, but when I return to London I will catch a plane over and book into the same Hotel as before, so with a bit of luck we will meet again within a week. Would that be OK?'

He could hear a sob on the line before Stefan answered with 'I'm looking forward to it already, take care my son' he said before he put the phone down. Jake could imagine that the old man was now quite distraught and in floods of tears. He thought to himself there was no mention of any other family that could help him during these harrowing times, therefore his visit to offer help would be gratefully appreciated he thought.

The more he pondered on the latest revelations the more he thought that his idyllic retirement was a long way in the future, however the items that had now come to light would certainly be taking priority. On his return from Sweden, he would take a flight the day after, returning to the States to help the old jeweller as much as he could to take as much stress off him as was humanly possible.

Next he would send off a message to Inspector Chi, confirming that he would be honoured to walk her down the aisle whenever the formalities were arranged, but obviously with prior knowledge of the date and time the ceremony would take place, although at present it appeared to be still in an embryonic stage.

Bringing him out of his pondering, his mobile was ringing with an incoming call, looking at the screen he realised it was Henry Bates, he quickly answered with 'Thank's for ringing me back sir, how are things?'

'Hi Jake, you obviously know about the French situation by now, and I wondered what else you were up to?'

Jake smiled to himself, assuming that Henry knew about the invitation he had received to visit Sweden so he replied with 'I wanted to know if you had received a note from the Swedish Police in Stockholm of my invitation to an award ceremony the day after tomorrow?'

'I do indeed, that was why I wanted to speak to you, have you any idea what it's about?' Henry queried.

'Unfortunately, no I don't, I was compensated really well on my previous visit, and together with the invitation letter there were First Class airline tickets enclosed for this visit, I assume therefore there must be an additional award from the higher up's. On my return I am flying off to the States again for a few days to visit an old Jewish Jeweller I met whilst I was over there with George Adams, he has had some tragic health diagnosis and is winding up his business. Whilst there I built up quite a rap-ore with him and would like to help him with clearing up as best I can, as he doesn't appear to have any relative's'.

'You have a considerable amount of empathy with people Jake, and you should stand back sometime and think of yourself as a good and kind human being'.

'Thank you sir, I appreciate your thought's, just to confirm I'll be flying to Stockholm the day after tomorrow. I assume my stay there will only be 48 hours at the most, then I'll return to the UK and take a flight to the States the following day. I propose to stay there as long as required to sort out Stefan's business, then I'll return home for a bit of quiet time, whatever that is these days'.

There was a pregnant silence for a short period before Bates interjected with 'George unfortunately is taking early retirement as the beating he received has undermined his confidence and mental health and he feel's that he would be better off carrying out an alternative occupation, leaving me with a big hole in the team'.

Jake thought to himself, he is going to ask me to return full time, so he replied with 'I expect there are a lot of good people out there that could take up George's baton sir?'

'I have a couple of people in mind, perhaps on your return from the States you could spare me an hour or so to look over the possible candidates?'

'My pleasure, but I could only give you my honest opinion, the final decision would have to come from you'.

'I fully understand Jake, have a nice couple of trips and I'll see you soon'.

Chapter 49

First things first, he needed to ring the girls and tell them he had to make two unexpected visits abroad and wouldn't be coming down to see them for at least another few weeks. Clare picked up the phone and said 'Hi Dad are you on your way down today?'

'I'm afraid not luv. I have to go to Sweden tomorrow for an Awards Ceremony which could involve me staying there a couple of days. Then as I return to London I'll be catching a flight to the States again to help out a dear old man I met on my last visit. That should take at least another ten days. But the day after I return home I'll ring you and arrange a visit, OK?'

'That's fine with me Dad, you have to do what you have to do, will you ring Sharon or would you like me to tell her?'

'If you could tell her for me I would appreciate it, I'll be travelling up to London this evening and staying at a Hotel there, as the flight is early tomorrow morning, so once I return I'll give you a call, take care luv and I'll see you soon'.

'OK Dad don't overdo it, you're not getting any younger you know, bye for now'.

Realising he would be absent from his Cottage for at least a couple of weeks he checked his supplies in the kitchen and decided to make up a couple of meals with the disposable ingredients in the fridge and freeze them down for another day. If there was too much there he would have a meal with the leftovers before he departed for London.

Up in his bedroom he packed two separate cases of clothes and toiletries, one for Sweden and the other for the States then took them out the front door and packed them in the Lexus.

Opening the safe he took out his passport, a bundle of euros for his upcoming Swedish trip, together with two thousand GBP's for his visit to America and packed them in his briefcase. The flight to Stockholm tomorrow was scheduled for midday, this would allow him to leave the Hotel reasonably early and call into the office before driving back to Heathrow.

Now with time to spare he thought he would run the vacuum cleaner over the house as he wouldn't be returning for at least a couple of weeks. Once finished he put the washing machine on and put in all his dirty clothing together with the tea and bath towels he had used, allowing time for airing before he left.

Packing his cases and briefcase into the car, he checked all the windows and doors to make sure they were all secure then after activating the alarm he locked the front door and started the Lexus for his journey to London.

An hour and a half later he drove into the underground car park to the Hotel, he had used previously and made his way to Reception to book in. The young lady that he had spoken to before was on duty and gave him a radiant smile as he walked towards the desk. 'Good evening Mr Tordale, are you off on your travels again sir?'

Jake appeared quite gobsmacked with her greeting, but quickly regained his composure, and replied with 'I am indeed, off to Sweden tomorrow for a couple of days, then I stay here overnight before flying off to the States for a week or so. Could I book in overnight now, then when I return stay a further night. Also book my car in for the duration, approximately two weeks?'

'No problem sir' she answered, typing away on the computer.

As he waited he gave the young lady the once-over, guessing she would be in her middle thirties, natural blond hair tied back in a ponytail, minimal make up, small gold ear rings, no apparent tattoo's or rings. She had a full hour glass figure and would certainly turn the eye of many a male and even female tourists that frequent the Hotel.

Jake was still looking her over as she completed the booking form, she blushed slightly as she realised he had been giving her the 'stare', not uncommon in her line of work.

Handing him the room key she just smiled as he returned to his car to retrieve his luggage. Once settled in the room, he felt quite peckish so he walked down to the restaurant and gave the menu his full attention. As the waiter approached he had already decided on a soup starter, main course of gammon with the trimmings, and cheesecake for dessert,to accompany the meal he asked for a bottle of white wine.

An hour later he felt quite satisfied as he sat nursing the last of the wine, contemplating his return visit to Stockholm and what he would encounter on his second visit to the country. The time was approaching

9pm as he stood and walked back to Reception to settle the bill for his evening meal. The young lady was still busy at her station, booking two more customers in, so he sat on a couch patiently waiting his turn.

Ten minutes later she was free so he approached the desk and explained what he had just had in the Restaurant and duly paid the bill. He glanced at her name badge before taking his receipt and thanking 'Nancy' for her attention and bidding her goodnight.

Chapter 50

He walked down to the Dining Room early for breakfast as he wished to meet Henry Bates at 9am for a chat before checking in at the Terminal for his flight to Sweden.

He had a full English and a pot of black coffee together with toast to help him on his way, as he was unsure what, and when his next meal would be.

Nodding to the Receptionist as he walked out the front doors, he made his way to the car park and drove his trusty Lexus out of the complex and joined the lines of traffic entering the Capital. As expected the journey was quite laborious and it took three quarters of an hour before he drove into the car park.

Taking the lift up to Reception, he signed in after speaking to the young man, explaining he was there to see Henry, then he took the lift up to level three, knocked on the Director's door and walked in.

Henry stood and greeted Jake with a firm handshake before saying 'Another trip to Sweden, you are indeed a popular fellow old man'.

'I'm quite intrigued really sir, on my previous visit I was presented with a medal and a monetary gift, and as I have done nothing since I cannot for the life of me wonder why I have been asked to return for another award ceremony, it also appears quite a 'to do', as included with my plane tickets was a programme outlining the various categories and persons due for an award, and to my surprise my name is included'.

'Well when you get any further details please let me know and I'll send a formal thank you from me, what time will you be flying?'

'I have to check in by 11am so I will need to get back to the Hotel and park up the car and catch the shuttle to the terminal within the next hour, so if there is nothing else to discuss I'll ring you when I return from Stockholm'.

'There was just one thing, how is the delectable Olivia and are you meeting up with her again over there?'

'As you know we are going on holiday in a month or so, so I would be surprised if I come across her on this visit, as I guess she will be on duty, but you never know !!'

'Well you'd better run along I won't keep you any longer and I'll see you when you return' he concluded, turning back to the paperwork on his desk.

Jake turned and walked out of the office, taking the lift directly to the underground car park. As he settled into the driver's seat and before he started the engine his mobile rang, without looking at the caller ID he answered with 'Jake Tordale'.

There was a female purring sound on the device before it was answered with 'I'll collect you from the airport, this is an unexpected visit you are making' Olivia questioned.

'Lovely to hear from you, I have a lot to tell you. Just one question, will you be at the awards ceremony and have you any idea why I am on the list?'

'I'll tell you more when I pick you up later today, enjoy the flight' she answered and disconnected the call.

No wiser he started the engine, drove out of the car park, and made his way back to the hotel to deposit his car there and collect his luggage.

He walked into the entrance of Terminal 2 after being dropped off by the regular bus shuttle, and walked over to Departure's and then into the First Class Lounge. He received a nod from the Manager, who remembered him as he had become a well known figure that frequented the Lounge on a number of occasions in the past. He walked over to a table and plush seat in the corner of the room, carefully placing his briefcase between his feet. A waiter approached him and asked if he required anything food or drink wise. He asked for a large gin and tonic and a mixture of nuts, together with The Times newspaper. The man returned after a minute or so with Jake's requirements. Looking around there were quite a few individual's that were intent on their laptops or mobile phones, and a few couples that were deeply in conversation, but no one that stood out to him as a threat.

Of course the Lounge catered for a number of Airlines and it was impossible to notice anyone of those travellers that would be heading to Stockholm on the same flight as himself. As he finished his drink and nibbles he glanced at his watch to check the time just as his flight was called.

Casting his eye around the room he noticed three people stand up and walk towards the exit, realising that they would be accompanying him on his journey, as they left he stood and followed in their wake, taking out his boarding pass and passport. Twenty minutes later the aircraft taxied down the runway gathering speed before soaring up into the bright sunlight and turning East heading towards Scandinavia. The journey would be just over two hours so he settled down to read his newspaper, before the Hostess appeared asking what he would like from the menu in front of him.

By the time the plane landed and the hour difference, it would be late afternoon before he would be sat alongside Olivia in her work vehicle, so he decided to have a meal.

The young lady that approached him was similar in appearance to the blond lady in the group ABBA, what was her name he pondered, before remembering it was Agnetha Faltkog, however that was when the group first appeared. She realised that he was looking her up and down before she asked in perfect English 'have you decided on your meal, sir?'

'Thank you, I would like the casserole and green vegetables, with roast potatoes, and a bottle of red wine No.14 on the list. Then once I finish I will glance at the dessert menu, but the cheese and biscuits certainly look inviting I must say'.

'A good choice sir, are you on holiday or making a business trip, if I may be so bold to ask?'

'Business, I will only be in Stockholm for a couple of days, before returning to London, and then off to the United States for a couple of weeks, work again I'm afraid'.

She looked him up and down before turning and returning to the galley. As she walked Jake was sure she gave an extra wiggle as she disappeared behind the curtain.

Halfway through the flight he had completed his meal, and bottle of wine and was feeling quite drowsy, so reclined his seat to have a doze. He stirred after a short while as he felt a hand on his neck, opening his eyes he was face to face with the hostess who was putting a cushion as support for his neck. Her perfume was intoxicating, and as he focused on her face he noticed that her lips were parted, before her tongue swept across them moistening the skin.

'Sorry to disturb you sir, I was afraid you would wake with a stiff neck so I wanted to place the cushion to support your head'.

Even her breath was sweet, so he thanked her for her concern as he felt a movement in the groin area at the closeness of this delectable and sensuous young woman.

'Is there anything else I can do for you Mr Tordale?' she asked with a toothy grin.

'In other circumstances I would say yes, but as there are over two hundred people on the plane I think my answer would be inappropriate, but thank you anyway'.

She smiled and pulled away from him before saying, 'Landing will be another one and a half hours, I'll call back and see if there is anything I can help you with in half an hour'.

The sap was rising in Jake's nether regions, as the suggested comment didn't go unnoticed, and unless he misread her intentions he would be in for an interesting second half of the flight.

He relaxed back into his seat and contemplated what his visit to Stockholm would entail, with eyes closed he was unaware of the young ladies presence until the waft of her perfume invaded his nostrils, and he was forced to open his eyes.

'I return with a small offering that is not on the menu, but you will have to control your emotions and noise, as there is only a curtain between us and the rest of the First Class passengers. I am a red blooded Swedish spinster, I am 30 years of age, however my work takes me all over the world and gives me little time for leisure. Do you understand what I am talking about Mr Tordale. I am extremely attracted to you and would ask if you feel the same. As you can see I am dressed in a suit, however I have nothing else beneath, so if you are willing I will help you, if you help me with my needs'.

Flabbergasted at the hostess's suggestion, he could only reply with 'I'm all your's but the curtain will not stop anyone coming to find you, and I would hate to be disturbed'.

'Do not worry, I have spoken to my superior, explaining that you are a little under the weather, and I will stay with you until we land to ensure you are OK', with that she stood and removed her cap and jacket, exposing a firm pair of pert breasts which she thrust into Jake's face.

Her hand moved down to his crotch which she stroked until it stood up to greet her.

She undid his belt, pulled down the zip and released the beast, kneeling in front of him she took the whole of his manhood into her mouth and with great dexterity massaged his member with the back of her throat. As she felt him become totally aroused, she stood up, lifted up her skirt eased towards him and carefully took him inside her. 'Don't move, let me do the work' she said with some urgency.

Slowly at first. until she gained momentum, then with vigour she whispered 'I'm coming anytime now so thrust with me'.

They carried on this movement for at least 5 minutes before neither of them could hold out any longer. Jake took a nipple in each hand as he bored into her with gusto. She groaned in his ear, as floods of love juice spread over their thighs, and they sunk into each others arms.

She stood, pulled down her skirt, then put on her hat and jacket back on, then turned towards him and kissed him fully on the lips. Jake was speechless and only smiled as she pulled away from him, allowing him to adjust his clothing. 'Could you bring me a glass of brandy, as I think I need a pick-me-up for the rest of the flight'.

'Certainly Mr Tordale, I'll be about 5 minutes' she replied, pulling the curtain open and walking back to her station.

True to her word she returned after a few minutes with a large brandy, in that time she had applied new makeup and most likely had a quick wash.

'When will you be returning home Mr.Tordale, only I could be on the return flight and we could indulge in round two?'

'I should be in Stockholm for two days only, but as I said I will be flying out to the States the day after I get back to London'.

'You never know, what will be will be, I hope you have a nice stay in my Country'.

As she left he downed the large brandy that was in his hand, then tried to relax and get his composure back before the plane landed and he had to disembark.

An hour later he was pushing his trolley out of the exit doors and was met by Olivia who came running towards him.

'Nice to see you Jake, it was a total surprise to me that you had been put forward for another award, more Importantly they are to be given out by none other than King Carl XV1 Gustav of Sweden. The ceremony takes place tomorrow morning at 11am local time, this will be followed by a formal luncheon finishing around 3pm. I will drive you to the hotel where you stayed before so you can book in and take your belongings up to your room. As you can see I am on duty at present, so I will have to leave you until I leave work at 6pm, perhaps you would like to go out to eat then and have a couple of beers, and tell me what you have been up to since we last met'.

'That sounds good to me' he replied whilst loading his luggage into the boot of the car.

They quickly sped out of the Terminal, headed towards the City before pulling up outside the Hotel's entrance. He retrieved his luggage from the boot and strode into the Hotel. He gave his name to the receptionist who handed him his room key. He turned and kissed Olivia on the cheek saying he would see her this evening, then he took the lift up to the second floor.

After hanging up his clothes in the wardrobe, he stripped off and had a long hot shower before dressing in new clothing. As it was only a couple of hours before Olivia's return he decided to have a little shut eye and settled down in the luxurious bed and drifted off to sleep within minutes.

Chapter 51

He woke up with a start, then after quickly checking the time realising he had been asleep for an hour and a half, but he certainly felt refreshed and invigorated.

Olivia would be calling at the Hotel in another hour's time so he thought he would go down to the Bar and have a nice cool beer or two. Strolling into the room he approached the Bar and asked for a glass of local lager from the tall bartender who spoke perfect English, and also remembered him from his previous visit. A short but polite conversation took place as the beer was slowly poured into his large glass, then he walked over to a table in the corner of the room. The beer was ice cold and strong tasting, but certainly cleared his palette, in a refreshing way. There were no other customers in the room so the man approached Jake and asked if he was staying for a while, and if it was business or pleasure. Jake smiled and said 'A bit of both' without further elaboration.

The bartender took the hint and returned to his position behind counter and busied himself with cleaning a few glasses and stacking them below the bar.

Having thoroughly enjoyed the beer he returned the glass to the young man and walked out into the foyer just as Olivia walked in the front door.

She smiled as she saw him exit the Bar and said 'Have you just had a little pick me up before our meeting?'

'To tell you the truth Olivia, after you left I had a shower and all of a sudden felt quite tired so I settled on the luxurious bed and drifted off to sleep, awakening an hour and a half later. I then decided to have a drink before meeting you, so what's the plan?'

'What ever you fancy, shall we eat at the restaurant that I took you to before, or would you prefer to try something different?'

'I'm quite hungry actually, so if there is a nice steakhouse nearby that would be fine with me. But again we have to be on the same page, so what and where would you like to eat?'

Olivia smiled and said 'You are a very considerate man Jake Tordale, I'm quite happy to take you to a steakhouse, but we will have to travel into town, which should take about half an hour, OK?'

'I can taste it already, so let's go' he said with enthusiasm.

As they pulled up outside the Restaurant Jake was underwhelmed by the front of the premises as it looked quite small, however his motto was 'never judge a book by its cover'. So he got out of the car and stood on the pavement waiting for Olivia, who quickly joined him, then as they walked inside they were approached by what looked like a Manager. Gabbling away in Swedish towards Jake, he quickly looked at Olivia and asked her what the man was saying. She smiled and explained that he was welcoming them to his Restaurant and would show them to a table. The man realised that he was talking to a non-national and reverted to English before shaking Jake's hand. The room Jake quickly decided would seat around fifty people and although early was at least half full which was a good sign indeed.

As they wound there way between the many tables Jake took in the enticing smell of cooked meat and was impressed by the size of the steaks that were on view on the customers plates. This he thought was going to be an enjoyable evening of gastronomic delight.

Olivia watched his face all the way to their allotted table and as they sat down she smiled and said 'What do you think so far?'

'The smells are intoxicating and the portion sizes appear impressive, so I can't wait to view the menu and make a decision on what is in store'.

They ordered two bottles of red wine, and after perusing the menu for five minutes or so they both plumped for a 14oz fillet steak medium rear with all the trimmings.

She was eager to talk to him and find out what his latest escapades had been all about, but he declined to elaborate at present, due to the cacophony of noise that was emanating around the room, from the diners who were indulging in animated conversations and he said they would have to shout to enable her to hear his report.

Halfway through the first bottle of wine their meals arrived, and Jake's mouth opened in shock at the bulk of food that covered his plate, however his gastric juices started flowing and he started to tuck into the lovely food in front of him. Olivia also ate with gusto as if she hadn't eaten for a while. The only time cutlery was put down was when

Jake refilled their glasses, which wasn't often, not a word was uttered until both their plates were clean, and they both gave a satisfied sigh.

Olivia spoke first with a smile 'Well, you wanted a steak and by the look on your face you certainly got what you asked for'.

He smiled at her before replying with 'I certainly did and more besides, what a dream of a place this is, if you haven't anything planned following the presentation I would have no compunction in returning here and sampling another steak before I return to London'.

She looked at him thoughtfully before answering with 'I have to agree with you Jake, this is certainly the place for a meat eater and I would also like to try another cut of meat, so perhaps we'll book a table for tomorrow evening'.

As Jake paid for their meal he booked a table for the next evening at 7pm, whilst saying how much they had enjoyed their food this evening, he also left a generous tip.

As they sat in her car outside his Hotel, Jake was deep in thought regarding the presentation the following day and asked Olivia what the dress sense would be. He had brought a suit with him he said, and she confirmed that it would be the correct dress for the occasion.

She turned to him and pecked him on the cheek, before saying that she would have to have an early night as she was working from seven until mid day, and would save herself for tomorrow evening, said with a glint in her eye.

'That's fine with me, I feel quite tired to be honest and a good eight hour's sleep wouldn't go amiss'. They kissed again before he alighted from the car, turned and waved her goodbye.

Although they had consumed two bottles of wine between them, he decided to have a nightcap in the bar before retireing to his room.

As he approached the counter to the Bar, he was asked what he would like to drink, 'A large vodka and tonic please, with plenty of ice'.

'I'll bring it over for you sir' replied the bartender.

Twenty minutes later he wandered up to his room, after carrying out his ablutions he removed his suit from the case together with a clean shirt and hung them up ready for the next day's business.

Chapter 52

He awoke bright as a button at 7am local time, had a quick shower and dressed in casual clothing for breakfast.

The Dining Room was already busy with four or five tables already occupied by other guests, Jake smiled as he passed the various tables before seating himself in the corner of the room adjacent to the buffet ensemble. A waiter approached asking what he would like to drink, he asked for a pot of black coffee, which was brought to him.

He stood and walked along to see what was on offer, food wise, and decided to have cereal and toast only, as he expected to be fed quite royally at the Police Station.

Mulling things over in his mind he decided to return to his room, and run through the programme for the presentation, as he didn't ask Olivia what time he had to be there or even how he would get there.

He removed the programme from his briefcase and scanned the front page, it was unfortunately written in Swedish, but he could at least read the date and time of the event. It commenced today at 11am, allowing him plenty of time to arrange for a taxi, unless of course the lovely Olivia was collecting him.

He dialled her mobile and after a few rings she picked up with 'Sorry Jake, I forgot to say to you last night that I would be collecting you at 10.30am if that's OK with you?'

'You didn't give me chance to ask the question, but that was the answer I hoped for, I'm sorry I didn't ask you last night' he replied weakly.

'OK, I'll see you soon' she replied finally and rang off, obviously in work mode he surmised. He had a couple of hours to waste, so decided to go for a short walk and view the shops in the locality. He was not disappointed, two shops caught his eye for presents he wished to buy for his family, and after completing his purchases he returned to his room to prepare himself for collection by dear Olivia.

He was stood in the hotel foyer as she pulled up outside dead on 10.30am, and rather than her get out of the car, he rushed out the door and got into the passenger's seat, quickly buckling up his seat belt. 'Got morning to you beautiful lady' he exclaimed.

'Good morning to you, you handsome and attractive Englishman' as she turned and kissed him fully on the lips, which was reciprocated.

After a few seconds he asked 'Will there be a lot of people at this presentation, and have you any idea why they have asked me to revisit Stockholm?'

She smiled before replying with 'I'm in the dark as much as yourself, the details are way above my pay grade, but I'm sure there must be a good reason for them to bring you all the way to Sweden, with all expenses paid'.

The remainder of the drive was taken in silence before they pulled into the huge car park at the rear of the Station building. 'Here we are Jake, there is nothing to worry about, just enjoy the occasion, and think of another steak tonight which will take your mind off all these Swedish people'.

He smiled, unsure what the next hour or so had in store for him, however he got out of the car and followed Olivia into the building like a little lapdog.

As they entered the room there was a considerable mumbling sound enhanced with occasional laughter as the accumulated attendees engaged in animated conversation that was completely alien to Jake, as it appeared to be all in the local language.

Olivia turned to Jake and noticed his unease and said 'Don't worry the main people know of your attendance and will revert to English when it is your time to collect the award'.

'Thank God for that' he replied 'I think otherwise I would be out of my depth when it came to any acceptance speech if it is necessary'.

The room was laid out with a row of seats behind a long table, along one wall for the main Officials, with the remaining area laid out with chairs in rows at least ten deep and at least fifteen horizontally.

Olivia introduced Jake to her Boss, whom he had met on his previous visit, and they were shown to their seats by an Officer, that stood alongside them.

Checking the Officials that were already in position, he was surprised to see that there were a number of seats empty, but as the Master of Ceremonies spoke into the microphone to bring the throng to order, a rendition of the National Swedish Anthem made everyone stand and welcome the Guests of Honour, non other than King Carl XV1 Gustav and Queen Silvia, dressed in their fineries. As they took their seats the Anthem came to a halt. The next three quarters of an hour was taken up in Swedish with the Awards being presented and explained as the Awardee collected it. It then came to Jake's presentation as Olivia pointed to his name in the catalogue and the Official commenced his introduction in English.

'It now gives me great pleasure to ask Mr Jake Tordale of England to come forward to collect his International Award for Services above and beyond those required, trapping a Drug dealer and his associates in his own house before Special Forces detained the people, and had them extradited to Sweden. These men were the scourge of Europe and through this man's diligence, showing incredible courage in the face of adversity these men are now locked away for a considerable time. If you would please come to the front Mr Tordale to collect your Award'.

The remaining people broke out in loud clapping as Jake walked forward, bowed to the King and shook his hand. A few words were exchanged thankfully in English, before the King handed him his award, which was completely different than all the other awards, as it was encased in an A4 sized box. Feeling quite humble he walked slowly back to his seat, sure in the knowledge that his face was bright red.

As he sat down alongside Olivia he just said 'Blimey, what an honour, I'm in total shock at what has just happened, is my face as bright red as I think it is Olivia?'

'Unfortunately it is, however you conducted yourself very well and it was nice to see you receive a smile from His Majesty'.

Scanning through the programme they realised that the Ceremony would last at least another hour, so they both sat back and clapped with the crowd as and when necessary.

Once over the Master of Ceremonies advised all those present that there would be a Buffet Lunch set out in the Canteen, and would everyone follow on, after the Top Table had left the room.

Olivia and Jake chatted for a while until they were the last to leave, or so they thought, however as they made their way to the doorway a call made them stop and turn around, It was Olivia's superior who asked them to stop for a minute.

Somewhat concerned they looked at each other before shrugging their shoulders and waited in anticipation to what the Inspector was going to say.

'Could I have a quick word before you go?' he enquired.

'Certainly' replied Jake, 'How may I help you?'

'Your approach at the ceremony was exemplary, especially the way you spoke to His Majesty. However that is not what I wanted to say to you, your Award is rather a unique item for an International recipient, the significance of it needs to be explained to you, which I'm sure this Officer is quite capable of carrying out when you are back to your Hotel. Therefore before you leave Sweden I would like to receive a phone call from you to confirm that you understand the significance of the article. That was all, I hope you enjoy the buffet Mr Tordale and the remainder of your stay in our Country'.

They shook hands before Jake replied with 'Thank you very much sir, I will treasure this article, even more when its significance has been explained to me'.

With that the three of them strode out the door and followed the Inspector to the Canteen where everyone else had congregated.

Olivia collected two plates of food for them as Jake was spoken to by a few of the other recipients, who all appeared to speak extremely good English with the occasional lovely twist in expressions. However he was pleased to see the lovely Olivia returning with their food, before he apologised to the people he was in conversation with, and went over to join her. 'You appear rather popular today Jake' she said as she handed over a plate of food that covered the whole plate.

'They were all asking me what I did for a living, how come I am in Sweden, and how long I am in the Country, that's all' he replied.

'OK, I have to get back to work after we disperse, are you able to get back to the Hotel all right or do you intend to look around Stockholm for a few hours and I could catch up with you at the end of my shift?'

'I assume this gathering will be over in another hour or so which will take us to around 2pm, so I'll make my way into town and when I have finished catch a taxi back to the Hotel, then catch up with you later' he said, answering her enquiry.

True to Jake's assessment an hour later he was making his way out of the Station and walking towards the main shopping area. After his plate had been filled twice more he needed to walk off the excess and also the air was quite refreshing.

He called into various shops but this time he was not looking for presents for his family in Devon, he decided he would like to surprise Olivia with something special. However nothing caught his eye until he spied a number of Jeweller's on the opposite side of the road, he thought to himself this requires a bit of 'window shopping'.

He noticed that since he had known her she only wore one pair of earrings, so he scoured the windows searching for something a little different that he could buy for her in preparation for their upcoming return trip to Santorini.

The third window he looked in had a number of trays of earrings, so he decided to enter the shop and inspect up close what was on sale. As the door opened the tinkle of a bell indicated that the assistant had a client, and had entered the premises. As Jake approached the Sales Counter a rather rotund elderly man appeared from behind a black curtain. He was smarty dressed in a three piece striped suit attired with the ubiquitous pocket watch, chain and fob, blue shirt and polka dot bow tie. He looked at Jake through his half rimmed glasses and asked in perfect English 'How may I be of service sir?' quickly observing Jake's right arm where his Patek Phillip watch was on show, obviously unintentionally.

'I am in search of a pair of earrings for a friend of mine, and was drawn to your displays in the window, could I take a look at them please'.

'Certainly sir, take a seat and I'll be with you shortly'.

Jake sat down and looked around the shop, thinking to himself that he could be in any quintessential property anywhere in the World, especially around Hatton Garden in London.

The Jeweller returned after a few minutes with four trays for Jake's inspection and placed them on the counter for his perusal.

'If there is nothing here that catches your eye, I have two additional trays that I keep in the safe. But first cast your eyes over these and see if there is anything you think would be appropriate'.

'Thank you, you are most accommodating, as a matter of interest how did you know that I was British?'

'My Jeweller's eye sir, I have visitors from all over the world and am quick on the uptake by first their dress attire and then their demeanour as they enter the shop, then if unsure await their first comment'.

'You remind me of a friend of mine who I will be visiting shortly in the States, he has a similar eye and is certainly an extremely shrewd man as you are yourself, anyway lets get back to business. These are extremely impressive, but I anticipate that the ones that are in your safe are significantly more desirable'.

'I see that you are a man of extreme taste, let me get them for you sir' with that he took the trays off the counter and placed them on a shelf below, out of sight. Although friendly he was still cautious, as of course he should be.

On his return he placed the two trays on the counter, then explained 'The tray on your left are earrings that I have taken in part exchange for other jewellery or watches, and although better quality than what you have inspected on the previous trays will be sold at a discounted rate. The tray on the right contain brand new earrings, but are of the highest quality and any women would be besotted by them'.

Jake scanned both trays, there were no sign of price tickets, however he had already decided on two sets that caught his eye, realising how they would offset Olivia's blond hair, so he pointed to two from the right hand tray.

The jeweller took them out of the tray and placed them in velvet box's before asking Jake which he preferred.

Jake smiled, knowing full well that the question was loaded, and that he would be buying both of them. 'How much are each of them please?'

Rubbing his chin, he took off his glasses and quickly cleaned them, before tapping away on a calculator as if he didn't already know the figure he was going to come up with, he replied, 'If you take the both they will be two thousand seven hundred euros, but separately they would be fifteen hundred each. They are solid 22 carat gold, with a diamond centre piece, what do you think?'

Jake hesitated for a few seconds whilst looking the man in the eye, then without a word from the rotund man he gave a belly laugh which was quickly joined by a chuckle from the jeweller. Jake looked at the earrings for a second time before putting in his final bid, 'I'll take the both for two thousand five hundred euro's in cash, however I don't carry that much on me but I could collect it from my Hotel and be back here within the hour, giving you plenty of time to gift wrap them separately for me, what do you say?' whilst offering his hand for a shake. It was quickly gripped and with a nod of his large head the deal was agreed.

'Could you possible ring for a taxi for me, it will save me a lot of time and I can ask the driver to wait until I collect my money from my room'

'Certainly sir, I'll ring a company that I deal with a lot and he will be here within ten minutes. Whilst you are waiting I notice that you have on your arm a Patek Phillipe watch, is it possible for me to look at it?'

Jake smiled before taking off his treasured possession and handing it over to the delight of the jeweller.

'I have never held such a wonderful timepiece, how long has it been in your possession, if I might ask?'

'I bought it on holiday two years ago, having negotiated a reasonable discount for the watch, it has been admired by a number of jewellers where I have purchased other goods in various parts of the world'.

Handing it back to Jake, he looked out the door and said 'Your taxi has just arrived outside, please don't pay for your journey I know the Company well and will pay the fare'.

'You are most generous, thank you I'll be as quick as I possibly can' he replied whilst exiting the shop and clambering into the Volvo.

Explaining the name of the Hotel and the circumstances the driver nodded his head and drove off. When he was dropped at the curb on the return journey the door was opened for him to enter the shop and the taxi pulled away.

'That was certainly a fast turn around sir, I hope it was a comfortable ride for you'.

'It certainly was, the driver was very polite and not at all irritated for the wait as I retrieved my money'.

As Jake approached the counter he was pleased to see there were two parcels ready for him, so he handed over the money for the man to count. The deal completed he asked if Jake required a receipt. 'Only if you need to issue one, perhaps you could sign one of your business cards in case I need to visit you again so you can remember me?'

This was quickly done and the money went straight into his wallet that he had taken from his back pocket.

They shook hands and Jake left the shop feeling as if he had negotiated well, but no doubt the earrings were already marked at an inflated price, however he felt happy.

Still some miles from the Hotel he rang Olivia's mobile which was picked up at the third ring, 'Hi Jake, is everything OK?'

'Yes thanks, I wondered what time you would be available, only I'm stranded downtown and would like to get back to the Hotel and prepare myself for another evening out with you' he said tongue in cheek. 'I'm actually within walking distance of the Station, but if you aren't ready yet I'll hail a taxi'.

'If you could hang on for about half an hour I'll meet you in the car park, my car hasn't moved since this morning, so I'll see you in a while and with that she rang off.

Half an hour he thought to himself, I think I'll pop into a cafe up the road for a quick coffee before making my way back to Olivia's car.

True to her word as he walked up to the car, she exited the building at the rear entrance door, and strode towards him. 'Have you waited long?' she said, as they were seated.

'No. I popped into a cafe and had a coffee before I made my way here, thanks'.

She swirled in her seat and gave him a long sensuous kiss on the lips, which he reciprocated. Coming up for breath she asked 'What time shall we eat this evening?'

He smiled and said 'Around eight I think, so by the time we finish at the restaurant and get back here it will be almost eleven o'clock, so I'll pack ready for the trip back to the Airport in the morning as its an early start, my flight is at ten o'clock'.

'I think I'll pack an overnight bag and drop it in your room before we head off to eat, then we can spend some quality time together there, what do you think?'

'Sounds good to me, I might need a little practice ready for two weeks together in Santorini in a months time' he replied with a beaming smile.

She dropped him off half an hour later, and said she would return and collect him as arranged just before eight.

Chapter 53

As he settled in his room he was determined to pack the majority of his belongs before having a quick nap. Surprisingly he completed his first task in twenty minutes, also laying out his clothes for his return to London, and leaving his washing accessories in the bathroom. He opened his briefcase and took five hundred euros out of the wallet in the secret compartment and tucked them into his jacket that was laid out on the bed.

Feeling pleased with himself, he then had a shower and shave in preparation for the arrival of the delectable Olivia for their evening out.

He put one of the parcelled earrings in his jacket pocket that was hung up in the wardrobe, and the other back in the briefcase. Checking his watch he noted he had a window of some hour and a half before Olivia was arriving, so he stretched out on the bed and was asleep within minutes, his time clock in his head allowed him an hour before he needed to wake up, and to the minute he awoke feeling completely refreshed.

Dressing ready for going out, he thought he would go down to the foyer awaiting her arrival, then they could go up to the room together to deposit her overnight case.

As he looked at his watch for the tenth time, he saw out the corner of his eye her car pulling up to the curb.

She quickly got out, retrieved her case from the boot and strode into the foyer, they took the lift up and deposited the case in his room.

Standing back he gave Olivia the once over, she was dressed in a yellow dress cut short just above the knee, hugging tightly to her hour glass body. Her blond hair was cascading down her back, and the little makeup she had applied only emphasised the beauty of the Swedish Goddess that Jake had been smitten by.

'Do I pass your British eyes for our evening out?' she asked.

'One hundred percent, however I noticed that all the time I have known you, you only appear to have one set of earrings, and that is the ones you have this evening' he answered with a smile.

'Don't you like them Jake?' she asked.

He fumbled in his pocket before handing over the little package containing the new ones.

She gave a little giggle, like a child at Christmas, before attacking the paper and exposing the blue velvet box. Opening the lid, she shrieked as she saw its contents, then flung her arms around Jake thanking him profusely. She walked into the bathroom, took out her old earrings and put in the new ones, before returning to face him.

'Well' she said, 'Do I meet with your approval'.

'More than that, they look as if they were made for you, mind you anything would look lovely on you, my dear'.

'Well if we're now ready, I'm starving and ready for another lovely meal, how about you'.

'Ravishing, as my company is also, so let's go'.

Down in the elevator they kissed with Olivia thanking him yet again for his generous gift, saying that she could only give him the gift of her body later, he replied that was the only thanks he needed.

They pulled up outside the restaurant half an hour early but the maitre de took them to their seats, which was the table they had sat at the previous evening. Jake asked for a bottle of champagne as he was handed the food menu.

Olivia quickly made up her mind and plumped for the Surf and Turf, with the steak being a 16oz fillet, Jake swallowed at the thought of it, but ordered the same, confirming that both steaks to be cooked medium rare.

Another wonderful couple of hours of gastronomic heaven quickly sailed by with another bottle of champagne, before they left the establishment feeling full to the brim and ready for a good workout.

It was indeed eleven o'clock before they prepared for bed, with Jake under the sheets first, Olivia slowly took off her yellow dress revealing matching bra and g string underwear, then said 'Shall I take everything off or would you prefer to remove them'.

'Off' he said, 'But I need one of your special massages first'.

She smiled, walked into the bathroom and returned carrying a tube of oil which she placed on the bed. Quickly removing her underwear she asked him to turn onto his stomach, then after straddling him applied the oil to his neck and shoulders which she massaged into him, working down his spine, along his legs before finishing with his feet.

She then asked him to turn over, which confirmed the state of arousal he was in as she spied his erect organ. Ignoring it completely she started massaging in the opposite direction, starting with his feet then legs, missing his nether region she worked up across his stomach and chest before finally around his head and ears.

Jake was panting in anticipating, waiting for what was to come as she poured more oil around his genitals before finally caressing his erect penis.

She slowly lifted herself off him, before returning to him backwards and letting him enter her completely. She worked herself up and down his shaft as they both started moaning in pleasure with Jake caressing her nipples and Olivia stroking his scrotum. After only a few minutes they knew they were both about to climax, as she uttered one word 'Now' they accelerated their movements until they both groaned in ecstasy and flopped back totally spent.

Jake dropped off to sleep after his exertion, however Olivia wanted more and half an hour later her lips surrounded his flacid organ and it quickly came back to life for round two. Jake however was still dozy and thought he was dreaming before her movements became more frantic, and for the second time he went through a second orgasm.

Not to be outdone he reciprocated by prising her legs open and licking and sucking her clitoris until she screamed with a huge orgasm.

After a shower they both fell into a deep sleep, waking at seven o'clock the next morning.

Chapter 54

Being Saturday Olivia had the weekend off and would be able to take him to the Airport directly after they had had their breakfast, and Jake had completed his remaining packing. However there was one thing that had passed by, that needed addressing and that was the Award he had received at the presentation. To date it still remained in its packaging, and Olivia was keen to see what it contained. So Jake carefully removed the adhesive and carefully pulled apart the paper wrapping to reveal the contents. There was a coloured glass figure of an explorer complete with ski's and poles, and at its base there was a nameplate with the words ROALD AMUNDSEN AWARD TO JAKE TORDALE. As Olivia looked at the wording her hand covered her mouth before tears fell down onto her cheeks and she said 'This is one of the highest Awards for a civilian not of Swedish descent, you should be very proud. Putting the statue to one side he opened the envelope that it was resting on and pulled out a letter from the Head of the Government, that explained the significance of the Award and how thankful the Swedish people were at the bravery he had portrayed in apprehending the criminals that had caused mayhem within their Country and across Europe. There was also a slip of paper at the base of the envelope which he pulled out, It was in fact a cheque made out to him in the sum of £10k.

Lost for words he handed the letter and the cheque over to Olivia to inspect, her mouth opened wide in astonishment at both pieces of paper and she could only say, 'That must be the highest Award ever given out to a foreign National that I have ever heard of since my time in the Police Force, but it is certainly well deserved'.

'When I return home I will send a thank you letter to your Inspector asking for a copy to be sent to all those involved in the Award Ceremony. I think we should go down for breakfast now don't you, I'm feeling a little peckish after all the exercise I had last night'.

'I'm ready when you are, Jake' she replied.

They made their way to the Dining Room and sat at the table Jake had used previously, the waiter followed them there and asked what they required. They both asked for black coffee, then made their way to the Buffet counter for cereal and toast.

They made small talk over the meal, before checking the time Jake suggested they went back to his room and collect the baggage ready to drive to the Airport.

Twenty minutes later they pulled up at the Terminal and Jake put his luggage onto a trolley and walked into Departure's. Saying a short farewell to Olivia, they confirmed the travel arrangements that she would be making in a few weeks time for their upcoming holiday to Santorini, he walked to passport control and deposited his suitcase before clearing the area and waving goodbye to her as he walked into the Departure Lounge. He still retained his carry-on case that housed his briefcase and made himself comfortable to await the call for boarding.

Half an hour later his flight was called and to his surprise there were only a trickle of passengers that stood to the call. However he would be glad when he landed on British soil again, albeit for only a short time. The walk to the plane only took a couple of minutes and once shown to his seat in First Class by a steward, he made himself comfortable and was relieved to see that the Stewardess on the flight from London was nowhere to be seen, so hopefully he would have a quiet and relaxing trip.

A quarter of an hour later the plane shot down the runway and up into the clear sky on its way to the Capital of England, London. Once they had attained cruising height a Steward came and took his order for food and drink. The choice was quite varied so he plumped for a rare venison sandwich with a bottle of red wine, followed by black coffee. The remainder of the flight was uneventful so he dozed most of the way before the Captain gave out over the tannoy that they would be descending into London Heathrow, and they should touch-down in twenty minutes time.

After landing, then through Passport Control, he collecting his suitcase and walked to the bus stop to catch the Shuttle to take him back to his Hotel. After booking in he took his baggage up to his room, then down to collect his other suitcase from the car park.

Chapter 54

Ringing the office he was put through to Henry Bates who asked how he had got on in Stockholm, after a quick resume of his couple of days away, he said if he could spare a few minutes he would call and see him.

'Fine Jake, what time is you flight to the States?'

'Not until silly early time tomorrow morning' Jake answered.

'OK, I'm in all day today, so call in when it suits you' his Boss offered.

So he cancelled the call and made his way to Reception to order a taxi for the MI6 office.

The vehicle arrived, and Jake gave him his destination address, twenty minutes later they pulled up alongside the Thames across the road from the famous building.

He walked into the underground car park and took the lift up to Reception, after a few polite words with the young lady he took the lift up to the Director's Office.

He knocked and walked into Bates's office, as he approached the desk the main man stood and shook his hand. 'Everything go OK old man' was Henry's opening gambit.

'Better than I expected, firstly the Awards were presented by none other than the King and Queen of Sweden, when I collected mine His Majesty had a few words with me and appeared quite interested in why I had been proposed for the overseas Award.

In fact I have brought it with me, I thought when you looked at it you would be suitably impressed'.

He fumbled in his bag and passed the statue over to Henry to inspect. 'What an incredible statue, mainly for its design depicting the famous explorer in the medium of glass. You must have felt quite humble to have receive such a beautiful item, was anything else with it?'

Jake smiled and took out the letter and cheque that he had in the bag.

Henry read the letter and saw the amount on the cheque and blew out his cheeks.

Before he could say anything Jake said 'I intend to send off a letter of thanks when I eventually get home from the States, asking for copies to be forwarded to all those involved in the presentation'.

'Very honourable Jake, and the cheque is a worthy reflection of what you went through with the criminals that followed you around Europe and eventually to your home. I would say that the money is thanks from the European countries that suffered with the drugs problems that were inflicted on them by those perpetrators'.

'Well that's my story sir, is everything OK here and have you drawn up a short list of people to replace George Adams position?'

Henry shook his head, stood and looked out of his office window before answering Jake's question with 'I couldn't persuade you out of retirement could I?' without turning around.

Silence for a while as Henry returned to his seat and looked Jake in the eye.

'Not on your Nellie sir I'm afraid, these last couple of years have worn me right out, if I was twenty years younger I would have jumped at the opportunity but after my visit to the States and on my return a two week holiday in Santorini, I will be settling down in my quiet retreat of Wisteria Cottage to possibly write a novel or two based on my adventures over the past few years'.

'I fully understand Jake, but it was worth a try. I have three people that certainly have the credentials, one of whom is an extremely talented women, perhaps you could sit in on the interviews which I intend arranging the day you return from America. Is that a possibility before you make your way home?'

'I haven't decided the length of my stay away, however when I have carried out the work I envisage I will ring you the day before I leave, I hope that will be enough time for you to arrange for the three of them to attend'.

'Thank you Jake, you are most helpful, I hope your visit to the States is fruitful for you and you are able to assist your old man there to complete the clearance of his shop'.

'Thank you sir, I'll see you soon' he then stood shook Henry's hand and walked out of the office. He called a taxi and returned to the Airport Hotel, up in his room he re-arranged the clothing in his suitcase and packed everything for tomorrow's journey. Feeling drained after his latest run a round he settled down for a nap before having an evening meal in the Hotel's Dining Room later in the evening.

Chapter 54

Awaking two hours later he felt quite refreshed, but decided to have a cold shower to liven his body up, then a nice meal with a bottle of house wine.

After his meal he called around to the Reception Desk to confirm that he would be leaving in the morning, however his car would remain in the car park until he returned from his American trip where he would be staying another night, so could he pencil in a room for ten days time. His flight the next morning was at seven am so he booked an early breakfast at six.

Chapter 55

The usual routine was carried out first thing the next morning, bags down to the foyer, quick continental breakfast, catch the shuttle bus to the Terminal, book in, through Passport Control and relax in the First Class Lounge. He refused any food or drink as he would be well looked after on the flight over, and awaited the familiar call to board.

The early flight passenger's were mostly American holidaymakers, with a smattering of people engaged in their laptops and tablets either on conference calls or working on whatever projects their Company was involved in. The remainder were newbies to First Class travel and mopping up the free food and drink that was on offer.

As he settled into his comfortable seat twenty minutes later, he contemplated how he would help the dear old Jeweller with his final moving, and where in fact did the old man live. He wouldn't find out until later today after he had booked into his Hotel and walked the half a mile or so to the shop. He quickly sent off a message to the Jeweller, giving him an approximate time he would be walking down the sidewalk to meet him, and to his surprise he quickly received a return message that said 'Looking forward to seeing you my son'. Jake welled up for a minute or two after seeing those few short and sincere words. Take-off was on time and following the usual food and drink breaks together with a film watch, he eventually reclined his seat and drifted off to sleep for a few hours.

Landing on time he followed the usual routine of Passport Control collecting his suitcase from the carousel, and taking whatever cab was available to the Hotel, where he booked in via the Receptionist that had been so helpful on his previous trip. He took all his belongings up to his room before walking to the Jeweller's shop. Feeling quite sad as he viewed the large front window that was painted over in white, that prevented anyone looking into the almost empty shop. He knocked on the front door and was greeted warmly by the old man who in fact looked very poorly. He gave Jake a fatherly hug, then followed the old man into the shop. 'As you can see most of the stock has been sold off,

I just have a few items in the safe I wish to discuss with you, and then I need to dismantle the counter, shelves and window display's ready for selling on'.

'You have got on really well, now what plan of operations have you for me, shall we get on with it today, I know I have only just arrived but I'm willing an able to carry out whatever work you want me to do for you'.

Smiling at Jake the Jeweller stood and looked him up and down, and thought to himself that this unselfish man had just flown from the UK to help him with the conclusion of his lifetime's work, who else would have dropped everything like he had done today.

Jake looked at him and said 'Are you OK, you seemed to be gazing off into a different world?'

'I'm sorry Jake, I'm just overwhelmed by your kindness in travelling such a distance to help me, it's not as if you are part of my family, which unfortunately I have none, but you are a son to me in another way' he stopped before he broke down.

'It is my pleasure to help another human being who has been through so much during his lifetime, before finally being diagnosed with this awful illness, say no more of it, let's get to work shall we?'

'OK my friend, but first I'll lock the front door before I open the safe in the back room' he said before walking past him and locking the door. He gestured for Jake to follow him to an area only Stefan was privy too, behind the curtain. To his surprise it was more spacious than he imagined, there were washing facilities and a toilet, together with a separate, albeit minuscule kitchenette, where he could prepare any food he had time to consume. In the corner of the room was quite a substantial safe tucked under a work surface. 'Come, come' said Stefan, gesturing for Jake to enter this sacred part of the shop. Jake was bemused at the small but efficient room and said 'You have everything you need here, especially if you have a quiet day. You're able to prepare a meal and relax, and should a customer enter the shop you're only a curtain away from your Client'.

Stefan smiled at Jake's resume of his premises, and felt quite proud of his friend's assessment of the shop, however it was time to open the safe and show Jake the remaining stock he had within.

Dialling in the combination he opened the door of the safe for possibly the last time and handed Jake an array of blue bags and boxes of watches, which he placed on the worktop. Then took one last item out that was obviously special as it was in a sealed box.

'Before I show you the bits and pieces there, I want to let you view what is inside this container, it was the only item my family were able to hide during the Second World War that decimated my Country, I found it amongst my late parents belongings some forty years ago. My father was not blessed with wealth but certain things he obtained during his working life led to the purchase of this item.

I have not been able to have it valued, as for my late family it was an heirloom to be treasured, but as I am in my twilight years and suffering from an incurable illness I would like your assistance in getting it valued and sold to enable, when the time comes, it will pay for my medical care and finally my funeral. Would you take on that task for me Jake, my son?' Stefan opened the box, and Jake was blinded by the intricate ornament held within. The delicate diamonds and other precious stones surrounding an Icon of some beauty, and it was enclosed in a solid gold frame.

'Dear me Stefan, I fail to see how your parents were able to hold on to this wonderful item, and then for you to be the custodian for all these past years, don't you think it would be best displayed in a cultural museum. If you are happy for me to take it I will visit Sotheby's Auction House in New York where it would be displayed on the internet, allowing people from all over the world to inspect the items and enter their bids.

I would first visit Sotheby's website and send a photo of it to obtain guide prices, once I have it I will discuss it with you, and if you are happy to sell it, at an acceptable price, then we will see what happens from there, how does that sound?'

'You're brain works extremely fast Jake, but I think that would be my best option, as time is short', he then closed the lid and handed the box over.

'I will take it personally to New York, together with all the other items, then once agreed we will let the Auctioneer do his best for you. There is an Auction in a week or so, I'm hoping therefore to enter the items in the Jewellery section and once sold they will forward a cheque directly to you, obviously less their commission'.

Chapter 55

'You are one in a million Jake, thank you so much, now let's look at the other items on the worktop' he said shuffling over to the bags and boxes.

They checked all the items, which as far as Jake was concerned were all of high quality, before Stefan spoke again. 'I would like you to take all these as well, then once you get back from New York you can decide on which you would like for yourself, then sell the remainder. Of the money you collect, take the cost out for your expenses, how does that sound?'

'Quite a responsibility on my part, but I'm glad to help you Stefan. I'll ring Sotheby's after lunch, I expect they could possibly give us an estimate for all the various items if we forward photographs to them via email but let's see what they say after I speak to them'.

Stefan beamed a toothy smile at Jake, showing two gold incisor teeth, before saying 'I knew the minute I saw you that you would be my saviour if I was ever in trouble, thank you Jake.'

'My pleasure Stefan, now would you like a break, I would like to take you out for lunch if you feel up for it. Of course I would be pleased to go to whichever restaurant you choose'.

'What a kind thought, I sometimes visit a small but extremely cosy and personal place only a few hundred yards from here, if you like I will give them a call and book a table'.

'Fine with me, but I insist on paying for the meal Stefan' Jake said unsure if he had overstepped the mark.

But he didn't have to worry as the old fellow nodded whilst he talked on the phone to the restaurant, obviously as the conversation went on for a while he realised that it was somewhere that Stefan frequented often.

'The table is booked for half an hour's time, leaving us a few minutes to return these items to the safe and for us to amble down the road for lunch'.

'OK, whilst you do that I'll obtain Sotheby's number and ring them with the details and see what they say they need from us'. He looked up the telephone number on his Google app, wrote it on a piece of paper and dialled the number.

A Receptionist answered, and after he explained the reason for his call he was put through to one of the Auctioneer's. He then set out in great detail the reason for his call, the various items he had to hand that he wish valued and put up for Auction. He realised that the man was writing down word for word what he had explained, then after a few seconds silence, he asked if photos could be taken, transferred to a laptop and forwarded to him. He gave his name and email address and confirmed that the items could be included in the upcoming programme in a week's time, of course once a valuation had been made the items would have to be delivered to their New York address.

Finally Jake explained who he was and assuming everything was agreed regarding the sale he would make the journey and deliver the goods himself.

After finishing the call he went through everything with Stefan what he had just explained to the Sotheby's representative, and after they had enjoyed their lunch he would photograph all the wares and input them onto Stefan's laptop, to forward to Sotheby's.

They then closed up the shop and ambled down the sidewalk to the Restaurant. As they walked in the waiter welcomed Stefan like a member of his family, with a kiss and hug, before Jake was introduced with a warm handshake. They were shown to their table and handed menu's. Jake smiled at his companion and said, 'I would like you to order for the both of us, and I am sure I will enjoy every morsel'.

Over the next hour and a half they dined like Prince's and with the waiter calling every few minutes asking if everything was OK, the time appeared to fly by.

After Jake handed over his Debit card to pay he turned to Stefan and said 'I think we had better return to the shop now, as I would like to take the photos and get the email off today to enable the valuation to be made and returned tomorrow, which will allow me to get to New York no later than is practically possible'.

'I understand Jake, thank you for lunch and we'll head back there right away'.

Chapter 56

Back in the shop Jake decided to set out all the objects on the counter, and take photos one at a time on his mobile phone. After taking the first photo he had a quick look at it in the Gallery section and felt quite pleased with the result, over the next half an hour he had taken a picture of all the articles they wished to Auction. However, transferring them onto Stefan's ancient laptop took a lot longer but in the end, having written small details under each photo he felt happy with the result.

Heading the email with Sotheby's representative's address, he wrote a small note, saying who he was and whom he was representing, finally expressing the urgency of the matter as he had to return to the UK by the end of next week, and he would be available from receipt of his reply to travel to New York with the goods.

As the email pinged off he sat back totally drained, with a worried Stefan looking at him, he quickly stood up and asked how he wished to proceed with the taking down of the counter and display units.

With the time approaching 4pm Stefan said to Jake that he had done enough for the day and it was time for him to return to his Hotel and relax for a while. With that Jake suddenly had a lightbulb moment and realised he had been here for almost a day and he hadn't bothered to ring Charlene, which was something he would do as soon as he got back to his room.

They shook hands and arranged to meet in the morning at 9am and finalise the work required in the shop, before hopefully running through the reply Stefan had received on his laptop from New York.

He took his shoes off as soon as he entered his room and flopped down on the bed feeling extremely tired. He picked up his mobile and rang Charlene's number, she picked it up with a high pitched 'Jake, how are you?'

'All the better for hearing your voice, I'm sat in the Hotel I was in only a while ago and wondered how you are fixed for an evening meal tonight'.

'What do you mean, are you actually here in Washington, if so why?'

He quickly explained why and what he was doing for Stefan, but confirming he would be returning to the UK no later than the end of next week, and also to say that one of the days would be taken up on a visit to New York.

'What a busy man you are, I'd better grab the little time we will have together and accept your invitation for a meal this evening then, I suppose. What time and where would you like to eat?'

'The choice is your's dear lady, there is only one problem, I will need to be collected and returned, if that isn't too much trouble?'

'Not at all, I'll collect you around 7pm and we'll take it from there shall we?'

'I can't wait, see you in a few hour's' he answered, finally completing the call.

He then stripped off to his underwear set a timer on his phone for 6pm and got his head down for a nap.

As his phone gave him a wake up call he took off his pants and dived under the shower, then having a quick shave he applied a considerable amount of aftershave and deodorant before dressing in preparation for the arrival of the lovely Charlene. He retrieved the other box containing earrings he had purchased on his trip to Sweden, which he intended giving to her at the table this evening, and put them in his sports coat pocket.

As he settled into the plush armchair in the foyer the Receptionist asked if he was waiting for someone or if she could be of any assistance. He replied he was waiting for a lift from his girlfriend. The words were out before he realised what he had said, but he didn't elaborate to the young lady.

A few minutes later a car pulled up outside, and out stepped the lovely Charlene dressed in a warm overcoat. Jake stood and opened the door for her and kissed her on both cheeks before a word was said. She turned on her heels and they made their way to the car, somewhat confused Charlene said 'Don't you want to be seen with me or something Jake?'

'It's not that, the young lady on Reception is an inquisitive soul and will question me when I see her again who my lovely date is'.

'You're not ashamed of me are you? if so we can cancel and I'll be on my way' she answered firmly with a hint of aggression.

'Nothing of the sort, I'm a bit ragged after the flight and a session with the lovely old Jeweller who I'm helping to clear his shop, as due to Ill health he is retiring to enjoy what little life he has left'.

'That's OK then, slate clean, let's head off to the restaurant for a lovely meal and you can tell me everything that has happened since last we met'.

As they sat at the table of their plush restaurant Jake scoured the menu trying to decide what fare he would be having. He had already ordered a bottle of white and a bottle of red anticipating Charlene's bias towards white, with his being red.

Charlene made up her mind almost immediately, she would go for the melon starter followed by Clam Chowder. Jake being more adventurous went for the crab claws starter, with his main course of mixed seafood and charred sourdough.

Whilst they waited for their meal Jake commenced his rhetoric of what had transpired since they last meet. Explaining about his trip to the rugby International in France, his visit to Sweden to collect an Award from the Royal Family, then his reason for his visit to the States. After that he asked if she had any interesting snippets of what had happened in her life. However her's was only about work and visit's out with her flatmate.

Thankfully the waiter arrived with their starters, and conversation ground to a halt as they tucked into their food.

The waiter popped back a couple of times to refill their glasses, and before they knew it the main course arrived, and to Jake's delight the huge plate of seafood was most impressive, and he said to Charlene that he might need a little help in clearing the huge amount of food on display. She smiled and said 'I'm here if you need any help, you lightweight'.

An hour later with their plates clean and the two bottles empty the waiter handed over a menu for them to look at, regarding dessert.

They sat back and gave the page the once-over, and with finality she decided on Cheesecake and Jake creme brûlée.

Once again the plates were totally covered with the sweet but true to form they finished every last morsel. Jake fancied coffee and brandy, however as Charlene was driving she just had the coffee.

Full to the brim Jake asked for the bill, and paid it with the usual 10% tip for the waiter who had been most attentive. Before they got up from the table Jake took the box from his pocket and passed it across the table to her, and said 'I purchased these earrings when I was in Sweden, and as I was coming to the States hoped I would see you as when I viewed them on the Jeweller's counter I thought they would be ideal for you'.

'That's most generous of you Jake' but her face was a picture as she opened the box, then her mouth dropped open as she viewed the beautiful stones that surrounded the gold base. For once she appeared lost for words, but quickly closed the box, stood up and said 'Let's get out of here I think you need a reward for your generosity and I can think of one way I can give that to you'.

The journey back to the Hotel appeared to be a lot faster than when they left it, Charlene was panting and getting into a frenzy with the slowness of the traffic, so Jake said there is no rush. However with a glance across to him she said 'Oh yes there is, I cannot wait until we are up in your room'.

No more was said until she parked the car in the Hotel car park and they made their way up in the lift. As Jake put the key in the door and opened it Charlene was removing her clothes, no sooner had Jake locked the door, before he was doing the same. Not a word was said as they sank into the bed and spent the next half an hour enjoying each others bodies. They had a quick shower before round two commenced which was less frantic and more sensual.

As the time reached ten pm Charlene said she would have to go home to get some rest before work in the morning, Jake kissed her and followed her down to the car and waved her goodbye.

Now completely knackered he slept through until 8am, after rousing himself for a shower, he went down for breakfast before it was time for his walk to the Jeweller's shop at 9am.

Chapter 57

He was no more than a few paces from the shop, when he saw Stefan striding purposefully towards him. They arrived at the door at the same time and greeted each other with a hand shake and smile. 'Good morning Stefan are you ready for viewing of the Auctioneer's assessment, if indeed he has replied yet?'

'I certainly am Jake, I presume it will only be guess figures before he see's them in the flesh, however it will give us some idea as to the total valuation' and with that they walked into the shop. Stefan opened his laptop and brought up his emails, there was indeed a reply from New York, and he worked busily writing figures on a notepad before Jake had viewed the pages. The old man turned the laptop around for Jake to see and passed him his written notes. Jake's mouth opened wide as he viewed the figures Stefan had written down and was amazed to see that the total exceeded thirty thousand dollars. Looking at the laptop he was gobsmacked to see that the estimated figure for the main item was fifteen thousand dollars, with a note attached saying that it was possibly a low estimate. The final paragraph asked for the items to be brought to New York no later than the next day at 5pm, for it to be included in the Auction. Jake looked Stefan in the eye before saying 'I think you had better reply to this email and say your colleague will be there tomorrow early afternoon with the goods'.

Stefan smiled and asked 'How will you travel to New York?'

'I'll hire a rental car and leave first thing tomorrow morning, if that's OK with you. We'll spend the rest of today clearing up here so that arrangements can be made to collect the demolished counter and display cases. Also we can take away any personal items you wish to retain'.

Stefan smiled and looked at Jake in amazement 'You are such an organised man Jake, I cannot thank you enough for doing all this for me, once it is all sorted I will reward you generously'.

'Do you have a phone number of Hertz Rentals, if not we could look the local number up on your laptop, then I'll book a car and collect it last thing today'.

Stefan nodded and passed over the laptop, a couple of minutes later he had the number, dialled it and booked the car for delivery to his Hotel at 6pm this evening, paying the deposit and explaining where the car would be going and returning the following evening.

With the most important jobs completed they set about taking down the pieces of furniture, whilst Stefan busied himself in the back room, then stacking the various parts that Jake had taken apart.

Come lunchtime Jake asked if Stefan would like him to collect some sandwiches and drinks from a local Deli, he knew just the place and ordered the food and drink to be delivered paying over the phone for them, they arrived twenty minutes later. They stopped for half an hour to demolish their lunch, afterwards they continued their work until the last screw was removed and all the sections of counter were stacked alongside the front door.

Jake swept thought the shop and brushed out the build up of dust in the front window before saying that they were finished.

The valuables were still laid out on the kitchenette worktop and the old man asked Jake how he would be carrying them to New York. He admitted he hadn't given it a thought, however alongside the sink Stefan passed over a briefcase to Jake that would house all the items he would be taking to the Auction House, there was also a digital lock under the handle the number of which was written on a piece of a paper inside the case.

Between them they carefully stacked all the goods before Jake locked it and spun the numbers on the lock. He put the piece of paper in his wallet for safe keeping but had already memorised the five numbers he would require to open the case in New York.

Something that had struck Jake was that he had no idea where Stefan lived or even if he had a car, so he asked the question, mainly for the simple reason of carrying the items he wished to retain back to his house.

'I'm sorry Jake that I haven't given you that information, as it wasn't relevant before but now I understand you're concern. I keep my car in a little lock-up down the end of the road, no more that two hundred metres or so away. My house is another three miles away, where I live alone, perhaps if I collect the car we can load it up and you could come with me to unload it there. Whilst we are there I'll give you some money for the hire car and fuel for the journey together with spending money for food and drink for your trip, please don't argue with me on that score'.

'OK, I'll wait here whilst you collect the car, I need to make a few phone calls so will do that whilst you are away'.

The old man was gone almost an hour and Jake wondered if he was OK, but he needn't have worried as he heard a car pull up outside.

To his amazement Stefan's car was a reasonably new shooting brake with ample room in the trunk for all the items he wished to keep, and fifteen minutes later the vehicle was loaded, they locked the shop and for once Jake got in the passenger seat for his trip to Stefan's home. It was a well kept detached single storey premises, the front garden of which was tended neatly and was covered with flowers and mature bushes to the whole perimeter of the property. 'Welcome to my humble home Jake, you are the first person to come here in a few years' he said as he backed up to the garage door that opened electronically with a key fob attached to his keyring. The car pulled into the beautifully kept garage and the door closed as the engine was turned off, and they both got out and walked into a modern, well equipped, smart kitchen.

'Can I offer you a coffee Jake or tea if you so require?'

'Black coffee for me Stefan thank you' he replied.

'Please sit down Jake we have a lot to discuss before you depart for New York tomorrow'.

Jake sat in a comfortable chair at the kitchen table, and then cast his eyes around the homely room, imagining that the whole premises would be as immaculate as this room.

As Stefan sat down having brought the drinks to the table, he again thanked Jake for all he had done for him, then sat back and explained what he wished Jake to hear.

'Since you first walked into the shop, I knew you were a special person Jake, someone I knew I could trust and rely on, I cannot think of anyone who would travel all the way from the UK, at the drop of a hat, to help out an old Jewish Jeweller he had only recently met, who had also relieved him of a reasonable amount of money' he stopped for a laugh at his small joke, but then unfortunately started a coughing fit.

He waved Jake's concern away with a sweep of his hand, then said 'Just a cold, nothing to worry about. Now I must continue, as I told you I have no living relative's in fact the closest I have to family is Jake Tordale. I have never made out a Will, and assumed that after my demise the Government would end up with the little I had saved over the past years. So I will now rectify that situation by contacting my Solicitor tomorrow and drafting out a Will with you as my sole beneficiary, please do not say anything in response to my statement. When you return from New York I will give you a copy of my Will and I will lodge your full details with the Solicitor, i.e. Your name and address, telephone number and email address, do I make myself clear Jake?'

'Are you sure there is no-one at all that is related to you, in the whole world, only I didn't come over here to help you, then expect to inherit your life's savings if that's what you think?'

'No Jake, it's the exact opposite to your theory, I think you are the least money grabbing person I have ever met in my whole life, even taking into consideration my long deceased family, so you can forget that idea right now.

Before we hail you a cab to take you back to the Hotel I wish to give you spending money, including the car hire, fuel etc, if you wait there I will just go and get the cash'.

Jake stood and stretched as Stefan left the room for a few moments, just as Jake had sat down again he returned and handed over a number of hundred dollar bills to him, then said he would ring for a cab.

The number of hundred dollar bills he had been given appeared excessive but he thought it best not to say anything as he didn't wish to upset his friend.

As he re-entered the room he said the cab would be five minutes, Jake therefore picked up the briefcase that contained all the jewellery etc, then stood and walked to the front door to await the cab. Stefan walked with him and wished him a safe journey tomorrow, asking him to ring him before he left New York in the afternoon to tell him how the meeting had gone. With that the yellow cab pulled up outside. They quickly shook hands and Jake walked quickly to the car, then turned and waved to his friend Stefan, before they pulled away from the curb.

Walking into the Hotel he nodded to the Receptionist and took the briefcase up to his room, had a quick shower before making his way down to receive the hire car that was due in a quarter of an hour's time. Whilst waiting in the foyer the Receptionist asked if he was eating in or out tonight, as she would book him a table if he was eating in.

He said he would be eating in and thanked her for looking after his interests. Right on time the Hertz car pulled alongside the kerb and a tall elegant man got out of the driver's side and approached Jake. 'Mr Tordale I presume'.

'I am he' replied Jake, 'How will you get back to your Depot?'

'It's no problem sir, the car just down the road is another of our vehicles that we have just collected so that driver will take me back, thank you for your concern, your receipt is in the glove compartment, the tank is full and I hope you enjoy the vehicle, you have a nice evening sir'.

'Jake smiled, and said 'Thank you very much' then shook his hand which contained a twenty dollar note as a tip.The driver nodded his appreciation, turned and made his way back along the road to the other car that was waiting for him.

Jake drove the car in the rear car park and returned to the Hotel and walked through to the Dining Room.

It had been a long and exhausting day, and he intending making an early start in the morning, as the total distance there and back was around five hundred miles it would certainly take it out of him.

Checking the menu he quickly decided on a chicken salad, followed by a fruit salad dessert, which was quite plentiful and with additional sauces really tasty. After the meal he made a few phone calls, first to Charlene explaining where he would be going tomorrow and why, then to his eldest daughter Clare and finally he sent a text to Olivia as he was unsure what the time would be in Sweden. With that completed he thought he would have an early night, then be up early for breakfast and attempt to be on the road by 8am.

Chapter 58

Walking into the Dining Room at 7am Jake was one of the first to dine, so took his seat at his favourite table. The waiter brought his coffee and asked what he would like today.

He decided on eggs and bacon with toast, as he would not stop on the road until he reached New York. Whilst he waited for his food his mobile rang and it was Stefan 'Just checking if you are OK and ready for your journey, I wanted to tell you that I have arranged for the collection of the remaining items in the shop at 11am, I am seeing the Solicitor at 2pm and will be putting the shop on the market later today'.

'OK Stefan, I'm just finishing breakfast and will be leaving soon after, I will ring you from New York later'.

Back up in his room he collected his briefcase, and walked to the car park. He stowed the briefcase in the boot, set the sat nav for Sotheby's address and pulled out onto the road heading for the Interstate.

The two hundred or so miles would take him four hours plus so he set the cruise control at sixty miles and hour, relaxed back in his plush seat to let the comfortable vehicle do all the work.

As he approached the Big Apple around midday he released the cruise control and followed the directions given to him for the Auction House. He parked as directed in the large car park at the rear of the Auction House, retrieved his briefcase and walked into the building. At Reception he explained who he was and the person he wished to see and was directed to a room just off the foyer. He knocked and was asked to enter, where he was welcomed by a tall elegant man in a pin striped suit who shook his hand strongly and said 'It's good to meet you Mr Tordale, I assume the items are in your briefcase'.

'They are indeed, shall I take them out and spread them on your desk or do you wish to go somewhere else?' he asked.

'Please wait a moment I will clear my desk and put a soft liner over it to protect your items'.

There were only a few bits and pieces on the desk, photo frame, pens, pencils, and notepad together with the requisite bank of telephones, and a couple of minutes later he spread the liner over the cleared desk.

Whilst he was waiting Jake had opened the case in preparation for removing the items, which he then started to take out. First the boxes with necklaces, followed by rings and earrings. There were five boxes of watches until the main event the box containing the encrusted jewels.

Jake opened the boxes and as he took them out and put them facing the Auctioneer he was surprised at the man's face as he looked carefully at each item. He took out his notepad and pen and started to write furiously, Jake unsure what was going on just sat back until the man put the pad and pen down.

'I'm going to have to readjust the figures I sent you I'm afraid, now I have seen the goods I realise how rare some of these articles are. Do you have any idea what you have here?'

Jake was shocked at his statement but shook his head before saying 'These are items that have been with the Jeweller for a number of years, the big one came out of Germany during the Second World War and was passed to him when his parents died. I have only known him for a short while, and unfortunately he has a terminal illness, no family and I am the only person he trusts to sort out his business. As you no doubt notice I am from the UK and have visited the States a number of times in the past year on business' he then took out his MI6 card from his wallet and showed it to the man who scrutinised it before handing it back.

Let me run through my adjusted figures for you, and be prepared for surprises. You have one of the earliest Rolex watches I have ever seen. One of the other Swiss watches I have never even heard of but checking the number it was constructed in the 1920's. The necklaces are natural pearls of the highest quality, the earrings of top quality material and are as modern today as when they were first made. Which leads me to the main event, I have seen a picture of this wonderful item in a book many years ago when I was training as an Auctioneer, the book was printed in 1925, therefore the item was made prior to that date, its a one off, and my lowest starting price at the auction will be one point five million dollars, and together with the other items you should expect a collective figure of not less than two and a half million dollars, less our fee of course'.

Jake looked at the man quite stunned 'That it most unfortunate that dear old Stefan has had these items in his possession for all these years and will not live to benefit from his collection, however I will make sure that the remaining time he has will be spent in luxury and his needs will be seen too'.

The man smiled before replying with 'You must remember that these are only my estimated figures and could easily exceed my total. Will you be staying for the Auction

Mr Tordale, or will you be watching online'.

'I will be glued to Stefan's laptop with him on the day, I might just give him the basic details when I ring him later I don't wish to give him such a surprise over the telephone, however when I get back to Washington I will explain to him how rare the objects are. As I am late for inclusion in the brochure will it be the last to sell and if so how will the people know what they are bidding for?'

'I was ready with an answer to your enquiry, you need not worry I will photograph all your items again and produce a few additional pages to the online brochure, therefore all the people interested will have prior knowledge of these additional beauties'.

'I understand, how does the payment situation work, at this time I do not have Mr Cohen's bank details, but could forward them to you when I return to Washington if that's OK'.

'That's OK Mr Tordale, the payment for each item will be in our hands the following Monday and once cleared a Bank Transfer will be made to Mr Cohen within 48 hours'.

'Just one other thing, will you give me a receipt for these individual items so I can pass it to Stefan on my return to show that they are lodged with you?'

'Of course sir, that will be done within the hour, perhaps you would like to go for something to eat in the meantime, I could recommend a superb restaurant no more than fifty metres walk from here'.

'Ideal, thank you very much I'll see you in an hour or so'.

As he walked through the door of the restaurant there was a hustle and bustle about the place, with diners in animated conversation, and as a waiter approached him he was unsure if there was a table available for a single person. However when the waiter said one word 'One' he was shown to a table around the corner from the main area. The menu was all American so he decided on a beef burger with fries and salad, together with iced water. The meal arrived within minutes and it was placed in front of him he realised how hungry he was and tucked into the meal with relish. After finishing the substantial meal he checked his phone for messages, there was one from Charlene and another from Stefan, asking how the drive was and did he have any further news for him. He quickly sent off a reply saying he was waiting for revised figures, but wouldn't send them but see him tomorrow morning. His reply to Charlene was short and sweet, confirming his visit to the Big Apple and he wouldn't be returning until early evening when he would ring her.

The waiter called at his table and asked if everything was OK, and would he like the bill. Jake thanked him and said how much he had enjoyed it and asked for the bill which he paid with a generous tip.

He then walked slowly back to the Auction Room and was directed back to the Office, where a smiling Auctioneer greeted him. 'I hope I'm not too early only I had a lovely meal and am waiting in anticipation regarding your results'.

'As you walked in I have just finished, I think you had better take a seat Mr Tordale. I have put out a sounder on the net after printing off the additional pages to the Brochure, and the enquiries have gone ballistic. There have been emails from all over the Globe and I anticipate there will be a multitude of bids when the Auction goes live'.

'I assume it is difficult to assess what sort of figure we are talking about for the whole of the items?' Jake asked in anticipation.

'It is almost impossible to give you a logical costing, however, and this is only my guess at this stage but I could see my original figure being double or possibly triple that. However auctions can be quirky things so I would like to keep my original figure as a guide for you and we will see what happens on Friday. I assume that you will be able to watch the Auction on line in Washington with your old Jeweller, and once your items have all been sold I will ring you with the final figure'. He stood and shook Jake's hand before passing over an envelope to him 'This is your insured receipt for all the objects, together with my initial estimate. I hope you enjoy the event and the eventual outcome will be to both your approvals'.

'Thank you for your efficient time and effort on our behalf, now I'll make my way back to Washington before the rush hour' then he turned and walked out of the office, back to the car park where he sat and scanned through the paperwork in the envelope. His feeling was just like the birth of his children, euphoric, but tinged with a little sadness that Stefan wouldn't enjoy the funds that would be raised with the sale of his valuables, that had been part of his family for such a long period of time.

Before pulling away he rang MI6 and asked to be put through to Henry Bates, he wished to give him notice when he would be returning to the UK. He was greeted with 'Where are you today you reprobate galavanting around the States?'

'I'm just leaving The Big Apple and returning to Washington, I thought I would give you a call to say I'll be travelling home on Sunday and wondered if that would give you enough notice for the interviews, if not, I'll stay here a few days longer'.

'That would give me enough time if you could be in the office by 10am for the first interview on Monday morning, then the other two we will see afterwards. How are you getting on with your old Jeweller?'

'Completed the clearance of the shop, however I have just come to New York to put some really valuable items in Sotheby's Auction this Friday, so hopefully we will have some good news at the close of the event as to the value of them. There is more to say regarding the old man but I will give you that information face to face. Now I must be on my way the drive back will take me a few hours and I'm feeling a little tired already'.

'Take care Jake and drive carefully, I look forward to seeing you next week'.

Starting the engine he slowly pulled out into the traffic and onto the interstate for his lonely journey ahead.

He pulled into the Hotel car park just after 6pm feeling absolutely exhausted, although the car was luxuriously comfortable almost six hours of driving highlighted the varying injuries he had sustained over the last couple of years and he was looking forward to a long, hot soothing shower.

He stripped off in his room glad to get out of his day clothes, but before going in the shower he rang Stefan to say he had arrived back from New York, complete with the estimate and receipt for the goods.

'Thank you Jake you must be exhausted, I'll see you in the morning at the home, say around 10am?'

'Ok Stefan, see you then' he replied whilst finishing the call.

Chapter 59

He had a lie on until 9am as he felt completely spent after the driving yesterday, but then quickly dressed and went down for a hasty breakfast. Whilst sat at the table he gave Hertz a call to say he would hang onto the car for another day, but it could be collected in the evening from the Hotel.

Back in his room he picked up the envelope and put it in Stefan's briefcase, then drove to his house pulling up outside just before ten.

As he stepped out of the car the front door opened and Stefan stood there with a welcoming grin on his face and said 'Welcome back Jake, you must be shattered after the journey yesterday?'

'I am a little, but truly buzzing with the information I wish to pass onto you'.

He stood to one side and said 'Come in, come in, tell me all about it my boy'.

As they sat at the Dining Room table Jake opened the briefcase and took out the envelope. He took out the Valuation and receipted papers and handed them over to the old man whose face went from happiness to disbelief in a matter of seconds.

'Is this kosher Jake?' he questioned.

'Not only that he has had enquiries from all over the World and anticipates that his estimate could in fact triple at the end of the Auction. However I would like to sit with you at your laptop on Friday and see how the programme of events transpires'.

'I am absolutely gobsmacked Jake, I cannot thank you enough for going to all this effort for me. However I have something to say to you, what I have been up to since you have been away. The shop is virtually sold, as seen, the Solicitor has all the details I gave him and the Will should be in my hands by Friday morning with a copy for you. What are your intentions for the remainder of your stay here?'

'I have to return to the UK either Sunday or at the latest Tuesday to carry out a number of interviews, of course it depends on how the Auction goes and if any paperwork needs to be sorted out for you.

I also need to catch up with a lady friend of mine who I will see on Saturday apart from that I intend to relax unless you have anything else in mind that you would like me to see for you'.

'If you could spare an hour or two now I would like you to walk through the property with me and let me give you a tour of my possessions'.

'Certainly, it would be my pleasure, lead on my friend' as Jake gestured with his hand.

Obviously a religious man there were items in each room depicting his faith, then they walked silently into the spare bedroom which was a shrine to his late wife, not a word was spoken and Jake even felt a little uncomfortable at the prolonged silence, before Stefan turned without a word and left the room. They returned to the Dining Room and sat back down at the table, whereupon the old man scanned through the estimated sale prices of the items that Jake had taken to the Auctioneer's.

He looked Jake in the eye and said 'These are unbelievable figures for items that have been in my possession for more than half a century, just imagine how much is still tucked away with all the other Jewish families, unaware as to their wealth'.

Jake was lost for words, unsure how to reply to his friend until he said 'It is most unfortunate that your illness has forced you into possibly parting with all these family heirlooms, the proceeds of which you most likely will be unable to enjoy. However I will be at your beck and call, just because there is a huge expanse of water between us, I could be with you within half a day if there was anything you needed me to do for you'.

Tears streamed down Stefan's cheeks at the words Jake uttered, and as he composed himself all he could utter was 'I will enjoy what I can, but I'm sure you and your family will reap the benefit of my legacy'.

'I haven't asked any personal questions about your health, but what was the layman's forecast from the doctor at your last visit?'

'Not good Jake, the scan showed that the cancer had spread and his prognosis is six to nine months'.

'I'm so sorry Stefan, may I be rude and ask how old you are?'

'Three weeks time I will be eighty nine, but I feel blessed that I have lived a long and fulfilling life, however I miss my dear wife everyday and will look forward to meeting her again in the after life. My time spent with you has taken me out of the doldrums and helped me considerably in sorting out the shop and my affairs, I will be forever grateful for that Jake'.

'Unfortunately, as you know I will have to return to the UK either Sunday or Monday, so I intend organising a birthday party for you before I leave Washington, so don't argue with me, as I am happy to do this for you. Now if you could eat anywhere in Washington where would you that be?'

'There is only one place in Washington that I have always fancied visiting and that is the Michelin Star establishment called Rose's Luxury on 8th Street, unfortunately its not the place to go for a single person'.

'Considerate it done Stefan, there is only one thing I wish to add to that, I would like to invite a lady friend of mine as well, if you have no objection. How about if I book a table for Friday evening after we hear the results of the Auction, that would then make it a double celebration'.

'Excellent idea Jake, I'll leave you to organise the event, perhaps we can have a taxi there and back and you can organise the young lady's transport for her?'

'No problem at all, I'll give the Restaurant a call and book for Friday at say seven thirty, then I'll call Charlene and give her the invitation'.

He walked to the kitchen and made the calls before walking back and joining Stefan at the table. 'All sorted, i think Friday will be a good day indeed' Jake said to him.

'I'm looking forward to it already, of course a copy of the Will should also be with us on Friday morning, what a day it's going to be Jake' remarked Stefan with a beaming smile.

'If there is nothing else to do today Stefan, I'll head back to the Hotel and ring Hertz to collect the car.'

'No, I'm fine it does feel strange not having to go to work, I expect I'll get used to it. You spend a bit of you're time and go shopping for whatever you fancy doing for the rest of today and tomorrow before Big Friday arrives'.

'OK, I'll see you on Friday, early around nine, so we can make ourselves ready for the Auction, although I expect your items will be last on the Programme as we were late entering, however it will be an enjoyable experience seeing how all the other lots perform'.

'See you on Friday my son, and thank you again for everything you have done for me'.

'Think nothing of it, I enjoy your company and am looking forward to an enjoyable Friday, from start to finish'.

Chapter 60

As he pulled into the Hotel car park his mobile rang, he didn't recognise the number so just answered 'Hello'.

'There was a short delay before a man said 'Hello Mr Tordale its Andrew from Sotheby's, I thought I would give you a bit of information before the Auction on Friday. We have received an extremely high bid from a museum in Israel that we are leaving on the table in preparation for the Auction, however I doubt if any other bidders will be in the running, but you never know'.

'May I ask what figure you are talking about Andrew?'

'Certainly, however this is only for the main boxed item alone, the confirmed figure is three point five million US dollars, for which even I'm astonished. How do you feel about this surprised offer?'

'Astonished is a very underrated word, but I agree with you, in fact I am totally gobsmacked, I am sure that Mr Cohen will be also, thank you for phoning. Before you go could you give me an idea when you anticipate our items will be selling on Friday?'.

'It's always difficult to give a time as some lots take longer than others, however as your's will be the last to go I would guess at 3pm, with all your lots taking approximately three quarter's of an hour'.

'Thank you Andrew, we will be watching the whole Auction on a laptop, as neither of us have been involved in high end bidding before and find the whole occasion fascinating'.

'I hope both of you enjoy the day, bye for now'.

Jake found it most difficult to prise himself from the car seat whilst trying to remain calm following this astonishing news he had just been given, so he was deep in thought as he walked past the Reception desk without looking at the young lady, before taking the lift up to the second floor and his room.

Feeling rather drained from first the news of Stefan's diagnosis and estimated demise, then more positive news from Sotheby's he thought he would have a nap before walking back down the busy street where the Jewellery shop was one of many outlet's, to look for a suitable present for his friend's birthday, although early he intended giving it to him at the Restaurant on Friday evening.

Of the numerous shops advertising their wares, very few were of interest to him, in fact what do you buy for someone who will be an eighty nine year old Jewish Jeweller, in poor health. Of course something to remind him of his birthday, but more importantly something he would enjoy.

As his mind wandered he turned, and looked at the latest shop window he was beside and there was his inspiration. There, on a stand was an A4 card with the words 'Memories for you and your loved ones' and below it said photos, videos, etc, call in and see us.

Into the shop he walked and approached the man behind the Counter who greeted him with 'Good afternoon sir, how may I help you'.

'I noticed the advert in the window regarding memories, firstly how long has this shop been here?'

'This will be our tenth year, why do you ask?' he said with a quizzical look.

'I'm sorry, let me explain, Stefan Cohen had a Jeweller's shop up the road, he has just retired and is about to sell the shop. He is a great friend of mine and I wish to give him a present for his upcoming eighty ninth birthday. He has virtually all he requires, but unfortunately is in rather ill health, I would like to give him something completely different for his birthday and hope you are the person to help me in my quest'.

'I've known Mr Cohen for quite a while and have had many a conversation with him, may I suggest contacting previous Client's of his and the various shops along the Street and arrange for everyone to put a message on Whats app and send to yourself, or if you like I will do it for you'.

'The only problem I have is that we are celebrating his birthday the day after tomorrow and I am taking him to a nice restaurant to celebrate it, I would like to present him with something memorable, which I believe is what you have suggested. However, I am afraid I don't know anyone here apart from Stefan himself, and if you could see yourself possibly doing it for me, I would make it worth your while'.

'Well I'de better get my skates on Mister?'

'Tordale, Jake Tordale, if I give you my mobile number you can keep in touch and let me know what you come up with' he wrote his number on a scrap of paper.

They shook hands, and Jake left the shop feeling quite pleased with himself as to how that meeting had gone.

With the rest of the day to himself he thought he would visit the Hospital and see if Nurse McDonald was on duty and see how she was, also to speak to her about George Adams early retirement due to his debilitating health issues.

As he walked past the Hotel he thought to himself he must also thank the Receptionist for her help with Stefan's details, and sending the parcel to him whilst she was over in the UK.

The weather was still a little nippy so the walk to the Hospital was quite pleasant until he walked through the entrance doors and was hit by a different temperature, it must have been at least 15 degrees hotter than outside, so he removed his wind cheater as he approached the Main desk.

A delightful Mexican Receptionist smiled and said 'How may I help you sir' most likely repeated hundred's of times every day, however the smile was genuine.

'Could you tell me if Staff Nurse McDonald is on duty today, only I'm over from the UK visiting a friend, and she kindly helped me, when a colleague of mine was admitted to Hospital a few weeks ago, and as I'm here I would just like to say hello?'

'I'll check for you sir, could I have your name please'.

'Certainly it's Jake Tordale' he answered hoping that firstly she was on duty, and secondly not wrapped up in an emergency and could spare a few minutes to say hello.

'Yes Mr Tordale, she is on duty and could spare you a few minutes, if you take the lift, I assume you know the way from there?'

'I certainly do, thank you for your help young lady'.

'You're most welcome sir, have a nice day' she answered, blushing.

He walked over to the lift and pressed the requisite button, and as the doors opened, there stood the lovely Staff Nurse. 'Nice to see you again Mr Tordale, how may I be of assistance?'.

'I'm actually on a mercy mission helping out an old man I met the last time I was here, and thought I couldn't visit Washington without calling here and keeping you up to date with my friend George Adams'.

'I trust he is in good health and on the mend?'

'Unfortunately due to the nature of his employment and the damage to his body he has taken early retirement, however he is in good spirits and decided to start a new career in writing'.

'I'm sorry that he had to leave his job but perhaps he will now become a famous writer and make millions' she said with a laugh.

'I won't keep you any longer Staff Nurse but it was good seeing you again, I assume it is just as manic as ever here?'

'In fact I think since I saw you last we have lost 10% of Staff and the work load has increased by 15% with most Nurses now working 50 hour weeks, which in the end is untenable, however the work is a vocation and when you qualify you know what you are letting yourself in for.

So you buckle up and get on with it, anyway I must get back to the 'grindstone' as you English people say' with that she pecked Jake on the cheek turned and walked away.

He thought to himself what a remarkable women, and also all the other staff that work in this Hospital and all Hospital's throughout the World.

With the time approaching midday, he walked back to the Hotel and into the Dining Room and had a spot of lunch. For a brief moment he felt quite lonely until his mobile rang. Checking the number he realised it was Stefan's, 'Hi Stefan, what can I do for you?' he asked. 'Hello Jake, what are you up to, are you busy, only I would like to talk to you about a few things, could you come over to mine?'

'OK Stefan, I'm just having a spot of lunch at the Hotel, so I'll be with you in about an hour'.

'Thank you Jake, see you later'.

After finishing his meal he realised he still had the hire car, so gave them a ring and asked if he could keep it for another day, they confirmed that his invoice can easily be adjusted.

Back in his room he had a quick shower and change of clothes then walked to the car park and drove out to Stefan's abode.

He knocked the door and Stefan shouted 'come on in its open'.

Jake smiled but decided to say to his friend that the door should be locked at all times, due to the current wave of burglaries in the area.

Stefan bowed his head and said 'Sorry, I have never locked my doors when I am here, only at night but I fully understand your concern my son, and will do so from today, I promise'.

'I'm only thinking of you Stefan, the offender's have no thought for human life I'm afraid and would have no compunction in causing you serious harm just to get what they want'.

'I understand Jake, your concerns are noted, shall we get to what I called you here for?'

'I'm sorry, yes I will keep quiet from now on' he replied with a cheeky grin as if he had been reprimanded by his teacher.

'OK, please sit at the Dining Room table and I'll run through a few details that I have had since we met before'.

As they sat down Stefan gathered a few pieces of paper that were already stacked on the table and shuffled them in the order he wished to discuss with Jake.

'Firstly I have a buyer for the shop, the offer I accepted was ten times what I originally paid for it, secondly I have here the Draft copy of my Will to run through with you, and thirdly I have a current Bank Statement and the deeds of this property that have been kept there'.

Jake was flabbergasted at this statement, as he couldn't work out how Stefan had been able to coerce all those involved in organising all these documents in such a short period of time, however he decided to keep quiet and let his friend carry on with his explanation.

'I think before I start we will have a drink of some kind, what would you prefer Jake hot or cold, I have plenty of choices, but it's up to you?'

'I would love a cup of black coffee please Stefan'.

'OK, I won't be a while sit back and relax, and prepare yourself for some extraordinary facts that I have on this table'.

Stefan returned with a tray containing their drinks and a plate of mixed biscuits, then sat down and commenced his oratory.

'Right, first things first, the shop, I purchased it in 1949 for the princely sum of fifteen hundred dollars, quite a sum then, especially just after the Second World War. Now the sale price was just over one hundred and fifty thousand dollars, the sum of which I am completely happy with. Now if you would like to peruse the Draft copy of my Will for a minute or two as we drink our coffee, and ask me any questions once you have finished. Whilst you are doing that I will also hand you my current Bank Statement and the Deeds of this property'.

Some fifteen minutes passed before Jake replied, but before he could open his mouth Stefan spoke. 'I know you are surprised what I have put in the Will but as you know I have no living relatives, and the brief time we have known each other I feel that you are the son I never had, and I wish I had more time to spend with you'.

Jake took a deep breath and answered with 'This is incredibly generous of you Stefan, I think you are a wonderful human being, how you have gone through all the troubles and strifes of the Second World War then built up a successful Jewellery business which at the grand old age you are, you deserve enjoyment which I intend to make true over the next few days'.

'Well of course there is one other item we haven't discussed and that is the Auction tomorrow, and what will become of the proceeds. May I suggest that a sum is forwarded to the Hospital that I have been going to for my diagnosis and treatment, and possibly a cause that is close to your heart. The remainder I will put in an account in your name. then it will be accessible when the day comes for me to return to my dear wife'.

Jake then took his leave explaining to his friend that he needed an early night, as he wished to have an early breakfast in the morning and be back with him before the Auction begins, enabling them to have the laptop fired up and the notepad and pen available.

Stefan understood and shook his hand before replying with 'Tomorrow I think will be a special day, goodnight my boy'.

Chapter 61

After a quick breakfast he made his way to Stefan's for the big day, Auction first, followed by celebrations of his birthday at a swanky restaurant in the City. As he walked in he felt that Stefan was quite agitated regarding the upcoming sale, and the celebrations of his last birthday, however as Jake shook his hand and wished him a Happy birthday, the strain appeared to disappear from his face.

There followed a period of quietness, before the silence was broken by Jake who said 'I think it's time to turn on the laptop, as the Auction begins in ten minutes time'.

Bringing Stefan out of his memories, he smiled then opened the machine and logged into the website, which lit up with colourful flashing lights indicating the countdown to the commencement of the Event.

Neither man had been privy to this type of Auction before and they were almost salivating in anticipation, aa the light display finished a close-up of the Auctioneer came in full screen and he announced 'Welcome to Sotheby's, New York to all those present, and the prospective buyers from around the World, we will start the Auction with Item No.1 in your brochure'.

This first item took only three minutes to sell, the various lots sold rapidly for the next two hours until they came to Item 100 and the Auctioneer said there would be a twenty minute break after this item was sold, as the gavel came down the clock struck one pm.

Stefan stood and walked into the kitchen where he retrieved a plate of sandwiches he had prepared earlier and put the kettle on for a cup of tea. When he sat down, they relaxed back in the Lounge's armchairs and ate their food before Jake said 'The sale is quite rapid don't you think, I wonder how many lots there are in total, what am I saying you have the brochure here somewhere Stefan, don't you?'

It was in fact still on the table in the Dining Room, so he stood and collected it, as he walked into the Lounge he said 'There are three hundred and twenty lots, plus ours, so it would appear that the total sale will take until 6pm, making it quite tight for us to get to the Restaurant, but priorities first, I think'.

As they finished their lunch Jake carried the plates, cups and saucer's into the Kitchen and returned to the Dining Room table just as Stefan opened the laptop in time for the resumption of the Auction. They muttered a lot as the various Lots were shown, before being sold, and as 5pm approached it was getting to the end of the Official Programme.

They looked at each other before Jake spoke first with

'Now the fun starts Stefan, do you have a pen and paper and I'll put the sale prices against the notes that I was given to give us some idea what sort of figure we will end up with, less fees'.

Stefan collected the items from his bureau and handed them to Jake who was poised as the Auctioneer, made a short speech to everyone. 'The following items were handed in at short notice, and were obviously not included in the Official Programme of Lots, however they have been posted online, and everyone here in front of me has been handed a copy as they entered the facility. Some of the articles are extremely rare and to let everyone know in advance I have numerous bids already logged on the computer from Clients around the World. Let's now start with the first item one of the earliest Rolex watches ever built. This item is boxed and has never been worn, it has all the relevant information, obviously there is no receipt as it is being sold on behalf of a Jeweller, as are all the other items. Could I start with a bid of $50,000 dollars'. Half a dozen numbered paddles were raised in the air, there were also three people on mobile phones. The bidding quickly raced to $100,000 with the hammer finally going down at $135,000.

Three quarters of an hour went by before the main event went up for sale. This was the final item, and the Auctioneer gave a short speech explaining to everyone what in fact the article was and the approximate date it would have been constructed.

There was a hushed silence before he looked at all of the people gathered in front of him, took a deep breath and spoke quietly into the microphone and said 'I have an opening bid from Israel of $1,500,000, I see all the paddles raised and telephone bidders, I will ask for offers of $20,000 increments'. The sale took fifteen minutes before the man said, For the third and last time I sell this beautiful item for $3,255,000' and the gavel crashed down, as applause broke out throughout the room.

In a Dining Room in Washington DC two stunned men looked at each other, and without a word spoken stood and hugged each other.

Using the calculator on his mobile, Jake quickly totted up the value of their total sale and turned to Stefan and said '$4,335,000 less fees'.

Stefan with tears running down his cheeks, looked as Jake, opened his mouth, but no words came out. Jake answered for him and said 'Well that wasn't what I expected, how about you?'

'To think that item has been in my possession for approximately forty years and has sold for that astronomic figure beggars belief, also the total figure is astounding Jake'.

'I agree, but feel saddened that we, or you alone, have only discovered the items worth at the eleventh hour of your life and will not benefit from the proceeds, however I will make the money work for you when I return here again after a three week break back in the UK where I have a holiday booked to Greece for two weeks. I have given a few items some thought and wondered if you would like to return to your former home in Europe or perhaps make a visit to Israel one last time?'

'You are most thoughtful Jake, I still hold a passport as I have visited a few Countries over the past few years buying and selling my wares, so a possible visit to Europe and Israel seems a lovely way to enjoy a few dollars from the sale proceeds. But of course you would have to accompany me on the journey?'

'That is agreed then, all that's left to do now is to prepare for our meal out. I have to pop back to the Hotel to change and I'll be back as soon as I can and we can order a cab'.

'Excellent Jake, see you soon, I'll be ready by the time you return'.

'As he sat in the car he dialled the number of the shop and spoke to the Owner, asking how he had got on with the various messages he was hoping to collect. 'Hello Mr Tordale, I have done even better than I originally thought, not only do I have the present Shop Owners. but they contacted the previous owners who knew Stefan, and I have received notes from them. What time are you off for your meal?'

'Time is not on my side, I have just left him and have to return to the Hotel to change clothes and then I'll be with you to collect the item'.

'I can do better than that' the man said, 'I'll drop it in Reception for you to save you a little time in your busy day, and you can call in tomorrow to pay my invoice'

'That is extremely kind of you, I really appreciate the effort you have put into this gift for Stefan, I'm sure tears, albeit happy tears will be shed later on, thank you again for your help'. Then before the old man became suspicious he pulled away and raced back to the Hotel. Twenty minutes later he stood in front of the Receptionist and asked if she had a parcel for him. She smiled, then nodded, leant under the counter and brought out a gift wrapped parcel for him. He returned her smile and said 'This will make Stefan extremely happy, thank you'.

It was twenty to seven when Jake pulled up outside Stefan's home, he parked on the drive, he had decided as time was tight that he would drive to the venue. He leapt out of the car, knocked the door and walked in to find Stefan suited and booted and ready for an evening out. 'Forget the cab Stefan, I've decided to drive you there myself as time is short, I'll ring Charlene on the way and tell her to go to the table and advise the Staff we will be there at seven, OK?'

Chapter 62

He rang Charlene as they walked to the hire car, and she agreed to go in and sit at their table in preparation for Stefan's grand entrance. They pulled into the rear car park two minutes late, the waiter that greeted them was understanding, and showed them over to where Charlene was already seated and nursing a drink. The Manager approached the table and explained the various menu's that were on offer. Decisions were made following the formal introduction of Charlene to Stefan, and the waiter walked away to collect their drink orders.

The four course meals were delivered at regular intervals, as and when diner's were ready, more drinks flowed, before Jake excused himself and asked the Manager to keep his companion's happy whilst he collected a present for his friend's impending birthday. The man smiled and walked back to the table and engaged in conversation with Charlene and Stefan. Jake returned five minutes later with his parcel and handed it over to his friend with 'As I won't be here for your actual birthday, I would like to give you this item as a small token before I return and take you to Europe in a months time'.

Stefan was speechless for a moment or two before he accepted the gift, then asked if he could have a bottle of champagne, to keep his friends entertained whilst he opened the gift. The cork popped and as the waiter poured the champagne, Stefan carefully opened his parcel, he scratched the side of his head, before the penny dropped, and he realised what he actually had in his hand. Going through all the messages on the cards brought the tears streaming down his cheeks, and he was unable to complete all the messages before he took a sip of his drink.

'I know it's short notice, but it's amazing how much you are respected and held in high regard throughout the retail shops in your street and beyond. I think it best after you have a cursory inspection, you save your actual viewing until you get back home'.

Stefan patted Jake's shoulders and said how honoured he felt to receive so many nice thoughts from the various shopkeepers, and he vowed to write to each and everyone of them, he then turned to Charlene and smiled before remarking 'You look lovely this evening my dear, please forgive me for not saying so earlier, only Jake has caught me on the hop with this lovely gift, and we have spent a lot of time consuming this lovely fair'.

She smiled at him, stood and gave him a peck on the cheek before saying 'It's your evening, I'm just glad Jake invited me tonight to meet you in person and enjoy your company'.

Jake butted in and quickly said 'Don't start us off babbling my dear, it doesn't take a lot for us to start, and I must agree with Charlene it has been a lovely evening, now if you'll excuse me I'll just go and settle the bill' he stood and walked over to the Manager.

When he returned to the table his two companions were indulging in conversation and neither noticed him until he sat down, just as Stefan completed with the words 'Like a son to me'.

The Manager approached the table and handed an envelope to Stefan, wishing him a Happy Birthday, and not to open it until his actual Birth Day. Stefan smiled before saying to all those present 'You have all made an old man very happy tonight and I thank you all'.

Jake said if Charlene could spare the time he would drive Stefan home, and then drop her back to her flat rather than ordering a cab.

She smiled at him ands replied 'Thank you Jake, it will give me more time to enjoy this lovely man's company'.

Stefan blushed and said 'The pleasure is all mine my dear'. Charlene and Stefan sat in the rear seats and talked all the way back to his home, only stopping as Jake pulled into the kerb. 'Would you care to call in for a drink of some kind, or would you rather head home'.

Charlene smiled at the old man before answering with 'Perhaps another time, I have work tomorrow that has to be completed over the weekend, and I need to have a clear head in the morning, thank you anyway' she kissed him on the cheek then got back in the car.

Jake saw him to the door, shook his hand and gave him a hug before turning and walking back to the hire car.

Now with Charlene in the passenger seat beside him he could converse with her quite freely. 'Do you really have to work over the weekend, I was hoping we could have tomorrow to ourselves and I am flying on Sunday, back to the UK?'

'I'm sorry Jake please forgive me' she said, before breaking out into a grin and saying and adding 'I had to think quickly, so I hope Stefan will forgive me for telling a white lie'.

Jake turned and returned her smile before asking 'So you will be free tomorrow?'

'Yes I will, I'm your's for the whole day, what would you like to do?'

After giving her a quizzical look he said 'Nothing too strenuous, however I would like to see other parts of the Capital if possible, but I'll leave the itinerary to you my dear'.

The journey into the City was reasonably quiet and he pulled up outside her flat at 9pm, gave her a long, sensual kiss and said he would see her in the morning. He added that he would collect her again as the Hire car was his until he returned it to the Airport on Sunday. They agreed on a start time of 9am, for their next adventure together, and with that he pulled away and returned to the Hotel.

Chapter 63

The Dining Room was quiet as he walked in, his favourite waiter approached him and said 'Usual black coffee Mr Tordale?'

'Yes please Daniel' he replied, 'I'll also have eggs sunny side up, bacon, tomatoes and hash browns, with toast, please'.

'Right away sir, are you leaving us soon?'

'I am, why do you ask?'

'I am leaving the Hotel and moving to Texas for another position there on Monday, I want to make sure I say goodbye to you before you leave' he replied blushing slightly.

'I am also leaving tomorrow, so I'll see you at breakfast before I depart'.

'OK, I'll go and get you're coffee sir, and put the order in for the food' he turned and walked away from the table.

Daniel returned with the coffee, then a few minutes later came back with a huge plateful of food, and Jake's side dish of toast.

He had just completed his breakfast when his mobile rang, he checked the number and realised it was Charlene ringing. 'Good morning young lady, I'm just finishing my breakfast and I can be with you within the hour, if that's OK?'

'Your words have saved me a few questions I had for you. I'll be ready and waiting, to take you for another adventure around the Capital accompanied by my good self as your guide' she joked.

'I'll meet you outside your apartment as soon as possible, bye for now'.

Back in his room, he quickly sent off an email to Henry confirming his flight details back to the UK, and promising to be in his Office by 9am Monday morning for the impending interviews. Then a quick call to Stefan to make sure he was in good spirits, and to say he would ring again before he boarded his plane on Sunday.

Getting into the Hire car he drove as fast as he could into the centre of Washington to collect the lovely Charlene for their trip around the Capital, for whatever she had in store for him.

As the weather had brightened over the past couple of days, she was dressed in a floral outfit of multiple colours but still carried a warm coat in case the weather turned.

As she sat in the car and made herself comfortable Jake turned and looked at her before asking 'Which way?'

Charlene laughed and told him to take the car into the rear car park that was allocated to the various apartments and to swop positions with her car, as it would be far easier for her to drive as she knew exactly where they were headed, and it was too complicated to issue instructions to Jake as he drove.

'You're a remarkable lady Charlene, always thinking about the best of circumstances for other people, I do appreciate it, and must insist that I cover all costs today, no arguments'.

'Fine with me, you handsome English Gentleman'

Having swopped positions she sat back before pulling away and explained 'Today will not be as intense as our previous adventures, but I trust you will enjoy the experience on your last day here'.

'I'm read for it, let's go driver' he said as he turned and smiled at her.

As they drove away she said 'The first visit will be somewhere that we both found interesting, The International Spy Museum, we could spend a little more time exploring, as we do not have a timed itinerary today'.

'Fine by me, I agree it was interesting and I did skip a few area that I would like to explore in more detail this time'.

Two hours drifted by as they went their separate ways around the Museum, and with time approaching midday Jake suggested that their next stop was for a food break.

'Already organised Mr Tordale, we have to head into the Centre for today's chosen extravaganza, I hope you are hungry as we will be feasting at the best Italian in Washington, none other than Fiola's. It's difficult to get a table at short notice, however I have eaten there a few times and explained the circumstances, and they have reserved a table for us. The meal is extortionately priced, however its all about the experience, and the wonderful service that is provided by its attentive staff. I think it will match any establishment that you have in the UK, however I'm a little biased'.

'If I'd known we were visiting such an upmarket facility I would have dressed more formally however they will have to take me as they find me'.

'Exactly right Jake, never judge a book by its cover, I think is the quaint old English saying' she answered whilst smiling at him.

She pulled into the curb twenty minutes later, outside the Restaurant, and a valet approached the car as they alighted and Charlene handed her keys to him.

They were only two strides away from the Entrance when the door was opened by a swarthy looking Italian man dressed in a dark suit, white shirt and beige tie, and said 'Welcome to Fiola madam, welcome back, I assume this is your English gentleman?'

She nodded and the man shook Jake's hand, whilst repeating his welcome.

They were shown to a lovely table for two and handed the wine list. They discussed what they would be eating and what wine would suit them before placing their order for drinks.

Charlene had already giving their food requirements when she placed her reservation, and their starter arrived almost immediately after their wine was served.

Over the next hour they were treated with delight after delight, until finally the Manager returned with a complimentary drink for Jake. Nothing for Charlene as she was the driver today, however he also brought something for her, a small bouquet of flowers.

As Jake enjoyed his final drink he turned to Charlene and said 'You are an excellent judge of a restaurant, this was a fantastic meal and well worth every penny of the 'extortionate' cost, however as someone who was very close to me used to say 'you only get what you pay for' and I totally agree with that comment'.

Jake handed over his card and dropped a $100 dollar note on the silver salver as a tip.

As they stood the Manager handed Charlene her keys saying that the car was parked outside. He opened the door and shook hands with both of them, opening the car door for her to slide in.

As they settled in Jake asked 'What's next?'

She smiled and replied 'The National Theatre have another show on this afternoon and we have seats booked for 3pm, so I'd best get my skates on, buckle up'.

Chapter 63

An enthralling two hours later they walked out of the Auditorium having witnessed a wonderful rendition of Romeo and Juliet, with a twist of modern day life, however they both agreed that it was most interesting.

With the time approaching 6pm Charlene told her companion that the tour was over for the day, and inquired what time his flight was in the morning.

'I need to be at the Airport by midday as it will allow me to drop off my Hire car, go through Customs, then sit and enjoy the First Class Lounge before take-off'

'I'll drop you back to the car park you have a lot to sort out for the rest of the day, looking in on Stefan, packing etc, then I'll see you again when you return, to collect him for your journey to Europe for his final Birthday treat'.

'Thank's Charlene, I'm sorry the time is short on this visit, but it has been a whirlwind visit this time spent with the people who mean a lot to me, unfortunately cut short by my return to the UK, however I will be returning in a few weeks to accompany Stefan to Europe. Thank you for your time which I will make up to you on my next visit'.

Chapter 64

Back at the Hotel, he collected his belongings and packed ready for an early start in the morning. Checking through his remaining items he put his passport and ticket to one side and laid out the clothes he would be wearing on his flight to England.

He would ring Stefan before he left the Hotel in the morning explaining his intentions to return to the US as soon as he had cleared up all the urgent items in England. that would take him at least a month. Then once back in Washington he would arrange flights to Europe for both off them to enable Stefan to visit his roots one last time.

He then sent a text to Henry Bates advising him of the flight details, he would be taking the next day, followed by quick messages to his daughters saying he would be back in the UK tomorrow but had interviews in London for most of Monday. Another message to Olivia confirming her forthcoming flight to Heathrow, then onward journey to Bristol, where he would pick her up ready for their holiday to Santorini.

What a busy chap, he thought to himself.

He then settled down for a good night's sleep.

Waking early he had a final shower in the Hotel, dressed and went down for breakfast and say goodbye to Daniel the waiter who was also leaving the Hotel for other ventures. After finishing his food Daniel came to clear the plates and Jake handed him a $50 dollar tip, whilst wishing him good luck in his new career.

He stood and walked to the Receptionist to pay his bill, and thank the young lady for all her help with Stefan.

Back in the room he collected all his belongings and placed them in the hire car, before returning to the counter and handing over his room key.

A slow drive to the Airport before parking near the Hertz Rental unit, he collected a trolley and placed his cases on it before walking into the Offices to pay his bill.

Chapter 64

Walking into the Terminal, as he done on numerous occasions recently, he went through the routine almost like a robot, before walking into the First Class Lounge. His flight, he thought wouldn't be called for at least another hour and a half, so he settled back and read a paper whilst caressing a coffee and brandy chaser. Casting his eyes around the room there was no-one that caught his attention as someone he knew, so he returned to the pages of the tabloid reading from front to back of the huge paper.

There was only a five minute break before the flight was called, and he joined the throng of bodies making their way onto the huge jet.

Settling into his seat, he was quickly approached by a Steward who welcomed him on board, saying his name was Bryan and if there was anything he needed to just press the bell on the arm of his seat. Jake nodded and smiled in return and closed his eyes ready for take-off.

The flight went by without a hitch, and following the usual food and drink breaks, he took a number of naps to help with the jet lag that would hit him later after landing.

Depositing his belongings in the boot of his car he walked into the Hotel, smiled at the Receptionist and booked a room for the night.

Feeling extremely tired he went up to his room and had another nap, he thought to himself age is catching up after all his latest globetrotting journey's.

He woke a couple of hours later and went down to the Dining Room and had a late evening meal, before retiring for the night.

Chapter 65

Up ready for a different day, he had an early breakfast as he intended being in the Office by 9am ready for the interviews for George Adam's post.

Driving into the City in the rush hour is never an enjoyable event and he was glad he was in a taxi, as the journey was horrendous, however the vehicle pulled alongside the pavement at five minutes to nine.

Taking the lift up to Reception from the underground car park, he nodded at the young lady before taking the other lift up to Henry Bates's office.

Henry stood and shook hands with him as soon as he approached his desk, and asked if he was OK and ready for the interrogation of the interviewees.

'Are there any obvious questions to ask, I assume you will take the lead, then look to me for any additional questions?'

'We have their CV's to scan through first, the initial interview is 9.30, the other four will be at hourly interval's. I assume with your 'people understanding', the possible obvious candidate will stand out to you, but we will discuss each applicant as we go along. Right Jake, let's go in the other room and ready ourselves for the first one'.

The room was set out with a table away from the door with two chairs and a telephone, then in front of the table sat a single chair for each Applicant. The table had numerous files enclosed in manilla folders on it, together with notepads and pens for Henry and Jake's use.

The first Applicant was a young lady, ex SAS trained, aged thirty one, with an extensive CV, she was single and lived in a flat in Surrey.

Jake turned to Henry and said 'She looks impressive sir, what are your thoughts?'

'After reading her file I wanted to interview her first, as it would give us a benchmark of what the others had to live up to, however let's wait and see what she is like, CV's can be impressive, however sometimes the actual person can be something completely different'.

'I agree, well let's see what she can provide, eh?'

Five minutes later the telephone rang, and the secretary said that the first applicant was here and ready for her interview. Henry said 'Show her in'.

There was a knock on the door and Henry bellowed 'Enter'.

In walked a tall, athletic woman with dark hair, dressed in a grey sombre suit and topped off with black flat shoes. She had no jewellery on her, ears, nose, etc and light makeup.

Jake thought although not unattractive, she could mingle unnoticed in a crowd if she was doing undercover work, but if needed could impress someone.

She approached the table and before sitting on the chair confirmed her name, Henry nodded before asking her to sit.

Henry opened her file and scanned the pages within, for a couple of minutes before lifting his eyes and looking at the young lady and starting with his opening gambit, "Why have you put yourself forward for this post Miss Freith?'

'I pride myself in fitness and presentation, together with a fluency in French, German and Italian which I think would help in the post you have advertised. With my training in the SAS I have close skills in hand to hand fighting and have had use and skills in various armaments should it be needed'.

'You have an excellent CV, but what about the private side of you as a woman, what do you do in your spare time, do you have any hobbies or interests that you can tell us about?'

She flushed slightly before answering this question with 'I play squash to a reasonable level, my fitness is kept up with cycling and running. My only hobbies have been a spell of orienteering and rock climbing. I have no partners either male or female, anticipating your next question. However, once I almost decided to enter a convent to get away from the turmoil of my life, but that quickly faded when I joined the SAS'.

A short silence followed before Henry looked a Jake and nodded for him to ask her the next questions.

'What about a social life, do you have one, and if so what does it involve?'

She smiled before saying 'My social life tends to involve the people I work with, I'm not a drinker or party girl, so apart from my sporting activities my life is quite mundane'.

Jake looked her in the eye before continuing with 'Do you consider yourself a team player, only this post is not a James Bond one, but more of a follow, report and occasionally chase, one. Your work could involve being in Europe or quite often, somewhere else around the World. Although I mention it as a team situation, a lot of the time you are flying solo. How do you feel about that?'

'I understand fully what you are saying sir, but I feel that as I have no immediate companions, and I am my own person, I feel available to carry out any situation that MI6 requires of me'.

Henry nodded to Jake, stood and thanked Miss Frieth for her honesty and said they would be in touch with her as soon as possible.

She shook Henry and Jake's hands then thanked them for their time, before turning and leaving the room.

As the door shut they looked at each other before Henry said 'Impressive, don't you think?'

'I must admit she'll take some beating' Jake replied.

The remaining interview's were taken at hourly intervals, and as the last applicant left at 12.40pm, they stood, stretched and said to each other, 'Lunch before summary, I think'.

They spent a couple hours in a nearby Chinese Restaurant indulging in a sumptuous meal together with a bottle of wine, whilst mulling over the four people they had interviewed. Although there were two outstanding candidates, one male and one female it was almost impossible to separate them after the initial interview. Jake therefore suggested that they get them back for a second chat before finally making their decision.

Henry agreed and rang his office secretary to telephone the two people concerned and ask them to return for a second interview, that afternoon.

As they were returning to the office, Henry's phone rang and it was confirmed that she could only make contact at present with Miss Frieth who said she was still in London and could return at 2.30pm. She said she had left a voicemail message with the man and was still awaiting a reply.

'Henry said to Jake 'Miss Freith is coming in at 2.30pm, but at present there is no answer from Mr Johnson's phone, however she left a message for him to reply as soon as possible, so at this stage there is a definite tick for Miss Freith'.

As they walked into the Office Henry's secretary said 'Mr Johnson has just replied and said he could be here at 3pm, I've told him that would be OK'.

'Fine' said Henry, 'When Miss Frieth returns send her right in please'.

'Certainly sir' she replied.

They took their seats behind the desk, then scanned both folders again. Jake asked Henry 'What additional questions do you intend asking her Henry?'

'To be honest I'm a little worried that her life is a bit off key, not like a normal 30 year old, she appears almost like a robot, what do you think?'

'I see where you're coming from, however the job is a little like that when you are out in the field, you need to be a bit of an individual animal, not worried about a loved one, or the party you have to get to over the weekend. However I understand what you mean about a team player she appears very black and white, so a few additional questions into her lifestyle might reveal something that she hasn't divulged, like the Convent situation'.

'Yes, that was going to be one of my first questions to her, if I hesitate at all, please fill in for me with your own thought's'.

'I will indeed' Jake replied, and with that there was a knock on the door, and Miss Freith walked in and stood by the chair.

'Please sit down' Henry acknowledged with a hand gesture. 'We asked you to return, as there are a couple of other items we would like you to elaborate on, to enable us to make a final decision between yourself and another candidate who will be following you. So you hinted on your possible removal from general life and taking vows to become a Nun. What in your life made you have strong thoughts on this decision, and then why did you not carry through with this vocation?'

Her face turned crimson and she appeared flustered with his question, she coughed before replying to Henry with 'There have been certain things in my life that have questioned my mental health, even my existence, and when I was at a severe low I thought of retreating to a simpler life, such as in a Convent. I do not wish to go into specifics however but it happened over ten years ago, and I am now a more stable person and OK with my life'.

Henry first eyed her facial expression, before looking her straight in the eye and saying 'Thank you for your honesty, I do not wish to bring up things from your past that bring unpleasant memories to you, however I trust these do not come to the surface often as they would give you negative thoughts when you're under pressure in the post you have applied for'.

'I understand sir, however I cannot say definitely that it wouldn't happen again, as no-one knows how their brain would react to circumstances beyond their control' she answered.

Jake cleared his throat before asking 'You say you have no commitments at the moment, for a young attractive lady like yourself I assumed there must be someone, either now or in the past that you are or had been close to?'

Again she blushed, looked Jake in the eye and answered his query with 'Yes there was someone in my past, but in wasn't a viable relationship once I joined the SAS and it fizzled out over a period of time'.

Jake turned to Henry and nodded, to say that he had finished.

Henry looked at her and said with a final few words 'I would like to thank you for your honesty, and if you would be so kind as to take the lift down to Reception, the young lady will offer you refreshments. We have another interview to perform and once that has been completed then we will make our decision and inform you of our decision', She nodded, stood, turned and left the room.

A few minutes later there was a tap on the door and Mr Johnson entered the room and Henry asked him to sit in the chair again.

There was a long pause before anyone spoke, then Henry looked up from his paperwork and said 'If you were offered the post today when could you start?'

Johnson looked Henry in the eye and then over to Jake before a smile spread across his face and he replied 'Tomorrow if you want me'.

Henry didn't smile, he just said 'Thank you for your time, I'll be in touch'.

Chapter 65

Johnson stood and walked out of the room without another word. Henry turned to Jake before saying 'I knew there was something wrong with him, but I just couldn't put my finger on it. He's an arrogant, out of work mercenary and not someone I want on the team. I'm sorry I didn't warn you what I was going to say, I only thought about it as he entered the room, something was off with him'.

'By your reaction I assume you will be taking on Miss Frieth then?' he asked.

'I'm still unsure, if you would like to call into Marcus W's this evening we could mull over everything over a nice meal and finalise our thoughts on the matter, what do you say'.

'It would be rude to turn down your offer, what time shall we meet up?'

'I'll ring the restaurant now and book our table for 6pm if that's OK with you?'

'Excellent, I am in fact quite peckish, as I'll have to stay here for another hour I'll spend the time looking through both of the files on the finalist's to give me a head's up'.

Later they were greeted by Marcus as they entered his establishment and shown to the table that Henry always used.

The meal as usual was delicious and fulfilling but the conversation was about the possible employing of Miss Frieth to replace their friend George Adams. In the end they decided that she was easily the best candidate and wasn't burdened by any ties, however they would have to watch her mental health issues for the first six month's probation.

Their meal finished at eight, and Jake said he would order a taxi to take him back to the Airport Hotel, for him to have a good night's sleep before heading home to Dorset.

As he walked into the Foyer of the Hotel at 9pm he thought he would have a nightcap before retiring and walked into the Bar and ordered a pint of lager. The room was extremely quiet, no doubt flight arrivals and departures were not due at present, or had been at an earlier time and the passengers had either left the Terminal or had retired to their Hotels.

After finishing his drink he made his way to his room and settled down for the night as he expected to be awake early the next morning for breakfast, then he would make a swift drive back to the sanctuary of his home.

Chapter 66

He was wide awake at 6am, had a quick shower and shave before dressing and going down for breakfast. He fancied a good old 'English' with toast and black coffee to set him up for the day, which went down a treat. Then he called to Reception, paid his invoice before heading back up to his room to collect his luggage and make his way to the car in the parking area.

Heading West the traffic was lighter as most of the vehicles were heading into London , he pulled into his drive an hour and a half later and let out a sigh of relief that he was at last back home.

Unlocking the front door he quickly walked into the Hall and disconnected the alarm system before retrieving his luggage from the car.

There were a number of letters on the floor, together with a couple of thin parcels, which he placed on the Dining Room table.

He then took the luggage up to his bedroom and sorted what needed washing, and what could be put away, then taking the dirty washing into the kitchen he put it in the washing machine.

After making a coffee he sat down at the table and went through all the letters before opening the two small parcels.

One of the parcels contained a copy of his new will from his solicitor, and the other was from Olivia, it contained a copy of her two flight details, together with a photograph in a cardboard frame of her family at Christmas time.

Most of the letters were innocuous, however there was one from the USA, when he opened it he was astonished to find it came from Stefan. There was a one page explanation and a cheque in the sum of £1.5 million pounds, the letter read 'A downpayment from me to you for the work you carried out, in selling my goods through Sotheby's, in New York. I have paid the remainder into the Bank and sent another cheque to the Hospital as discussed, I hope you had a nice flight back, and that you enjoy your two week holiday. I look forward to seeing you when you return to arrange our short visit to Europe. Yours Stefan'.

Chapter 66

Good grief Jake thought, I can't get over the generosity of the man in sending me this amount of money so soon. The remainder of his post were either Bills or begging letters.

He sat back contemplating what he would do next, as Olivia would be arriving at Bristol Airport the following day. He decided to go into Dorchester to pay in his cheque, but not before ringing the Manager of the Bank, to arrange an appointment with him for the coming afternoon. The Manager was glad to speak with him and could spare a quarter of an hour around 2pm, if that was OK with him. Jake thought he would drive to Dorchester for lunch before visiting the Bank, for his meeting.

He pulled into the town centre car park and walked along the main street and into an Italian Restaurant that was only a hundred or so yards from the Bank. The place was quite busy, he noticed, as he was shown to a table at the rear of the premises. The waiter asked what he would like to drink whilst handing him a menu, he asked for a sparkling water and ordered spaghetti carbonara for his meal.

The food was excellent and as he checked his watch he realised he had time for a dessert, looking at the menu he was surprised to see rice pudding there, so when the waiter cleared his plate he ordered his dessert.

Completely satisfied he didn't order coffee as the time was now one fifty, so he paid the bill, and walked along to the Bank. Introducing himself to the teller, he advised her he had an appointment with the Manager for 2pm. She opened a side door and ushered him into the bowels of the Bank before knocking the door and opening it for Jake.

'Good afternoon Mr Tordale, I'm Arnold Granger it's a pleasure to meet you in the flesh how may I be of service to you?'

'I assume that you have looked at my details prior to my visit, however I expect I will be making your day, as I have a substantial cheque to deposit with you' he said handing over the piece of paper.

Granger could not contain his surprise as his eyebrows lifted considerably and his eyes almost popped out, before he controlled himself and replied 'Quite a sum Mr Tordale, do you wish me to put it in your current account or divide it into a few accounts to gain a little interest?'

'I'll leave that up to you as you are the experts, however should I need to extract a couple of large items, I will telephone you prior to doing so. I also have a copy of my will which I would like you to put in one of your deposit boxes. Finally over the next 12 months a valued friend of mine who is suffering from a terminal illness will no doubt pass away, it his intention to leave me a house in Washington DC which I will sell, also as he has no living relatives leaving me as the sole beneficiary of his will, therefore additional large payments will be forthcoming. In the meantime I would like you to investigate the best investments I can make for these monies, also I wondered if I should put certain amounts in other establishments to reduce the tax element with the the HMRC?'

'No problem sir, I understand your thoughts regarding the HMRC, however wherever you place your funds the Banks are bound to advise the Tax Office, may I suggest you employ a good Accountant to look after your affairs, but I will certainly forward a list of Investments for you by tomorrow'.

He stood and said 'Before you go, I'll get you a receipt for your deposit which I suggest you keep in a safe place until you receive your latest statement'.

Jake was left in the chair with a huge beaming smile on his face, as it was a joy to see the man looking like a 'child in a sweet shop' as he walked out of the room clutching his valuable piece of paper.

A couple of minutes later he returned with Jake's receipt, they shook hands and the Manager ushered him out of the inner sanctum of the Bank, whilst thanking him for calling to see him. Walking back to the car he mulled over what was next on the list of things to do, his thought wandered to Olivia's visit tomorrow and his drive to Bristol Airport to collect her. As there was nothing more pressing for the rest of the day, he thought he would tidy up the Cottage when he returned, in preparation for her arrival, then once finished pop down to the Pub for a couple of beers and a catch up with whoever of his pals happened to be there. The tidy up took a lot longer than he thought and it was gone six before he was ready to walk down the lane, and as he hadn't had anything to eat since lunch in Dorchester he would have a snack at The Swan.

Approached the door to the Bar he could hear a lot of talking and laughter so assumed that a few of his pals that went to France with him to see the Rugby International were in there and in fine voice. As he opened the door there was a loud cheer, and he realised they were playing an early game of 'spoof', with the last person involved in the game buying a round of drinks. The trouble with the game is that each round involved downing a pint of beer so the chaps had obviously been through a few rounds already, but it was all good fun. At the centre of it all was his friend Tony Bailey, who shouted over to him to join the throng, however Jake said he was going to have a snack first and walked to the Bar to order his food and drink from Bert the Landlord.

'Good evening Jake, long time no see, been on your travels again, I assume?'.

'Yes I have Bert, long story as usual, and it's not the time to tell you about it. I was hoping for a quiet couple of drinks before I go on holiday in a couple of days. But it appears that I will be getting involved with the other chaps once I have had my food'.

Bert handed over a pint before saying 'The've been at it for over an hour, so even the heaviest of drinkers will only last another couple of rounds, so I think you might be safe as they slow down and start behaving like adults, however It's all good fun'.

Jake ordered a ham and mustard sandwich to go with his pint and sat on a table alongside his mates who were still playing the knockout game, which by the look of them would be their last. They all acknowledged his presence before returning to the game.

Having finished his sandwich and beer he walked up to the Bar to ordered another beer just as the game reached its conclusion, with loser Tony standing alongside him to get the last round in. 'Hello Tony, looks like you drew the last straw of the evening, how are you everything OK on the farm, busy as usual I assume?'

A smile spread across Tony's face as he slurred out a response with 'Yes, its my only round though, and again yes everything is good at home. How the devil are you I haven't seen you for ages, where have you been?'

'Here, there, and everywhere mate really, I'll fill you in when things are a little quieter. But just to say the day after tomorrow I'm going on holiday for a couple of weeks back to Santorini before I go back to the States again'.

'Christ Jake you're always on the move, when will your globetrotting days come to an end, so you can relax and enjoy your lovely Cottage in peace?'

'I've got at least another couple of month's travelling, and following a trip to Devon to see the family, then travels should cease for a while, anyway the troops are beginning to look a bit restless you'd better take them their winning drinks'.

'OK Jake, nice to catch up, give me a ring before you leave again, perhaps we can have a little chat and mull over a few things' he said carefully carrying a tray of beer back to the table. Bert sidled up to him and said 'They've had a good evening, they are a good bunch of mates, it was a great weekend in France for the rugby don't you think, perhaps we could go to another International next year, what do you say?'

'I would be the first to sign up for another away weekend, when do the fixtures usual get announced, it would be nice to travel to Italy if that was an away game'.

It certainly would, do you want another or are you making a move?' Bert asked.

'I'de better just have the two I have to travel to Bristol Airport to pick up a friend who is coming to stay for a day, until we jet off to Santorini for two weeks'.

'It's alright for some' he replied, 'Well have a nice time and send me a postcard if you've got time' he said with a grin, knowing full well that his friend was female.

He shook Bert's hand and said goodnight, and on the way out he called at the large table and shook hands with all his pals saying he would see them soon, then made his way out the door, for his walk back along the lane to his Cottage.

He watched a little TV before making himself a drinking chocolate and retiring to bed.

Chapter 67

Waking to a crisp, clear morning he busied himself around the house for an hour or two, spraying here and there with fragrance to welcome Olivia. Checking his letter from her with a copy of Arrival times at Bristol Airport, he realised she should land around 2pm, which would allow him to leave home around 12.30pm.

Checking through his freezer he realised it was still well stocked, and the fridge had enough salad ingredients to make the meals they would require before heading off to Santorini the following day.

He made himself a sandwich and a cup of tea before checking the car inside and out to make room for the huge amount of luggage he expected Olivia to arrive with.

As the time approached 12.30pm he drove down the lane, before heading onto the M5 towards the turnoff for the Airport. The road were reasonably quite on the B road and he made good time, parking in the short stay car park.

He walked through the front doors to wait for the Arrivals from Heathrow, she would be travelling on a small aircraft as it was only a short hop from London, and usually the scheduled flights were on time.

He only had to wait fifteen minutes before he could hear the noise of suitcases banging as their owners retrieved them from the carousel, then the few passengers walked out in single file to be greeted by their waiting relations or friends that surrounded Jake.

He was beginning to feel a little concerned as there was a short delay between the last couple that came out, but there was no need for him to worry as Olivia made her entrance as he expected she would being the last to arrive.

The trolley she was pushing was stacked up with two suitcases and what looked like two carry on bags. As she spied him a broad grin spread over her tired face.

He looked her up and down and was surprised to find that she was dressed in a yellow blouse and fawn trousers, and her feet were covered in flat shoes, before he noticed a jacket slung over the handle of the trolley.

With quite an effort she pushed the trolley towards him before falling into his arms for a lingering kiss. 'So good to see you Jake, how are you?' she asked.

'All the better for seeing you my dear, I trust both flights were OK?'

'Surprisingly they were, and although they were not long haul I feel as if I've been travelling all day'.

'Right then let's get you and your luggage in the car and back to Wisteria Cottage where you can relax, then I'll cook you a nice meal'.

'Sounds good to me, after that we can relax with a glass of wine and you can tell me all about your travels since I saw you last'.

As they drove back Olivia enthused about their impending holiday break, extolling her thoughts at staying at the luxurious Five Star Hotel, rather than just calling there for a meal as she had done on their last visit to the Island.

Jake just drove and let her chat away, and before they knew it they were heading past The Swan and down the lane to Jake's abode.

'It's good to be back here again Jake, I love the countryside and the quietness it must surely be a delight to wake up here every day and listen to the birds singing before it's time to get out of bed'.

'Yes it is' he replied with a smile, 'I am truly blessed to have inherited this property from my brother, and all the work that has been carried out recently I feel that it is at last my home, that I intend to retire into in the next few months'.

Olivia turned and looked at him before commenting with 'What do you mean retiring, have you finished all your adventure's with the Secret Service?'

'Yes, I'll tell you all, once we settle in' he finished, with not wanting to elaborate until they were ensconced in the property and sat having a cup of something.

He parked the car outside the garage, and let her into the property before collecting her luggage and taking it up to the bedroom. Walking into the kitchen he put the kettle on and asked her what she would like to drink.

'Coffee, please my love' he answered.

Jake fussed about for a few minutes before bringing in their drinks with a plate of biscuits of varying types.

Chapter 67

They stared at each other for a while waiting for one of them to start their narrative, however Jake just sipped his drink and nibbled on a couple of biscuits so Olivia started the conversation first.

'OK, well first of all I was overwhelmed at Christmas with the family, we had a wonderful time and I think it did everyone a power of good, as we all chatted away in our native language, together with playing our childhood party games the whole time. Obviously I have seen you since then for a fleeting visit, but again a most enjoyable time.

Since then work has been a little hectic, we have at last rounded up all the criminal's around Europe that were part of the gang that you apprehended here in this very Cottage, therefore cutting the heads off a huge portion of people that were involved in drug supplies. Unfortunately you can remove the head but the body still remains, as an old Swedish saying goes, the demand for drugs doesn't go away, therefore someone else will fill the void and carry on the sordid business. But we must remain vigilant and Interpol continues to have eyes throughout the World and will keep us up to date of their findings as time goes by. We have also had a spate of murders culminating with a mass shooting at a cinema last week with the offender fleeing before we attended the scene, however we have a description of the felon'.

Jake scanned her face and thought to himself that she looked exhausted, before replying to her explanation with 'I thought I had been busy, but it appears this break has come at the right time for you, as it will allow you to recharge you're batteries for your return to work'.

'It will indeed, especially as I will be in your company, right now it's your turn to give me details of the breaks you have had in France and America'.

'Well I'll give you an abridged version, as a lot of it is quite boring however my latest trip to the States involved me helping an old Jeweller that I met previously, who had decided to close his shop through health reasons, and required my assistance in clearing out the stock and selling a pile of valuables through Sotheby's Auction House in New York. The details of the valuables were initially sent online, however as the Auction was only three days after, I hired a car and drove to the Big Apple to deliver them in person. We had no idea of their value but when the whole collection was sold last Friday, after commission we were astonished at the cheque my friend Stefan received. It totalled over $3 million dollars. The shame of it is that he will not be able to enjoy the fruits of his windfall as he only has a maximum of 6 months to live. He had a wish to fulfil before his demise, of returning to his hometown in Germany, then whilst in Europe go to Israel, and I have agreed to accompany him after our holiday is over. But before that I went to France to locate a drug dealer and his cronies, and through a bit of good luck and detective work they were apprehended and brought to justice. I told you that I was visiting France prior to that with my friends from the Village, to attend the conclusion of the rugby tournament in Paris, with France at home to England. Following a wonderful game, England were the victors, and this enabled them to win the Championship. There, that is a potted version of what I have been up to recently, I think its now time to rustle up some food for my guest, does madam fancy anything in particular. or could I just prepare you a light English salad, which would then leave room for an evening meal at The Swan'.

'Sounds good to me, I'll just go up and unpack, then have a shower and change into something casual for the rest of the day' she said and tootled off up the stairs.

Before starting lunch he rang Bert at The Swan and booked a table for two at 6.30pm, Bert answered and had to ask who the plus one was, however Jake just replied with wait and see later. Checking his fridge he took out a cucumber, tomatoes, lettuce, avocado and radishes, before heading to his veg rack and selecting some new potatoes. That was the base of the salad, he thought he would boil a couple of eggs to cut up, then grate some cheese over the plate and have a separate dressing on the side.

He could hear the shower running just as the potatoes were ready, and the eggs had boiled, so he assumed she would take another 10 minutes or so before she came down giving him time to lay the table, plate up and open a nice bottle of white wine.

He had completed his tasks just as Olivia walked into the Dining Room looking resplendent in her outfit and smelling divine.

She eyed the concoction that he had prepared before saying 'This looks good enough to eat, I must admit I am feeling extremely peckish'.

Jake smiled at her and pulled the chair back to allow her to sit, then took his place opposite her, and poured the wine.

'The dressing on the side is one of my specialities' he remarked with a sense of pride, however I have salad dressing or mayonnaise if you prefer'.

'I'm fine Jake, this looks delightful' she said lifting her glass and clinking it with Jake's before saying 'Here's to a lovely holiday'.

Jake smiled and before replying with, 'Your good health Olivia, I'm sure we will enjoy every minute of the trip, we will relish the culinary delights of Santorini, and possibly visit another island or two over the two week period. Right let's tuck in and enjoy a simple English meal shall we'.

'It looks delicious Jake, you certainly have hidden talents' she said smiling.

'And so do you my dear, some of which I hope to enjoy whilst we are away'.

An hour later, the bottle was empty the dishes were washed and cleared away and they were sat in the Lounge enjoying a coffee and brandy, whilst chatting away about life in general, what time they were going to the Swan, and clarifying when they would be leaving in the morning for Bristol Airport.

Olivia chose a book from Jake's extensive library and sat down to read for an hour or two, whilst Jake went upstairs to pack his suitcase.

Joining Olivia in reading they spent a couple of hours in silence engrossed in their tomes, then as 6pm approached they made their way down to the Pub.

Although early, they had a drink before Bert said their table was ready in the Restaurant, perusing the menu Jake plumped for a Surf and Turf, whilst Olivia chose Sea Bass.

The food as usual was excellent and following a couple more drinks, Jake walked up to the Bar and paid Bert for their meals.

Bert smirked at Jake as he waited for the payment to go through, before saying 'Your daughter is looking smart this evening Jake'.

'You cheeky bugger Bert, Olivia is a friend of mine and we are going on holiday for a couple of weeks from tomorrow to Santorini'.

'I wish I was going on holiday with your friend, she is certainly an extremely attractive young lady, but good on you Jake, I hope you have a lovely holiday, don't forget to send a postcard to the pub'.

'I'll be sending quite a few Bert so I'm sure another won't break the Bank, thank's for a lovely meal and see you in a couple of weeks' They shook hands and Olivia joined Jake as they left the pub and returned to the car.

Chapter 68

Their flight was leaving at 6.30am the next day so they retired early as they would need to leave the Cottage around 3am, allowing time for the drive to the Airport, booking in and the usual fuss through passport control and luggage search. Before settling for a while in the VIP Lounge that Jake had pre-booked for them.

There were no holdups, they boarded on time and soared up into the sky before heading for their Greek destination. The flight went as planned and they landed around lunchtime, local time. Quickly going through the repeat procedures they collected their luggage and as expected Jake spied a large card with TORDALE written on it, held by the Hotel driver he had used on his last trip.

The man quickly walked towards them and took control of the trolley. 'Welcome back to Santorini Mr Tordale, its good to see you again and also your lovely companion'.

Jake thanked the driver before replying with 'This is Miss Olivia, she is my guest for the two weeks we are staying at the Hotel, and we will most likely be requiring your services from time to time'.

The driver smiled before replying with 'I will be at your service sir, whenever you need me. Now I think it would be best if I got you into the car and out of this heat, then we'll get you to the Hotel where you can relax and enjoy the delights of our lovely Island'.

They both got in the back seats as the driver loaded the vehicle with their luggage, and a few minutes later they were on their way. The drive was taken in silence as they both made small talk whilst enjoying the view.

As the car pulled up outside the Hotel entrance, the Manager was stood waiting for them, he opened the door for Olivia and the driver opened Jake's door. 'Welcome Mr Tordale its so good to see you again, I have taken the liberty of putting a complimentary bottle of champagne in your room and whatever meal you require this evening is also on the house'. Whilst they were talking to the Manager the driver had deposited their belonging inside the foyer, and members of staff had then collected them and taken the luggage up to their room. After signing in they made their way up to the room and unpacked their clothes before popping the champagne and enjoying it alongside their infinite pool.

Before he left home Jake had jotted down a number of things he would like to do whilst on holiday and he ran through the details with Olivia to gain her approval.

Once he had completed his thoughts he looked at her for approval 'That sounds wonderful Jake, I enjoyed our boat trip and the snorkelling, and I think your trips to other Greek Islands is a great idea. I know we have only just arrived so what particular order do you have in mind for them?'

'Well, I thought today we will relax here, enjoy the pool with a bit of sunbathing. Then this evening have a lovely meal in the restaurant. Afterwards I'll talk to the Manager and arrange with him for our boat trips as and when they are available, after that we will have a couple of days touring Santorini with a bit of Retail Therapy thrown in'.

'Excellent idea' replied Olivia, 'I'm going to have a quick shower, change into my sun wear and relax on the sun loungers'.

'I think that is an excellent idea, I will join you, shall I order some sandwiches in the meantime?'

'That would be lovely, perhaps some melon as well' she replied.

Twenty minutes later there was a knock on the door, it was the waiter with their food on a tray, Jake took it from him and palmed him a ten euro note tip.

Relaxing in the sun loungers they devoured their food with a relish whilst finishing off the champagne, within ten minutes they had drifted off to sleep.

Jake woke with a start as he realised that the noise he heard was a splash as Olivia dived into the pool, splashing Jake as she swam towards him, he quickly got up from his seat and 'bombed' her as he jumped in alongside her. The water was quite warm and relaxing to them both and after a few lengths racing each other they got out and sat back again, letting the suns rays dry them in the afternoon heat.

They chatted for a while about the days ahead before Jake said he would be getting dressed and going to see the Manager regarding the trips they intended going on.

Chapter 68

Olivia said she would stay in the room and prepare herself for his return, with a glint in her eye. Jake returned her smile as he walked out and down the stairs to the Reception Area to talk to the Manager. He booked a long sailing trip as before over three days touring the Greek Islands, a snorkelling morning with the boat he had been with before, and finally a day with the Hotel's driver to take them around the beautiful island of Santorini, in the opposite direction they had taken on their previous visit. Jake paid for all their trips there and then, so the only outlay he would have later would be for food and drink, together with any presents he wished to purchase.

Back in the room he saw that Olivia was still soaking up the sun so quickly stripped off and donned his trunks to join her.

'All sorted?' she asked.

'I've booked a few trips for us, together with the driver for a day to take us around the Island, but that won't be until our second week. Our first trip will be snorkelling, the day after tomorrow, then the following day we are on the Hotel's schooner for a three day tour to four smaller islands'.

She smiled at him then said 'You are an incredible organiser, and I am really looking forward to this holiday with you my love' before laying back down and applying sun lotion to herself.

Jake smiled to himself before settling down as well and contemplating the next two weeks with relish.

Chapter 69

At 6pm they decided to have a quick dip in the pool before, enjoying a shower to remove the remnants of sun cream, then dress for dinner.

Jake had booked a table for seven o'clock, so they took their time making sure they looked tip-top before sauntering into the Dining Room on the stroke of seven. They were shown to their table by a waiter who remembered Jake from his last visit, he shook hands with them both and welcomed them back. Once seated he brought both drink and food menus for them to peruse at their leisure.

They decided on a bottle of red wine for their meal, and as Jake studied the food menu he was surprised to see that they still had Beef Wellington on there, albeit with a heavy supplement charge attached, most likely to restrict the numbers who would order this course. However he thought he would wait to see what Olivia would like for their first meal. He noticed that she was hovering over a couple of items, and quietly asked if she had a favourite, or was she undecided over a couple of the items.

'To be honest I fancy something light this evening, and I'm torn between the shellfish and the elaborate vegetarian salad, what about you?'

'To be honest any item on this fantastic menu would be devoured if placed in front of me, but I will have whatever you fancy, however I'm swayed by the seafood, which I have had before'.

Olivia smiled 'The seafood it is then, look out if I don't like it' she said with a cheeky grin on her face.

The waiter brought the wine which he poured for approval, then took their food order, returning ten minutes later with two huge plates containing shellfish of all types accompanied by a Greek side salad, and a separate dressing.

Her eyes almost came out on stalks as she viewed the delicious looking food that had been placed in front of her, then turned to Jake and smiled 'I think you have chosen well'.

Over the next half an hour not a word was said as they tucked into the delicious food and wine. With the plates empty the waiter cleared them away and asked if they would like dessert. They looked at each other before declining, however Jake asked for coffee and Ouzo to complete their meals.

Small talk followed before they decided to walk up to the viewing point and watch the setting sun.

The crowds had built up to see this world renowned event and as always it didn't disappoint, for all those gathered there, as the 'ow's and ah's' and clicking of camera's and iPhones confirmed.

As they slowly walked back to the Hotel hand in hand, they were overcome by a sudden tiredness as they realised that their holiday had started almost a day earlier when they left the comfort of Wisteria Cottage, so they were looking forward to charging their batteries up with a good night's sleep. As they approached the Hotel, Olivia turned to the left and Jake realised they were stood outside the holiday apartment she had previously occupied, and surprisingly where they had first met. Jake pondered at how much had ensued in his life since then, then they carried on down the steps and walked into the Hotel. Back in the room they decided on a nightcap outside by the pool and watch the final setting of the sun and its incredible afterglow as it disappeared below the horizon.

They talked about the next day's snorkelling, that both of them would be enjoying in the caldera, with Jake outlining what he had witnessed on his previous excursion there.

Before retiring they both outlined what they had been up to over the last few months since they had seen each other, obviously Jake had more to tell than Olivia, however it took them over an hour to complete their stories.

Chapter 70

They woke early, excited, and looking forward to their snorkelling adventure later on in the morning. They both had a light breakfast, and agreed to eat out in the centre of the Island once finished. Their trip commenced with a Health and Safety question and answer instructions, with the Captain and Expert on diving running through everything with them and the other couple that would be joining them.

Once on board Olivia looked slightly apprehensive after the talk, but Jake held her hand and said 'Just listen to what is said and follow the instructions to the letter and everything will go smoothly, and you will enjoy the experience'.

Somehow she didn't look convinced.

The outboard motors roared into life, before they shot away from the quay and out into deeper water with the anchor being lowered almost at the edge of the caldera.

Once in the water both ladies doggy paddled for a while before feeling more comfortable and ducked their heads under, moving away from the craft they bobbed up occasionally saying how wonderful it looked below. The men joined them afterwards, but as they were more experienced they had donned scuba gear and said to the girls they were going down and joining the skipper.

They were at least 20 minutes down below, and as they appeared a few metres from the boat the ladies were already drying off and chatting away on board.

The dive was most enjoyable the four of them agreed, and following discussions regarding their work, hobbies, homes etc they decided that when they were back on dry land they would eat together at a harbour side restaurant.

The men carried the bags whilst the two woman carried on chatting about womanly things and lagging behind them until they approached the agreed hostelry. Jake addressed the Owner who remember him from his previous visit, anticipating a generous tip from his diners, he took them to a table with the best view.

He offered them complimentary drinks and handed them menus to peruse. All four of them agreed on seafood and when it was placed in front of them the looks on their faces made the waiter smile.

To go with the meal Jake ordered two bottles of wine which disappeared whilst they were still eating, so his companion Sergio ordered two more bottles anticipating that a dessert course would follow and possibly cheese and biscuits, he wouldn't be disappointed.

An hour later with everyone feeling quite sated the two men split the bill and gave a healthy tip to go with it.

Jake rang the Hotel and booked a pick up in an hours time, whilst Sergio and his wife walked back to their car that was parked alongside the harbour. After they exchanged goodbyes Jake and Olivia walked into the town's shopping area to browse and walk off their indulgences.

The temperature had risen considerably since lunch but thankfully they were dressed in thin summer clothes and with a slight breeze they felt quite comfortable, slowly walking up and down the narrow street's doing a little window shopping. They made their way back along the harbour side just in time for the Hotel's limousine to pull up alongside them. The air con was on full as they entered the car and they were thankful for that luxury as they returned to the Hotel.

Back in their room they decided on a quick swim and spend the rest of the afternoon topping up their tans. The position of the balcony gave them a wonderful vista below them and before long Jake drifted off in a contented sleep, Olivia stared at him for a while before lying back and drifting off herself.

After a couple of hours Jake came too and realised that Olivia wasn't there, but he heard the shower and decided to join her. As she stepped out he was transfixed as he viewed her beautiful body and quickly became aroused. However he stripped off and enjoyed a long cold shower himself, before drying off and flopping down onto the bed alongside her.

She looked at him and smiled 'Massage' she said.

He didn't reply, just turned over onto his stomach ready for the application of oils, then not long after two words were expressed by Olivia 'Turn over'.

The next hour was spent massaging each other towards a full blown sexual encounter, followed by a slow swim in the infinity pool.

They discussed the meeting between them and the other couple on the boat Sergio and Helena, and were amazed how easily they had bonded, so perhaps they would meet up again over the next two weeks.

The time was approaching 7 o'clock so they dried off and dressed, before going down for their evening meal, as following their recent exertions they were feeling quite hungry.

The waiter nodded to them as they entered the Dining Room and escorted them to their table. Jake ordered a bottle of champagne to accompany their meal of oysters for starter, followed by sirloin steak with a side salad and new potatoes, with cheese and biscuits to follow accompanied by two large glasses of Port.

They chatted away regarding their trip the next day, visiting three Islands they had yet to see, so decided to retire, pack the necessary clothing required for their three day trip and have an early night.

Chapter 71

They were woken as the sun shone through the bedroom window heralding another glorious day on Santorini. They had to be at the harbour by 10am, in preparation for their pre-sail Health and Safety instructions, whilst being shown the way around the craft, so a long time in the Dining Room was spent building up calories for the initial day of their trip, thus allowing them a base for the first leg of their journey. They would be taken by the Hotel's limousine to the harbour which would be leaving around 9.45am, so they were in position in the foyer ready just after 9.30am.

They had both applied plenty of sunscreen to their exposed skin, prior to leaving but would apply more once they were on board. They didn't know if there were any other passengers that would be taking the trip, however they anticipated at least another four minimum, would be joining them.

As they alighted from the car, and walked towards the yacht, they were joined by three men and one woman walking in the same direction, 'good mornings' were exchanged and smiles, before they were met by the Captain and mate who welcomed them, asking all to follow them into the shed, cum office, alongside.

The following twenty minutes or so was spent with firstly the Captain introducing himself, then his assistant. After that he introduced the passengers to each other by calling out each of their names for them to stand up and repeat names, then finally he turned to them and talked everyone through the Health and Safety regarding the craft. Walking to a blackboard which held a map in place, he explained the details of the islands they would be visiting, and the time allowed at each site. Finally he asked if anyone had any questions of him, surprisingly there were none, so he asked his guests to follow him onboard, and then they would be on their way.

They slipped anchor and the engine puttered along taking them out beyond the cove into the breeze to enable the sails to be raised.

The passengers were all sat on the main deck as the Captain explained that they would be heading for the first Island of Sifnos that was around seventy nautical miles away, and with a good wind they should be there around 8pm, so he suggested that today for them would be a 'plenty of suncream day' and to just enjoy the ride. The three couples took up their various positions and settled down for a lazy day. They had been travelling for a couple of hours before the crewman told them that lunch would be served below decks in 10 minutes.They all followed him down and sat around a table where a Greek meal was set out for them with bottles of local wine.

This took an hour or so as they got to know each other a little better. The Captain joined them at the end of their meal and informed them they were making good progress and he anticipated that they would be dropping anchor around 7pm.

The gathering then returned to their sun beds and applied more sun cream before settling down for another bout of sun worshiping. Jake and Olivia chatted for a while before joining the others in relaxing back on the sun deck for their long voyage to Sefnos.

True to the Captain's word the outline of the island came into view at 6.30pm, then as they dropped anchor just as the time approached 7pm. They were then gathered together and asked if they would like to go ashore for an evening meal or stay on board to be fed. Everyone suggested they eat on the island and rushed below to change. The little outboard only took four at a time so it wasted another twenty minutes until they were all gathered together on the shore. Having been to Sifnos numerous times the Captain led them to his favourite establishment, and was greeted by the owner with vociferous hugging and clasping of hands. The restaurant was lit with an abundance of light bulbs, that were on extended wiring around the property, that looked out onto the flat calm sea just as the sun commenced dipping below the horizon, spreading a fiery glow over the sea's surface, and bathing the surrounding area in a deep orange glow.

Before long the ensemble were talking loudly, whilst drinking numerous glasses of local wine, to help wash down their delicious Greek food that the waiters had brought to the table on numerous huge plates. The whole meal took the best part of the evening to consume and with the wine flowing readily the party couldn't have been in better spirits.

Chapter 71

The Captain settled the bill then the six guests followed him to the quay for their return trip to the yacht. Conversation back on board entailed each and everyone talking about their occupation, where they lived, and so on. before they decided to retire, as the Captain wished to get going early tomorrow, for them to discover the island and all its charm. Most of the party had stirred by 7am and breakfast was served half an hour later, a few were worse for wear after consuming too much local wine but after their food, they appeared to liven up ready for the next adventure.

The Captain explained that he wished to take them to Chrisopigi Monastery, the Agios Andreas and Museum, Church of the Seven Martyrs and finally Faros Beach. They would be travelling in a minibus which would meet them at the quayside in an hours time, so suggested that they collected whatever they needed as soon as possible.

The two journey repeat of last evening went smoothly and they all boarded their transport on time, making their way to the Monastery. They spent just over half an hour there which was most interesting for them all, then on to the Acropolis and Museum. They had a break for coffee, before making tracks for the Church of the Seven Martyrs, a few of the guests were quite religious and spent some time praying with the remainder just sitting in the back of the Church as a relief from the harsh sun. They got to Faros Beach in time for lunch and all feasted on fresh fish together with more bottles of the local vino.

The next couple of hours were spent either sun bathing or swimming in the aquamarine sea. The Captain and driver sat in the shade of the taverna until it was time to return to the harbour and back onto the yacht.

They were treated to a board game as they sat on deck watching the sun go down, with the Captain explaining the on going journey tomorrow.

They would stay at anchor until dawn then set sail for Tinos where they would land and explore the Island during the morning. Then back on board for the next stop which would be Naxos, the largest Island in the Cyclades This was the final Island before they returned to Santorini, so depending on timings they should return early evening the following day.

More wine was consumed as they chatted amongst themselves before the group broke up and went below.

Chapter 72

As dawn broke the passengers came to at the sound of the anchor lifting with a clanging that echoed around the vessel, then as they walked up on deck they were greeted by the most beautiful sunrise, that happens every day in Greece. The Captain was directing his mate with the rigging and advised the gathered group to take care as the sails were being raised. A little later on the mate prepared breakfast which they ate below deck, renewing the conversations that had started the evening before. Jake and Olivia were frugal with the description of their occupations, but explained where they lived and how they had met quite truthfully, here on holiday. Roger and Greta were from Canada and had retired last year after spending forty years running a Bakery business, they were rather sprightly for their age, but unfortunately Roger had been blighted with cancer during the previous year, however he had had an operation and chemo, and was at present in remission. The other couple were from Germany, named Gunter and Helga, they were in their early thirties, unmarried and both working in Finance in the capital Berlin. They both spoke fluent English with a slight guttural accent with some of their words, however they were certainly good company. As they approached Nexos around eleven with the engine deployed, they secured to a bollard alongside the harbour wall, and tied off, to let the passengers disembark much easier than previously. They had been briefed what was available to see on an organised trip, however if anyone wanted to do their own thing, it was agreed to meet alongside the yacht no later than 5pm so that they could all eat together. All six agreed to go on the trip, and after Captain Costos rang the company to advise on the number of passengers, a minibus arrived 10 minutes later to take them out for the day. Their first stop was in a beautiful village called Pyrgos which was famous throughout Greece for its Museum of Marble Crafts, then off to Tarambados where there were hundreds of Dovecotes, it certainly was an incredible sight and many photographs were taken.

Their last stop was the famous beach of Agios Fokas which was next to Hora, where they stopped for lunch and a couple of hours on the beach. The food as usual was exquisite and many bottles of wine were consumed over the lunch period.

At 4pm they returned to the minibus and slowly made their way back to the harbour side. They all had showers and changed clothing before meeting up on deck again to be greeted by Costos, who explained that the restaurant this time was in the middle of the town, but well worth losing the sea view for the quality of the food that they would be consuming.

Various strong perfumes and aftershaves emanated from the women and men as they made their way off their yacht, following Costas through the quaint streets until he slowed and stopped outside a white fronted restaurant. Out came a portly Greek man in traditional dress who welcomed Costos with a bear hug and a kiss on both cheeks, before turning to the others and welcoming them to his humble establishment.

They sat at a large table alongside the open kitchen that had already been set out for seven diners. Two baskets of bread and a few bottles of wine already adorned the table and as the diners sat down two waiters appeared handing out menus for everyone.

Costos laughed out loud at the strange looks his guests had on their faces, as the waiters had given them menus in Greek which looked totally unreadable.

He turned to everyone and smiled at them before saying 'This is a local joke when non Greek diners eat here, have no fear I have already asked for the Banquet which is a speciality here' and as he finished his explanation the waiters collected the menus and returned with a number of Meze dishes to accompany the bread they had in front of them. The waiters poured the wine and before long the table came alive with loud laughter and clapping as they demolished the first course. As the plates were cleared away a fish course arrived with Costos advising them that it would have been caught this very morning, however he was unable to say what the fish's name was in English. They all enjoyed it as no sooner had they started than there knives and forks were placed on the plate, whilst they licked their lips in approval.

There then followed a break where more wine was taken, with Jake raising his glass and toasting Costos and his mate for how well they had looked after them. Roger raised his glass for a second toast to the crew, then not to be outdone Gunter raised his glass and toasted the ladies. More bottles were brought to the table as the main course arrived which was Lamb Kleftiko with vegetables and sliced potatoes.

Following another break they had each to decide on dessert and coffee. As they finished Jake asked if everyone would join him in a nightcap, which they all did, the brandy bottle went around the table three times as each man ordered a round, obviously Costos only joined them in the initial round as he would be in charge of their craft on the journey back to Santorini.

The evening ground to a halt around 9pm, and after the men settled their Bar bill they all trundled back to the ship. The whole party was in good humour, so the Captain asked if they would like to join him in a quiz, it was only 20 questions based on Greece and the Greek Islands, there were six prizes, so he hoped that each of the couples would win a prize. He handed sheets of paper around the table with six pencils, asking them to put their name at the top of the page and number along the side one to twenty.

After they had completed this small task, he talked them through the twenty questions. Due to the amount of alcohol that they had each consumed this took over an hour. Once completed they handed back their sheets and Costos went to his cabin to decide on the first, second and third prizes.

He looked at the nervous passengers before saying 'Well I am quietly impressed at your knowledge of my Country and Islands, so I will give you the results of the first three places. Third place goes to Roger, our Canadian friend, second place goes to Gunter from Germany, and the winner with a 100% score is Jake. The prizes were third place a locally made tea towel, second prize was a bottle of wine and first place was a bottle of champagne. Needless to say that the two bottles were empty before they all retired below.

No-one woke at sunrise the next morning, as all the heads were a little fragile and only the men and Olivia decided on breakfast.

The engine started just after 9am as they made their way back to Santorini, once out onto the open sea the mainsail was deployed and they sped along towards their destination, with all the passengers laid back and enjoying their last day on board, whilst worshiping the sun stretched out on the deck.

Chapter 72

The yacht pulled alongside the harbour just before 4pm and once they all collected their belongings they bade farewell to the crew and each other at the quayside. Jake rang the Hotel for the taxi to collect them, and Olivia and him drank coffee at a Taverna, relaxing until the limousine arrived.

They were feeling quite tired as they eventually got to their room, therefore after unpacking their bits and pieces they took the opportunity of having forty winks before it was time to go down for their evening meal. Surprisingly they slept for more than an hour and a half, with Olivia coming back to the land of the living, she got herself ready before Jake had opened his eyes, to the delightful sight of his companion walking around the room in her underwear. Realising that the time was approaching 7pm he quickly got off the bed and headed for a shower and shave, then by the time he had dressed in fresh clothes it was time to go.

As usual the fare was fantastic and together with the usual delicious wine they spent a considerable time eating, drinking and chatting, before Jake asked if she would like to go up the steps to the viewing area and watch the sunset, which they did.

Chapter 73

The next few days were spent going into the town exploring the shops and restaurants that they had missed on their previous visit, together with another trip scuba diving, which they really enjoyed as they were the only guests on the boat.

The remainder of their holiday included trips around the Island with the Hotels taxi and the driver dropping them at isolated places to explore with the odd beach visit. They also spent a lot of time sunbathing and dipping into their infinity pool, as well as enjoying each others company.

However the holiday took a dive when Jake received a message from Stefan Cohen from Washington which read 'Dear Jake, I'm sorry to spoil your holiday but I'm afraid my illness has crept up on me, and your wonderful plans of taking me to Germany and Israel will have to be cancelled. However if you could spare the time I would appreciate you coming to the States to see me so that we can make alternate arrangements. Kind Regards, Stefan'. Jake's head dropped as he read the text and he quickly replied with 'Dear Stefan, Thank you for your message, the holiday will be concluded in the next couple of days, therefore, as soon as I return to the UK I'll book a flight to Washington so hope to see you in no more than 4 days time. Look after yourself. Regards, Jake'.

As he looked up he noticed that he hadn't spoke to Olivia for a while, so quickly explained the text he had received from Washington, and also his reply.

'I fully understand Jake, you'll have to go as you say as soon as we get back to England, I'll make my own way back to London so you catch the first available plane to the US' she replied.

'It's no problem I'll take you to Heathrow as I'll be flying from there anyway, this will give us more time at Wisteria Cottage and you can cancel your return ticket from Bristol and travel in the car with me, OK?'

'That sounds like a good idea, so let's enjoy the last two days at the Hotel, before we have to return home'.

Jake was deep in thought as he recalled the words in the text before looking at Olivia, smiled and replied 'Yes lets'.

However the text from Stefan had dampened the mood for the final couple of days, although they enjoyed their time it was is if Jake was just going through the motions and they were both glad when they boarded the aircraft to take them back to Bristol.

The flight was without mishap, they had a couple of drinks whilst making small talk on the three hour plus flight, whilst drifting in and out of sleep. Then through the airport ritual, collecting their luggage they made their way to the car, and onto Wisteria Cottage in the beautiful County of Dorset.

Opening the front door he was met with the usual swathe of post on the doormat as he rushed to turn off the alarm, he quickly turned and collected the post before Olivia entered the house. Unloading the car, realisation spread over him once more as his thoughts flashed to dear old Stefan Cohen who had taken a turn for the worse. Once they had sorted themselves out he would ring the airport and book a flight to Washington as soon as practically possible, and find out Stefan's current medical situation.

In the meanwhile Olivia had wandered into the kitchen and put on the kettle for a hot drink, giving Jake time to put the cases upstairs and go through his mail.

She looked up as Jake walked down the stairs and felt his pain. She gave him a wane smile and as he sat down said 'I think it would be a good idea for us to eat at The Swan this evening, then you can pack your new clothes and toiletries before we head back to London in the morning'.

Jake smiled and replied with 'You will make a good wife and companion for someone, as you always think ahead at the practicalities in life, and I love you for that'.

Checking his watch he decided to ring Bert at the Pub and book a table for 6.30pm, his daughter answered and confirmed the booking.

After finishing their drinks they freshened themselves up, changed clothes before making their way down the lane to the comfort of the local Pub.

As they opened the Lounge door Bert greeted them with a broad smile and poured Jake's pint before asking what the lady would like to drink. Olivia smiled and said 'I'll have a half of that please'. Bert smiled again at her request but quickly retrieved a half pint glass from below the counter and poured her drink. 'Take a seat and I'll bring the drinks over'.

'Thank's Bert, two menus as well please' Jake replied.

'Coming up' Bert concluded.

As he brought over the drinks and menu's he said 'By the colour of you both a good holiday was had by all, Santorini wasn't it, can't say I've been there but the pictures I've seen of it surely make's it a good destination for a holiday'.

'We had a lovely time thank's Bert, however I had some sad news regarding my friend in Washington, and I have to fly there tomorrow and my friend Olivia will be returning to Sweden also, so we thought we would have a nice quiet meal here this evening to complete our time together'.

'I'm sorry about that Jake, just give me a shout when you've decided what you would like to eat, and I'll be right over' then he turned and walked back behind the Bar as four other people walked in.

They browsed through the menu and Jake stood and went through the Specials' board, eventually deciding on Rib-eye steaks for both of them accompanied by an expensive bottle of red wine.

Jake then walked up to the Bar and gave Bert their order and asked for a quick refill of their glasses as the food would take around 20 minutes to prepare. They spent the time talking about Stefan and what Jake expected he would encounter once he got to the States. Then he asked Olivia, when she had to return to work, and what she was involved with. The conversation went back and forth and as they finished their drinks Bert approached the table with their cutlery and napkins and took away the empty glasses.

He returned with the bottle of wine and two glasses, with Jake doing the tasting before he filled them. He returned a few minutes later with their sizzling steaks, accompanied by grilled tomatoes, triple cooked chips and chestnut mushrooms. They had also requested a brandy sauce to go with the steaks.

Chapter 73

They ate their meal in silence with Jake topping up their glasses at varying intervals, until finally their cutlery was placed on the empty plates.

Whilst eating their food the Dining Room had filled up and Jake had nodded to two of his Rugby mates who were joined either by their wives or girlfriends and looked in good form.

After they had drunk the last of the wine Jake walked up to the Bar to pay for their meal, and asked Bert to refill the glasses of their friends sat close to them, before turning and returning to Olivia.

Twenty minutes later they were back in the sanctuary of the Cottage, and with the time approaching 10pm decided to have an early night as Olivia's flight was 11am, and Jake's Washington flight an hour later at noon. So they agreed that they would have to leave at around 7am, giving them enough time to book in to the Hotel to allow Jake to store his car in the car park, and to get Olivia through the booking in ritual for her earlier flight.

Jake packed his case apart from his toiletries which would give him more time in the morning to prepare breakfast for them both. Of course Olivia just had to change into another set of clothes and she would be ready for her flight.

Chapter 74

They stirred at 6am and after a quick cuddle Jake used the bathroom first and told Olivia that he would send her off with a good old English Breakfast, then made his way down to the kitchen.

Olivia came down after twenty minutes and sniffed the air as the aroma that was invading her senses of fried bacon, sausages, tomatoes, mushrooms and eggs, so quickly sat at the Dining Room table.

Jake placed the loaded plate in front of her before saying 'Toast is on its way Madam'. The percolator was popping away and would be ready once the toast shot up from the toaster. With all the breakfast items in place Jake sat himself down and said to Olivia 'Enjoy'. They tucked in like there was no tomorrow, and the plates were quickly devoid of food and the cups empty. 'You complete what you have to do my love, and I'll sort out the dishes, the I'll put the cases in the car. I'de like to leave by seven at the latest as we will hit the rush hour traffic as we approach Heathrow'.

True to his word the car was packed, the Cottage locked yet again, and they drove slowly down the lane, back on the road to London. As it happened, today was a clearer day and they parked in the Hotel car park at 9.15am. Jake booked in at Reception for his car advising the Clerk that he anticipated he would be away no longer than 7 days. They then collected their luggage and caught the shuttle bus to the Terminal, Olivia quickly collected her ticket handed in her luggage before kissing Jake, and making her way through to Departures.

Jake suddenly felt quite disconsolate having left Olivia on quite a downer but said he would call her as soon as he touched down in Washington.

He was extremely early for his flight but put his luggage through and made his way into the VIP lounge. Still feeling quite full from the breakfast that they had only recently consumed, he just had a coffee whilst he read the Daily paper and perused the other passengers in the Lounge area.

An hour later he was boarding the plane to Washington, and being shown to his seat in First Class by a twenty something polite young man who went through the ritual of explaining how he would be with him once they were airborne, to take his food and drink order that he required for the journey, then as Jake sat in his seat he handed him a copy of The Times newspaper. For all the journey's he had taken over the past couple of years it now appeared no different than travelling by bus or train, however the distances were more lengthy.

During the usual Safety briefing he thought of the poor old man he would be visiting and wondering if he would be capable of an internal flight within the US or even a journey by car, but to know anything at all he would have to talk face to face with his friend.

He slept for an hour or so as the journey began, then ordered some food and a bottle of wine for a late lunch. He didn't anticipate any further sustenance until he was in the Hotel he used on previous visits to Washington.

After the Steward had cleared away his dishes he told the man that he would not require anything more for the rest of the flight and would appreciate it if he was left undisturbed.

His dreams during his protracted flight were many and colourful, based mainly on the escapades he had been involved with over the past few years, but as usual with dreams they bore no exactness to events that had taken place. He was glad when he was brought out of his stupor by an announcement, that they would be preparing to descend into Washington, and would all passenger return to their seats and re-attach their seat belts, in preparation for landing.

After a smooth landing the huge aircraft taxied to its parking position and the engines slowed to a halt which was a time for the 'ants' to block the walkway as they scrambled to retrieve their carry on cases from the overhead lockers. As usual Jake smiled to himself at the way even seasoned travellers still carried on with this irrational rush to remove themselves from the metal giant forgetting that everyone on the plane wished to do exactly the same thing, however, this procedure was most likely duplicated thousands of times a day all over the world.

Being in First Class gave them some priority and they quickly found themselves inside the Terminal and through Customs, and able to retrieve their belongings before the majority of their fellow travellers.

Jake walked directly to the Hertz office and reacquainted himself with one of the Hire cars for his time in Washington. Loading his cases in the boot he made his way directly to the Hotel, booked in then rang Stefan to inform him of his arrival.

'Thank you for coming so quickly Jake' he said, 'Are you up to coming to see me, or would you like a rest and call in the morning?'

He thought for a while before answering with 'I'll just settle into my room, have a shower and a change of clothes and be with you in an hour'.

There was a short pause before Stefan answered with a soulful reply of 'Thank you my friend, I am really looking forward to seeing you again'.

An hour later he pulled the Rental into the driveway, got out, and was just about to knock the door when it was opened by his friend. Jake was shocked as he walked into the premises at how much his friend had aged after only the three weeks since he had last seen him.

As they walked into the Lounge Stefan looked at Jake before giving him a bear hug, albeit quite gentle, and said 'Would you like a drink before we settle down?'

'Yes please Stefan, could I get it for you?' he answered.

'No it's OK, I have taken the liberty of purchasing a nice brandy, and I thought now would be the time to indulge ourselves whilst we talk seriously about the future. It's only here in this cupboard with the glasses, so sit yourself down'.

Jake smiled and thought he sounded just like his Grandfather, giving him firm but quiet instructions. Handing Jake a large balloon glass of the strong smelling liquor they clinked glasses before Stefan made himself comfortable in his favourite armchair.

Looking at the aged and frail old man, Jake was almost brought to tears at how he had gone downhill so suddenly thus not being able to take his final journey home to Germany that he wanted nor even to Israel. However as he sipped the lovely brandy, he was impressed to see the way that his friend also took a large slug of the drink preparing himself for the hardest speech he had ever made.

Stefan took a deep breath and started with 'I expect you can see for yourself that the sands of time are running out for me and the tumour in my brain is gradually doing its dreadful deed. Please Jake let me finish my speech to you before I break down and lose control, once I have finished we can talk and I will try and answer any questions that you have of me'. He took a sip of brandy before continuing with 'I had to visit the Hospital just after you left for the UK, and the surgeon informed me that I have less than a few months left, I'm sorry that we will not be able to take the trips that you intended to take with me, but I am blessed to have you here with me now. The prognosis over the following weeks is that I will eventually be unable to move, before finally falling into a coma and eventually casting off this mortal coil. I do not wish you to be here when all this happens so I have set out what needs to be done now to enable my affairs to be put into place. I wish to visit my Solicitor tomorrow, with you at 11am to finalise my finances. After that we'll call at the Bank and see the Manager where an account is being prepared in your name, this will allow all my funds to be transferred to you.

The monies I have received for the sale of the shop and the balance of monies from Sotheby's are also in that account. The deeds to this house have already been transferred to you Jake, which I assume will be sold once I have passed. I have arranged my funeral with the local Synagogue which we will visit the following day, together with the Undertakers who I wish to employ. Please forgive me for being so blunt with you Jake but these things have to be done. There is just one other thing that no-one knows about, and I wish to give to you now and that is this' he unclipped a gold necklace from around his neck, that housed a gold cross which was encrusted with diamonds 'This article I purchased when I first started my Jewellery business all those years ago, and kept it with me as a keepsake but also as a guarantee that should times become hard I would always have some collateral. However it is now time to hand over the gauntlet to you, my dear friend, who came into my life too late, however the short time that we have known each other, it couldn't have been more precious to me. There I think I have finished by eulogy dear Jake' whereupon he drained his glass before tears streamed down his cheeks.

Jake was lost for words as he looked at the effort Stefan had made to complete his speech without breaking down, until eventually he replied 'Stefan I am hear for however long you need me, I have booked into the Hotel, however if you would like me to stay with you I will uproot and come here. You are a kind, thoughtful and generous person who I have the pleasure of knowing, the world needs plenty of Stefan Cohen's to enable it to survive. If you wish to visit anywhere in the US before your condition deteriorates I will make it happen, and I mean anywhere'.

He gave Jake a wan smile before saying 'I know you mean well my friend, however I will have to take it day by day, I hope you understand. W'ell just get over the legal stuff over the next couple of days then see how I feel.

If I could go anywhere I would like to visit Niagara Falls, its somewhere I should have been to during my lifetime but never found time, the only other attraction would be the Grand Canyon. So let's wait and see how things are later on, OK'.

Jake smiled and said 'Anything you want, I'll leave it up to you what we do, now I think that's enough for you for one day, I'll pop back to the Hotel and get some sleep then be up bright and early for whatever we need to do tomorrow'.

'Thank you Jake, firstly, before you go I would like to know all about your holiday, and the location details' he said with a smile.

'I'll be here just after 9am in the morning, now I'll leave you to get an early night's sleep' he stood and shook the old man's hand and walked out the door before he himself broke down. As he slowly drove back to the Hotel he couldn't help but think of Stefan as a courageous human being, who has led such a solitary life, he was therefore glad that he had brought some form of happiness to him in these depressing times.

Although early, he retired to his bed with sad thoughts, his joyful holiday far behind him, however he decided to ring Clare his eldest daughter to explain that he would be in Washington again, for quite a while, and would she kindly inform the rest of the family of his situation. As a thoughtful gesture he sent a text to his Boss Henry Bates explaining the recent circumstances as to why he had returned to the States.

Chapter 75

Awake bright and early the next morning he went down for breakfast, then walked to the Reception Area and explained to the young lady he had spoken to many times before, that he would be booking out and moving in with Stefan for the foreseeable future due to his friend's condition. However he explained how this might change as time progressed and he would possibly come back here at a later date. She said she understood completely and would organise his invoice for whenever he would be leaving.

Jake walked back to his room and packed his suitcase before returning and settling his bill. He trudged to the car park and put his belongings in the boot of the hire car before making his way to Stefan's house, ready for the busy day ahead. As he walked up the path the old man opened the front door for him, before directing him to the Guest bedroom where he placed his suitcase and carry on bag. Then he returned to the Lounge where his friend sat holding a manilla file of official looking papers.

Stefan hesitated before speaking with 'Shall we have a cup of tea or coffee before I run through these official documents Jake, or would you rather get these items out of the way first?'.Taken aback with these few words, Jake thought that all the official paperwork was either with the Solicitor, and the Bank, however he assumed that the old man would prefer to read through the documents with him first, so he just nodded his head and replied 'I think it would be preferable to run through them first'.

Stefan smile, noticing Jake's awkwardness from his initial enquiry, so explained the paperwork contained with the file 'Firstly I have a copy of the sale of the shop, next there is a copy of the Bank Statement you will be collecting from the Bank, of monies in the deposit account, this envelope contains the combination of the safe where I keep a considerable amount of cash, in fact enough to cover my funeral, together with a bit left over for any trips we may take over the next couple of weeks. There I think I'm now ready for a drink, how about you?'

Jake smiled weakly at his friend before answering with 'I'll have a black coffee, but I suppose you will be having tea. If I follow you into the kitchen, you can explain where everything is kept, as I intend being your butler, driver, cleaner, etc for however long I am here, and I will not take any argument from you'.

They walked into the kitchen and whilst the kettle boiled Jake was shown where everything was kept. After they had completed their drinks Jake washed and dried the dishes, whilst Stefan prepared himself for the visit to the Solicitor's and the Bank.

They arrived at the Solicitor's office and parked at the rear of the premises in the companies official car park just before eleven., and walked into the Reception Area. Stefan explained that they were here for an appointment with Henry Swartek his Solicitor, the young lady smiled and stood, before walking them through a corridor to his office.

Swartek stood as they walked in and shook Stefan's hand vigorously before introducing Jake. They sat in the chairs facing the Solicitor, then over the next three quarters of an hour he went through the official paperwork with Jake, that his friend had already been through. There were numerous signatures to be done by all three parties before finally he said that everything was complete and in order. The Solicitor stood before shaking hands with both of them and they returned to the car for the second leg of their official appointments. The Bank was about a mile away but this time they had to park in a multi-storey car park opposite, they made their way across the road and approached a teller, explaining to her they had an appointment with the Manager. The teller stood up just as the door opened to the Manager's Office and with a knowing gesture he asked the young lady to escort them through to the inner sanctum. The legal bits and pieces were carried out over the next 20 minutes, finally with Stefan and Jake signing the forms that were placed in front of them. The Manager enquired how long Jake would be staying in the States, to which he replied for a few weeks at least. He finally took Jake's details of address, various telephone numbers, and email address to store in his file.

With everything completed they stood, shook hands with the man, and left the Bank walking slowly back to the car park. Before driving off Jake asked if Stefan would like to have lunch out as the time was approaching noon, and to his surprise his friend said he would, also that he knew of an extremely fine restaurant only a couple of hundred metres from the Bank. They left the car where it was parked and walked along the pavement to the impressive premises that advertised first class cuisine from around the world. Suitably impressed Jake pushed open the door to let Stefan walk inside. The room was bright and airy and they were quickly seen by a suited gentlemen who welcomed them to his establishment, and showed them to a table within the bowels of the room. There were already a dozen tables laden with guests, which appeared a good enough reason for them to eat there. As they sat down the man handed them menus and asked what they would like to drink, they both said iced water.

The menu was quite extensive, as Stefan looked up he could see the smile on Jake's face as he perused the numerous pages. Jake looked at Stefan and asked 'What do you fancy, its a great cross section of cuisine's but as I'm in the States I will be eating local food. The steak's in America are a sight to behold so I'm going for the Sirloin medium rare with all the trimmings'.

Stefan smiled and said he would have the same, but steady on the trimmings.

Jake laughed at this remark, and ordered a bottle of red wine to accompany their meal.

A little while later with plates empty, Jake paid the bill, they left the restaurant then made their way back to the car park and drove home.

They spent the evening preparing themselves for the next day's visit to both the Synagogue and finally the Funeral Directors to put things in place for when he passed.

This was talked about in clinical, but objective ways in which Stefan outlined what he wanted and would be informing the necessary people, whilst paying for their services.

They then had hot drinks and watched a little television before settling down for the night.

Chapter 76

They got up quite early the next morning and indulged in a cooked breakfast preparing themselves for the busy day ahead. Whilst sat at the table Jake explained that he had researched the possibility of going to both of Stefan's idyllic holiday sites. They would first visit Niagara Falls by rental car, then leave the vehicle at the Airport after viewing the spectacular falls, before taking a flight to their next destination. He also suggested that whilst there they go on an organised helicopter flight to take in the best features of the Grand Canyon.

Stefan smiled at him before saying 'I'll leave all the details to you my boy, you look so organised and excited at the prospect of the tour, it even makes me quite excited myself'.

After clearing up the breakfast things, Jake went to his room, so that Stefan could prepare himself for the Synagogue visit, when they met in the Lounge Jake suggested to him that when they arrived Jake would sit in the car to give him some space. Stefan smiled before answering with 'You are so thoughtful and I would assume that you would be out of your comfort zone, so I agree with your thoughts entirely'.

Their destination was a distance of 5 miles by car, then as he pulled into the car park, he turned and smiled at his friend, with 'Take as long as you like, I need to make a few phone calls back home, so I'll have plenty to occupy me'.

Stefan nodded and got out of the car, after a minute or two disappeared from view into the house of Worship.

Before making his calls he reflected on what the old man was going through and vowed to make his remaining time on earth enlightening and as comfortable as he could make it.

Next he rang his daughters, then Olivia before finally having a short conversation with Henry Bates who kept him up to date with the new recruits status. With that over he scrolled through his Google account to see flight availability from Niagara Falls to the Grand Canyon, also what notice was required for the helicopter flights there.

Chapter 76

No sooner had he received the information than he was joined by Stefan, who smiled at him as he got in the passengers seat.

Jake looked at him and asked 'Everything sorted?'

'Yes, when we see the person in charge at the Funeral Home I have to give him details of the service and for them to contact the Synagogue'.

'Right, onwards and upwards' Jake said, then he drove off to the Funeral Home as it was only a couple of blocks away.

'I'll direct you' said his friend.

When they arrived outside the premises, Stefan asked him to join him, as he felt quite nervous at this location, which Jake did after parking at the rear of the premises.

As they entered they were met by a young attractive lady in her thirties who asked 'How may I help you today gentlemen?'

Stefan approached her desk and explained why they were there, she picked up an internal phone and spoke quietly into it. A few minutes later an elderly grey haired man appeared from a door to the right of her and introduced himself as Eugine Spoitek the owner of the premises. 'How may I be of assistance today?'

Stefan shook his hand before saying 'I wish to talk to you regarding my funeral arrangements'.

'Please step into my office gentlemen, and we will discuss your requirements'.

The office was quite spacious, there was a large office desk with a leather chair behind it for Spoitek, then in front of him two additional chairs for visitors. There were two metal cabinets, each containing four drawers, and to one side a number of framed certificates. The air felt quite fragrant and Jake noted an air freshener concealed behind a framed photograph of the Companies hearse, and fleet of cars.

When they were sat comfortably in their chairs, Spoitek commenced his questions with the initial inquiry of 'May I ask when you require the arrangements to be made?'

Stefan could only stare blankly at his question, before replying with 'Its a little premature, however, as its for me I'll explain, I have a brain tumour which is trying extremely hard to finish me off, however I have a few things to do before that happens. So I thought I would call and see you and run through my requirements'.

Spoitek was taken aback by Stefan's bluntness and humour, however having been in the business for a considerable time he was not fazed by the comments and continued his sales talk. 'May I ask if it will be a burial or cremation when the time comes, what casket you would like, will there be family flowers, and finally which religious ceremony you require?'

Stefan thought for a while on these questions before answering with 'Cremation, I'll look at pictures of the caskets you have, no flowers as Jake is my only family, and I have just left the Synagogue the details of which I will give you later. Finally I would like a firm estimate of these arrangements before I leave to enable me to pay for the affair prior to my demise'.

A look of surprise spread across the man's face as he listened to the coldness of Stefan's answers, but he quickly regained his composure, stood and collected a bound copy of photographs showing a multitude of caskets.

'As you have requested a cremation, I would recommend examining pages one to fifteen to determine your preference. I assume you will only require one funeral car, I will allow for four bearers'. There was a hushed silence as Stefan thumbed through the pages before settling on a casket on page four. Spoitek made notes on an A4 sheet of paper and said he would be back in a few minutes with a typed copy of costings.

As he left Jake turned to his friend and said 'You are an extraordinary man you know, how you discussed your funeral in such a cold and calculating way amazes me'.

Stefan smiled in return and said 'I'm going to die Jake, it's best to do it while I'm able, then once these details are out the way, I can enjoy a couple of trips away with you'.

As Stefan finished his reply the man returned and handed over the costings contained within an envelope.

Both Jake and Stefan examined the costings, before Jake produced his Debit card and paid for the funeral, the man signed the paper with PAID IN FULL and handed it back, attaching a receipt for the payment.

They stood and shook the man's hand, before he said 'Please let me know if there is anything I can help you with at any time, I am available 24 hours a day' he then handed over his business card which housed all numbers for him.

Back in the car Stefan let out a deep sigh before saying to Jake 'I'm glad that's over, shall we indulge in some lunch now, all that depressing conversation has made me hungry'.

Chapter 76

Jake bellowed with laughter as he started the car before asking 'Where may I take you sir, for another gastronomic journey?'

'I think back to a little place I have used previously its close to my house, within walking distance actually, so you can park in the drive and we can indulge ourselves in some exercise, before and after our meal'.

After parking in the drive they walked down the road and into an extremely small venue, they were intercepted by a young lady who recognised Stefan, she greeted him with a handshake and and said 'So lovely to see you Mr Cohen, long time no see, who's your lovely friend?'

Stefan smiled before saying 'This is Jake from England he's here on holiday at present, so I thought I would bring him to the best eating establishment in Washington'.

'You teaser, let me show you to a table' she replied whilst directing them to the rear of the small Dining Area.

The decor, Jake noticed was quite plain with beige wallpaper with a number of photographs of local landscapes. The tables and chairs were quite old but comfortable and spaced out so no table was tight to the other.

The waitress handed over two menus and asked them what they would like to drink, both plumping for beer.

The menu was quite extensive, and after much deliberation they decided on burgers, french fries and salad, accompanied by a couple of beers.

During their meal they discussed how soon they would be off on their adventure to Niagara Falls and the Grand Canyon, however Jake was prepared for the question and said that once back home he would book the itinerary, assuming everything was available they would start the first leg in a couple of days time.

Although not Five Star food the meal was substantial and satisfying and as they left the establishment they felt quite fulfilled as they walked back to the house.

They drank coffee as Jake went through the ritual of booking various flights and a Hotel facility, then feeling quite happy with his work he settled down with a welcome cup of coffee. Tomorrow they would have a free day, so Jake said he would like to do a bit of present shopping whilst leaving Stefan to carry on with his daily ritual.

Chapter 77

Jake rose early and set out to prepare breakfast, so he was ready for when Stefan got up. He fancied pancakes and grits and as the ingredients were in the cupboard he assumed that his friend would also like to start the day with a similar decent meal.

Stefan walked in sniffing the air and said to Jake 'Something smells good, I think it could be an American's favourite start to the day, pancakes and grits if I'm not mistaken?'

'I took a chance after checking the fridge and food cupboard, I've also put on toast and coffee. Sit yourself down and food will be ready in five minutes'.

'My mouth's watering already, before I have it though I'de better take my medication and wash it down with a cold glass of water' He walked to the bathroom with his water and came back soon after, just as Jake placed the food in front of him. They talked for a while over their food, before Jake said that he would be driving into town and spending a few hours there, to buy a number of presents for his family, then possibly eat out whilst he was in town.

'That's fine with me, I need to carry out a bit of housework, so I'll have plenty to occupy myself whilst you're away. Take as long as you like my friend, if I need you I can always give you a call'.

Before setting off into the City Jake decided to visit a few of the shopkeepers who were part of the celebrations for Stefan's birthday bash, to explain the recent news and check if when the time comes they would be part of the celebration of his life. It was a delicate conversation that would have to be done sympathetically and a certain amount of tact, however it helped that he wasn't on first name terms with them.

An hour later having explained the situation to them he made his way into the City, as he parked up in the multi storey car park close to Charlene's flat, he noted to himself that he needed to ring his friend and arrange a meet up. Walking onto the street, he was familiar with the location, having shopped there on his previous visit, so knew exactly the outlets he would be visiting.

Thinking of Stefan, he thought a little something for the time he had left would be acceptable and as he had a liking for whiskey, he would search for a vintage bottle to take back for him. Clare and Sharon, together with their spouses and children had already been looked after on his previous visit, so he was only looking for friends tokens, Bert at The Swan, Tony and Joyce Bailey, plus a little something for his Solicitor Bryan Fairfax and his long suffering secretary Joan.

Having collected 50% of the presents he intended purchasing he decided to stop for something to eat and continue his search afterwards. He dropped his items back to the car then walked to the Chinese Restaurant he had eating at before. The place was busy and when he asked for a table for one he was placed close to the kitchen area which he was certainly happy with as the intoxicating aroma's invaded his senses. Although he had an enjoyable breakfast with his friend, he decided to have a three course lunch accompanied by a cold beer. The food as usual was exceptional and he finished off with a coffee and a small brandy.

Back out on the road he quickly located the remaining shops he needed for presents which just left him with Stefan's whiskey.. Walking another quarter of a mile brought him to a huge Liquor Store, as he walked into the huge premises he was amazed at the quantities of alcohol on display, however as he was only after one item he checked the overhead signage before locating the Spirits section. The majority of items were American based with Mexican influence, but as he walked further along the shelving he came across Scottish and Irish Whisky. There were only around twenty five separate Vintages to choose from, however to his surprise there was one that caught his eye. He lifted the bottle off the shelf, read the label and was amazed to see that it was a Ben Nevis 1991 Platinum old and rare whiskey, priced at $1200 dollars, as it was the only one on the shelf he walked to the till and paid for it. As he walked back to the car he felt quite pleased with himself, so as he settled back in the car seat then sent off a message to Charlene with a quick note explaining that he was in Washington, but would be off for a few days sightseeing with Stefan. There was no immediate reply so he drove back to the house. Taking all his purchases out of the boot, he struggled up the path to the front door, which opened for him to enter the premises. A smile spread across Stefan's face as he noticed how much Jake had with him, and said 'Did you find everything you wanted?'

'I certainly did' he replied, 'More than I thought in fact. I'll just put them in the bedroom and we can sit down and have a chat'.

Returning with the whiskey in a plastic bag he sat in an armchair and outlined where he had been, before finally saying. 'I bought you a nice surprise, it has to be drunk extremely slowly as it was bottled in 1991' he then handed the package over to his friend.

As the old man removed the bottle from the package, he slowly read the label before looking Jake in the eye and saying 'This isn't you're usual $25 dollar bottle, I certainly appreciate this wonderful gift, but hesitate to ask what you had to fork out for it, in fact I won't even embarrass myself by asking you. Thank you again for your generosity, I will savour every mouthful'.

'I'm glad' Jake replied 'You deserve a little treat every now and then, and to confirm that statement everything is booked for our adventure and we have to be at the airport early tomorrow morning. So I think we had better organise a case of clothing, along with toiletries and any medication we require, but of course the most important thing a passport, after that you can sit back and enjoy the adventure'.

'When you say early tomorrow morning Jake, how early are we talking?' Stefan questioned, thinking of an early night.

'We have to be at the airport by 10am, so I suggest if we are packed and ready to go this evening we'll just have breakfast in the morning and make our way to the terminal'.

'Fine by me, so let's get to it' Stefan said with a toothy grin.

An hour later two suitcases were positioned by the front door ready to put in the car the following morning. They both had a cup of hot chocolate and a snifter before retiring and getting a good night's sleep.

Chapter 78

As they sat at the dining table eating their breakfast Stefan looked at Jake and said 'I feel like I'm ten years old again and looking forward to my latest adventure. Thank you for organising the visits Jake I truly appreciate it'.

'Think nothing of it, in fact I'm almost as excited as you, having never been to either iconic locations before'.

'What time do we need to set off Jake?' he asked.

'In half an hour, we'll just run through the essentials we need to confirm that we have them. and then we'll be off'.

Within the hour they had parked the car in a long stay car park and caught a bus to the Terminal. Jake collected their tickets, then they made their way through the various book in sections before settling down in the Departure Lounge. Jake collected a couple of coffees from the Cafe before they sat and waited for the flight announcement. Just as they had finished their coffee's, and Jake had despatched the empty containers in the trash can, the flight was called.

They stood and followed the various passengers, to line up for boarding, then having cleared the final hurdle they made their way to the waiting aircraft.

The seats were at the front of the plane and as they settled down, an elderly gentleman took up the aisle seat.

The estimated flight time was four hours, so a certain amount of conversation would take place during this period. To break the ice Jake asked the old man if he was visiting the Falls or not. He hesitated for a while before saying that he was going home as he lived close by the Falls.

Jake thought to himself, don't ask any more questions of the old man, if he wants to talk just let him. With that the engines roared into life, they cruised along the hardtop to get in line for take-off, all the while the Stewardess was explaining the Safety features over the tannoy. Straightforward take-off and flight followed, with both Stefan and Jake dozing throughout the journey.

Collecting their cases they exited the Terminal and collected a car from the Hertz Rental Company, then drove to a Hotel a mile or two from the Airport and booked in.

Jake had already booked the tour before they left, so the rest of the day was their own, and rather than tire Stefan unnecessarily, they agreed to stay within the confines of the Hotel. They were collected the next morning at 10am for their visit to the Falls, the vehicle being a minibus which contained twelve seats. They collected the remaining passengers from two other Hotels close by, and were at the site an hour later.

The boat trip to the base of the Falls was amazing and both of them felt like children as they laughed and screamed with the rest of the passengers as they got soaked through. However the volume of water that fell from the upper level hour after hour, day after day was mind boggling, but the sight itself had to be seen to fully understand the power that was generated from the volume of water that congregated at the higher level.

After they returned to shore the group were directed to a Cafe that overlooked the Falls and a stop there was arranged for lunch and photo opportunities. The group were a mix of local Americans, Japanese tourists, plus Jake and Stefan, they sat in huddles, sipping coffees before ordering their lunch. Jake walked to the Viewing platform and took numerous pictures at their location, to show his family when he returned home.

When he got back to the table their food had arrived and Stefan had already started tucking into his Cheeseburger and fries. Jake smiled as he sat down and joined in the fare with his Gammon steak and salad.

They had another coffee before the driver explained that they would be leaving in 20 minutes, and for his guests to make their way back to the minibus at their convenience.

On the return journey there was a buzz of animated conversation between the tourists of how wonderful a day that everyone had had, and Jake and Stefan totally agreed with their comments. By the time the other guests had been dropped at their Hotels and the minibus pulled up outside their Hotel, both Jake and Stefan were totally exhausted, so they made their way directly to their rooms for a nap, agreeing to meet up a few hours later for their evening meal in the Hotel's restaurant.

Chapter 78

Jake slept like a log and was amazed when he came too and noticed the time, it was now 6pm, and just as he stirred the phone rang, answering it Stefan said 'Good sleep, I went off like a baby, but I'm now quite hungry, so I'm going to have a shower, change and go down to the Dining Room where I'll meet you'.

'Fine bye me, see you in half an hour or so'.

Jake smiled to himself at the stamina of his friend, who was suffering from a debilitating terminal illness, but still was going to enjoy every last minute of life.

They walked into the Dining Room together and sat at their directed table, the waiter asked what they fancied, then took their order.

Afterwards they walked around the ground for a while to digest their food, before the retired to their rooms for an early night.

Up early for a quick breakfast, then half an hour later they returned to their rooms, collected their luggage for their onward journey to the Grand Canyon.The taxi collected them and took them to the Terminal, where they booked in and walked through to Departure Lounge and took seat close to the windows. Boarding was called after 30 minutes so they took their positions in the line of passengers and within 30 minutes they were sat in their seats preparing for take-off. Flight time was a smidgen over four hours, giving them both time for a catchup nap and while away the time.

The flight was smooth and it was extremely pleasant as there were no noisy passengers to disturb them, then frequent flyer Jake's body recognised the change in engine noise and realised that they were commencing their approach to the Airport, he stirred looked at his companion who was in a world of his own looking out the small window, 'Did you have a nap Stefan?'

'Only for a while, I'm fascinated how these huge metal objects stay in the air, and I also have a morbid thought that one of the engines could fall off at any minute, so I'm just keeping my eye on this one' as he finished he turned to Jake and smiled.

'As you can tell we are now descending on the final approach to the Airport, so in a couple of hour's time we'll be heading off to the Grand Canyon for our final treat. I've booked a Hotel within theTerminal's grounds as the helicopter will be taking us from its confines'.

'Excellent Jake, you appear to have everything under control, I can't tell you how much I'm looking forward to this experience'.

As they exited the huge building they caught a shuttle bus to their Hotel, where they booked in, dropped off their luggage, and met up again in the Hotel Bar for a much wanted drink.

Jake contacted the helicopter provider, confirmed that they had arrived and were in the Terminal, and arranged to be dropped off an hour later for their magical experience.

There were another couple who boarded with them, the pilot went through basic Health and Safety regulations for them, before they took off and then their journey commenced.

Both couples had arranged to be dropped at the floor of the Canyon after they had traversed the route giving them an idea of the enormity of the gouge in the earth, it was mind blowing they all agreed. They spent an hour and a half on the ground before the pilot politely asked them to return to the helicopter. On the return flight he deviated and took them over the glitzy sight of Las Vegas which was a bonus and had the passengers amazed at the City that had grown out of the desert.

Back at the airport all four of them thanked the pilot profusely for his time and agreed that it was the most amazing experience they had ever had, and something that they could tick off their bucket lists.

They went their separate ways with Jake and Stefan returning to the Hotel, and preparing for their evening meals. The food at the Hotel was not what they had been used to recently, however it was plentiful and quite tasty. Over coffees they talked about the two sites they had been on and Stefan thanked Jake yet again for organising his surprise trip. The flight back to DC took off at 10am they next morning so they decided to get an early night as they would have to book in around 9am.

Chapter 79

After a hearty breakfast they boarded the shuttle to the Terminal and went through the usual routine of booking in, Passport Control, then made their way through to Departures.

Internal flights in the US and to all large Countries throughout the world that ran scheduled flights, generally left on time and their's was no different. Within twenty minutes they were through the Gate and on board the aircraft, as they buckled up their seat belts the plane commenced its taxi to the runway and a quarter of an hour later it lifted off the ground and levelled out at its cruising height on the way to Washington.

Surprisingly the occupancy was only around 50% leaving no-one seated next to them ready to ask innocuous questions, so the two of them had a nap for part of the journey.

As Jake came too, he checked his watch and realised they were only a quarter of an hour away from landing and at that moment the plane started its descent. Jake lightly nudged Stefan and informed him of the situation, the old man adjusted himself in the seat and put on his seat belt ready for landing. He stared at Stefan for a second or two and thought to himself that he was looking rather pale so asked him 'Do you feel OK Stefan, you're looking a little pale?'

'I feel a little exhausted, we've done quite a lot recently and I think my body is telling me to slow down for a few days after we return home'.

'I'm sorry if I've given you too much excitement recently, but what a few days we have had, to have visited two of the Worlds greatest sites was mind-blowing so at least I was able to take you to them, to enjoy. So when we get back home, I want you to relax and I'll be your 'mother,' to wash, cook and clean before you recharge your batteries'.

A smile spread across Stefan's face as he tapped Jake's leg and just said 'You are definitely the son I never had, and I'm so glad we met'.

A tear drifted down Jake's cheek as he looked at the old man before saying 'Time is a precious thing and I hope we can enjoy many more days together'.

Stefan smiled before replying with 'I'm afraid what's going on inside my head is getting the better of me, and I will arrange an appointment with the Doctor as soon as we get home, as I think I am on my final journey. Don't make any other plans for me my son, after I see the Doctor I feel he will only confirm my self diagnosis, but he will be able to give me a rough guide to the next stage of my illness. If the prognosis is weeks, I wish to go into a Hospice for my final days where I will be treated with the necessary drugs to reduce the pain I anticipate I will be in. You can visit me as often as you like but I don't expect it to be that long, its not a surprise as I have had little pain so far but I know how bad it will get at the end so I do not wish to put you through the heartache of looking after me, do you understand?'

Jake's tears flowed down his face after listening to his friend's calm explanation, and there was silence before he could answer with 'I'll go with whatever you require Stefan, I didn't realise how bad you felt, so we will make a phone call to the Doctor as soon as we walk into home, then take it from there'.

'Yes mother' Stefan replied, with not a hint of amusement.

Jake carried the cases into the house whilst Stefan made himself comfortable in his favourite armchair, then picked up the telephone. Jake took the cases into their bedrooms giving his friend a little space as he talked to his doctor, however as he returned to the Lounge the conversation was still in full flow. Obviously Jake could only hear one side of what was being discussed, and there were long periods where Stefan just listened before he finished the call with 'See you in the morning at 10am, thank you'.

Jake waited in anticipation for Stefan to explain what was happening next, obviously he would be seeing the Doctor in the morning, however he thought that more had been said regarding the situation ahead.

'Shall I make us a cup of tea Stefan, and you can tell me all about it'. Stefan just nodded his acceptance for tea, and appeared lost in thought.

A few minutes later Jake returned with a tray on which held a teapot, milk jug, two cups and saucers together with a biscuit tin. He poured their drinks and sat opposite his friend, waiting for his explanation.

Stefan gave Jake a wan smile before saying 'There is no easy way to say this, but it sound like the beginning of the end. My doctor is fully aware of my symptoms and anticipates I have weeks to live, as you heard I have an appointment in the morning at 10am and would appreciate it if you would accompany me, in case I misinterpret the diagnosis and its following stages. As I said to you before if it is soon I wish to be looked after in a local Hospice, and I'm certainly glad that all my business is in order so you won't have complicated issues to deal with once I've gone. Now enough of the long face my dear friend, I want the next week or so to be happy, then I would like you to return to your home to see your family. You can contact the Hospice whenever you like, and no doubt if I'm in good spirits we will be able to talk, but please don't ring every day. They will have your contact details and ring you as and when required'.

Jake hesitated before he replied with 'We knew it was coming, however we are never really ready. Certainly I'll come with you in the morning, then do whatever you require of me thereafter. Assuming after the visit to the Doctors, and he recommends that you arrange to go into a Hospice, after you are settled in I'll head back home for a while to see my family, then we'll take it from there. I'm going to check on the fridge and freezer and see what's lurking in its bowels, then prepare a nice meal for us to celebrate our return from two wonderful visits'.

'Excellent idea Jake, I have no idea what is in there, however I'm sure there's enough for a small banquet for two hungry travellers. A nice bottle of wine, then finished with a nice slug of that lovely whiskey you bought me'.

Jake smiled 'Sit back and relax, I'm looking forward to preparing a nice meal for us both' he said as he walked out to the kitchen.

Looking through the freezer he came across some steak mince which he would defrost whilst preparing the other elements of his dish, in the food cupboard he found two sauces to accompany the mince together with lasagne sheets to construct their evening meal.

He walked back into the Lounge and informed Stefan of his choice of meal from the ingredients that were available. Stefan smiled 'Sounds like a meal that would be good with a fine red wine. I'll find one in the back room and let it breath whilst you are involved with the cooking'.

When Jake walked into the Lounge a second time he found the table laid out in the corner with two glasses and a bottle of wine. He smiled again towards his friend and said 'Food will be served in ten minutes sir, with a side salad, I hope you enjoy the meal' he said with the words of a waiter, and backed out of the room. Stefan clapped and smiled as Jake walked backwards towards the kitchen.

Half an hour later they were tucking into the meal, whilst sipping an excellent wine, and attempting a little light conversation without touching on the subject of a visit to the Doctors the following morning. As the cutlery was put down on their plates and both sighed with satisfaction, Jake suggested coffee or tea with a 'wee dram' of whiskey to complete the meal. Stefan nodded in agreement and stood to retrieve the whiskey bottle, whilst Jake cleared away their dishes and brought in two cups of coffee.

The remainder of the evening was tense with both men resorting to reading a book and sipping more whiskey, leaving them to retire around 10.30pm.

Chapter 80

Both men were dressed and ready for breakfast before 9am, they were content with cereal and a cup of tea. An awkward hour was spent pottering around before they got in the car and made their way to the Surgery. Stefan approached the Receptionist who knew him well and explained that he had a 10am appointment. He was ushered through with Jake following in his footsteps, as they entered the room the Doctor stood and shook Stefan's hand and asked both of them to take a seat. A number of questions were asked by him which Stefan answered truthfully, before a slight delay incurred, and after a deep breath he said 'I don't think there is anything left to do but book myself into a Hospice'.

The doctor lowered his gaze for a split second before replying with 'I'm terribly sorry Mr Cohen but your time is very short as the cancer in your brain has spread like wildfire, so before the pain becomes intense I agree with you that a Hospice is the best place for palliative care, to enable your last days to be comfortable. Before you came today I had spoken to the local Hospice and have reserved a room for you anytime after today. There is no pressure as to when you go but I think the sooner the better, I assume Mr Tordale will be staying in the States for a while to tidy up your estate?'

'Once I enter the Hospice I want Jake to return to his home in England as he has quite a large family who he hasn't seen for a month or so, and I'm sure he will be in contact with the Hospice quite frequently, with the possibility of speaking to me every so often'.

'You appear quite organised between you, so all I can say is if you require any medication in the meantime for pain, please let me know and I'll arrange for anything you require'.

'Thank you doctor, you have been extremely kind and helpful during this dreadful period of my life, but I'm afraid the curtain is slowly closing and I don't wish to be a burden to my friend here any longer than is necessary'.

They stood, shook hands and left the Medical Centre without another word said, until they got in the car.

Jake started the car, but before they pulled away Stefan held his arm for a split second before saying 'It's for the best Jake, I think whilst we are out, I'd like to visit the Hospice and see where I'll be staying, OK?'

Jake turned and stared at his friend, then smiled and said 'I'm your driver and I am at your disposal, please give me directions' that was all he could manage before his voice stuttered. Stefan relayed the directions and fifteen minutes later they pulled into the car park at the rear of the Hospice.

They walked into the Main Entrance and approached the Reception Area where they were met by an attractive thirty something lady dressed in a white medical dress, who asked 'How may I be of help today gentlemen?'

Stefan smiled at her before explaining his name, and that of his doctor, to her. She fumbled through the pages in a large tome in front of her before looking up, smiling and answering 'I see I have a reservation for you Mr Cohen, with the date of occupation to be confirmed, would you like to see the room whilst you are here?'

Stefan smiled again and answered 'We would indeed, thank you'.

She pressed a button under the desk and within seconds a nurse appeared and approached the desk, the Receptionist explained who the two gentlemen were and that they would like to look at the room. The nurse asked them to follow her, as she turned and walked away with Stefan and Jake following in her wake. The room was only ten yards or so along the corridor, and as she opened the door they were both amazed to see that the room was private and had a window that looked out onto the road. The walls were decorated in bright blue and red colours, there was a large hospital bed that took up a lot of the space available, in addition there were two side cabinets and two chairs, one armchair and a visitor's chair. There was a plush carpet covering the whole floor and off to one side was an en-suite bathroom. Stefan nodded and turned to Jake and said 'Quite nice' before tears gently ran down both of his cheeks. And with that Stefan turned and walked out of the room followed by the nurse and Jake bringing up the rear. As they walked into the Reception Area Stefan said to the Receptionist 'I'll call you tomorrow and confirm when I will be booking in, OK?'

'Certainly Mr Cohen, I'll await your call, bye for now'.

Both men quickly walked out of the Hospice and back to the car. Jake unsure where to start, just said 'It certainly is a lovely place and everyone appears quite friendly, the decision is yours my friend, there is no hurry, and I'll do whatever suits you'.

Stefan looked into Jake's eyes before replying with 'I think it best if I pack this evening and get booked in tomorrow, then you can sort out what you need to do and go back to England to see your family. At the moment I'm OK so its nice to have your company but we agreed between us that as I am beginning to feel unwell I'm better off at the Hospice'.

'OK by me, now shall we have lunch out I'm famished, let's enjoy a 'pig out' for a good farewell, for now?'

Stefan grinned from ear to ear, then looked into his friend's eyes before replying with 'Good idea, my treat, I fancy a nice Mexican meal, there's a good place not far from here. If we turn right when we pull out onto the road it's about 2k from here'.

They drove along nattering away about nothing in particular, but mainly about food and what each of them fancied. There was a small parking area to the rear of the Mexican eatery, so they parked up and walked into the front entrance to be greeted by a waiter.

'Table for two is it?' he asked. 'Yes please' Jake replied. They followed him to a table close to the kitchen area and as they sat down, he handed them each a menu. 'Can I offer you both some drinks' he enquired. 'Two beers please'.

They quickly scoured the menu before deciding on a mixture of dishes, just as the waiter returned with their drinks. Jake asked for Buritos, Enchelados, Esquites (corn stew) and Camarones a la Diablo (Devilled shrimp), and smiled at the waiter as he took the order.

'You are looking at two extremely hungry gentlemen, I hope we can do the meal proud'.

He just smiled, turned and walked away.

An hour or so later two bloated but completely satisfied diners sat back in their seats and sighed with contentment, not everything was eaten but they managed at least 90% of the wonderful food that had been placed in front of them. The waiter approached their table together with another suited and booted man who smelt of Management, they both smiled, before the new man said in broken English, 'Am surprised how much you fellows eat but pleased you come to this place, thank you'.

'Jake smiled at the man before replying with 'I love my food but even I am flabbergasted that we have eaten so much of your delicious food, if we could have a Tequila shot to finish with I would be obliged'.

The waiter rushed away, however the main man looked at Jake and said 'You English, friend, I have extended family in North England, so glad you come here, Tequila on house' he turned and walked away.

'Strange fellow' Jake said to Stefan, who appeared overcome with the amount of food that they had just demolished. 'He must be the owner Jake, it's not often they approach a diners table, but to speak in English is an honour indeed'. With that the waiter returned with their shots. They toasted each other and knocked back the drink in one.

Before Stefan could say anything Jake paid the bill with a decent tip added. They then stood and left the restaurant shaking hands at the door with the owner and waiter.

Back in the car Stefan again thanked Jake for paying the bill then said 'Our last meal out together was most enjoyable and certainly fulfilling, let's go home now I have a lot to do'.

Jake put the car in gear and they headed back.

Chapter 81

After packing his case the evening before, Stefan was up later than usual. It was a sombre breakfast as they sat at the Dining Room table, there was little conversation until they were on their second cup of tea. Jake could not stand the silence any longer and started the conversation with a guarded 'Are you contacting the Hospice this morning and giving them a date when you will be moving in?'

'Very subtle Jake, however I have already contacted them and said you will be dropping me off this afternoon around two, leaving me to sort out a few things around the house before I leave, for the last time'.

There then followed another silence as both men felt unable to restart the broadside remarks that had just taken place, so Jake stood and cleared the breakfast dishes and washed and dried them leaving Stefan to mull over what he had just said, thus preparing himself for further comment when Jake returned. But he was still not in the right place and retired to his bedroom to put together the few items he needed to take with him.

Jake in turn returned to his room and sorted out his packing for his imminent flight back to the UK. One of the things that hadn't been spoken about was what was going to happen to Stefan's car, so he thought he would mention that when they met up again, putting it as tactfully as possible, so as not to cause any undue distress to his dear friend.

An hour passed before they met up again in the Lounge, Jake felt he had to speak first and addressed his friend, firstly with an apology, then a couple of questions starting with 'Please accept my apology for the blunt way I spoke to you, however I feel that we need to talk bluntly about what remains here after your move, and what you would like me to do with the house contents. Secondly your car will have to be sold, and I wondered if you had any thoughts on donating the proceeds to any charity. Those are my two main concerns before we head off this afternoon, and then of course if you have any questions of me before I return to the UK?'

Stefan had looked Jake directly in the eye since he had opened the conversation, then he gave his friend a sad smile before replying to the questions that had been put to him, 'First I have packed a few personal trinkets to take with me, the remainder of the house contents you can either arrange for a House Clearance Company to remove them, or sell on eBay.

With regards to my car I would suggest you keep it in the garage until my demise, so that you can use it whenever you return to arrange my funeral and clear up the estate. Afterwards you can sell the car and put the proceeds towards the Hospice upkeep. In the safe I have kept a few items which I'll leave you to sort out, when you return from the Hospice. My Will is with the Solicitor and a copy is with the Bank, you will need to contact both establishments once I have gone, finally I would like to thank you most sincerely for our latest escapade to Niagara Falls and the Grand Canyon, neither sites would I have visited without your intervention, and finally I thank the day you walked into my shop and made your first purchase from me and I hope I have repaid the kindness you have given to me, my son'. He then stood and embraced Jace and kissed both cheeks.

On the Dining Room table there were keys for the safe, the front and back doors to the house, the garage door and car keys. They had all been fitted with a plastic tab that indicated what they were for, alongside them was a manilla envelope marked JAKE - OPEN WHEN YOU RETURN, marked on the front.

Stefan stood by the table and went through the various items with Jake so there would be no misunderstanding. Finally he asked Jake if he would make a nice lunch for them before they left for the Hospice.

A quick look at his watch and off he went to the kitchen. Scouring the fridge and freezer, he selected a number of items together with the remaining fresh vegetables, to make a roast lunch, together with fruit and cream for dessert. He laid the Dining Room table, then noticed that Stefan had decided to have a final nap in his lovely home. He quietly closed the door as he left and commenced the preparation work for their lunch. Putting the vegetables on first, he took a roasting tin out of the cupboard in which he placed a beef joint, then put them into the pre-heated oven, he par-boiled some potatoes before adding them to the roasting tin. An hour and a half later he was just dishing up when Stefan came into the kitchen. 'My nostrils guided me here Jake something smells delicious, what are we having?'

'I found a nice piece of beef, so that's been roasted, we have roast potatoes, carrots, broccoli, swede and stuffing balls, and for dessert some mixed fruit in a light syrup, with ice cream'.

'Sounds delicious, I can't wait' Stefan replied, turning and walking back to the Dining Room.

'Sit to the table, I'll bring it in in 5 minutes, what would you like to drink?' Jake asked.

'I'll have a large glass of whiskey after my dessert I think' he said with a grin.

As Jake plated up he felt quite pleased with the outcome and after filling a jug with dark brown luxurious gravy he carried everything in on a tray and placed everything on the table. Stefan licked his lips and mockingly said 'A delightful meal for a condemned man I think, sorry Jake I mean it looks delicious'.

As they ate small talk between them was sparse, however Stefan cleared his plate with a smack of his lips, before uttering 'Thank you Jake that was lovely, fruit and ice cream next I presume'.

'Yes, I'll just clear these dishes away and return shortly' in the kitchen he smiled to himself thinking of Stefan's expression of the condemned man, that his expression was indeed quite accurate in one way.

Bringing in their dessert plates he was surprised to see his friend tucking into a large glass of whiskey, and as he placed the dish of fruit in front of him Stefan smiled and said 'I need a little bit of 'Dutch Courage' for the remainder of the day'.

'Would you like a coffee as well? he asked.

'Please, but not until we have eaten this lovely looking dessert, sit down and enjoy it with me, I didn't pour you a glass as you have to drive after lunch'.

'May I suggest that we take the rest of the bottle into the Hospice, so that you can have a tipple whenever you fancy, I'm sure there will be no objection from the staff'.

'Good idea Jake, otherwise you would have to finish it for me' he replied with a smirk.

A little while later after Jake had cleared the table, washed and dried the dishes the time had come to prepare for leaving. As Jake walked into the Lounge, Stefan was sat looking out the window, he was ready with his coat and hat on, with his case alongside him.

He turned and looked at Jake before quietly saying, 'This must have been what it was like during the war when the Germans had rounded up my family and loaded them on a train for their last journey'.

'The only difference between them and yourself my friend is that you have had a long life, before the powers above, have decided they wish you to join your relatives in the after life. No words of comfort will make your next journey any easier, but I can say that I know you will be well looked after in your final days, and I will be with you all the way in mind and spirit, whether here or when I return home to England'.

'I wish we could have spent more time together Jake. but as you so eloquently explained I have been blessed with a long life and now its time to leave, so lets make our way there'.

Jake took his case which felt quite light and put it in the car, he opened the passenger door to let his friend in, then turned and locked the front door. Stefan stared at his home one last time before the car backed down the drive and onto the open road.

Walking through the entrance doors to the Hospice it felt to Jake as if they were walking into the waiting room, it reminded him of the sitcom he used to watch years ago called 'Waiting for God' and he inadvertently smiled to himself as they approached the Receptionist.

She smiled at them and gently said 'Good afternoon Mr Cohen, so lovely to see you again. She pressed a bell below the counter and a nurse appeared from a side door and walked towards them. 'Jennifer this is Mr Cohen he will be staying with us in Room 20 if you would kindly take them there.

Stefan smiled at the Receptionist and Jennifer, then both Jake and him followed her down the corridor to Room 20. Once in the room Nurse Jennifer explained where everything he would need was situated, then left them to unpack.

Stefan sat in an armchair by the window and took a key out of his pocket and handed it to Jake. 'This is the safe key Jake, there is no combination, its an old fashioned type however its situated behind the landscape picture in the Hall, there are items in there I haven't told you about, so whatever you find are not to be spoken of between us, do you understand'.

'Certainly Stefan, but why the secrecy?'

'You will find out once you open the safe, now that's the end of that. I'm going to unpack and you will have things to do back home before you return to the UK, so leave me to my unpacking and I'll see you soon' he shook Jake's hand, turned and opened his small suitcase in preparation for taking out his limited possessions.

Feeling that the conversation was at an end, Jake rose from his chair and quietly said 'See you soon my friend' and walked out of the room easing the door shut as he left.

He nodded to the girl on Reception as he left and rushed to the car before he broke down in tears at the abruptness in his friend's attitude as he had left the room.

It was obviously difficult for Stefan, and no-one can say how you feel, unless you yourself are in the situation that Stefan has now found himself in, but Jake knew he would be well looked after in the Hospice, and given the best palliative care possible on his last journey.

As he drove the car up the drive, he found it increasingly devious of Stefan to give him this puzzle to solve in the secret safe, but he would do his best to sort it out.

Chapter 82

As he walked into the house it felt strangely quiet and uninviting as if Stefan had already departed and his ghost had infiltrating the entire fabric of the property. This was quickly dispelled as he entered the kitchen area and switched on the kettle for a cup of coffee.

Sitting in the room with the cup warming his hands, an overwhelming sense of loss enveloped him and he felt suddenly quite alone. Attached to the fridge door was a message on a post-it note from Stefan, he hadn't noticed before, so he assumed that it was the last thing his friend did as they left earlier on. He collected it and scanned the short message that read 'THANK YOU FOR EVERYTHING MY DEAR FRIEND AND ADOPTED SON, I WILL REMEMBER YOU TILL MY LAST BREATH. STEFAN'.

He hadn't felt this emotional since the funeral of his late wife many years ago, so he quickly drank the remnants of his coffee and decided to make a list of things he had to do before he returned home. He scrolled up on his mobile and entered numerous reminders for himself, after a few minutes he was satisfied that everything was noted so he got down to the jobs that required doing in the house, firstly taking the safe key from his pocket, he removed the painting in the Hallway and put the key into the safe's lock and turned the handle. There were numerous items inside together with a small metal box. After removing all the items he put them on the Dining Room table and slowly went through them all until he came to the small box. On opening it he was confronted by a smaller box that contained an antique wrist watch and to his surprise he realised it was one of the initial ones produced by the famous Company Rolex, this item was dated 1929 it also included the original paperwork and under the watch was a note that just said 'Jake.' The other items included a list of the furniture in the house and the purchase prices, all other movable equipment and the name of a Removal Company that he had used before. Jake sat quietly, somewhat astonished at the information that was in front of him, then realising how efficient and thoughtful his friend had been to help him with the disposal of the house's contents.

The question now was what next, it didn't take him long to decide that the house and its contents could wait until his dear friend had departed and the funeral ceremony was over, as this could take a while he would stay a few more days and visit the Hospice daily to see his friend together with looking through the house and itemising its contents, before returning to the UK for a short while to visit family in Devon.

Checking the contents of the fridge and freezer he realised there wasn't enough there to sustain him for more than a few days, so decided that for the main meal of each day he would eat out in the locality.

Feeling slightly peckish he donned his coat locked the entrance door and walked down the street to visit the Restaurant both Stefan and he had enjoyed recently.

As he entered the front door he was approached by non other than the Manager, who shook his hand and enquired after his friend. Following a short explanation he was shown to a corner seat and handed a menu.

The full Mexican menu offered a host of dishes of varying cuisines, however Jake decided on a Mexican three course Special accompanied with a beer to start. The food as before was excellent, however the absence of his friend for conversation made the time spent there somewhat overpowering and he was glad when he had paid the bill and exited the building to make his way back.

The remainder of the evening was spent watching TV, and then he started reading a book from Stefan's extensive library.

Going to bed around 10.30pm Jake suddenly felt very lonely and looked forward to the plane journey back home in a few days time. Mulling over what he would be doing over the next few days, other than visits to the Hospice, he thought it would only be polite to give Charlene a call and arrange to meet up when convenient for her.

She answered the phone almost immediately with 'Hello big boy, what do I owe this pleasure'. After a lengthy explanation, he told her that he would be returning home in a few days time and wondered if she had the time to meet up for a chat and a bite to eat.

A short pause before she answered with 'I could meet you tomorrow evening around seven, for something to eat, can you come to me and we'll eat locally?'

'That's fine with me see you tomorrow' Jake confirmed.

Back to the book for a while before he turned off the light and fell into a troubled sleep.

Chapter 83

After a fitful sleep he woke at six and decided to make a start on the inventory of the house in preparation for the inevitable. He made a coffee and some toast, then after locating an old notepad made a start in Stefan's bedroom, followed by his bedroom, the Lounge, Dining Room, Kitchen, Hallway and finally the Garage. He was overwhelmed by the amount of furniture, appliances and miscellaneous items he had to clear away but when the time came it all had to go. Surprisingly he found one or two interesting items that would not be going to the Clearance Company but back to the UK with him to remember his friend. This took him a couple of hours and to make it more easy he decided to type it up using Stefan's computer, after he had finished he took off a couple of copies, one for himself and another to give to the Clearance man.

As he was seeing Charlene later he thought he would collect a small item to give her as a present as they wouldn't be seeing each other for a while after his visit this evening.

Locking up the front door, he wandered down the town and walked into a 'bric-a-brac' shop, he hunted around for a while before the proprietor approached him and asked if he could be of assistance. 'I'm looking for a gift for a young lady, preferably an unusual item, could you point me in that direction' he asked.The man looked bemused for a few seconds, before a light bulb moment lit up his face 'Follow me' he said with a wide grin spreading across his face.

They walked almost to the back of the shop before he suddenly stopped, scratched his head, struggling to get his brain cells to tell him where the article was, that he visualised when Jake asked for his gift, before stretching and locating what he assumed would be a suitable present and handing it to him. Jake smiled as he looked at the object on all sides before saying to the man 'That will do nicely'.

It was an electric hand warmer, ideal for the cold conditions that Washington residents have to put up with each year, and something a little different from the gifts that he had given Charlene in the past.

The man walked back to the checkout and asked if Jake would like it gift wrapped at no extra charge. 'Thank you that would be much appreciated,' he replied.

Walking out of the shop a few minutes later he had a bounce in his step as he walked back to the home and decided to spring clean the property from top to bottom as he wanted to feel at home for the next few days before returning to the UK. He was meeting Charlene at seven, so he would go and see Stefan later in the afternoon for a catch up, then drive to her apartment afterwards.

Searching out the vacuum cleaner and dusters he started his domestic duties too clean throughout the property. Afterwards he polished the timber surfaces and sprayed the rooms with air freshener, before finally applying bleach to the toilet, basins and sink throughout the property. Feeling satisfied with his work there was just one other job to carry out and that was to find a long handled duster to clear the cobwebs around the ceilings.

Jobs complete he made himself a sandwich and coffee and sat down at the Dining Room table to relax for a while. With lunch finished he cleared away his dishes and sat on the Lounge chair and caught up with the local news on the TV, but in no time at all he had dropped off to sleep. He woke with a start an hour later, then had a shower and changed into another set of clothes before setting off to visit his friend at the Hospice.

The young lady on Reception greeted him with a smile, checked with the nurses that Stefan was not being attended to and ushered Jake through to his room. Stefan was sat at a chair by the window reading a paper, turned to greet his friend as he entered the room. 'Don't get up Stefan, I'll pull my chair over to you' Jake said.

'Good to see you Jake, how's things?' he asked rather weakly.

He smiled before replying with 'I have been a 'person that does' this morning, and spring cleaned from from top to bottom, double checked the list of furniture and cleaned the car. I'm meeting Charlene this evening and we're going out for something to eat, I will only be seeing her this one time as I will be returning to the UK in a couple of days. Anyway I digress how are you my friend, I hope they are looking after you?'

'If I wasn't dying, its the equivalent of a five star hotel' he quipped, 'The nurses are the same during the day as in the hours of darkness, if there is anything I want they will oblige'.

Jake smiled before saying 'That isn't what I asked, how are you?'

Stefan returned the smile and said 'There are no flies on you young man, I tried to dodge the question, but didn't get away with it did I, well I can say honestly that I am in no pain, mainly due to the medication that my doctor has prescribed, but honestly I think my time here will not be a long one. Does that answer your question?'

Jake's demeanour changed as soon as Stefan had replied to his searching question, however they both knew that once he had entered the Hospice it would only be a matter of time before his demise. 'Yes it does my friend'. They then chatted about World affairs for twenty minutes, before they were interrupted by a nurse who needed to carry out a few tests and administer Stefan's drugs, so Jake excused himself and said he would see his friend the following day.

Driving away from the establishment his mind was in turmoil, thinking about the short time he had known his friend, the enjoyment they had with the Sotheby's sale, their trip to Niagara and the Grand Canyon, together with Stefan's birthday. He had tried his best to lighten the burden that his friend was carrying and attempted to make his last few weeks of 'freedom' enjoyable if that is the right word.

Walking back into the building he concocted a 'work' plan for the next few days that would entail contacted the various people that would eventually empty the house of its contents, together with putting Stefan's car up for sale. During the few hours he had left before his meeting with Charlene he made good use of the time by exploring what was in the attic. To his surprise the whole area was bathed in light once he turned the one switch on. Jake smiled and thought to himself that Stefan hadn't ventured up there in a while as there were numerous boxes spread around the boarded out loft space. However on further inspection he found that they all had a note attached to the lid explaining what each box contained.

Quickly counting the number of boxes and what they contained he realised there was a lot of work involved in sorting them out, so he set too and took them down and put them in the Lounge for him to sift through. Once he had completed his task he prepared himself for his visit to Charlene. Taking the hire car he arrived outside the Apartment block at 6.46pm, and gave her a ring, but to his surprise she answered the call and stepped out the front door at the same time.

As she sat in the passenger seat she asked where he would like to eat. He smiled and said he enjoyed the restaurant they had eaten at the last time they met, she nodded in return and off they went. The food as before was splendid, accompanied by a bottle of wine. They spent two hours over their meal talking profusely about her work and the latest details of Stefan's illness. Jake spent most of the time talking, whilst Charlene sat listening intently, nodding occasionally, not wishing to interrupt his narrative.

Eventually Jake stopped and smiled at Charlene before apologising about his tirade, but she just smiled and said 'You have quite a burden on your shoulders, and I'm glad that you have shared it with me. What would you like to do now, come back to mine, or will you set off back to the Stefan's?'

He smiled at her before replying with 'I'm going back home in two days time, and I still have lots to do, would you mind if I dropped you back to your's and perhaps we could meet up tomorrow, and I'll show you the premises, unless of course you have other things to do?'

'That will be fine, tomorrow's Saturday and I won't be going into work, so I can meet you whenever you like. If you pick me up say 10am we could spend the day together'.

He leaned over and gave her a kiss before saying 'That sounds splendid, I'll pay the bill and drop you home'. He pulled up outside the Apartments, quickly got out and opened the door for her, he took her in his arms a gave her a lingering kiss, before standing back and saying, 'Thanks for listening to my tale Charlene, I had no-one else to speak to and I feel a lot better now I have shared it with you. See you in the morning' he said whilst walking her to the door. As she passed through the door he turned and made his way back to the car and drove off without looking back.

Chapter 84

He rose early, had a quick breakfast and made his way to Charlene's apartment block, on the way he rang her giving his approximate arrival time, so she was stood on the sidewalk when he pulled up. He switched off the engine and rushed to open the passenger door for her with a quick 'Good morning madam, where would you wish to be taken this morning'. She smiled as she took her seat, and as he started the car she replied to his question with 'I hope to spend a quiet day with an 'acquaintance of mine', but I would also like to visit a friend of his who is not very well, could you help me with that please?'.

He smiled at her and said 'It would be my pleasure madam, I have pencilled in an appointment this afternoon at three o'clock for that, so the rest of the day can be spent with your 'acquaintance', he replied, pulling into the traffic and smiling to himself.

He pulled up into the drive and ushered Charlene into the house, 'Care for a coffee before I give you a tour of the premises'.

'Thank's, that would be lovely, he directed her to the Lounge before heading to the kitchen to make their drinks. As he sat in the chair he had used previously he handed her a mug of coffee and commenced his explanation of Stefan's medical condition and how he would be returning after a week or so to arrange the selling of the house and car, together with the clearance of contents. To his surprise Charlene enquired as to the proposed selling price, as she would be interested in purchasing it at a later date. Jake felt slightly confused at her comment as he thought she was settled in her apartment, however he realised she must have a tidy sum invested after her recent inheritance, so perhaps she was interested in the property as an investment. That's something to think on, it would make the transition a lot simpler for him if it was someone he knew.

With coffee's drunk Jake walked around the property to enable Charlene to gauge if it was the property for her, indicating the quirky areas he had recently discovered. She smiled throughout and a joy seemed to engulf her when they returned to the Lounge.

She looked at Jake and said 'I think if the price is right this could be my home in the future. Obviously once the furniture is removed it would need some updating and redecorating but the property as a whole would be ideal for me'.

He was quite overwhelmed at the thought of her living there in the future, but as Stefan has said in the past, 'life goes on'. 'Well my dear, on Stefan's demise I will inherit the property so I'm sure that we could come to an amicable figure, obviously discounted for you'. She stood up and hugged him before asking him for an approximate valuation.

His face turned grave before he replied with 'I'm afraid I would rather not talk on this subject anymore as when I visit him this afternoon I will have this conversation on my mind, so I would rather discuss this further once my friend has passed'.

'Please forgive me Jake I got carried away with my excitement regarding the property, I'll mention it no-more, what shall we do next, have a spot of lunch locally?'

Jake smiled as he had felt unhappy for a few moments regarding the house sale, but perked up once food was mentioned. 'There is a nice little restaurant down the road which I would like to take you to, its within walking distance, so if you fancy some nice Mexican cuisine we'll wander down there'.

She returned his smile and replied with 'You know I like something hot, and Mexican is one of my favourites, so lead on'.

They both stood and made their way down the road and fifteen minutes later they were seated and perusing the extensive menu, whilst sipping a small beer. After much deliberation they placed their orders, which got delivered within 10 minutes. They made small talk over the meal with the subject of the property sale not mentioned in their conversation.

An hour later feeling sated, they walked back in preparation for their visit to the Hospice to see Stefan and discuss Jake's return to the UK the next day. Jake had asked if she would like to accompany him, and as she had met him whilst celebrating his birthday at the swanky restaurant she said it would be her pleasure.

Jake made a cup of tea for them before they took the car for the short trip to the Hospice. As they approached the Receptionist the young lady greeted Jake with a 'Good afternoon Mr Tordale, I'm afraid that Mr Cohen is busy at the moment, the doctor is with him, however as soon as he leaves you can go to his room, would you please take a seat whilst you are waiting'.

'Thank you' Jake replied with a frown, he wondered if his friend had taken a turn for the worse, but then thought that he must not speculate, it could just be a general check up.

Ten minutes passed before the doctor whom Jake had met previously walked along the corridor, as he noticed Jake he walked over to him. They shook hands and before a word was said Jake feared the worst, he sat in the adjoining chair and quietly outlined the reason for his visit. 'Unfortunately Mr Cohen has taken a turn for the worse, and I fear that the cancer in his brain is spreading more rapidly than expected,

I have explained everything to him but as I said at our meeting there is no time limit on this dreadful disease. I can only give you an approximate prognosis but I think the end will be one week or at the most two. When you go in I think the brave man that he is will be quite honest with you and confirm what I have just said to him, but you know Stefan quite well now and he is resigned to his fate. As time goes by he will be heavily sedated against the pain and will eventually drift away. I understand you will be returning to England tomorrow, so if you could give me your mobile number I will keep you informed daily'.

He stood and they shook hands again, issuing just one word before he left 'Sorry'.

Jake took out a handkerchief and blew his nose before turning to Charlene and asking her 'You haven't got to come in with me you know'. She gave a warm smile and replied with 'I want to'. They slowly walked along the corridor, knocked on the door and walked in to see Stefan in his chair by the window. He turned and smiled as he saw the two of them and asked them to come in. 'What a pleasure to see you young lady, your appearance has brightened up the room. And my dear friend Jake off back to England tomorrow, how are you both?'

Jake walked over to the old man and shook his hand as a knowing message passed between them. 'We're fine my friend, how are you?'

'I can't lie Jake, I feel rubbish, I've just had my doctor here and he has given me the good news, which I expect you know, as he would have seen you in Reception, that the end is nigh, however the staff are looking after me with the necessary drugs, so you can pop back to your lovely family and catch up with them, knowing I am in safe hands'.

The hanky came out again as Jake blew his nose to cover his distress, he then turned to wipe his eyes before saying 'We both knew it would be a short ride, but at least we were able to go off and enjoy ourselves for a few days after the exhilaration of the sale at Sotheby's?'

'Indeed, I'm sorry to say that I feel quite tired at the moment so before I have my afternoon meds I'll take a little nap. Charlene I'd like to thank you for coming today, however would you mind if I have a private word with Jake before you both go?'

Charlene stood and shook Stefan's hand and gave him a peck on the cheek before saying 'Goodbye' and leaving the room.

Jake sat alongside him, waiting in anticipation as to what Stefan wanted to say to him. He looked in turmoil as he prepared himself for the final conversation they would be having.

'I want you to return to England tomorrow and do what you want to do, my doctor will keep you informed of my condition, as you know everything is in place once I pass, so there will be no need for you to return immediately after I pass. Now is there anything you need to know before you leave?

Nothing at all my dear friend, it's been a pleasure, and make sure you drink all that whiskey'.

'No fear of that, it's already gone' he answered finally with a weak smile. Jake stood up and hugged his friend one last time, turned and left the room.

As he walked into the Reception Area Charlene stood, turned and walked towards the exit door with Jake in her wake, he rushed forward to open the door forgetting that they were automatic and they both walked silently to the car. As they got in he turned to her and said, 'Well I think that will be the last time I see my friend, as I'm sure he will just give up now that I will be out of the Country, if I'm honest I'll expect a call from the Hospice after a couple of days back home.

However I do not wish him to suffer after such a long working life that he has enjoyed'.

Charlene sat with tears in her eyes and didn't reply for a minute or so before replying with 'You have done all you can for your dear friend, when he finally departs it will be a happy release for him'. With that Jake started the car and drove back down the road, and back to the property in a somewhat morbid mood, almost fazing out his companion, however as he pulled up the drive and got out of the car he brightened up as he opened the front door to let Charlene pass. 'I'm sorry about that my dear, realisation has just set in that I am returning to the UK for my own ends, and my friend will be battling for his life, alone'.

'He won't be alone Jake the staff at the Hospital will tend to his every need, and he will be free of pain with the medication they will administer to him, and I think quite honestly he is ready.'

'I agree but I feel quite helpless, at least I was able to give him a little happiness with our trips together to Niagara Falls and the Grand Canyon which hopefully he will think about'.

She smiled and gave him a hug before saying 'You have made an old man very happy in his twilight years, just imagine if you hadn't come into his life, he had no relatives to do what you have done for him, I think whilst his brain is functioning he will recall the good times he has had with you, as he said you are 'the son he never had'.

'Thank you my dear, I know what you are saying but the reality of it all has just begun to sink in, I have a lot to sort out in the future however let's just chill out for an hour or so before I drop you back home. I'll make us a coffee and we can have a last catch up before I return home tomorrow'.

The next couple of hours was spent on various things, with Charlene's final mention of the property again. Jake thought for a while and promised to give her an approximate figure when he returned to the US following his home visit.

He drove her back to her apartment a little later and they parted as firm friends with Charlene kissing him on both cheeks before alighting from the car and striding to the front door, passing through it without turning or waving to him.

Unsure why her attitude had changed, he drove off slightly peeved and back to the house where he decided to pack his cases in preparation for his early start in the morning.

Chapter 85

Rising early, he made breakfast with the last of the cereal and milk in the fridge, then after his cup of tea he put the cases in the boot of the car. The perfectionist that he was he decided to hoover throughout the ground floor and wipe down the kitchen and bathroom surfaces before leaving. He then turned off the electrics and gas heating whilst checking through each room making sure that everything was in order. His flight left at 10.30am so he intended arriving at the Terminal by no later than 9am, allowing him time to fill out the paperwork for the hire car and pay for the time he had had the vehicle.

Locking the front door he felt a little twinge of regret at leaving when his dear friend was in the last stage of his life, but his life must go on, and his family in the UK were his priority, plus the state of his property in Dorset which most likely was in need some TLC after his long absence.

Starting the car he drove quickly down the road as his mind gradually changed from US to UK thoughts, then after sorting the hire car out he strode into the Terminal and approached the ticket cubicle. He handed over his 'fluid' return ticket then after a few minutes he was handed boarding cards.

Through Passport Control, then after handing over his two cases, he settled into the First Class Lounge that was almost empty. He was greeted by a waiter who asked if he would like any food. He decided on poached eggs on toast and coffee and settled down with the local paper. As he was eating his food the Lounge started filling up with more travellers and as he completed his meal the room was bursting at the seams. Twenty minutes passed, and just as he had finished with the paper, boarding was called for the flight to Heathrow, London.

The journey was as expected in First Class, revolved around eating, drinking, sleeping and reading in his expensive but comfortable seat, and as the Captain gave out over the tannoy that they were descending he realised that he had slept a lot longer than usual on his homeward flight. On landing, then going through the regulations and collecting his luggage he caught the shuttle back to the Hotel. Dropping his luggage into the boot of the Lexus he started her up, running the engine for a few minutes to recharge the battery.

Then he called into Reception to pay his bill, returning to the car he sat in the drivers seat and mulled over the happenings whilst he had been in the States, thinking about his dear friend languishing in the Hospice awaiting the inevitable. He quickly pulled himself out of his negativity and fired up the engine and made his way home.

Pulling out of the Airport it felt strange adjusting back to the left hand side of the roads, but after a few miles it was as if he hadn't been away, after a couple of hours he pulled into his driveway. Stretching as he got out of the car, he anticipated there would be a considerable amount of post on the other side of the front door, he therefore gently eased the door open and before he looked at the accumulated paperwork he rushed to disconnected the house alarm. Turning around even he was surprised at the volume of paperwork that was strewn over the floor. He picked it all up and placed it on the Dining Room table to look at later, then before collecting his luggage from the boot, he turned on the heating as the house was almost polar after his latest excursion

Retrieving both suitcases he removed his dirty clothing and put them straight into the washing machine and took the remnants left in the cases up to his bedroom, to be sorted after he had opened the post.

He separated the paperwork into different piles, flyers to one side, bills next to them and written correspondence in front of him. Recognising the writing on the first envelope and the stamp marked Australia he assumed it was from Mrs Choo, but on opening it he was surprised to find that it was from Inspector Chi of the Brisbane Police, included with a latter was an invitation for her forthcoming wedding in two months time, with an RSVP attached. There were two letters postmarked Plymouth which were from his two children wishing him a Happy New Year. the final envelope was from the States, he didn't recognise the writing so he opened it quite gingerly, but to his surprise it was from Stefan, he had obviously written it before he went into the Hospice. He picked it up and sat in his favourite armchair to read it. The envelope contained two pages, and they were written on each side of the paper. It read 'Mr dear friend Jake, I decided to write this note rather than tell you how I feel at the moment. The day you walked into my shop and uttered a few words I was overcome with a feeling of a kind, thoughtful Englishman who I would like to know. Over the time you had in the States I looked forward to your frequent visits to purchase items for your friends and family, but also I was pleased to get to know you better, and as I have told you before you are the son I never had. I feel confident that you will handle my affairs efficiently like the gentleman you are and although I will soon be entering the Hospice and didn't want you to see me during my final days.

I know you have to return to the UK for a while but I hope to see you again before I shed my mortal coil. May God take care of you in the future and I hope you enjoy your retirement, thank you for being there with me when I needed you. Your friend Stefan'.

Jake stood and walked to the kitchen to make himself a cup of tea, whilst trying to contain his emotions over Stefan's letter. Returning with his tea he sat again at the Dining Room table and opened the remaining post, there was nothing of interest so he collected the envelopes and unwanted mail and placed them in the recycling bag.

Checking his watch he realised he hadn't altered it to GMT so he quickly adjusted it and noticed that the local time was approaching 6pm, too late for shopping so a visit to the Pub would be a good idea.

A lovely pint of local ale and something from Bert's vast menu seemed a good idea. He rang the Pub and booked a table for 7pm with Bert's daughter, then went upstairs to change into a replacement outfit.

Whilst in the bedroom he rang both his daughter's saying he would be coming to Devon over the weekend and was looking forward to seeing everyone. Half an hour later he set the alarm, locked the front door, and drove down the lane to the Pub and pulled into the side parking area.

As he approached the bar Bert appeared from the kitchen with a broad grin on his face before asking Jake 'Hello mate, where the hell have you been, we thought you'd decided to take your custom to another hostelry'.

'I've been to America again, a dear friend of mine has brain cancer and had to go into a Hospice, and I have been in Washington for the last 10 days sorting out his affairs. I'll only be back here for a week then I have to return again. Anyway I'll put that to one side at the moment and enjoy a pint of your lovely real ale, in preparation for some of your delicious food'.

Chapter 85

Bert grinned from ear to ear as he placed Jake's beer to front of him before saying 'I've put you on your usual table 2 my friend, sit yourself down and I'll bring over a menu'.

There were only half a dozen people in the Dining Room at present tucking into their meals, so Jake took his seat, and whilst waiting for the menu he glanced at the Special's board and his decision was made. The second item there was 12oz gammon steak with all the trimmings, his favourite. As Bert walked towards him he had noticed that Jake was scanning the Specials and knew that what he would be having 'I'm not a physic but I can guarantee that the menu is superfluous and you'll order the Gammon, am I right?'

Jake laughed and replied 'Am I that predictable Bert?'.

'Not always, however I saw a slight smile as you looked at the board, so I would say I made an educated guess'.

When his meal was placed in front of him the Gammon almost covered the plate, he therefore had to have a side dish with the chips and peas for him to apply himself, on top of the meat was a generous portion of pineapple. Bert also brought another pint for him.

Bert said 'That's what you call a special for a dear friend, enjoy'.

'Thank's Bert its nice to have a proper English meal, although there is nothing wrong with American and Mexican food but this is right up my street'.

Twenty minutes later as Jake finished his second pint he felt completely bloated and wished he had walked down the lane as on the return journey at least he would have moved his indulgence around a little, however he had brought the car. Walking up to the Bar he paid his bill, shook Bert's hand and thanked him for the service and lovely food.

Walking back into the house he decided to catch up with the news on the telly and settle down for the night. Nestling a warm cup of drinking chocolate he read through his letters again interspersed with looking at various headlines on the Sky news channel. Scrolling through the various channels he made up his mind to watch a film and tuned into one, unfortunately he only watched twenty minutes or so of it and dropped off to sleep in the chair. Stirring an hour or so later he turned the TV off and made his way up the stairs to bed, feeling absolutely shattered.

Chapter 86

Up early the next morning he gathered together the presents he had purchased in America and put them in a bag to take down to Devon. As the weather was dry and sunny he got the MG out of the garage and put the Lexus in its place. Checking the oil, water and tyres on the sports car, he was satisfied that the old girl would be up to the round trip so he walked back into the kitchen and prepared himself breakfast and a cup of tea.

As it was Saturday he knew that most of the family were home, or in Sharon and Lottie's case at the stables, he thought today was a good day to hit the road early to Devon.

Once he pulled onto the M5 the traffic was considerably heavier than normal, due to the football and rugby games being played that afternoon, however there were numerous caravans, together with huge camper vans bunched up together frustrating the single car drivers. However the traffic thinned a little when most of them took the A30 near Exeter leaving numerous 'Lewis Hamilton' type drivers to accelerate along what was left of the motorway. Jake was left trundling along in the inside lane quite happy to enjoy the scenery at a steady 60mph, however Haldon hill was a different story and he had to drop down a gear or two as he reached the summit.

The remainder of the drive to his home town took a little over 30 minutes and he felt quite excited as he pulled into his daughter's driveway just after 10am.

The front door opened and his daughter rushed down the steps to meet him. 'Hello luv, how are you, it seems ages since I saw you last. Are the rest of the crowd around today?'

'Come on in Dad' Clare said, 'Its a nice day but there's still a chill in the air, cup of tea?'

'Thank's luv, I'll just get some bits and pieces out of the car' but as he turned the family Golden Retriever launched herself at him, with her massive tail shaking in delight. Jake stopped and gave her head a rub and smoothed her back. She followed him to the car and back and shot past him as he opened the front door.

Clare shouted out 'I think she's glad to see you don't you think?'.

Jake smiled and said 'If only she could talk, I wonder what she would say'.

'Most likely, whilst you are here what about a walk' Clare replied.

They sat at the kitchen table nursing their mugs of tea before Clare quizzed her father about his time in America.

Jake looked into his cup before outlining his time with Stefan and the situation regarding his returning to the States within a week to sort out his friends estate, and visit him during his final days in the Hospice.

'Quite a sad time for you Dad, however it would be a lot easier if you were both in the same Country, but it is what it is. Do you have a time scale as to when you will return again to the US or is it an open ended situation'.

Jake huffed and puffed for a few seconds before replying with 'I can't say really my love, the prognosis is basically Stefan could go at any time, even as we speak. However when I spoke to the Doctor at the Hospice he said he wouldn't be in any pain as the drugs that he has administered will keep him free from that. But eventually he will go into a coma and slowly pass away, I intend to be back in the States before that happens'.

The whole clan arrived at Clare's just before noon, so another 20 minutes explanation was needed to keep everyone up to date with his latest exploits in the USA. He distributed the remaining presents to everyone and the various family members returned to their own homes to have their lunch. With just Clare and her father left they both thought that fish and chips would be a good idea and so they headed down to Fore Street to collect their takeaway lunch. For a variation Jake plumped for scampi and chips with mushy peas and Clare had her usual fish and chips with mushy peas. They returned home and sat at the kitchen table to enjoy their meal, chatting away like they hadn't see each other for ages. Having a second cup of coffee they retired to the Lounge with Jake asking questions about the ins and outs of family life, and checking if everyone was in good health and happy with their careers at present. Once they finished their drinks they washed and wiped the dishes, then Jake said that he would get back on the road to enable him to get back to Wisteria Cottage before dark. The drive home was straightforward and he trundled down the lane just as the twilight made its appearance. He changed over the cars in the garage, locked the door and settled down to watch the news on the TV with a small brandy.

Just after 6pm his mobile rang, checking the number it just said WITHHELD so he was unsure wether to take the call, but it might be someone he knew, so he pressed the button and said Tordale.

There was a crackling sound for a couple of seconds before a women's voice said 'Good evening Mr Tordale its Nurse Graham at the Hospice in Washington. I don't wish to alarm you but I'm afraid that Mr Cohen's health has deteriorated since you returned home and we fear that he is in the last stage of life. We knew you wished to be informed if there was any changes in your friend's health, however he is comfortable'.

'Thank you for calling me Nurse, do you think if I catch a plane tomorrow I would be in time to see him?' he asked almost knowing the answer.

'The doctor has visited him in the past hour and giving him a sedative, our thought's are that his demise is quite imminent. I know you would like to see him, therefore i can only say with uncertainty if you arrive tomorrow you might be in time, however we cannot say if he would know you or not'.

'Thank you nurse, I will catch an early flight tomorrow, and make my way straight to the Hospice, if I am in time well and good, if not my journey will not be wasted as I have a lot of things to do when I get there, thank you again, goodbye', he put the phone down and felt quite sad to receive the inevitable call.

He phoned through to Heathrow and booked a First Class open ticket to Washington for the next day, then rang his daughter to tell her his news, that he would be returning to the States the next day.

Walking up the stairs he packed two suitcases for the morning, opened the safe and retrieved his passport and his remaining US dollars, putting these in his carryon case. It was a good job he hadn't had time to restock his fridge with food, as he didn't know when he would be returning.

His flight departed mid morning so an early start would be required to allow him to get there in plenty of time, firstly to drop the car off at the airport Hotel, then to collect his tickets, put his cases through, and spend some time in the First Class Lounge prior to take-off.

Chapter 87

It only seemed 5 minutes ago that he had travelled the path from London Heathrow, now he was taking the reverse journey yet again, to return to Washington DC. The drive today was exceptionally busy he was therefore glad he had allowed himself half an hour's grace as he was travelling to London at a peak time of the day, with commuters going into the City to carry out their working day. He pulled the Lexus into the car park at the rear of the Hotel, collected a trolley from the foyer and loaded his cases on board. He approached the front desk and booked his car in yet again, thankfully it was the same Receptionist he had spoken to only a few days ago. Therefore she knew what Jake required, she booked the car in with an open available date for his return. With that done he stationed himself near the front door and within ten minutes the shuttle bus arrived and he placed his luggage on board for the short trip to the Terminal. Collecting his tickets he booked his luggage in and made his way to the VIP lounge and indulged in a good old Full English breakfast coupled with a pot of Earl Grey tea. The room quickly filled up with early morning passengers, and an hour later his flight was called. Between boarding and take off it only took three quarters of an hour, so he quickly settled down to the routine of a seasoned First Class traveller. His priority once landing was to collect a hire car from Hertz and make his way to the Hospice as soon as practically possible, then once he was there assess the situation, then hopefully he would be in time to see his friend and have a final conversation with him. After he left the Airport it took him three quarters of an hour to arrive at the Hospice, on approaching the Receptionist he felt somewhat dismayed at her sad face and thought the worst. However after explaining who he was and who had come to see the young lady brightened up and said to him 'Carry on through Mr Tordale you know the way, a nurse is with Mr Cohen at present however I expect both of them will be glad to see you'. Jake nodded at her and turned towards the corridor with a frown on his face, unsure what he had meant by 'glad to see you'.

Chapter 87

He knocked on the door and waited for the nurse to open it and let him enter. She smiled and greeted him with 'Mr Cohen is comfortable, the Doctor has seen him this morning and we have given the patient his medication, and I'm afraid now it is a question of time before his release from pain.

Unfortunately at the moment he is asleep, however when I spoke to him earlier I told him you would be with us today, so if you would like to sit beside the bed and talk to him I'm sure he will eventually wake up and be able in small bursts to converse with you'.

Jake smiled and walked over to the chair and sat down, he turned to the nurse, smiled and thanked her as she left the room quietly.

Casting his eyes over him he saw such a difference in his friend's face, all colour had drained from him and he looked critically ill, which of course he was. What to say, he was at a loss for a while before he quietly explained to Stefan what he had been up to in the UK since they had last seen each other. Jake had been talking for at least fifteen minutes before there was a knock on the door and the nurse returned with a cup of tea for him, which he took and thanked her. Between sips of tea he carried on his recital on his visits to family and friends, before there appeared a flickering of Stefan's eyes and eventually they focused on Jake's face and recognition slowly spread over him and he gave a weak smile. Jake unsure wether to speak first or not smiled in return before quietly saying 'Hello Stefan its Jake' gripping his friend's hand. Stefan opened his mouth and whispered in reply 'Thank you for coming my friend, it's almost over and I wanted to see you one last time'. Even this sentence took a lot of effort, and his eyes closed again. Jake remained quiet for another five minutes, then Stefan opened his eyes again, obviously he was building up for more conversation but it was a tremendous effort to do. 'I think you only want to make this one visit, my friend' he whispered again 'The doctor said that my time is running out, and in fact I have made my peace now that I have seen you for the last time. Please just prepare for what you have to do once I have departed' then gripping Jake's hand he muttered something in Yiddish and finished in English with 'Thank you for everything you have done for me my son, enjoy your richly deserved inheritance I will be looking down on you' then he relaxed the grip on his hand and drifted off to sleep again. Jake felt extremely emotional as he stood and left the room, then as he entered the Reception Area he said to the young lady 'Please let me know on my mobile of any further developments'. She smiled weakly before replying with 'Certainly Mr Tordale'. He nodded then strode out through the front doors and back to his car.

Feeling a little lost after his visit and the now certain demise of his friend he made his mind up as soon as he returned to the property he would set about making lists for himself, of firstly the people he would contact, Solicitor, Bank Manager, Funeral Director, plus the various shopkeepers that Stefan had been in contact with.

Next on the list would be the House Clearance person who would remove all the unwanted furniture and electrical goods. Priority would be contacting Charlene to tell her he was back in Washington, and they needed a meeting regarding her possible purchase of the House.

He settled back into the guest bedroom and deposited his clothing in the wardrobe before returning to the kitchen and putting on the kettle for a cup of coffee.

The fridge and food cupboard were almost empty so he needed to pop to the local supermarket to obtain food and drink to sustain him for the next week or so, as the time was approaching 3pm he would go there after finishing his coffee.

Although the supermarket was only half a mile away he decided to give Stefan's car a run, plus he would require a number of bags to carry his goods, so therefore it was impractical to walk there. As he walked into the huge establishment he realised he was out of his comfort zone, as he was unsure where he had to go first. A young assistant was stacking shelves and noticed his confused expression and asked if she could be assistance. He quickly explained that he was from the UK and unsure of the layout of the supermarket.

She laughed before pointing above Jake's head, where in bold letters it explained what each aisle contained together with its number.

Slightly embarrassed Jake blushed and thanked her for the instructions, and walked down the first aisle picking up items as he went. After 10 minutes he was glad that he had taken a trolley rather than a basket, as it was already three quarters full and there was plenty more items he was looking for.

The final aisle contained alcohol and he put in three boxes of beer, and a bottle of brandy in case he had visitors during his stay. As he filled the boxes provided he was surprised at the cost of items against that of the UK and the final total came to an acceptable $150 dollars.

He pushed the trolley to the rear of the car and put all the boxes in the boot then returned it to the enclosure where they are stored.

Ten minutes later he pulled up onto the driveway, carried in the boxes and stored his goods in the fridge and food cupboard. With that completed he sat down and phoned Charlene, she answered on the second ring with 'Hello, and welcome back, how are things?'

Slight hesitation before Jake gave her the full story of his friend's situation, then he asked if she fancied eating out that evening or tomorrow whichever suited her.

'Unfortunately I am still at work, however I would love to dine out tomorrow evening. Shall we say around seven?'

A slightly disappointed Jake said 'Fine, see you tomorrow' and disconnected the call.

Chapter 88

He made himself some dinner and sat down to watch TV for the evening, however he nodded off just after 8pm, and slept until ten. He was woken by the cheers from fans on the TV watching a baseball match, so he scrolled through the channels until he found a revamped UK soap that he watched after getting himself a beer. Around eleven he had had enough viewing and wandered along the corridor to his room for a good night's sleep.He slept like a log and didn't open his eyes until 8.30am which was extremely late for him, however his first thoughts were, there is nothing of any urgency for me today. However not one for lying in bed unnecessarily he got out and eventually sat down for his breakfast. A strange melancholy swept over him as he nursed his cup of tea, he was thousands of miles away from his home and family, and in limbo waiting for the demise of a dear friend of his before he could carry out the necessary work he had come back to the States to carry out. This evening he would be meeting Charlene for a meal and chat, mainly for him, as to wether she was still serious about purchasing Stefan's house, as before he returned to the UK he wanted to complete the sale of his friend's assets that had been bequeathed to him prior to his entering the Hospice.

Breakfast finished he washed and put away the dishes, before settling down to list everything in the property, room by room. Partitioned into lists of items to sell, items that, should Charlene buy the property she might like to retain, and finally items that just needed to be cleared away. The next item was the car, Stefan had taken great care of his beloved car, so he decided to give it a good clean inside and out, remove anything that shouldn't be in there and put it up for sale in the local rag.

After he had completed that task, he discovered all the relevant paperwork in the glove compartment and placed it in a large manilla envelope marked CAR. There were also one or two items that reminded Jake of his friend which he put to one side.

He rang the local paper and put an advert in under Classified Ads for Cars for Sale with all the necessary information and a guide price of $5000 dollars ono, together with his mobile number. Feeling pleased with his work over the last few hours he made himself a cup of coffee and sat in the Lounge to contemplate what else he could do for the rest of the day. He prepared a light lunch for himself after which he would set aside items room by room that he wished to retain, or to sell, then box up items that required removal. Then as late afternoon approached he would finish for the day and get ready to meet Charlene for their evening out.

He felt tired around 4.30pm so had a shower and shave and sat down with a coffee and relaxed for a while, which turned into a power nap of an hour. There was still plenty of time to have a shave and change of clothes before taking the rental car into the City to collect his friend.

Then his mobile rang, his body shook as he knew without looking who the call was from, he answered with a shaky voice 'Jake Tordale'

There was a two second silence before the caller said 'Hello Mr Tordale, it's Jemima from the Hospice, I'm afraid that Mr Cohen passed away a little while ago, and I'm extremely sorry for your loss. If you could spare some time and you would like to see him one last time before the funeral home comes to collect him I would suggest a visit within the next hour'.

Jake took a deep breath before answering with 'I'll be there in 20 minutes, thank you for calling', he disconnected the call and a wave of relief spread over him as he thought now his dear friend was out of pain and at peace. He quickly left and locked up, took the rental car and drove to the Hospice. The Receptionist who he assumed was Jemima was sat at her desk and stood as he walked in, and with a sad voice said 'Thank you for getting here so quickly Mr Tordale, if you would kindly take a seat I'll just contact the Nurse in Charge who is with your friend at present and inform her you that you have arrived and she will come for you once everything has been prepared'.

Jake could only nod, so he turned and sat in one of the comfortable armchairs.

The Receptionist made a call, which Jake presumed was to the Nurse, to advise her that Jake had arrived and ten minutes later she appeared along the corridor. Jake stood as she approached him, they shook hands and she offered her condolences to him and said that Stefan was ready for him and would he follow her.

They entered the room, the Nurse stood to one side to allow Jake to approach the bed and see his friend one last time. Tears spread across his cheeks as he mumbled quietly to his dear friend before turning and leaving the room.

Outside in the corridor the Nurse confirmed that the Hospice had phoned the Funeral Home and they would be collecting Mr. Cohen later that evening, and returning him to their premises. The remaining formalities would be left for him to take care of, the doctor had confirmed the death and certificates would be available in the morning, for the relevant authorities.

Jake shook her hand and thanked her and the Hospice for the care that they had given to Stefan who now thankfully was out of pain. He made his way back to the car, and drove back to the home without any knowledge of the journey. He walked in, made himself a cup of coffee and sent a text message to Charlene explaining the recent events.

She replied immediately asking if he would like to cancel their evening out, he quickly replied with 'No, I think being on my own at the moment is not what I need, so I'll call for you at 7pm as agreed'.

As he was already changed to go out all he had to do was clean his teeth and make his way to Charlene's apartment and collect her before going to a restaurant for supper.

As pulled up alongside the apartment building Charlene opened the door and quickly made her way to the car. She got in and kissed him on the cheek before saying 'I'm sorry for the loss of your friend, but at least he is out of pain now. Where would you like to go Jake, its your evening so whatever you want to do I'll go along with?'

He turned to look at her warm and beautiful face and said 'If I'm honest I haven't eaten much today, and as well as needing a drink at the moment I am in your hands'.

She gave him a soft smile before replying with 'I know somewhere that's quiet, intimate and doesn't have blaring music playing as you dine. It's the other side of Washington and around 20 minutes drive. I'll direct you as you drive'.

Her directions were superb as the drove in to the small private car park at the rear of the premises. They walked to the entrance and were greeted by a waiter who asked them to follow him to a table in the centre of the restaurant. The dimmed lighting and delicious smells emanating from the kitchen made Jake feel a little happier as they took their seats, they perused the menu's that they had been given. Jake ordered a bottle of red wine for them to have whilst deciding on their food order, and he began to talk to Charlene about what he had to do next, before finally asking if she would like to inspect the premises again to enable her to make up her mind about purchasing it. He didn't say it quite as bluntly as that but it was said as a loaded question.

Charlene smiled before replying with 'Shall we decide what food we would like, and enjoy this lovely red wine whilst we are doing it, and talk about everything else once we have finished our meal?'

'I'm sorry my dear, my mind is in turmoil at present with all I have to do, now that Stefan has departed, and I'm so glad we could meet as you are the only friend I have here' he said as he finished his first glass of wine.

The waiter returned just as they had made up their minds on what to order. The starter arrived as they made small talk. but the gap between their plates being removed and the main course was considerable, leaving a gap for their conversation to begin again. Charlene commenced with 'Could I help in any way with the various things you have to do, or is it something only you can perform?'

'That's very kind of you Charlene, however I make it appear considerable, but it is mainly phone calls to the Bank, Solicitor, Church, Funeral Parlour etc, the sale of his car and premises. But I'm going to take it slowly, all the people I mentioned I have already been in contact with, so they were anticipating Stefan's demise, it was just when it happened. I have placed an advert in the local papers Ads Section for the car, and I'm hoping there could be an interested party for his home, but I'll have to wait and see. Please accept my apologies for the way I appear today but as you know I was very fond of the man that was 'Stefan Cohen' and with that their food arrived before she could reply to his extended rant.

They ate and drank in silence, but no sooner had their knives and forks been placed on their plates Charlene looked directly at Jake and with a deep sigh said 'I know you are grieving and have a lot on you're plate at present but please don't pressurise me into making a decision on the property'.

Quite shocked Jake was taken aback for a few seconds before he replied with 'I'm sorry my dear, there wasn't meant to be any inference in my rant regarding yourself purchasing the property I was just outlining everything I have to do before I return home' he then leant over the table and clasped her hands before smiling at her.

That broke the ice and she returned his smile and said 'I am most interested in the property but would like to look at it again before I make any rash decisions. The positive is that I will be a cash buyer and I can pay with my inheritance that I squirrelled away in a high interest account a while ago'.

Jake spoke quickly before she said any more with 'There is no urgency in the sale of the property as nothing will take place until Stefan's funeral is long passed. Now would you like some dessert?'

'To be honest Jake I am quite full, however I think I would like a coffee to finish off the meal'. The waiter cleared their table and took their order for drinks.

Ten minutes later and after Jake had paid the bill they stood and walked back to the car in silence. As they sat in the car with the engine running Charlene asked if he would like to come back to her apartment for a while or did he want to head back.

Jake turned to her and kissed her on the lips and as he pulled away said 'That would be nice'. As they approached the apartment door Jake quietly asked her if they were alone or not. Charlene gave out a titter before replying with 'Why did you have something in mind?'.

'No, there was no ulterior motive in my question, just a general interest'.

'Well we will in fact be on our own, in answer to your question' as she opened the door and walked into the Lounge, and then through to the kitchenette.

Jake walked to the Lounge and sat on the armchair that he had done on a previous visit waiting for Charlene to emerge from the kitchenette with the drinks.

The next couple of hours were spent in mutual conversation about everything and nothing in particular, but with Charlene attempting to lighten the mood with details of her work and a holiday she was going to book in Europe the following year.

Jake thanked her for a lovely evening and took his leave, saying that todays news had drained him and he felt extremely tired and wished to drive home before he fell asleep.

She said she would ring him the next day as soon as she got home from work and perhaps she could call to see him one day the following week to look around the property, after he had carried out his urgent chores.

Chapter 89

The following morning he was up bright and early and ready for a busy day of telephone calls and organisation for the upcoming funeral. All the calls took the best part of the morning, with appointments being made to visit the Funeral Home, the Hospice and the Bank the following day.

He made himself a coffee before removing a ready meal from the freezer and putting it in the over for an early lunch, as the afternoon would be spent boxing up items in each of the rooms. He imagined that his stay in America would be at least another 10 to 14 days, as he wanted to clear up everything, if possible, on this visit, however time would tell. A visit to the supermarket was required to purchase the basics for his nomadic life whilst here, anything major food wise, he thought would involve eating out.

The afternoon was spent packing most things up and labelling what the boxes contained, come 4pm he felt quite satisfied with his day's work. He decided to eat at the local Mexican restaurant after he had received his call from Charlene, so he booked himself a table for one at 8pm. Feeling quite pleased with himself he sat in the Lounge with a drink waiting for Charlene's call. He didn't have to wait long as his mobile alerted him of an incoming call at 6.30pm, then looking at the screen he recognised her number and pressed the button and asked 'Good evening my dear, have you had a good day?'

She gave a sign and replied with 'Extremely busy, how about you with your mountain of jobs?'

;Well, I am quite pleased with what I have achieved today, I've made all my calls, and appointments are confirmed for tomorrow. Then this afternoon I have boxed up and labelled everything that was in the living spaces, which just leaves me with the kitchen to sort out, but that will be a last minute work in progress area. Oh and rather than shop for a lot of disposal items to eat, I am just going to have the essentials for breakfast and the usual bits and pieces you rely on to exist. Then for the remaining time I'll be in the States I'll eat out in local establishments'.

'OK, well I have something to say now that I think will make your day, I have been on to my Financial Planner and he has put in motion the transfer of funds for me that if your price is within my budget I could buy Stefan's property, so if you could work out a figure for me then perhaps we can strike a deal.

However I just need another look around the property, whenever its convenient for you, say this coming weekend?'

He hesitated for a while before replying with 'Sounds like a plan, it will give me chance to completely tidy everything for my 'prospective buyer' to inspect'.

She chuckled down the phone before saying 'There is no need to be so official Mr Tordale'. Jake laughed before answering with 'We could make a day of it, and eat out for lunch as well if you like?'

'Sounds good' she said 'Come Saturday I'll need a change of environment, and a day with my gorgeous friend is what I definitely need'.

Jake finished the conversation with 'Will you make your own way here, or would you prefer if I collected you?'

A slight hesitation before she said 'I'll make my own way to you, say around 10am?'

'Fine' he said 'See you at the weekend, don't work to hard my dear' then he ended the call. He decided to tidy up the kitchen before doing anything else as this is the quickest room to tidy, then make plans for tomorrow's descent on the remainder of the property.

Feeling satisfied with his day's progress he wandered down to the local Mexican Restaurant for his 8pm meal. The food as usual was excellent and an hour and a half later he made his way back home for a cup of coffee before sitting in front of the TV for some relaxing viewing.

Chapter 90

Up bright and early the next day he dressed in formal wear for his meetings with the Funeral Home, the Bank and the Hospice. He had spaced the appointments at hourly intervals with the Funeral Home first at 10am. The Owner was very sympathetic, and carried out his duties fastidiously and with compassion. He confirmed that he would organise whatever flowers Jake needed, plus he would liaise with the Church once the hymns etc. were agreed. Checking his watch he had another 15 minutes before he was due at the Bank and agreed on the hymns after perusing various songs that were popular.

Back in the car he headed towards the Bank and his appointment with the Manager. He was asked to wait for a few minutes before the man appeared at the counter and ushered him in to his Office, offering Jake tea or coffee. The drinks were brought in a few minutes later by one of the Cashiers that Jake had seen in the Bank on his recent visit.

The legal documents were put in front of him to sign and explained by the Manager as just being a formality, but as Stefan was now deceased confirming the transfer of funds and deeds of the house to him was required officially for the Banks accountants. He was also asked if he required the funds to be held at the Bank or would he prefer them to be transferred to his Bank in the UK. Jake explained that he had a prospective buyer for the property so therefore if the sale went through in the next 2 weeks, there would be additional funds to be transferred to this account. He would then make another appointment at the Bank prior to his returning to England, to discuss the transfer. Finally he explained his next visit to the Hospice was to make a donation, based on the sale of Stefan's car, at present unsold. So he will make a payment of $5000 dollars gifted in advance to the Hospice when he called later.

The Manager smiled and said 'That is an extremely generous gesture Mr Tordale, I'm sure they will be most thankful for your donation'.

Jake stood, shook hands with the man and thanked him for the refreshments before leaving the room and walking out of the Bank, next stop the Hospice he thought.

Chapter 90

Parking in the rear car park as he had done many times, it was with a sad heart he took the few paces to the front door and walked up to the Reception desk.

'Hello Mr Tordale how are you today' she asked whilst smiling weakly.

'Fine thank you, under the circumstances, could I have a word with the Director please'.

'Certainly sir, there is no-one with her at the moment, and I'm sure she will be pleased to see you' she lifted the receiver and explained that Jake wanted to have a word with her.

She appeared from a side office almost immediately and greeted Jake with a firm handshake, asking him to follow her through to her office.

As they sat down she asked Jake 'What can I do for you Mr Tordale?'

Jake bowed his head with emotion before explaining Stefan's wishes regarding the sale of his car and the proceeds of which would be donated to the Hospice. 'However' Jake started, 'as yet the car hasn't been sold, but I have a rough idea what it is worth, and am here today to give you $5000 dollars for all the hard work you do and the kindness you gave to Stefan for the short period of time he was here with you'.

She was taken aback before thanking him profusely, then asking him if it was a card payment, Jake smiled and said yes it would be.

She lifted the phone and asked the Receptionist to come in with the card reader to enable the gift to be given. Ten minutes later Jake was sat in his car, feeling that the last few hours had been most fruitful.

Starting the car he made his way back to start work on the rooms.

Two areas he had yet to visit were the Loft and Garage, but he would leave those for the next day, so started in the bedrooms, removing the bed coverings and folding them ready to take to the Laundrette that was close by for cleaning. He thought that if the sale of the house went through with the property she might retain some of the furnishings, but if not he would arrange for them to be removed by the house clearance firm he had already spoken too.

Part way through the tidying his mobile rang, looking at the screen he didn't recognise the number so answered with 'Tordale' as usual. The man on the other end said he was replying regarding the car that was for sale, as advertised in the local rag, and wondered if he could look at the vehicle today. He explained he was a car dealer, but that he was interested in the model for his own use. Jake said no problem, gave the address and the man Mr Wolenski said he would be there in an hour or so and looked forward to viewing the car. Change of plan for Jake, he had to look through all the paperwork spread out on the Dining Room table to locate the cars detail, and after pushing and pulling the numerous papers around he located the items he required and placed them on the kitchen worktop.

He returned to the bedrooms and completed the removal of the bedding, placing all the sheets, pillow cases etc in three large plastic bags and putting them in Stefan's room.

Returning to the kitchen he made himself a cup of coffee just as the front door bell sounded. On opening the door he was confronted by an extremely tall man with slicked back grey hair sporting a handlebar moustache, dressed in blue overalls, he introduced himself as Carl Wolenski 'I rang earlier about the car'.

Jake ushered him inside and explained who the car belonged too and that his friend had died quite recently. Wolenski didn't take a seat inside but appeared on edge, obviously waiting in anticipation to look at the car he urgently wanted to inspect. Jake noticed his obvious haste and suggested they look at the vehicle that was inside the garage. He collected the keys, opened the door and drove the car out onto the driveway, lifted the bonnet and boot together with all four doors for the man's inspection. He tried extremely hard to contain his excitement, but the more he inspected the car he couldn't contain himself as a broad grin spread across his face as his survey was complete. 'Lovely vehicle Mr Tordale, as I expected, what figure were you looking for. As you can see although I am a car salesman who would usually haggle for every penny, I really want this car'.

'Well Mr Wolenski, my friend spent his last few days in the local Hospice, and proceeds from the car are being given as a gift to the establishment, so I am asking $6000 dollars which I think is a fair price for such a beautiful vehicle'.

Wolenski rubbed his chin before looking at Jake and holding out his hand and saying, 'I'll give you $6500 my friend, as I feel the gesture you have put forward is worth an extra $500. Is cash OK?'

'Certainly, I take it that's your low loader down the road, you obviously wanted the vehicle and came prepared, if you would like to come inside I'll let you peruse the paperwork and issue you with a receipt. I've just made a coffee would you like one whilst you look at the paperwork?'

'That's most kind of you, that would go down nicely, I'll just pop to the van and get my briefcase, I won't be long'.

As they sat at the lounge table he quickly perused the documents whilst Jake counted the cash and wrote out a receipt. They finished their coffee's shook hands on the deal and paperwork was exchanged before Wolenski negotiated the car onto the back of the van and tied it in place. A quick exchange between them, before the van pulled down the road. Feeling quite pleased with himself he looked to the sky and thought of his late friend, who he thought would be smiling down at Jake's wheeling and dealing with this car salesman.

He was feeling quite peckish after the last couple of hours work and sales, so he rang the Mexican and booked a table for 8pm.

He was shown to his usual table by the friendly waiter and placed his food order accompanied by a large beer. As usual the fare was quite impressive and as he left there 2 hours latter he was glad of the walk back to the house to allow his food to digest.

Back at the house he made himself a coffee and sat and watched the News before retiring just before 11pm.

Chapter 91

Up bright and early the next morning he set too with clearing the loft, then he intended to attack the garage unsure what he would find in both areas.

The loft area was quite tidy, as Stefan had boxed up most things as they had been put up there, however he was surprised to see an area which had bundled items wrapped in newspaper behind the boxes as if the items had been put there first. He carefully placed them on the edge of the loft hatch, then after numerous treks up and down the ladder he had placed all the items on the Dining Room table. As he had brought them down he realised they were part of a Dinner service, then after removing all the paper and placing them, as if setting a table layout, he counted up the items and saw that it was a complete set for twenty four people. including terrines, dinner plates, side plates soup bowls, cups and saucers, plus condiment sets. He looked at the base of the plates and noted the maker. He looked on his mobile for details of the Company and was amazed to find that they had ceased trading in 1824, thus making them either Stefan's grandfather or great grandfathers initial purchase. The report online said that there were only two complete sets left in the World which Jake found astonishing, that his old friend had kept them in his loft for so long. On a whim he rang the man he met previously at Sotheby's in New York for advice. After the usual introductions Jake explained what he had discovered and his revelation as to what he had seen on Goggle regarding the items. He therefore needed further advice from Sotheby's as to its authenticity and possible value.

The Auctioneer asked Jake to forward photos to him and said he would look into it immediately and call him back.

Jake returned to the loft and brought down all the boxes, then just as he closed the hatch his mobile rang, on answering it he realised it was from Sotheby's.

The man on the other end of the line cleared his throat before saying 'Mr Tordale you have found a real gem there. I have contacted numerous colleagues regarding your enquiry, and am satisfied at how you described the set, that it is authentic.

What are your intentions next, as the valuation I am about to give you is a 'change in a lifetime' figure. The people interested in this set will be Museum's and wealthy Client's around the Globe who would purchase it as an investment, are you sat down sir?'

Jake looked bemused as he took the chair and replied 'Yes I am'.

'Well a conservative minimum starting figure would be $10,000,000 but I think it will make more. The only other set is held by a private collector in Russia, and I know that he would also be interested in this lot. So if you would like us to represent you again at a future Auction it would be my pleasure to carry out the sale for you and your friend'.

'Unfortunately its just me, my friend died recently without telling me that this was wrapped in paper up in his loft space, God only know's how long it has been up there. Yes I would like you to Auction this lot for me, would it mean that I'll have to travel to New York to deliver the set to you, if so when would the next Auction date be?'

'Mr Tordale due to the rarity and fragility of it I would be prepared to arrange for someone to visit your house, securely package the items and transport them back to New York for you. There would be no fee for this work as it would be taken out of our selling fee. If you would kindly send me your address and postcode I will arrange for a conservator to contact you as soon as possible to arrange for its collection, he will also issue you with a receipt for the product, how does that sound to you?'

'I'm absolutely gobsmacked as how such an event can happen in just a few hour's, I thank you for your help in this matter, and look forward to the date of the Auction which I will attend in person'.

'It's my pleasure Mr Tordale, items like this gives coming to work a real buzz, as most Auctions we carry out involve the usual run of the mill items, albeit expensive, but this is in a different league, quite intriguing and exciting, I'll be in touch, have a nice day'.

Jake just sat there with his mouth open wide, trying to take in what the Auctioneer had just told him. But then he realised that his dear friend Stefan was most likely oblivious as to this valuable dinner set that had been sat in his loft space for such a long period. He carefully wrapped up each item, but before he had finished he noticed that the newspaper was dated 14th February 1888. Yet another surprise for him, which confirmed how long it had been in his family. He wondered where Stefan's past family were from to have such a large service, but unfortunately he has no-one to ask now.

He shook his head to bring himself back to earth, then sent an email to Sotheby's explaining what he had just noticed, that the items were wrapped in paper dated 1888.

He busied himself with the boxes he had brought down, checking what indeed they contained and writing a list of their contents. Halfway through his mobile buzzed with a message, it read 'Please do not throw away the paper, it will confirm the dates as we hoped, and are in themselves quite valuable. I have contacted my conservator Mr. Graham Barnard and he will be in contact with you today, on your mobile'.

Enough for one morning he thought, then he set about making himself a sandwich and coffee for lunch. As he completed his meal his mobile rang, 'Tordale ' he answered, 'Hello Mr Tordale its Graham Barnard, Sotheby's Conservator, is it possible to arrange an appointment with you. I'm in New York at present but could be with you in 48 hours if convenient, say Friday at 11am'.

'That would be fine, would you require any packaging, or will you be bringing your own?'

'I'll bring everything I need with me, thank you for your concern. So I look forward to meeting you on Friday' then he rang off.

He spent the rest of the day clearing the loft space and itemising all that was left, then in the afternoon tackled the garage. Thankfully there wasn't a lot of items to sort out just the usual car related one's such as oil, shampoo, antifreeze, tools, together with a few items spilled over from the main building, such as blankets and sheets. Most things he would leave for Charlene assuming she would be purchasing the property, but he would get the 'House Clearance' man to remove the remainder of the unwanted items.

He sat down for a cup of tea at 5pm feeling extremely tired, but exhilarated at his loft find, then thought he would eat at another restaurant today and rang and booked a table for one at a local French eatery.

A shower and a change of clothing and he was ready for his short journey into town, the food there was delicious, accompanied and washed down with a bottle of red wine, making the aches and pains of his recent work appear to drift away.

Chapter 91

Back home just before nine, he switched on the TV to watch the news channel, and then the American football that followed it. However he had drifted off to sleep before the game started and came to about 10.30pm. Making the doors secure he wandered off to bed and slept like a log until 7.30am the following morning.

Chapter 92

Although the house was a shambles with marked boxes and disassembled furniture in various places Jake felt quite satisfied as he received the call early on Friday morning that the Conservator Graham Barnard had arrived in Washington and would be with him within the hour. He decided to remove the paper around the china and fold it ready for Barnard to take with the dinner set. By the time he had completed his task it left only fifteen minutes before the Conservator's arrival, giving him a short time to have breakfast and put the percolator on for coffee for them both.

Surprisingly when he arrived Barnard wan't the frumpy professor type individual that Jake expected, but a blond haired man of mid thirty's, heavily built and wearing a conservative dark suit, blue shirt and tie. After introductions had been made they unloaded his car containing various boxes and packing materials and assembled them beside the Dining Table. Jake offered his visitor a coffee before he commenced his work which he gratefully accepted. As they sat down Jake explained the discovery of the items on display and who they had belonged to and his unfortunate recent demise. Barnard made all the right noises in his sympathetic reply, before he started on the business that he had been tasked to perform. His eyes glistened as he viewed the array of items displayed on the table and made a lot of unintelligible noises to himself as he walked around making notes on his iPad. Taking a separate look at the newspapers that Jake had put in a pile on one of the chairs he nodded to himself before turning to Jake and exclaiming 'You have a wonderful set and associated papers here Mr Tordale, I think it best if I make a start on the packing. I don't wish to be rude but I would appreciate it if you don't hover whilst I am working as due to the astronomic value of the crockery, any distraction could seriously affect the sale and we wouldn't want that would we sir' he said with a smile to Jake.

'I appreciate your frankness Graham, I'll busy myself with tidying up the garage, shout if you need anything?'

Chapter 92

Three hours later and the garage as tidy as it required, Graham popped his head around the corner and told Jake that he had completed the boxing and all the items had been put into his vehicle. 'If you could just scan through the receipt sir, I'll be on my way' Barnard exclaimed.

Jake walked into the Dining Room, scanned the receipt his was shown, and signed the form, Graham tore off his copy and handed it to him. He then shook Jake's hand and said he was off, and that he hoped to be in New York early the next morning. After he left the building appeared to take on a hollow sound as if the property was totally empty, Jake mused, but he quickly adjusted his thoughts, and boxed up the items from the garage that he would be getting rid of. Feeling that he had accomplished a lot that day, he hoovered through the property in preparation for Charlene's visit the following day, then he sat down to make a few phone calls to the UK and Sweden to bring his family and Olivia up to date with the happenings in the US. With that done and with the time at 5pm he realised he hadn't eaten since breakfast and decided for a change he would order a takeaway meal from the local Chinese shop, as he didn't feel up to another trip to the Mexican restaurant he had eaten at for the past few days.

His meal arrived three quarters of an hour later, and as he sat at the kitchen table his thoughts returned to Australia which was where he had last consumed an oriental meal, but he had to admit that this was on a par with it. After putting the various containers back into the plastic delivery bag he deposited it in the rubbish bin, then sat with a glass of whisky to watch the local news channel, followed by a film, where as usual he missed halfway through the programme as he fell asleep.

Chapter 93

Up early the next morning he prepared again for the arrival of his dear friend and prospective house buyer Charlene, hoovering top to bottom and wiping down all surfaces and polishing the exposed woodwork. The boxes remained cluttering the Lounge for now until a decision was made about the sale, and if positive he would arrange for the House Clearance guy to collect everything that needed removing. Strangely for once he felt a little ill at ease regarding the sale, especially before Stefan's funeral. However by the time all the Legal paperwork had been sorted, things wouldn't be permanent for at least another three weeks or so. Running through his diary for the week ahead, he had final arrangements to make with the Funeral Directors which he would be doing on Monday. He would also ping off an email to the Shopkeeper that he had contacted previously in the precinct near Stefan's jewellery shop, to advise him of the date and time of the funeral and its location. He would also ask him to tell the other shop keepers if they could also spare the time to attend. On Tuesday if things progressed today he would be seeing the Clearance Man. Wednesday he needed to know how many people would be attending the funeral as he was going to ask the Mexican Restaurant if they could have the wake there with a buffet type meal and drinks which he would pay for. Thursday was the funeral and wake that would take up best part of the day. Just to make the week even more chaotic he had just received a text from Sotheby's to say that the Auction would be taking place between 10am and 4pm on Friday. However in retrospect at least it would tie everything up by the weekend, thus allowing him to book a flight home the following week, assuming everything went to plan that is.

With his notes complete he was taken out of his thought as the front doorbell rang, no doubt heralding the arrival of the lovely Charlene. He quickly rushed to the hallway and opened the door and welcomed her in with a kiss on the cheek.

'It looks like you've been busy since I called last Jake, and the house smells as if it has been cleaned from top to bottom. I hope it's not just for me?'

Jake chuckled before replying with 'To be honest I have two other people calling today who are interested in the property' then he was unable to contain himself before bursting out into laughter at the crestfallen look on her face which quickly changed to a broad smile.

'Shall I make us a coffee before we take a tour of the house?' he asked.

'Yes please, I hope we can have a simple day today, as this past week has been rather hectic and I have really looked forward to this weekend'.

'Take a seat in the Lounge and I'll be with you shortly'. It only took him a few minutes to put some biscuits on a plate and pour two cups of coffee from the already prepared percolator and then he returned to the Lounge.

They sat and chatted for a while whilst drinking and eating, then 30 minutes later they were up and walking around the property, with Jake explaining what all the boxes contained, whilst asking if she would be interested in any of the objects, as they visited each room. He explained that the loft space and garage were empty of any clutter, also the boxes were marked as such for the House Clearance man to check through after he had cleared everything. Charlene took a notebook from her handbag and wrote a few details in it as they walked around, obviously to discuss with Jake later.

Tour complete they went and sat back down in the Lounge with Charlene waiting for Jake to mention what figure he was going to say he required for the property. They stared at each other for a while before Jake asked her 'Well, are you interested my dear?'

She smiled, retrieved her notebook and asked if certain items would be staying with the property, namely the beds, wardrobes, kitchen equipment, carpets etc.

'Everything or whatever you require could stay its up to you my dear. But the most important question you wish to ask is how much for the property. I have consulted a local Estate Agent and he valued the house in its present condition at around $650,000 dollars, however I only asked for a rough figure as I had no intention of selling it to anyone but you, assuming you were still interested after our tour. I personally would prior to moving in, decorate the property from top to bottom, have new floor coverings and furniture which I would anticipate would cost in the region of $10,000 dollars or more depending on what you prefer. The structure of the house is in good condition, so I cannot think there would be any repairs required in that area. So taking everything into consideration the house could be yours for $495,000 dollars and I'll pay all the fees, how does that sound to you?'

Charlene stood and walked over to him and gave him a hug, which he assumed meant the deal was done, before she spoke with 'I was prepared to pay quite a lot more for it, as I am still tempted to retain my apartment and rent out the property here on a long lease. But let's just agree on the sale and get the paperwork moving. Now with the business out of the way shall we have a lovely lunch somewhere to celebrate?'

He gave her a renewed hug and a loving kiss before picking up his mobile and ringing the Mexican Restaurant to book a table for two. They made their way there and were greeted by the Manager as they walked in, he showed them to a table that Jake had sat at previously and asked them what they would like to drink, they both plumped for a bottle of local beer, to go with their exquisite lunch. Before he left Jake asked about the wake on Friday afternoon, the Manager was delighted to accept, and said he would lay on food for a minimum of thirty guests if that was OK. Jake also said that whatever drinks were consumed to be put on the final bill which he would settle before he left.

They had consumed quite a substantial meal together with another bottle of beer, then finished up with a glass of Tequila each, on the house. Then they walked slowly back and sat in the Lounge to finalise the details, and what in fact she wished to retain of the existing contents. With that done she took her leave, but promised to ring him in the morning to discuss as and when the paperwork would be ready for signatures, and funds forwarded.

The next day being Sunday, he thought he would treat himself to a little ride outside the boundary of the City and stop wherever the mood prevailed, then have a solitary seafood extravagant lunch. By a fluke, or by well informed guesswork he parked on a beautiful waterfront vista around noon, walked around 100 metres from the car and came across the most inviting Seafood Restaurant he could've imagined and booked a table.

The menu he was given was quite lengthy but his attention was drawn to the spider crab salad which he ordered, accompanied with a bottle of 2010 white wine from the Region. The meal was outstanding and after paying, he had quite a spring in his step as he walked back to the car. At that moment he decided to make a call to Sweden to attempt to speak to Olivia, and to his surprise she picked up after the usual various connections through umpteen exchanges. 'Good morning Jake Tordale' her delicious voice said 'What may I do for you today, and where in the world are you?'

'High gorgeous, I'm in Washington DC in the USA, and I thought of you so I could tell you what a delicious meal I have just consumed. It was a sumptuous spider crab salad with a fine white wine to accompany it, how are you my dear?'

A chuckle came down the line prior to her reply with 'I'm very well, involved in yet another drugs situation here in Sweden. Anyway when are you due back in the UK, this call will be costing you a fortune?'

'I just needed to hear your voice to enable me to engage my thoughts with our last meeting.and other things'.

'It's lovely to hear your voice too, give me a ring when you are back in Wisteria Cottage and perhaps we can meet up somewhere soon'.

'I should be home in a week and as soon as I unpack I'll give you a call, bye for now' and after her reply he disconnected the call.

Chapter 94

Monday morning arrived, the start of an extremely busy five days for him. A quick check of his emails, found that most of the shopkeeper's in the Mall had said that they would be attending Stefan's funeral and would also be at the wake. Therefore together with two people from the Hospice, the Solicitor, Bank Manager and Charlene it would make the event quite poignant for a man who was quite reserved during his lifetime, but loved all the same. He needed to visit the Funeral Home today to finalise the service, flowers etc, together with the number of cars required to follow the hearse, and of course to pay the balance of the Directors fee, he rang the office and arranged an appointment for 11am.

Whilst eating his breakfast he received another email, it was from Sotheby's confirming the safe arrival of the Dinner Service, there was also an attachment detailing the Auction Catalogue's Lots. He noticed that his was Lot No 185 (with a side note saying it should take place around 2.30pm local time). Although he was only interested in the sale of Lot 185, he thought he would be there at the start in case something took his fancy, that he could purchase and take back to the UK.

After his breakfast he gave Charlene a quick call to ask if she had decided on any items in the house she wished to retain, as he wanted to contact the House Clearance man to find if he could either call this afternoon or tomorrow to remove the boxes. Charlene had only just arrived at her office and listed the items she was happy to leave at the house. Jake then separated the items and put them into Stefan's old bedroom, leaving the remaining boxed items to be cleared away. He rang the man's number and he confirmed that he had a slot at 2.30pm today if that was convenient, and Jake thanked him saying he would see him later.That changed the dynamics of the day, however it also freed up Tuesday for him to do other things, so he rang the Solicitor and asked if he could make an appointment for tomorrow morning at 10.30am which he agreed. He also needed to speak to the Bank

Manager again, so rang him and made an appointment for mid afternoon around three.

Monday appeared to fly by as he sorted out all his appointments successfully, tying up a lot of loose ends ahead of his adjusted timetable. He visited the Mexican Restaurant to confirm numbers for Thursday's wake and paid a deposit for the food and drink. Whilst there he had a quick lunch before returning in time for the arrival of the House Clearance Man in the afternoon. With help from Jake the large panel van was loaded with all the boxes he wanted removed and the man was on his way inside two hours. Another tick for the week, successfully completed.

Walking back inside it now looked like an empty shell, however come the weekend that will be what it is, if all things being equal, he would be on his way back to the UK and the property, apart from the final legal requirements would belong to Charlene.

Chapter 95

His first appointment was at the Bank at 10.30am, therefore after a scant breakfast he busied himself with the vacuum cleaner and went through the house yet again, mainly for his own satisfaction. The Manager was as ever curious when he arrived and over the next 30 minutes he explained the latest situation with the house sale, an invitation to the funeral, and what could possibly happen with the Auction on Friday in New York. When Jake had completed his explanation, the Manager offered tea or coffee to his Client, who quickly accepted. When the drinks had been delivered, he was told of the way the various payments would be dealt with and suggested another account was opened for the transfer of funds to his Bank in England. Jake replied that if things went smoothly for the remainder of the week he would be booking a seat to return to the UK on Monday, explaining he would be visiting his Solicitor after leaving the Bank to discuss the legal bits and pieces with him, then he would arrange for a letter to be sent direct to the Bank once all the funds were confirmed. As Jake drank his coffee the Manager excused himself to obtain the relevant documents to open an additional account which he had to sign. After the paperwork was completed he was asked if he would be leaving an account open with the Bank, if so he suggested the one that would now be opened, thus leaving him access to Dollars when he next returned to the States. Coffee cup drained Jake stood and thanked the Manager for his time and said he looked forward to seeing him at the Service on Thursday, also if he had time for a spot of lunch at the Mexican Restaurant. They shook hands and Jake left the Bank quite elated as to how the meeting had gone.

Feeling a little peckish he thought he would kill two birds with one stone and wander over to the Mexican Restaurant, confirm numbers with the owner and have a spot of lunch whilst there, before his second meeting of the day with his Solicitor.

As he sat in his usual seat the Owner approached him and asked how things were. Jake explained that the expected numbers were less than he thought, but said to still cater for thirty as agreed. He then ordered his meal which the Owner said would be on the house, then the waiter walked by and took his order.

The meal as usual was exceptional and not to be outdone he left a $50 dollar tip which he gave directly to the Owner, saying he would see him on Thursday.

He then drove to the Solicitors office for his appointment, albeit he was 15 minutes early. However the Receptionist said that Jake was his only appointment and asked him to follow her to the man's office. After explaining his requirements, whilst reiterating his visit to the Bank Manager and his opening of an additional account, he mentioned the house sale, and forthcoming Sotheby's Auction on Friday. The Manager said how organised Jake was and so efficient. However he made notes of all the things that Jake had explained to him. Finally Jake invited him to the Funeral and wake on Thursday, which the man enthusiastically accepted. With all the business completed Jake left the office and returned back home. The remainder of the afternoon he spent thumbing through Stefan's extensive library and took down an interesting book on Judaism which he spent time reading before falling asleep in his favourite chair.

Chapter 96

Today being Wednesday he had a free day, so after a pleasant breakfast he riffled through the house keys to locate the smallest one there that was for the wall safe. Prior to Stefan going into the Hospice to told Jake not to open it until his death. But as the past few days had been so hectic it had completely slipped his mind, so open it was the next item to be ticked off his long 'things to do' list. Turning the key and opening the heavy door he was taken aback by the size of the safe internally, he felt around inside and removed a bundle of paperwork together with a stash of dollar bills, obviously for emergencies, then in the corner was a square shaped box. After emptying the safe he carried the collection and spread it out on the Dining Room table for further inspection. The paperwork contained death certificates of his parents, the deeds of the house, various letters he had received over the years, and a personal letter to Jake, which after reading it started the tears falling.The letter was quite long and expressed his thanks to Jake Tordale (the son he wished he had known for a longer period of time), and thanking him for everything he had done over the last few months, and hoped what he had been bequeathed would remind him of his late friend. It also highlighted and explained what was in the small box that he had founds at the rear of the safe, which he opened next. The box contained a large ring and the note in the letter said he wanted it taken to a certain place in Israel and handed to a custodian of Jewish artefacts that had been retrieved from various World War Two locations around Europe. The letter continued 'The money within the safe should cover your air fare from London, however you will unfortunately have to do a little digging to find the actual location in Israel, my apologies' Tears streamed down his cheeks again which he wiped away with a tissue. Counting the notes he was amazed at the total of $3,000 dollars. Having never been to Israel he asked Google for the details he needed and was surprised how easy it was to locate the premises, the information of which he transferred to the Notes App on his mobile. He then typed in flight details from London Heathrow to Israel, detailing flight times and decided he would return to Wisteria Cottage first to change clothes and do necessary chores before carrying out Stefan's last request and fly to Israel before attending to any urgent items at home.

So much had happened and Stefan's funeral wasn't until the next day. So he quickly returned all the items to the safe and locked the door. He then rang the Solicitor explaining that he had a copy of the Deeds to the house, and would he also have a copy, or was it lodged at the Bank. The Solicitor said he could do with Jake's copy and could he take it to the funeral tomorrow and hand it to him at the wake to save him coming to the office again, Jake agreed that that was a good idea.

Picking up his mobile he rang his daughter Clare and explained what the latest was in the States and that he would be travelling home 'hopefully' next Monday, however after returning to Wisteria Cottage he had to jet off to Israel to fulfil a request for his late friend. After a few huffs and puffs from his eldest, he asked how everyone was, all in good health he hoped, and she replied that everything was normal in Devon.

After a few more question and answers she rang off. He then decided to contact his Solicitor Bryan Fairfax to explain the latest developments with his life and hoping to see him on his return to the UK the following week. Feeling quite drained and needing a caffeine injection he put the percolator on and brewed a strong cup of coffee for himself. Sitting at the table his mind went through all the things for the funeral the next day and realised he had no formal clothing to wear, from dark suit, white shirt or even black shoes. So he quickly looked up Gents Outfitters locally and thankfully found one about a mile away. He rang the number and explained what he required and was informed that they had everything. He said he would be with them within the hour, whilst out he would also have something to eat and then return back 'home' later in the afternoon.

When he returned around 3pm he was satisfied with his purchases and pleasantly fulfilled with the repast he had had at a small cafe close the the Outfitters shop.

He hung up his new clothes and put his associated shirt, underwear, shoes and socks in the wardrobe ready for the next day, then sat down and watch a little TV before his usual nap overcame him. Waking up he opened his eyes to be blasted by a boisterous game of American football on the TV which he quickly turned off as he allowed his brain to wake up. Checking his watch he was amazed that he had slept for over 4 hours, and he felt hunger pains emanating from his stomach. Checking the freezer he noticed he was down to three frozen meals to pick from, so he chose a spaghetti bolognaise concoction with meat balls and put it in the microwave for the allotted time, whilst taking a can of lager from the fridge to accompany his meal. The ring of the microwave alerted him that his meal was ready, so he took that out, and with the beer to have at the Dining table.

Having finished his meagre meal he cleaned up and then sat in front of the TV again, to check on the local news and weather, before dialling in to an old film that was due its third replay to his knowledge, but he had enjoyed it before in the UK. The film finished at 10pm so he toddled off to bed for a good sleep to prepare him for the emotional day tomorrow.

Chapter 97

As he had had a long afternoon nap the previous day he was wide awake at 6am, but rather than doze off again he made himself get up and have a proper breakfast. He ate the remaining two rashers of bacon, the last egg, two hash browns and toast, with a cup of Earl Grey tea which went down a treat. He knew that the Funeral entourage would be arriving at 10am so he intended to be ready by 9.30am. He filled his wallet with notes for what he assumed would be the final bill at the Restaurant for the wake, then cleared away his breakfast dishes leaving the kitchen clean and tidy. He didn't anticipate anyone coming back to the house after the wake, as most would return to work, but you never know. He put the house Deeds into a plastic sleeve for the Solicitor, then went to the bedroom and put on his funeral attire. For once there was no need to polish his shoes as they were brand new. The shirt and suit fitted perfectly, then once his shoes and tie were in position he was ready to be collected for the short journey to the Synagogue.

There was a knock on the door at 9.50am and he was greeted by the Funeral Director himself who escorted him to the funeral car that would be following the hearse. He glanced at the flowers resting on Stefan's coffin as he walked towards the car and felt that his friend would have approved of his choice.

There were no other vehicles apart from the hearse and car so they made good timing and arrived at their destination on time. There was no-one outside the Synagogue so Jake assumed those attending were already inside the building. He followed the procession inside and took a seat at the front alongside the coffin. The service went smoothly with Jake in a daze throughout, he hadn't noticed any of the congregation and the amount of people there until the service was over.

But as he stood to follow the coffin out he was pleasantly surprised to see the numbers that were there, and nodded to them all as he made his way back down the aisle and out of the doorway. Stefan was to have a burial and he followed the Funeral ensemble to the graveside.

The committal was carried out by the Rabbi and completed in a quarter of an hour. The various mourners were congregating in the car park awaiting Jake's return to shake hands with him. He told each and everyone of them where the wake was located and for them to make their way there whenever they could. He located his Solicitor and handed over the Deeds of the house and thanked him for attending. He also said to Jake he would be calling to the Restaurant for a further chat with him and to have a bite to eat. Finally he shook hands with the Funeral Directors, thanking them profusely for their professionalism.

After speaking to everyone he realised that as he arrived at the Synagogue he had no way of getting to the Restaurant so quickly rushed over to the Solicitor, smiled and asked him for a lift, they both smiled before he led the way to his car.

Walking into the Restaurant the Owner came over and greeted him, then he asked if he would peruse the buffet table. As he viewed the mass of food displayed he thanked the man and said it was a marvellous variety of Mexican food and the 'show' would begin as soon as he had spoken to the gathering.

Jake turned and clapped his hands asking for the crowd to be silent, before he graciously thanked everyone for attending, and to help themselves to the buffet and order whatever drinks they wanted at the free bar. It was if he had fired a starter gun as all the guests stood and lined up for the buffet food, whilst those waiting behind walked to the Bar for drinks. After half an hour everyone was sat down enjoying their food and drinks. The Owner approached Jake and asked if everything was to his satisfaction, and Jake replied yes and thanked him profusely. The guests started wandering off after a couple of hours, but everyone of them stopped at Jake's table to shake hands with him. Last to leave was Jake who settled the bill, and then walked back to the 'house' to get a change of clothing, before sitting down with a cup of coffee. Feeling relieved that this day was drawing to a close he thought back to the time he had spent with Stefan, and all the enjoyable things they had had together over the past few weeks, his birthday meal, their trip to Niagara Falls, and the helicopter ride along the Grand Canyon. It was just a shame that he had not witnessed tomorrow's Auction of the hidden Dinner Set, But at least his friend was out of pain and at peace. He checked online to confirm the departure time for his flight to New York and decided on an early night as he would have to be at the

Chapter 97

Terminal around 7am. to collect his boarding card, then go through the routine of security checks.

Chapter 98

Armed with just his wallet, passport and carry-on bag he headed for the Terminal the next morning allowing himself to arrive around seven. Parking the hire car in the car park he walked into the building and headed for the ticket desk where he collected his reserved ticket together with a boarding card. Then through the various checks before sitting down in the Departure Lounge with a cup of Expresso coffee. Boarding was called just before eight and he followed the snake of passengers heading for the gate. The flight was on time and the arrival at New York was approximately an hour and a half later. Once landed he walked to the Hertz Office to pick up a hire car for the day, to get him too and from the Auction House, which should allow him to get there prior to the start of the anticipated sale. On arrival he looked for and located Sotheby's representative who he had spoken to recently and was presented with a Programme of Events brochure, then shown to a reserved seat near the front of the room. He looked through the brochure and ticked a few items that were of interest to him, noting the anticipated time that they would be auctioned. The items of interest were small in size, so they could easily be carried in his suitcase when he returned to the UK. The room was filling up quickly and Jake noticed the large screen behind the Auctioneer which gave full coverage for those at the back of the room together with everyone that would be watching online. The man banged his gavel dead on 11am introduced himself to the crowd and commenced the proceedings with Item One. The first item of interest was a quarter of the way inside the brochure and number 37, he therefore waited patiently as the smaller items were sold, mostly near the anticipated auction figure. Before he knew it Item 37 was introduced, it was a group of gold bracelets and chains the Auction figure was $700 dollars, he got his card out ready to bid on the lot.

The starting figure was $500 dollars, which quickly rose to $1000, Jake bided his time and as the bidding faltered at $1250 Jake raised his card for the next bid which was $1300, there was silence for around twenty seconds before the gavel was banged on the desk with the Auctioneer pointing at Jake as the winning bidder.

The next item he was interested in was Lot 50 a gold medallion, which going by the bidding so far time wise would be around 12.30pm, so he stood and left the room to collect a coffee from the cafe alongside the building. He was approached by his contact and asked how many items he had his eyes on. Jake smiled and said he was pleased with his first purchase and the next one of interest was a gold medallion in Lot 50. Jake finished his coffee and followed his companion back into the Auction House just as Lot 49 was announced. The item was an old Chinese vase, the description of which caused interest to Jake, then as the bidding commenced he was amazed as the starting figure went from $500 to $5000 dollars in seven bids. he opened the brochure to see the full description of the vase, and noted that it was around 600 years old and quite rare. The bids were mainly online, and when they slowed to a trickle he thought he would dip his toe in the water and put in a bid, he tried $10,000 as a taster, the people around him turned in amazement, before he was outbid again with a counter offer from China of $15,000.

His contact appeared all of a sudden and sat next to him. He asked if Jake knew the actual value of the vase, he said he didn't before saying $50,000. Jake stared at him aghast then raised his card and said $20,000, there was silence as the Auctioneer going once, twice then he raised the gavel and was about to say for the third and last time before another bid came on line which caused a buzz in the room, it was for $30,000. The Auctioneer looked at Jake, who shook his head leaving the card in his lap, so therefore the vase was off back to China. Lot 50 was an easy buy as it was only between Jake and one other, and he eventually purchase the medallion for $350.

The time wizzed by as he put in the occasional bid before realising he didn't really want the article, however he enjoyed the fun of the chase. Before he knew it the time approached 2.30pm, the anticipated arrival of his Dinner Service. Glancing at the brochure again he noticed it had a guide price under its description of $10 million dollars. Barely able to breath the Auctioneer outlined the description of the next item, its rarity, explaining that only two sets were in existence and the other was held privately in Russia. He had just completed the description when the telephone and online bidding started. The Auctioneer took a breath before saying loudly 'I have bids already for 10, 20, 30, 40, 50 million dollars, sorry I have numerous bids I'm unable to keep up with them, the latest bid is 60 million. The latest bid is also from Russia, do I have any further bids, otherwise I will sell to my latest bidder, going once, twice, third and last time, and the gavel went down with a loud bang to rapturous applause around the room.

Jake turned to his companion who shook his hand vigorously and said 'Happy'. Jake was flabbergasted before replying with 'Absolutely amazed, it's just a shame that Stefan is not here to witness the last 20 minutes, he would have been astounded, not knowing what had been sat in his loft for such a long period of time'. 'What time is your flight back to Washington Mr Tordale, only I would like to take you out for a meal if you have time to celebrate this momentous occasion'.

'I could catch a shuttle at seven, so it would be possible if we leave before the end of the sale, I'm in your hands as to a venue but the meal will be on me, I just have to pay for my purchases first'.

'OK, the remaining items will sell themselves quite easily without me being in the building so the restaurant I have in mind is only 20 minutes away from here, so once you have completed your transactions we'll take a trip in my car for a bite to eat, I hope you like wholesome American food, if so you're in for a treat'.

Following a delightful meal he was taken back to collect his car, and drove to the airport where he returned the vehicle before boarding his plane for the return flight to New York.

A quiet flight took just under an hour and a half, then he walked to the car park and drove back home, feeling unbelievably excited regarding the sale of the Dining set.

He had arranged with the Auction house to forward the payment to the Bank in Washington, however he had brought his purchases, the chains, bracelets and medallion back with him on the plane. As he pulled into the driveway he wanted to celebrate, however there was no-one close that he could share the news with so he decided to have a few glasses of Stefan's whiskey and celebrate alone, but toasting his dear departed friend for his luck.

Chapter 99

The Bank was open until noon, so he rang early and spoke to the Manager regarding the sale of the house, but mainly to inform him of the huge amount that would soon be deposited into the account from Sotheby's in the next few days or so. Unfortunately however, he would be returning to the UK on Monday so he asked him if he would forward an email once he had confirmation that the funds had been paid into the account. He then rang Charlene and asked if she was available today for a catch up, unfortunately the number went unanswered, so he left a voicemail asking her to call back when she could spare the time. A strange feeling crept over him as he realised that he had become a multi-millionaire overnight, therefore when he returned home he would have to tweak his Will that was lodged with his Solicitor. Also before he made the trip to Israel he would need to have a 'pow wow' with his family in Devon. He shook his head and put the financial situation to one side just as his mobile rang, it was Charlene returning his call. 'Sorry I missed your call Jake, how are things?'

'I have just had such a hectic week, the details of which I would like to share with you later if you have a spare hour or so?'he asked.

'Certainly Jake, I'm in the office at the moment but could meet you for lunch, say twelve at mine, then we can go on from there'.

'OK, see you then' he replied, and disconnected the call.

He then dialled another number, to Sweden and it was answered after a minute or so with 'Nice to hear from my favourite man from England, where are you calling from today?'

'Hullo Olivia, I'm in Washington still, but will be returning to England sometime on Monday, since I've been in the States I've made a decision to purchase a Villa in one of the Greek Islands and wondered if you would like to accompany me to locate one in the Autumn. I know working for the Police isn't an easy occupation to take time off from, however I'm giving you at least a few months advance notice of my intentions'.

There was a pregnant silence before she spoke again with 'How long do you anticipate being away for in the Autumn a week or two?'

He chuckled before replying with 'Shall we say two, then if I see one I like, I could buy it and we could stay on for whatever time there's left of the two weeks'.

'Sounds like a wonderful plan to me, I'll book two weeks holiday as soon as you give me a date, so I'll wait to hear from you, speak soon, bye'.

As it was approaching 10.30am he thought he would have a quick cup of coffee and once he had finished it would be almost time to trundle off to meet Charlene.

He had five minutes to spare when he pulled into the rear car park to the Apartment Block and rang Charlene's mobile to say where he was, she said 'I'm ready, I'll be down in a sec'. A short while later she swept into the passenger seat with her intoxicating perfume enveloping the cars surroundings. She was dressed in a knee length red skirt and white blouse under a thick puffer jacket.

She leant over and kissed him on the cheek.

'Where are we off to today Big Boy' she asked.

'As usual, I'll leave it to you where we dine, but could we make it an upmarket establishment today, as I have something to celebrate' he said with a shy smirk.

'I know just the place, it's usually quite busy, however as we are out of season I think we'll be lucky today. Just to make certain I'll give them a ring and book a table' she scrolled through her mobile until she found what she wanted, and made the call. The table was booked for 20 minutes time, and she anticipated that it wouldn't take long to get there and park up, so off they drove. He followed her directions until he was shown a car park to the rear of an upmarket establishment, obviously somewhere that she had been previously. As they walked through the door they were approached by a smartly suited waiter, he welcomed Charlene and Jake with what appeared great delight. Jake could see the man's brain wizzing at 100mph until he blurted out with 'So nice to see you again Madam, its our pleasure that you have returned to our humble restaurant, table for two I presume'.

With the pleasantries at an end they were shown to a table for two, which was tucked away from all the other diners. They were each given a menu and the man asked then what they would like to drink, Jake asked for the drinks menu and plumped for a bottle of South African 2010 red wine to accompany their meal. When the wine was placed on the table, opened and a small amount poured into Jake's glass, he did the honours. swilling it around in his mouth before nodding to the waiter who then proceeded to fill both glasses, then he took his leave giving them time to choose their meals. The extensive menu covered all types of meat, prepared in different ways, Charlene was amused at Jake's reaction to the menu so to help him she said 'I'm going for the fillet steak with a green salad together with a side of king prawns, which I think you say in Europe is Surf 'n Turf', what do you fancy?'

He closed the menu before replying with 'I am celebrating today, so I am ordering a Tomahawk steak which is becoming popular in England, but it is very expensive there, however the sides are a problem, so I think I'll have french fries, onion rings and a peppercorn sauce for the steak'.

'Crikey Jake, you're in America now, so I hope you realise the size of meat that will come to the table, however if its too much for you we can ask for a takeaway bag and you can finish it for supper' she answered with a smirk.

The waiter came to the table five minutes later, replenished their glasses and took the food order. He asked how they liked the steaks, and confirmed that the meat would be finished at the table, so they could say when the meat was cooked to their liking.

Jake's eyes nearly popped out of his head when his steak arrived, it was massive, however he was feeling quite peckish at the moment and the aroma that invaded his nostrils almost made him drool. Watching the waiter perform, was like watching a surgeon, and once they were happy with the cooking he plated up for them. He bowed and said 'Enjoy your meals, if there is anything you require please let me know'.

Jake thanked him and started on his gargantuan plate of food before everything started to cool down. No words were exchanged for the next three-quarters of an hour as they slowly demolished their meals, Jake had managed around 60% of the steak but had finished all the trimmings, Charlene thoroughly enjoyed her's and all that was left on her plate was a leaf or two of the salad.

The waiter had been hovering in the background for the previous minute or two and approached the table as they placed the cutlery on the plates. He asked them if everything was OK with their meals, looking at Jake waiting for his answer to the steak. Jake turned and smiled at him, then asked for a takeaway bag for the meat, he explained how his stomach was full of the most delicious steak he had ever tasted.

'Could I tempt you for something off the dessert menu to cleanse your taste buds, a sorbet or something similar?'

Jake looked at Charlene who nodded and said 'Yes please, could we look at what's on offer'.

Jake excused himself and visited the Mens Room, mainly to move around the meat he just consumed, as however delicious it appeared to him his body wasn't used to this excess, he returned to the table five minutes later and sat down whilst being handed the desert menu by his companion.

'Have you decided on anything my dear?' he asked her politely.

'I must say it all looks lovely, but I'm going to take the waiter's advice and plump for a lemon sorbet'.

'Excellent choice Charlene, I think we'll make that two'.

The gap between completing the main course and the sorbet took a while so Jake decided to run through the latest events since their last meeting. The explanation took more than fifteen minutes, and as Jake looked at his companion throughout, her jaw was dropping open more and more, until he stopped his rhetoric to tell her to close her mouth, afraid she would dislocate it.

Once he had finished she said 'I can see why we are having this sumptuous meal together to celebrate your enormous windfall, as well as dining with your favourite lady I assume?'

'If I'm honest Charlene, I've been in a daze since Thursday, what with Stefan's funeral and wake, then my flight to and from New York the following day which culminated in the enormous amount of money that the Dining Set made at the Auction, I am all of a sudden a multi-millionaire, which although nice takes one's life to a different level'.

She smiled at him just as the waiter arrived with their sorbet's. Whilst they consumed the refreshing and cold dessert Jake intermittently continued speaking.

'My first thought are towards my family, they of course will be well looked after, then I intend to make donations to various Charities that have been helpful to me over the years. I intend to purchase a property in the Greek Islands to enable my family and friends to use in lieu of a package holiday. There are also friends I worked with, over many years in the Building Industry who many moons ago I said if I ever came into some money I would buy a nice watch as a memento, for each of them. Once all that has been done I intend to settle down in my lovely house in Dorset during the summer months, then jet off to Greece for the winter months and relax for however long I have left'.

As they completed their sorbets Charlene patted Jake on the hand and replied with 'You deserve everything that has come your way Jake, you are a kind and considerate person and I hope to enjoy part of the time you have available, if and when you visit the States in the future'

'You can certainly depend on that my dear, I would like that a lot, visiting you in the future and would also like you to accompany on various trips assuming you will be able to fit me in'.

'Perhaps when the house has been completely refurbished you could spare a week or so to return and give the place your blessing and we could spend some time together'.

'Sounds like a plan, however when I have returned home I have a few things to sort out, then I am off to Greece to look for this property I'll be purchasing. A friend of mine in Australia will need a bit of my time as she is getting married in the Summer and has asked me to give her away, so that will be ten days or so. I thought I was retired, however I have the busy life of a full time employee at the moment, once the main items are out of the way I'll be able to reschedule my life and compartmentalise it with a tidy diary'.

After the meal he dropped Charlene back to her Apartment and bade her goodbye for now.

Chapter 100

Sunday was a strange day, he had sorted all he could do within the property, the wheels were in motion with the sale to Charlene, the Bank and Solicitor were in the know of everything that needed attending to regarding the sale and the influx of funds that would be forthcoming whilst he was back in the UK. Therefore the only outstanding item for him was to pack up everything ready for his return flight to the UK tomorrow morning.

Feeling a little lost, he went through each room yet again together with the garage in case he had missed anything. The safe was empty, a last check in the loft space confirmed that it was free of any storage, which just left the fridge and freezer to clear out and use whatever food was available for his last day in Washington. He separate a few bits and pieces that he could dine on this evening and for breakfast first thing the next day, and put the rest in the recycling. For lunch he would visit the Mexican restaurant for the last time and enjoy a sumptuous meal from its extensive menu, and have a chat with the owner, thanking him again for his hospitality during the Wake and for all the times he had eaten there. He walked into the establishment just before noon and the waiter directed him to his table that he had eaten at for the duration of his visit to the States. Deciding on a set menu with a little extra on the side, he accompanied his meal with a couple of beers. The Owner called at his table for a quick chat, and Jake explained that he was leaving early the next day to return to the UK, a look of disappointment spread over the Mexican's face, he left Jake's table before returning with a bottle of Tequila and two shot glasses, and sat down next to Jake. He poured two shots and toasted Stefan. refilled the glasses and toasted Jake, thanking him for his generous custom, and looking forward to his return to Washington in the future. Jake left half an hour later feeling a little tipsy, as the Tequila continued to flow until Jake asked for the Bill, only to be waved off with the comment 'No charge my friend I look forward to seeing you again soon'.

The walk back took a little longer than his walk there, however he had a warm glow within him due to the kindness that everyone had shown him recently. Feeling a little melancholy he whistled as he walked back, oblivious of all around him, and before he really noticed he was walking up the driveway.

He locked the front door after he got inside and knew that he would have to have forty winks, as the alcohol began to envelope his brain but also leaving him feeling warm and comfortable. He slept for three hours, then as he came to he realised he would have to do the normal things when you leave a property, such as, disconnect all the services, inform the various Suppliers that the house would be vacant. He would then have to deposit the keys with the Solicitor for safe keeping until Charlene's people sorted everything for her.

With all that done he sent Charlene a text message to confirm that the keys were with his Solicitor and if any further inspections were required she was to contact them for access.

He rang home and spoke to his eldest Clare to check on the family, to confirm he would be returning to London the following day and would ring her again when he walked through the front door of Wisteria Cottage. To keep her up to date, he ran through a list of what urgent things he had to do during the following weeks, such as a visit to Israel, Australia for his friend's wedding and a visit to Greece during the Autumn to purchase a property that will be made available for family holiday's. However he said he would fill the family in of all the details, once he visited Devon, which would be his first priority.

Chapter 101

Incredible that over the last few years of his hopping around the World, it had made him quite blasé regarding the intricacies of booking in for a long haul flight, however he felt almost nervous this morning, as he scrolled through everything he had encountered since he had arrived in the States. Now with nothing left to nibble in the fridge, or cupboards he made do with a pot of coffee knowing full well that he could indulge in the First Class Lounge, of the delights that this luxurious room held.

He dropped off the Hire car at the Hertz yard and cleared the account, before making his way inside the Terminal building for some considerable time. He collected his First Class Ticket and boarding card, put his cases through the usual area and made his way to Passport Control and on to the Lounge area for a nice breakfast. The room was reasonably full of Client's waiting for their plane's to take then to various locations, as he found a table away from the main throng he was approached by a waiter who asked what food he required. Jake salivated at the menu in front of him and ordered Pancakes and bacon with a side of mushrooms and tomatoes, accompanied with a large black coffee. The food was wonderful and as he washed it down with the coffee he did a quick scan of the room in case anyone caught his eye. Over the past couple of years working for the Secret Service, it had become the norm to carry out this as a matter of course, however no-one was of interest, so he settled back into the plush seat and bided his time until the call for boarding was announced.

Climbing the stairs to the huge aircraft and settling into his First Class seat he felt a little moved at leaving the States, but he was really looking forward to his adorable but small picturesque cottage in central Dorset, and then having a proper pint of beer at The Swan whilst having a chinwag with the Landlord, Bert.

But before that he had the long journey back to Blighty to contend with, then once on terra furma to leave Heathrow, London, and continue the drive back to Dorset. The lift off was on time, and as the aircraft levelled out at its cruising height, the Steward popped his head around to see if there was anything his passenger required. Jake informed him that he would be sleeping for an hour or so, but placed his food and drink order some two hours into the journey. As he travelled frequently his routine kicked in and after five minutes he was sound asleep. A gentle nudge alerted him that he was still on an aircraft, and as his eyes opened he became aware of a young air hostess stood over him. 'Sorry to disturb you sir' she whispered 'only your meal is ready if that's convenient'. He sat up, rubbed his eyes and replied with 'I'm dreadfully sorry, I was away with the fairies, thank you for waking me'.

She handed him a tray with his food plates on and asked if he required any drink apart from the coffee he had ordered. He thought for a few seconds and replied with 'Half bottle of red wine please'.

She turned and walked quickly away to collect his drink and glass.

The meal was superb and washed down with the red wine he felt ready for anything, also the nap did him the world of good, and left him prepared for the day ahead.

On landing he followed the other First Class passengers through the rigmarole of Passport Control and baggage collection, then made his way outside the Terminal to catch the Shuttle Bus back to the onsite Hotel. He called into Reception to collect his car key and pay the parking fee then deposited his baggage into his Lexus. A quick sigh as he got into the driver's seat, then he took a few deep breath's, started the engine and pulled out of the car park on his way back to Dorset.

Pulling into his driveway a while later, he felt quite melancholy looking at his quintessential house in the depth's of the South West of England and realised how lucky he was to have such a wonderful family, a good set of friends, and in a position now, thank's to his dearly departed friend Stefan of being in a situation to enjoy life to the full as well as setting up his family in Devon. He quickly got out of the car, put the key in the front door and slowly pushed it open, as he imagined there would be a pile of mail waiting for him on the coir yarn mat inside. True to his thoughts there were a lot of envelopes that had built up since he had been away. He strode over them and turned off the alarm before it sounded at the local police station. Turning to face the telephone table he noticed the blinking light heralding a missed call, or he anticipated calls that would have to be answered later. He returned outside and brought in his luggage which he took up to his bedroom, then made his way downstairs to make himself a cup of coffee. He picked up all the mail and put the accumulation on the Dining table, and slumped down in a chair.

Sipping his coffee occasionally he separated the wanted from the 'unwanted mail', which were mainly flyers, or begging letters, so he set about opening the 'need to know' ones.

The first letter was from Maureen Donaldson, saying she would like a call from him when he was available for a quick catch-up, he put that to one side. Another envelope had an Australian stamp on it, so it was either Mrs Choo or his Police lady friend referencing her upcoming wedding, so he quickly slid open the paper and pulled out the note left inside, it was indeed from the latter. Explaining she had fixed a date for the wedding, and assuming he could attend the date was the 15th August. He made a note on the envelope to send a reply when he was settled. The third envelope was from his Solicitor, who wanted to know when he wished to arrange an appointment. Finally there was a hand written envelope, the writing of which he wasn't familiar with. On opening it, he was surprised to find it was from his old colleague George Adams, he quickly read through the wording which asked if Jake was in London anytime soon could he possible meet up with him for a catch-up. There was his home address in the top right hand corner, and underneath a mobile number for his mate. He scribbled a few notes on the front of the envelope and put all the letters to one side. The next thing on the agenda was to see what phone message he had on the answerphone. There were only three, the first was from Bert, Landlord of the Swan, saying he missed him and was looking forward to his return from the States. The second call was from his Bank Manager, asking him to arrange a meeting as soon as possible. The third and last was from his youngest daughter Sharon, hoping everything was OK with his visit to the USA, and that she was looking forward to seeing him when he visited Devon. After his flight back and the car journey from London he felt quite tired but also longing for a pint of local beer from The Swan, so he went upstairs and emptied his cases, changed outfits, then locked up and walked down the lane to his local pub. He was greeted warmly by Bert as he approached the Bar and his glass had been poured by the time he opened his mouth to say 'It's glad to be back'. Although it was only just approaching five there were a number of regulars already drinking and there were nods all round when Jake turned to face them. Bert was itching for information from Jake, so therefore asked the obvious question, 'Where have you been this time Jake?'

'I've just come back from Washington, my friend there unfortunately passed away, and I had to organise the funeral and wake, together with selling his car and house, so not a happy visit if I'm honest'. Bert realised his error so he turned and walked along the Bar to serve another customer.

Jake's pint went down like nectar and it was quickly refilled by the Landlord, he looked around to see if he could buy anyone else a drink, however there wasn't anyone there that were part of the 'Clan' that he was a member of. Bert asked if was staying for a bite to eat, and offered him a menu, and pointed Jake to the 'Specials' board on the adjoining wall.

'You've twisted my arm Bert, I'll have the pork tenderloin please' he replied, glad to have some good old British food for a change.

The food as usual was plentiful and tasty, and Jake demolished the lot and washed it down with the remnants of his second pint. A while later as the Pub started filling up he bade farewell to Bert and made his way back home. As he walked into the Hall he began to feel the beginnings of 'jet lag' setting in, so he walked to the kitchen and made himself a cup of cocoa, sat down and watched a little TV, then off to bed for a good night's sleep.

Chapter 102

He was in a deep sleep before the throbbing sound of the ringtone on his mobile stirred him awake. He groggily answered 'Jake Tordale', and he was surprised to hear the voice of Henry Bates with 'Good morning Jake, how the devil are you?'

'Fine thank you sir, I've just got back from the States, and as you can most likely hear a little tired, after being hit by the dreaded jet lag'.

'Sorry about that old man, I just wondered if you had heard from George Adams at all?' he asked quizzically.

'Strangely enough, as I opened my mail yesterday afternoon, there was a letter from George asking me to visit him the next time I'm in the Capital, why do you ask sir?'

'Well, I also have had a similar letter asking me to make contact with him, I rang his mobile this morning however it went straight to voice mail, so I was a little concerned regarding his welfare. I sent over an operative but the house was locked up and there was no sign of life at all. The gardens which I know he kept well maintained, are neglected and the lawns are overgrown, as if no work has been done there for a number of weeks. I last spoke to him in January to check on his welfare and he appeared a little low, however as we said goodbye I could sense a little reticence on his part, like he had more to say, but perhaps I'm being paranoid'.

Jake was taken aback at these remarks and countered with 'I'll give his number a call after this and then try again this evening if I hear from him I'll give you a call, sir'.

'Thank's Jake, how are you by the way, and what have you been up to in the States?'

He smirked at Henry's inquisitive questions, then explained all that he had been up to in America together with the demise of his dear friend.

As he finished his story he said goodbye to Henry and got out of bed to carry out his ablutions and get some much needed breakfast. He rang the Solicitor's office to confirm his appointment with Bryan

Fairfax for 11am today, then decided to visit the supermarket and butcher's to top of his cupboards and fridge/freezer with food.

Opening the garage door he removed the covers from his beloved MG., put the key in the ignition and started the 'old dear' to give her a run into the village. He parked the car outside the butcher's, approached the counter and gave a list of his requirements to the owner who smiled at him before saying 'Been off on your travels again Jake and looking for a top-up, as usual, it will take me an hour to sort things out, so I assume you have to go to the supermarket as well, so I'll see you back here later'.

'Thank you Frank, it's good to be back home again to enjoy good old English food' he replied and walked along the road to the supermarket. Twenty minutes later with a full trolley of goodies, he opened the boot of the car and placed all his purchases in, then returned the trolley to the covered area where they are stored. Checking his watch he noticed he had timed it just right as the town hall clock struck 11am, time for him to dash to Bryan Fairfax for his appointment.

He opened the door saying, good morning to Joan as he walked in, as just at the moment Bryan walked out of his office carrying a piece of paper which he handed to Joan, 'Come on in Jake, how are you today?'

'A little weary to be honest Bryan, I returned from the States yesterday afternoon after a busy time there'.

Bryan smiled, then Jake explained what had happened whilst he had been in America, and the wealth that he had received from his dear departed friend, together with the surprising figure he had got for a rare dinner service that Sotheby's in New York had Auctioned for him. 'That's why I think I need to tweek my Will, what do you think Bryan?'

'It's really up to you Jake, your Will is fairly fluid with all your goods and chattels split between your two children. If you like we could put an addendum itemising amounts to each if you like. However as your eldest daughter is also your Executor I think a generalisation on an addendum would be sufficient. When you have the details sorted just pop me an email and I'll address it for you, would you then like a copy for the Bank, if so I'll give you a copy'.

Jake stood and thanked him saying a copy would be fine, they shook hands, then he left. Walking back to the butcher's he assumed enough time had passed for Frank to have sorted out his order and he wasn't disappointed as the cheery man smiled as he walked into the shop. 'You love your meat Jake, there's enough here to feed the 'five thousand,' but I suppose your freezer's empty after your trips away. That'll be £120 please sir'.

Jake handed over his card, and Frank helped him to the car with four heavy bags. There was just enough room for all the shopping in the boot, he thanked Frank, got in the drivers seat and made his way home.

He drove the MG back into the garage, then emptied the boot of his purchases and put everything away. Time for a coffee and to try George Adam's mobile, no reply so he left a message for him.

Next on the Agenda was a scroll through the internet at properties for sale in the Greek Islands. As he tapped on the first listing, the variety of available places for each island was quite extensive, so he refined his interest to properties 'close to sea, detached villa's with swimming pool and four bedrooms. The search requested 'price range', Jake smiled to himself as he was now in a position to put a figure normally out of range of the ordinary punter. So he typed in one to two million pounds, then all of a sudden the page changed to 'fantasy' properties, the likes of which he would never have considered previously. For that amount his options were enormous, the first site he found was on the island of Mykonos, where he had visited last year. There were at least ten that looked interesting so he made a note of the Agents details and sent off an email requesting written information, explaining that he would be visiting the Island shortly and would be making an offer on at least one of the properties. A reply followed within 30 seconds, saying that details would be sent to him in the post and that they were looking forward to his visit. That was that, he would send off a note to Olivia explaining that their holiday would be in the Greek Island of Mykonos, and if she could advise him when she was available he would book their flight tickets. Checking the time he rang his eldest Clare saying he would be coming to Devon the next day Saturday, to have a chat with the family about his latest visit to the USA and his forthcoming movements over the next month or so. Thankfully she answered the call and said she would arrange for her sister and the children to be at her's by noon the next day.

Chapter 103

Before he left for Devon the next morning he rang George's mobile once again, but it again went to voicemail, feeling extremely concerned now for his friend, he sent off a text to Henry Bates expressing his concern and suggested that the Police should be informed and treat him as a missing person. He then put a few bits and pieces in the MG of items he had purchased in Washington for the family then set off for Devon.

He pulled into his daughter's driveway at five minutes to twelve, noticing that the others had parked further up the road, there was Sharon's truck, Laura's car was further away, thus assuming that the family were gathered in the house, ready for his arrival.

As he turned off the engine the front door opened, and Clare stepped out to meet him, just as he opened the boot to retrieve a shopping bag.

'Hi Dad' she said kissing him on the cheek, 'Good journey on the M5, I expect you fancy a cup of tea before you tell us all what the meeting is about'.

He smiled before replying with 'I'm gasping for one actually, is everyone here?'

'Yes, they're all in the front room awaiting your visit with anticipation, what you have to say, I'll put on a brew before you start'.

Jake walked into the Lounge and kissed his younger daughter and the three grand children before taking a seat in the empty lounge chair that was available for him. Everyone appeared in good health, then Clare joined them with Jake's cup of tea. She sat on the arm of the chair alongside her father and waited for Jake to explain the reason for his visit today.

He took a couple of sips of his tea before placing with cup on the table close by, cleared his throat and started his narrative regarding his recent trip to the States. Ten minutes or so later you could have heard a pin drop in the room, as all his family were taken aback by what they had just heard. Then he continued explaining what he intended doing with the money that he had inherited from his dear friend, saying that he had changed his Will but as soon as the funds were in his UK account he would be transferring some of the money to each and everyone in the room.

Rather than go through what each of them would soon be receiving he had written the amount each would be getting on a piece of paper, he therefore handed an envelope to each of them with a message on the front saying 'DO NOT OPEN UNTIL THE FOLLOWING DAY'. Then the chatter started between his siblings as they gathered around to kiss and hug him. He continued with 'I have never thought, or had this amount of money that is heading my way, so rather than wait for my demise I wanted to see how you all would react to an amount of money that we all dream of, please think before you spend, however I trust this will make life easier for all of you'.

Clare smiled at him and just said 'I knew you were up to something Dad, when I spoke to you on the phone, but I didn't expect this, thank you very much indeed'.

'There is one other important item I have to explain to you all, I'm off to Greece in a few weeks time, looking for a property to purchase, that can be used by all the family. I'm looking at a few properties that have six bedrooms, a swimming pool and bags of space, so you can all go together or if you want at separate times, all you need to pay for would be food and drink, and of course the air fare. The thing with the Greek Islands is that the weather is superb almost throughout the year. So you could visit out of season or during the main holiday times to suit yourselves. As soon as I have completed my purchase I'll send through photos and details as to its location. Finally at the Sotheby's Auction I attended in New York I was fortunate enough to have the winning bid for a bunch of gold chains and bracelets, I have them in the car, there is enough for everyone but I'll leave it to each of you to choose an item that suits you. 'Clare if I could stay over tonight, perhaps we could all go out for lunch tomorrow, I was so impressed with the pub in Ipplepen when I lived in Devon, may I suggest we go there for a Carvery lunch. Then once we have all finished our meal, I'll head back to Dorset'.They all agreed that it would be a lovely idea, and said they would all look forward to eating together, and they would make their individual way's to the Pub to arrive at noon the next day. Sharon and Lottie excused themselves then saying they were off to the stables, Laura and Jake followed shortly after. Leaving Jake and Clare to chat on their own, with her faithful Goldie nuzzled up against Jake's leg.

Clare suggested fish and chips for tea when her husband got home from work, Jake felt quite delighted with that suggestion, saying he would take the car and pick up whatever food they fancied. He spent the afternoon watching the sport on the TV, whilst Clare took the dog for a walk, before coming home and carrying out a bit of ironing and general housework. The Chippy opened at 5pm and he decided he would be there for the freshness of the cooked food, which would also give him time for a natter with the Owner who had been at the property for nigh on forty years. As he walked into the shop there were already two people in front of him, but they were only after a portion of chips, whereas his order was quite large, he asked for three large cod with medium chips and three portions of curry sauce, and three gherkins.

Whilst it was being prepared more people arrived and he was unable to have a proper chat, so collected the large bag, walked back to the car park and drove the MG back to his daughter's house. The food went down a treat with an accompanying brew of tea, twenty minutes went by before three empty plates were taken out to the kitchen to wash.

All three of them felt bloated and Clare laughed as both men were snoring after half an hour, so she watched a game show on the TV as they slept.

Chapter 104

Jake was up bright and early the next morning and thought he would take the dog for a walk, he left a note on the kitchen counter for Clare explaining where he had gone and what time he had left. They strode up the road towards the recreation ground, where back in the day he had played cricket from 'schoolboy to manhood' until he was lucky enough to play for his County. He let the Goldie off and she ran around, jumping with joy as she was free to do whatever she liked, this early there was no-one else there so Jake let her run around to her heart's content for 20 minutes or so, until he called her to heel and put her lead back on. They then walked out the gate, before Jake decided to walk down the lane and into the woods called 'Heala' where he had spent many an hour in his youth. He passed a number of early dog walkers, however no-one he knew, so he just spoke the necessary pleasantries to them as they walked by.

Although this was a roundabout way back to the house he was glad of the exercise as it helped digest last night's fish supper and he knew that the dog was also enjoying the walk. A little while later, he opened the kitchen door, where Clare was preparing breakfast and was greeted with 'Have a nice walk Dad?. I don't suppose you had anything to eat before your walk'

'No, as it was such I nice morning I thought I'd give my 'friend' a nice run out and enjoy the lovely fresh Devon air'.

The one thing above all that Jake liked to invade his nostrils was the smell of cooked bacon which Clare was preparing for breakfast. 'I'm doing bacon sandwiches Dad, as we will be having a large lunch and after last night's fish supper I think it best to have something light, is that OK'

'Fine with me my love, I thought to myself as I opened the back door, that the one thing I love is the smell of bacon, there is only two things to rival it, and that is first, freshly baked bread from Heywood's Bakery and freshly ground coffee from Edgar Reed's shop' Jake smiled as he sat at the kitchen table. It was not only Jake's nostrils that were invaded by the smell of bacon, but Mike was calmly sat at the table awaiting his breakfast with knife and fork in hand. Jake joined him at the table after wiping the dog dry, and asked if he was as hungry as he looked. He replied 'Best day of the week, bacon sandwich for breakfast and no work ahead, marvellous'.

As Clare brought in the food and drinks they tucked in with Becky sat next to his master just in case some food should 'fall' off the table. At breakfast unfortunately she would be disappointed. Knife and fork down the conversation returned to Jake's good fortune and recent windfall, as his son-in-law asked what his intentions were for the future.

'Well' answered Jake 'I have adjusted my Will to take into account this latest item, and as soon as the funds are available I will be transferring useful amounts to each family, so there will be no need for anyone to worry about money problems for the rest of their lives. I would trust that a lot of thought would go into the amount that you receive, and its not spent on anything other than good for the family as a whole. However that is up to each individual's requirements and expectations. Unfortunately you hear these days of people winning the Lottery and splurging their money on fast cars, huge Estates, and God forbid drugs, and their world falls to pieces in a matter of years. However I don't think my family would go down that line. Anyway enough of that negativity, I'm going to put a few things in the car, then once we have eaten our lunch I'll be heading back to Wisteria Cottage'.

'Forgive me Jake, for setting you off, I was more interested as to what you would be doing with your life, apart from the purchase of a property in Greece?' Mike replied.

'Sorry Mike, I got on my high horse for a minute there, in response to your query, even I am not sure what I'll be doing with the money. However I have a few engagements in my diary, which involved trips to Israel and Australia and I shall be taking two weeks in Greece in late summer, then I'll mull over what is left to do on my bucket list for the future, I hope that answers your queries?'

Mike blushed a dark red before saying 'Sorry Jake, I was only asking out of politeness'.

Jake stood and cleared the plates, cups and saucers off the table and took them out to the kitchen to help wash and wipe them with Clare.

Our of earshot Clare said 'Sorry Dad, he's always been the nosy one but he didn't mean to pry, really'.

'That's OK luv, it's a bit of a bombshell for all of us I think, however it is in a nice way'.

'It certainly is Dad, its a shame Mum isn't around to enjoy your retirement and the comfortable wealth that the rest of the family will. But I know she would love it that we are now comfortably off'.

Jake turned to her and gave her a hug, as fond memories returned to his brain and tears streamed down his cheeks, he excused himself and went up to his bedroom and pack his bag, whilst wiping his face. Bag packed he walked down the stairs and out to the car, to put the bag in the boot.

When he walked back into the house there was a silence, that was deafening in the Lounge, Jake assumed that Clare had had a few words with her husband and he felt embarrassed, as he didn't look up from the paper as Jake sat opposite him with Clare busying herself in the kitchen. Becky sat near his legs waiting for her head to be rubbed, but gave up and sat near the fireplace.

The time dragged by, before Jake said as it was a nice morning he would take a drive around, and head over to Ipplepen to meet everyone there at noon. As he left the house he could still feel the tension between husband and wife, he hoped that the air would be cleared before they arrived at the Pub.

The food was as wonderful as he had previously enjoyed, and with the whole family in fine voice, the couple of hours they spent together he felt was really uplifting. He settled the bill, then with kisses and handshakes all round made his way back to Dorset.

Chapter 105

As he walked into the house his mobile rang, looking at the caller he realised it was Henry Bates, unusual for a Sunday. However he answered with 'Tordale' as usual.

'Hello Jake, I'm afraid it's bad news about George. The local Police had to break into his house, unfortunately and sadly he has taken his own life. There was an envelope on the table with my name on it. On opening and reading it I found it quite disturbing, however I won't say what was on the paper, over the phone. In the meantime I have searched through his family history, and sad to say he has no immediate family I could contact, so I will sort his affairs out'.

'How upsetting sir, did the text involve the 'Firm' at all?'

'No, I think he felt useless, and not able to carry out any other type of work to occupy his mind, but I'll tell you more later. Sorry to ring you on a Sunday but I thought you would like to know as soon as I had'.

'Thank you sir, I have only just arrived home after a visit to my family in Devon, I did try to contact him before I left home yesterday and put a message on his voicemail. Oh how very sad, I'm quite upset after all we went through in America'.

A sigh over the phone from Bates before he replied with 'Don't blame yourself Jake, I think it was a hidden inevitable situation that was out of our hands and destined to happen, reading into the situation that George had found himself in. I'll speak soon' and with that the phone went dead.

His upbeat mood had suddenly fallen to despair at this news, and he realised how easy it could happed when you have no family to relate your situation, and he thanked his lucky stars that he was. Retrieving his overnight bag from the car he reversed the MG back in the garage and covered it with the fitted indoor sheet. Returning to the house he walked to the drinks cabinet and poured out a large brandy and toasted his late friends 'Stefan' and 'George' and downed the drink in one gulp, he poured another and placed the glass on a side table, then went to the kitchen and made a black coffee. He switched on the TV and was confronted with the BBC News Channel which was doom and gloom, lowering his mood even more, but that quickly changed when his mobile rang, then looking at the caller, he smiled, realising that is was none other than Olivia calling from Sweden.

'Hello my dear how are you?' he asked.

'I'm fine, I thought I would call you in person and tell you that I have booked two weeks holiday from the last week August if that's convenient for you?'

'Splendid Olivia, I can now book flight's for us. Unfortunately we will have to fly from Heathrow, so when you arrive from Sweden we will catch a connecting flight to Greece the same day if not we will stay over in an onsite hotel until the flight is due, but I will sort it accordingly depending on your arrival time. Wonderful, that will be a holiday to remember, and you have certainly lifted my mood from the awful News I have been watching on the television'.

There was a pause before she finished with 'Right Jake now that's all sorted out I'de better get back to work. Look forward to meeting up with you, bye for now' and she was gone, before he could reply.

He turned the TV off and started to make notes and prepare a timetable of all the outstanding things he had to do over the next three months, the list was quite formidable but that was how his life had been over the last three years. However they were mostly things to look forward too.

1. Visit Israel with Stefan Cohen's artefact, to be handed to the Jewish Museum.
2. Travel to Brisbane, Australia to attend Chi's wedding, and to walk her down the aisle, and whilst there, call and see Mrs Choo.
3. In the meantime call to London to attend George Adam's funeral.
4. Two weeks holiday in Mykonos with Olivia, as well as purchasing a holiday home.
5. Before all the above travel to the garage to get the Lexus serviced and MOT'd, then whilst there, to make a visit to the Bank and talk to the Manager about the large sum of money that would be deposited into his account soon.

With all details entered into his diary he made his way up to bed for an early night.

Chapter 106

Waking the next morning he felt quite invigorated and decided today was the day to prepare himself a full English breakfast. He cooked two sausages, three rashers of bacon, four mushrooms, two fried eggs and a round of fried bread. He was salivating as the food cooked, before the percolator signalled his coffee was ready, he transferred the cooked food onto his large plate and carried it into the Dining Room. He applied his salt and pepper and a large splash of ketchup, then started to tuck in just as his mobile rang. 'Sod it' he thought, checking the caller he noticed it was Henry Bates. He only liked eating cooked food when it was hot, so resisted answering the call, and tucked into his breakfast. Once he had finished he carried his coffee into the Lounge and returned Henry's call. It was answered almost immediately, by Henry, who said 'Thank's for ringing back, I've got a problem'. Jake's stomach a minute ago felt fully satisfied, however it rumbled a bit at what his Boss was going to say next.

'The young lady that we interviewed to replace George has been out on location, but unfortunately we have lost a signal for her. In fact she hasn't been in touch for twenty four hours. All my other 'workmates' are tied up so I wondered if you are coming to London in the near future we can have a chat regarding this latest situation'.

'Retirement hasn't lasted very long sir has it. I'll postpone what I had booked in for the next few days, and travel up in the morning, I'll be in the car park for 10am'.

'Thank's Jake, see you tomorrow' Henry finished with and disconnected the call.

Thinking about his visit to London he decided whatever the situation is, he mustn't get involved, as he was already busy for the coming few months and he was in fact officially retired, however Henry know's how soft a touch he is so could easily be persuaded. He walked up to his bedroom and packed a small suitcase should he have to stay overnight.

It was still only mid morning , and as the weather was warm and sunny he thought he would carry out a little garden maintenance as he hadn't been at Wisteria Cottage for a while and the season was still early for planting out anything.

So he went outside, opened up the garden shed and pulled out the lawnmower to cut the front and rear grassed areas. He had also forgotten about the seeds he had purchased last year, but hadn't planted, so on completion of the cutting he filled three seed trays with potting compost to bring on broad beans, runner beans and various flower seeds, then putting the seed trays in the Lounge window to get the sunlight. It was approaching midday when he had finished his gardening, although he had a good breakfast he fancied a pint, and a sandwich at the Swan for lunch and decided to walk there.

Surprisingly the pub was fairly full as he walked into the Bar, the throng of people already there were drinking and walking towards the Dining Room, which left the Bar almost empty with just two old boys sat on bar stools. Bert walked over to him, and without a word passed between them poured him a pint of bitter. Jake smiled and asked what the sandwiches were on offer today. Bert handed him the menu, turned and filled the glasses of the two men sat at the other end of the Bar, before returning to Jake.

'In again, lunchtime as well my friend, are you home for a while now?' Bert questioned.

Jake smiled and replied with 'Unfortunately I have to pop up to London tomorrow so I thought I'de call here for lunch as I've cut the grass at home today and worked up an appetite'.

'Let me know when you've decided on your poison and I'll rustle it up for you'.

'Thank's Bert I won't be long deciding' he replied as he scanned the plastic covered menu. He noticed that it had changed, as it was now springtime it obviously was designed to suit the passing trade, namely holidaymakers in the area as well as locals.

Bert walked back to him as he looked up from the menu, and asked him if had decided, 'This is a new menu Bert isn't it?'

Bert smiled and said 'You are an astute fellow, its only been changed a few days ago, my Accountant said to me that I need to deviate from the locals and cater more for the passing trade this time of the year, so it's really experimenting time for me'.

'Well' said Jake, 'I'll try the curried prawns on granary and see what my reaction will be'.

'Excellent choice my friend, take a seat and I'll bring it over to you'.

Jake turned and sat at a window seat table ready for the food that was being prepared in the Pub's kitchen. Finishing his pint, Bert brought a replacement for him just as his daughter carried out a large plate with his sandwiches, complete with side salad and lightly salted crisps. He tucked in to the most unusual concoction and was pleasantly surprised and pleased that it actually worked, and as he went up to pay he told Bert his thoughts on the food. Bert asked if he fancied another pint on the house, but Jake declined and walked back along the lane to return home.

He boiled the kettle and made a cup of tea before taking a book from his library and settled down to read for the afternoon, but after an hour or so he dropped off to sleep.

He woke with a start, disorientated for a while until he looked at his watch and noticed that he had been asleep for almost two hours, but then thought does it really matter as he was almost retired, and his time was his own.

He then hoovered the house through and polished all the woodwork, before washing the kitchen and bathroom floors. Finally he put his recent clothing in the washing machine, which he would then transfer to the tumble dryer to finish off. With all those chores completed, he returned to his chair and got back into his book again whilst enjoying a glass of brandy.

Chapter 107

Up early the next morning he just had cereal and a cup of tea for breakfast, and was on the road at 8.30am, with the knowledge that he would be encountering the rush hour as he approached the Capital, but he was used to the slowness on the outskirts of London and had allowed himself plenty of time to get there for his appointment with Henry Bates.

Unfortunately as he pulled into the underground car park it was in fact 10.40am, there being no sign of Henry he therefore made his way up to the office in the lift.

Another young lady was sat in the normal Receptionist's seat, so he introduced himself to her, and she said for him to make his way up to the Boss's office, obviously she had been pre-warned that Jake was arriving shortly. He thanked her and walked up to the next level, he knocked on the door and walked in to face Henry's desk.

'Thanks for coming up at such short notice Jake, I trust I haven't inconvenienced you too much?' he asked with a somewhat regretful tone.

'I've re-arranged the meetings that I had this week, hoping that my visit here would just be for the one day, however I anticipate it could be longer according to what you are about to tell me?' he replied.

Henry stroked him chin before saying 'The problem with our young lady's apparent disappearance from the grid is perplexing. She was despatched to a situation in the Gulf which impacted on a member of the Diplomatic Department of the UK, who was on leave there. The man who shall remain anonymous, unfortunately had a little too much to drink in an area where drinking wasn't permitted. So in a Country that isn't tolerant with this behaviour, no matter who you are, he was arrested and thrown into prison. I sent our Operative off to play down the situation there, however intrusion by another UK citizen wasn't taken lightly, it wasn't as if she was a Lawyer, so she was sent packing. Now she cannot be contacted, and the Prime Minister has become involved, saying it's an embarrassment to the UK Government, and together with my worry as to the whereabouts of our Agent, you can see that my problem is twofold Jake'.

'I can see your problem sir, however I feel that it is more of an inter-departmental situation rather than something that our Service should have to tackle. But as our Agent has got tangled up and is now missing I assume that is your main concern?'

'It is indeed, however should both situations be resolved and they can be repatriated to the UK it would be in the Governments interests for it to be sorted out low key, and without any fuss'.

'It still appears to be a minefield to me, I presume you are asking me to travel to the Gulf to firstly locate our Agent and then nullify the situation with the Government official?' Jake asked.

'If you put it like that Jake, yes I am' Henry could not hold Jake's stare as he answered.

'I have taken the liberty of booking you onto a flight leaving at 2.30pm this afternoon from Heathrow, it's booked in First Class as usual and I trust that you are able to nullify this problem for myself and the UK Government. If you able to return both the people, I promise that I will never ask you for anything ever again, and leave you to retire in peace'.

Jake smiled at his friend before replying with 'Trust me to just bring an overnight bag, that means I'll have to do a little shopping when I get there'.

Henry opened a drawer and handed Jake a bundle of bank notes before explaining 'There's £5,000 there, when you get to the Terminal you had better change a couple of thousand pounds into the local currency'.

With that the audience was over, as Jake stood, they shook hands, with a parting 'Good luck' from Henry. He took the lift back down to the car park, got in his car, and drove to Heathrow. Two hours later the huge plane took off on it's way to Abu Dhabi, the flight was comfortable and he was looked after all the way with food and drink.

Whatever was going to happen at the other end, he had no idea.

However that would be another story !!!

The End